Midnight at Malabar House

Midnight at Malabar House

Vaseem Khan

HODDER

First published in Great Britain in 2020 by Hodder & Stoughton
An Hachette UK company

This paperback edition published in 2021

15

Copyright © Vaseem Khan 2020

Map by Rodney Paull

A CIP catalogue record for this title is available from the British Library

Paperback ISBN 978 1 473 68550 5
eBook ISBN 978 1 473 68549 9

Typeset in Adobe Caslon by Hewer Text UK Ltd, Edinburgh
Printed and bound in Great Britain by Clays Ltd, Elcograf S.p.A.

Hodder & Stoughton policy is to use papers that are natural, renewable
and recyclable products and made from wood grown in sustainable
forests. The logging and manufacturing processes are expected to
conform to the environmental regulations of the country of origin.

Hodder & Stoughton Ltd
Carmelite House
50 Victoria Embankment
London EC4Y 0DZ

www.hodder.co.uk

To history's unsung female pioneers who, through obstinacy, willpower and an indomitability of spirit, have changed our world.

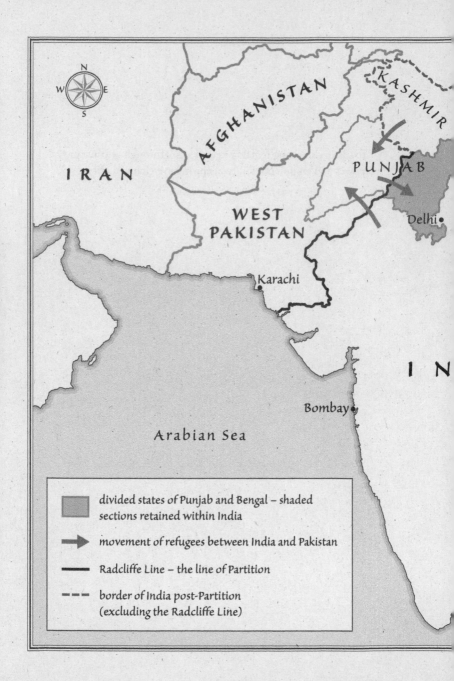

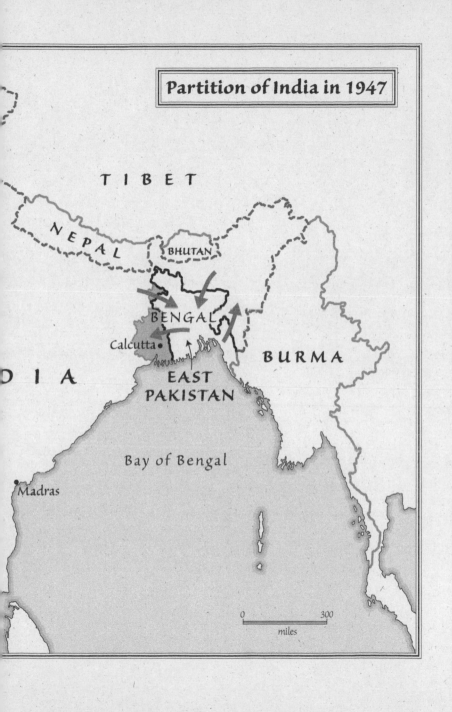

Partition of India in 1947

TIBET

NEPAL

BHUTAN

BENGAL

Calcutta

BURMA

INDIA

EAST
PAKISTAN

Bay of Bengal

Madras

0   300
miles

31 December 1949

The call came in the deepest part of the night, the telephone's lusty urgency shattering the basement silence. Persis paused, pen poised above the blank white page of the duty log she had been attempting to complete for the past hour.

There was little to report.

She sat alone in the office, the only sounds the gentle swishing of the ceiling fan and the scurrying of a lone mouse under the jumble of desks and battered metal filing cabinets. Occasionally a muffled bang would drift in from the world above. New Year's Eve fireworks. The entire city was out partying, the streets alive with drunken multitudes, celebrating the end of the most turbulent decade in the nation's history. In spite – or perhaps because – of this she had agreed to stand vigil for the night. Frivolity was alien to her nature and she had often been told that her tastes – in matters of dress and deportment – tended to the staid.

Perhaps this was the effect of growing up without a mother.

Sanaz Wadia née Poonawalla had died when Persis was just seven, taking with her the last vestiges of an already waning belief in a benevolent God. Her father had never remarried, raising her as best as he was able in the margins of his grief. Poor Aunt Nussie had tried her best, but Sam Wadia was a stubborn man.

The thought passed through her mind that the call might well be her father, ringing to assure himself that, an hour into the new year, she was still alive and well.

She plucked up the receiver of the black Stromberg Carlson: 'CID, Malabar House. Inspector Wadia speaking.'

A moment's hesitation, as her caller's incredulity filtered down the line.

It wasn't the first time.

Her appointment, seven months earlier, had occasioned hysteria in publications as far apart as the *Calcutta Gazette* to the *Karnataka Herald*. In Bombay, the *Indian Chronicle* had been particularly scathing: 'The commissioner's experiment in catapulting a woman into the service might well mirror our fledgling republic's forward-thinking ideals, but what he has failed to consider is that in temperament, intelligence and moral fibre, the female of the species is, and always will be, inferior to the male.'

That cutting, framed in glass, now looked up at her from her desk. Each morning it served as a shot across her bows, a trenchant reminder that if it was respect she craved, she faced an uphill task in earning it.

Her caller gathered his composure. 'May I speak with your superior officer?'

She stifled the urge to slam the receiver back into its cradle. 'I'm afraid that tonight *I* am the ranking officer. Sir.'

The shallowest intake of breath. 'In that case, Miss Wadia, might I ask you to make your way to Laburnum House on Marine Drive. The residence of Sir James Herriot.'

'Inspector.'

'I'm sorry?'

'*Inspector* Wadia. Not Miss.'

Silence. 'My apologies. *Inspector*, if you could make haste, it would be most appreciated.'

'May I ask what this is regarding?'

'You may,' said the voice coolly. 'Sir James has been murdered.'

2

Laburnum House: a two-storey cubist monstrosity, splashed in virulent shades of imperial maroon and beige, and imprinted from top to bottom with art deco motifs, including two startling elephant heads adorning the sea-facing main gates.

She was met at the front door by a house servant, a hand-wringing native with the look of an overdressed coolie. The man led her swiftly through a shimmering reception hall, an expanse of white marble from the centre of which sprouted a bronze of Prometheus. Some wag had stuck a turban on the Greek Titan's skull, imparting an air of noble sanctimony.

She was ushered into a drawing room where the man who had summoned her rose in greeting from a tan leather chesterfield.

His name was Madan Lal, Sir James Herriot's chief aide, a slender figure, immaculate in herringbone tweed. He wasn't quite tall enough to pull off the high-waisted trousers, but there was a smartness to him that signalled a sense of self-assurance.

He held out a hand. 'Inspector. Thank you for getting here so quickly.'

She noted the manicure, the clean-shaven cheeks, the black hair oiled back in a perfect widow's peak. Round, steel-framed spectacles gave him the look of a bookkeeper or an insurance broker. All in all, an attractive man, if one liked them a little on the well-pressed side.

It struck her that Lal, in his urbanity, was the very image of the modern civil servant. A man for the times: India in late 1949, more than two years after Partition, a nation struggling to redefine itself against a background of continuing social and political unrest. The dismantling of the old feudal system had seen a significant lurch towards the left, an attempt to even up the social scales. Set against this was the inertia of millennia, the hegemonies of old India, zamindars and noble houses frantically scrapping for their place in the new Eden. Independence had given them a bloody nose, but they weren't about to go down without an almighty scrap. Or so her father said.

She returned to the moment. 'Perhaps you could explain the circumstances of Mr Herriot's murder?' Small talk had never been her forte.

'Sir.'

'I'm sorry?'

'*Sir* James.' He gave a thin-lipped smile. 'We are all wedded to our titles, are we not?'

She coloured, wondering if he was chiding her for her earlier intransigence.

'In theory, you should refer to me as *Major* Lal. I served with the 50th Parachute Brigade in Burma. At any rate, let us dispense with formalities. Please come with me.'

She followed him through the lavishly appointed mansion, up a teak-banistered staircase, and along a series of corridors to the rear of the house.

Lal stopped before a lacquered black door. 'Forgive me, but I take it that you are not of a ... *delicate* disposition?'

She gave this insulting statement short shrift by brushing past him and into the room.

It was a study, lavishly decorated. Crystal chandeliers hung from a whitewashed ceiling. The furniture – a combination of bone-inlaid Burma teak and hand-carved rosewood – had been curated with impeccable taste. One wall was given over to a mural in red and black ceramic: Hannibal slogging over the Alps on elephant-back. The remaining walls were taken up by bookshelves, weighed down with identical-looking tomes, many of which had probably never been touched by human hand.

It was a room designed to impress, rather than a venue where midnight oil was routinely burned in lucubration.

Directly before them was a large desk, and behind that desk, slumped in a buttoned-leather captain's chair, was Sir James Herriot.

His head lolled on to his chest, arms slack by his sides.

She moved around the desk to get a better look.

The Englishman was in his late fifties and balding in that particularly aggressive way the British did, the top of his dome marred by a profusion of scarlet patches. He wore a red cape and a red tunic, unbuttoned to the navel, revealing a naked chest, pale and hairless. His stomach bulged above his crotch. He was naked from the waist down, something that had not been apparent from the door.

Instinctively, she averted her eyes, then chided herself. A police officer had a duty to examine every aspect of the crime scene.

Before she could proceed further, the door opened and a white man strode purposefully into the room. Tall, spare-framed, with thick, dark hair, and an uncommonly handsome face, he swung a boxy black leather bag by his side, like a doctor's carry case. A cream linen suit flapped around him, frayed at the elbows. A ratty tie was pushed up in an untidy knot towards a smooth neck. Green eyes flashed from under dark eyebrows. Black-framed spectacles sat on his nose. A sheen of sweat moistened his clean-shaven cheeks.

'Archie. Thank you for coming.' Madan Lal extended a hand to the newcomer who shook it warmly. He turned to her. 'Inspector, may I present Archimedes Blackfinch? He is presently serving as an adviser to the crime branch.'

'Archie, please,' he said, extending his own bony hand in her direction.

'Adviser?' she echoed, staring at the appendage as if he were attempting to palm her a live grenade.

'I'm a criminalist with the Metropolitan Police Service in London,' he clarified, lowering his hand.

Lal took up the baton. 'As you know our government is keen to breathe new life into the various state organs that have been returned to our patronage. If India is to uphold the rule of law we must have a police force worthy of the name. Advisers such as Archie have been retained to provide us with the necessary rigour to underpin our ambitions.'

It sounded like a campaign speech. She frowned. 'I take it you know each other?'

'We have had prior dealings. I assure you, he is most capable.'

'But he has no standing here as an investigative officer?'

Lal's smile became strained. 'Technically speaking. However, it is my hope that you will accommodate him. In fact, I am certain the commissioner would approve.'

She swallowed her objection. Clearly, Lal had the reach to pour discontent into the ears of a higher power.

Turning back to the body, she said, 'Why is he dressed like this?'

'I should have explained,' replied Lal. 'Tonight Sir James hosted his annual New Year's Eve ball. It is always a costumed affair.'

'Who was he supposed to be?'

'Mephistopheles. He is—'

'The demon to whom Faust sold his soul.'

He nodded. 'Quite.'

He seemed surprised. Perhaps women who could actually read and not just look pretty posing beside books and vases were unknown to him.

'Where is the . . . lower half of his outfit?'

'I'm afraid that his trousers have not yet been found. It is most puzzling.'

It was more than that. Why would Herriot's trousers be missing? Had the killer taken them? To what end?

'May I?' said Blackfinch.

She watched as he set down his case, opened it, removed a pair of gloves and pulled them on. She'd been taught the basics of crime scene procedure at the police training college at Mount Abu, two gruelling years as the only woman among a cadre of men who, for the most part, believed she had no right or reason to be there. It was here too that she had learned of the two Indians who had developed the fingerprint classification system that was now used throughout the service and which had been successfully exported to no less a home than Scotland Yard. Naturally, the credit for the technique had fallen to their English supervisor. She doubted that the Henry Classification System would be renamed now that the British had been shown the door.

Blackfinch stepped forward, laid his hands either side of Herriot's skull, and gently lifted his head.

She saw that blood had coagulated around his throat. Streaks of dried blood snaked down towards his pale belly, and over his thighs.

Blackfinch's gloved fingers interrogated the bloody mess until he found what he was looking for. 'The pathologist will have to confirm, but it appears as if a sharp blade was inserted here, at the side of the larynx, driven forcefully inwards, then yanked out to sever the carotid and jugular arteries. Death would have been all but instantaneous.'

Something caught his eye under the desk and he bent down to reach beneath it. When he straightened, it was with a balled-up handkerchief in his hand. He sniffed at it, crinkled his nose, then removed a waxy paper bag from his case and dropped the cloth into it. Not bothering to explain, he resumed his examination.

Persis turned to Lal. 'What was he doing up here?'

'I have asked myself the same question. I suspect he needed a moment's respite from the festivities. These functions can be quite trying.'

She looked again at Herriot's desk. It was of the pedestal type, fashioned from polished teak and waxed to within an inch of its life. The top was inlaid with a marble slab in bottle green, edged with rose gilt. The eight drawers making up the pedestals had reassuringly solid brass handles. A collection of objects ranged across the desk. An empty whisky glass. An ashtray in which lay a solitary cigar stub. A beige globe of empire, British colonies picked out in red, India still very much in the fold. A reading glass. A brass inkstand with lidded inkwells. A telephone.

There was something about the precise arrangement of the objects that bothered her, a subconscious itch. But she couldn't place it.

She moved to the far side of the desk and reached for the handle of the topmost drawer.

Both men all but cried out, startling her.

'If you're going to touch anything, you must put on gloves,' said Blackfinch.

Flushing, she cursed herself for not having considered this. The idea of appearing incompetent bothered her far more than being murdered or assaulted in the line of duty, a gruesome eventuality that Aunt Nussie predicted on a daily basis.

Lal's objection was more prosaic. 'Those are Sir James's private drawers,' he protested.

'I don't think privacy is of much concern to him any more, do you?'

'You don't understand. Sir James was working on many sensitive matters for the government. Those drawers may contain confidential documents.'

'Then it's a good thing,' she muttered, violently pulling on the gloves Blackfinch handed her, 'that I am known for my discretion.' She opened the topmost drawer – it was unlocked – as Lal's eyes bulged. The man was a bureaucratic heart attack waiting to happen.

The drawer contained a selection of papers, correspondence and handwritten scribblings, but nothing of note or of seeming relevance to Herriot's death.

Inside a battered leather notebook, she discovered a newspaper cutting taken from the *Times of India*. It included a photograph of four individuals: two Indians, a man and a woman, arm in arm, flanked by two tuxedoed white men. The article, dated two months earlier, detailed the gala opening of a club in Bombay.

She studied the individuals in the photograph.

The white men were nondescript – she pegged them as businessmen or civil servants – but the Indian couple were handsome, effortlessly glamorous. The woman, dressed in a sari, had one arm looped around the man's, the other at her throat, where an ostentatious necklace was prominent.

Scanning the article, she discovered that the Indian man in the photograph was the club's owner, Adi Shankar; the woman attached to his arm, 'socialite, Meenakshi Rai'. Aside from the article, the notebook was empty. She wondered briefly why Herriot had kept the cutting, then, on a whim, added the item to the evidence she had been collecting.

Quickly, she riffled through the remaining drawers, finding little of interest – scraps of paper, the odd trinket absentmindedly shoved in and forgotten about, a case of cigars. Lal had worried needlessly.

And then she opened the bottommost drawer.

She lifted out the revolver by the barrel and showed it to the two men.

'May I?' said Blackfinch. He took the pistol from her and sniffed at it. 'It hasn't been fired recently.' He pushed out the chamber. 'Fully loaded.'

'Did you know he had this?' she asked, directing herself to Lal.

'I knew he kept it there, yes. It's a Webley Mark IV. Standard issue for the British towards the end of the war.'

'Sir James fought in the war?'

'Not exactly fought. He was given honorary rank, for political reasons, and this entitled him to a sidearm. He kept it as a souvenir.'

'Was he a good shot?' asked Blackfinch.

'Yes. He prided himself on it.'

'Which means that if anyone had entered this room whom he perceived as a threat, his natural reaction would have been to reach for his gun.' Blackfinch waited, then added, 'Which he did not do.'

In time Persis would discover that the Englishman had a habit of belabouring his point. It was an instinctive and irritating aspect of his personality, made more so by the fact that he had no idea how irritating it was.

'There will have to be an autopsy,' continued Blackfinch.

'Autopsy?' Lal looked horrified, as if he had not considered this.

'We'll also have to search the house,' added Persis. 'How many people were at the party?'

'The guest list was forty-eight,' replied the aide. 'In addition, there were the house servants, the waiting staff hired for the evening, the jazz band and, of course, myself. A further total of nineteen.'

Impressed with his precision, she wondered if, perhaps, he had anticipated the question. 'Are they still here?'

'No one has yet left. Though many of our guests are growing restless.'

'You told them that Herriot had been murdered?'

'Not exactly. I said that he had been taken ill and retired for the night.'

She glanced at the dead Englishman. He was about as ill as it was possible to be. No tincture was going to get him up and jiving on the dance floor any time soon, that was for certain.

'I will need to question them. Can you gather them together?'

'You intend to question the *guests*?' He gave a shake of the head. 'I'm afraid you haven't grasped the nature of the beast, Inspector. Sir James's guest list runs to some of the wealthiest and most influential people in the city, if not the country. They cannot be treated as suspects in a murder investigation.'

'But that is precisely what they are.'

'I cannot believe that,' he countered. 'This is the work of a rogue. An opportunist stealing his way into the mansion, encountering Sir James in his study, and panicking.'

She considered this interpretation of events. 'Did you have guards at the gate?'

'Yes. But it was New Year's Eve. Even the guards take a moment to enjoy the celebration. I doubt it would have been difficult to evade them.'

Blackfinch spoke up. 'The killer was known to Sir James.'

Lal's brow furrowed. 'How can you be so certain?'

'Because the murderer had to get close to kill him. Even if we ignore the fact that he made no move for his revolver, had a stranger attacked him he would have attempted to defend himself. There would have been a struggle. Yet there appear to be no defensive wounds. The killer approached, looped one arm around his head' – he mimicked the action – 'and thrust the knife into his neck with the other hand. A practised manoeuvre, delivered with speed and precision.'

'What are you implying?'

'I mean that an untrained individual attacking another with a knife is liable to thrust and parry like a man fencing with a salmon. This isn't the work of a dilettante.'

Lal paled. 'You mean his killer was a military man?'

'Not necessarily. But someone who knew his way around violence, yes.'

'I will need a list of all those in attendance,' said Persis.

Lal's mouth flapped, his composure finally ruffled. He conceded with a short nod.

'Where is his family?' Persis asked next.

'Sir James is a bachelor. He has never married, nor does he have children.'

She paused to consider anything she might have overlooked. 'Is anything missing from the room or from Sir James's person?'

'If you mean anything valuable, then no.'

But there was a hesitation in the way Lal said this that made her look at him curiously. She was prevented from pursuing the thought by Blackfinch.

He had been examining a portrait behind the desk, set into the midst of rows of bookshelves. The painting was of Herriot, boorishly handsome, stuffed into a military uniform like a six-foot-tall sausage. Behind him, serving as a backdrop, was a large white mansion, reminiscent of Shimla or other wintering destinations favoured by the British. It was everything a colonial portrait might hope to express. Grandeur, sophistication, benevolence and disdain.

'There are scratch marks in the wood here,' said the Englishman. 'This painting has been moved around quite a bit. Ergo, I believe there is something behind it.'

Without waiting for Lal's permission, he reached up and lifted down the painting. It was a large, heavy-framed thing, and the awkwardness of the action lurched him backwards. Lal cried out, but it was too late. Blackfinch stumbled and fell, the canvas jamming against the corner of the desk. The tearing sound was appallingly loud in the silent room.

Blackfinch sprang to his feet, dusted himself off, mumbled an apology, then went back to the wall as if nothing had happened.

Persis glanced at Lal, who was still looking at the destroyed portrait in horror. The corner of the desk had spiked Herriot's face.

Blackfinch meanwhile had moved on to his discovery – a wall-safe ensconced in a niche behind the portrait. Pewter in colour, the safe sat inside a mahogany cabinet; the logo read: *Morris Ireland Safe Co.*

'It's unlocked,' he announced, turning a handle set into the safe's cast-iron door and pulling it open to peer inside.

Persis moved forward to look over his shoulder.

He reached in and came up with a key ring on which were two identical brass keys. He squinted at the writing etched on the keys. 'They're the keys to the safe.'

'What else is in there?' she asked.

He reached back in, but came out empty-handed. 'It's empty.'

She turned to Lal. 'What was in there?'

'Whatever Sir James kept in there was of a personal nature.'

'I doubt that he installed a safe like this only to have kept it empty.'

'Surely this indicates that the motive for his death was robbery?' ventured Lal.

'Too early to say,' replied Blackfinch. 'But the fact that the safe is open suggests that either he or his killer may have taken something out of it this evening.'

Persis looked around the room. Her eyes alighted on what she had at first thought was an ornamental fireplace. She saw now that a mound of ashes was heaped in the grate.

Walking over, she squatted down and reached out a hand. Still warm. Someone had burned a lot of paper. Recently. She picked up a poker and jabbed at the charred and blackened remains but there was nothing left to indicate their nature.

Another curiosity.

'Who found the body?'

'One of the houseboys,' replied Lal. 'The McGowans were leaving and wished to thank their host. They couldn't locate Sir James so asked me to fetch him. I sent Maan Singh. He discovered him here and had the presence of mind to come to me first.'

'When was the last time he was seen alive?'

'Impossible to say,' replied Lal. 'I myself saw him singing "Auld Lang Syne" with the guests out on the back lawn. That was at midnight.'

'And the body was found at what time?'

'Around one-ten.'

Somewhere in that witching hour after midnight Herriot had vanished upstairs to meet his fate.

'I'd like to speak with the houseboy,' said Persis.

The boy in question turned out to be six foot six and built like Everest. Maan Singh was one of those formidable Sikhs who'd made their reputation in the two great wars, as solid and implacable as tanks. There were still stories floating around from the Great War of Sikhs who'd shown their contempt for death by refusing to skulk down in the trenches, fairly eccentric behaviour in the middle of continuous bombardment.

'You found the body?' she asked, when he arrived.

Singh's shoulders straightened. He towered over her, eyes drilling straight ahead. Or rather, towards Lal. She sighed inwardly. Singh was from the north-west, a corner of the country not known for its sympathetic attitude towards feminine advancement. In manner and appearance, he seemed every inch the boorish Punjabi she had been warned to expect by Aunt Nussie, who, for reasons she would not disclose, held a particular grudge against the warrior clans of that region. He wore a scarlet longcoat, sashed at the waist, and a cream turban – the house uniform. The get-up reminded her of doormen at the Blue Nile, the Mandarin, or the Alibaba, popular nightclubs with a penchant for employing statuesque Sikhs to keep out the riff-raff.

'You may answer,' said Lal.

'Yes,' said Singh, still not looking at her.

'Yes, *ma'am*,' she said, unable to stop herself.

Singh's eyes swivelled down. She met his gaze unflinchingly. He had a handsome head, broad-faced, with shapely cheekbones, fierce eyes and a neatly trimmed beard.

'What time did you discover the body?'

'At one-ten. *Ma'am*.'

'What did you do when you found him?'

'I checked to see that he was dead—'

'You touched the body?' interrupted Blackfinch.

'I held his wrist and checked his pulse. That is all. He was dead.' This was said impassively, as if Singh were describing a batsman who had just been bowled during a game of cricket.

'How long have you worked for Herriot?'

'I have been in Sir James's employ for the past month.'

'What did you think of him?'

His forehead crunched into a frown. 'What do you mean?'

'Sir James? What did you make of him?'

'He was my employer. I did not make anything of him.'

'Did you like him?'

'It was not my place to like him. It was my place to do what he asked of me.'

'What *did* he ask of you? What was your role here?'

'I was a houseboy.'

'Really? You seem ill suited to the position.'

His eyes flashed. 'What do you mean?'

'A man of your size and strength . . .' She couldn't imagine him serving tea or delivering perfumed letters on silver swan trays.

He nodded, understanding. 'I was also Sir James's driver and his personal bodyguard.' Singh grimaced. 'I have failed him. I have failed in my duty. I must live with my shame.'

'There is nothing you could have done, Singh,' said Lal, but the big man was not to be mollified.

'Did you take anything from the room?' she asked.

His face darkened. 'Are you accusing me of stealing?'

'No. But Sir James's trousers are missing. And possibly items from his safe.'

'I know nothing about a safe.' His look could have felled a horse. She knew full well that accusing a Sikh of theft was a mortal insult. Had she suggested that he had put on a dress and danced the cancan, he would have been less offended.

'One last question: was the fire burning when you found the body?'

He frowned, then followed her gaze to the fireplace. 'No. There was no fire.'

'Very well,' she said. 'You may go.'

He marched stiffly towards the door, shutting it forcefully behind him.

'I must apologise,' said Lal. 'He is a singular man.'

She glanced at Blackfinch, who was busying himself collecting fingerprint samples, dusting with Lightning powder. Everything else around him had ceased to exist. She noticed that he had also taken out a camera from his bag and set it on to a tripod, presumably to photograph the scene. She debated the merits of calling out a team from the state forensic unit, but decided that the

Englishman would have a better grasp of the resources he needed and would be able to commandeer them with greater ease.

She turned back to Lal. 'I will interview the staff and guests now.'

Lal nodded. 'Follow me.'

Downstairs, scattered across various drawing rooms and receptions, she found Herriot's guests, well-heeled couples and a smattering of gay bachelors, smoking like chimneys and drinking the place dry. They milled around in a state of costumed uncertainty, subdued, but at the same time infected with a sense of nervous excitement. The cat was out of the bag, she realised. Word of Herriot's passing had reached them, a grisly but memorable ending to their bacchanalia.

She gathered them together in the ballroom and confirmed for them, tersely, that their host was now deceased. It was only when she informed them that she intended to question them individually that the bleating began. Many took this as a form of accusation and responded as one might expect of the rich and powerful. She listened silently to their oaths, threats, curses and protests, her face growing hot, and then repeated her intentions, stressing that she was merely attempting to gather information while memories were still fresh. The next couple of hours were spent in an anteroom carefully interrogating lawyers, bankers, managing agency officers, businessmen, and mid-ranking politicos and their doll-like wives. Each person was also searched, eliciting another round of furious protest.

But Persis was adamant. The murder weapon had to be on the premises somewhere.

Halfway through the interviews, Lal pulled her aside. 'I'm afraid this is taking too long. The remaining guests will mutiny if I don't allow them to leave.'

'They cannot leave,' she said. 'This is a police investigation.'

'Do you think you can stop them? Many of these people are on first-name terms with the commissioner.'

She bit back her anger. Lal was right. There was no real threat that she could employ to force them to stay. 'Very well. They may leave under two conditions. First, they must submit to a search. And, second, they must agree to be interviewed in the coming days.'

Lal nodded and went to deliver the news.

Ultimately, Persis was able to interview twenty-two of the forty-eight guests. It quickly become apparent that she would learn little of value.

Herriot was universally hailed as a 'damned fine chap'. No one had a bad word to say about the man. As for the evening itself, everyone remembered chatting to him – their host had been on fine form – but no one recalled the moment he had vanished upstairs.

Once she had finished with the guests she moved on to the staff and the jazz band.

Again, little of value bobbed to the surface. Aside from the house regulars, the others did not know Herriot and had nothing to add regarding his movements on the night.

One of those who seemed most affected by his death was the housekeeper, a widow by the name of Lalita Gupta, an elegant, reserved woman in a maroon sari. Gupta seemed stunned by her employer's sudden passing. In her mid-thirties, with streaks of grey beginning to invade her dark hair, Gupta spoke softly, in excellent English. She lived at the mansion, in a room on the ground floor, and had worked for Herriot for the past four years. She revealed that Herriot had spent much of the morning away from home, returning in the late afternoon to check on preparations for his party. She had noticed nothing unusual in his manner that day.

Finally, Persis called in the guards from the front gate.

One admitted that he had indulged in a few beers, but the other was a devout Mahomedan and had remained as sober as a nun. They were willing to swear on all that was holy that no uninvited visitor had slipped by them that night.

While all this was going on Persis had set in motion a second important aspect of the night's action – a search of the premises. To aid in this task she had phoned the nearby Marine Drive police station and argued with the imbecile in charge. A squad of *havaldars* had been duly despatched. Marshalling these Keystone cops – most of whom could not conceive of the idea of a female officer, let alone swallow orders from one – took up an inordinate degree of energy. It did not help that they glanced at Blackfinch for confirmation each time she issued an instruction.

In Herriot's bedroom, searching through his wardrobe, she discovered a ticket stub caught in the pocket of a gabardine driving jacket. The stub was stamped with the serial number 77183, and the series code 12, together with the message: PASSENGER TO RETAIN THIS PORTION OF THE TICKET. She recognised it as an intercity train ticket, but, frustratingly, the top half was missing, taken by the ticket inspector, no doubt. It was on that half that the date and start and end points of the journey were usually found. In a second pocket, she found a scrap of paper. It was torn at the top, clearly ripped from a pad. Just below the tear were the printed words: *By a pool of nectar, at the shrine of the sixty-eight.*

On the paper, in a scribbled hand, was a name – BAKSHI – and beneath that a jumble of letters and numbers: PLT41/85ACRG11.

She stared at the page, but could make nothing of it.

When the search was completed – with little else to show for the effort – neither the murder weapon nor Herriot's missing trousers had been found – she took Lal aside.

She asked him about the note, but Lal had no idea who Bakshi might be. The annotation meant nothing to him.

'I need a list of Sir James's appointments over the past weeks. I wish to establish his movements prior to his death.'

'I will provide you with a list.'

'There's something else: why do *you* think he was killed?'

'What do you mean?'

'Motive,' she said. 'What possible motive could someone have had to murder Sir James?'

Lal sighed. 'I have been asking myself the same thing. Sir James was a gregarious man, well liked and widely respected. He could be blunt when the need arose; yet he was a diplomat too and understood how to navigate the often treacherous waters of both British and Indian politics. I remember, a few years ago, we met Gandhi together. This was well before his death, of course, a year before the British finally caved in. Sir James took him aside and told him that he had won, that the British government had lost its stomach for the fight. There's just too damned many of you, he said. And every blasted one of you as troublesome as a wasp at a picnic. He actually made Gandhi laugh.' Lal smiled, reliving the memory.

'You don't seem overly upset by his death.'

Lal stiffened. Tact had never been her strongest suit. Aunt Nussie was constantly at pains to admonish her for her forthright manner. A lady, she had impressed upon her, must be demure, charming, gracious, and light of foot. Persis had rarely found herself praised for any of these qualities.

'He was not just my employer, Inspector. Sir James was also my friend. We first met years ago, at University College London. My parents had sent me abroad for the furtherance of my studies. Herriot was a trustee of the college. He gave that year's Disraeli Lecture, a vivid dissection of the state of affairs in India – he'd already spent the best part of a decade here. He was one of the few Englishmen at the time who believed in Indian Home Rule and was courageous enough to say so publicly. It is one of the reasons we asked him to stay on after Partition.' He sighed. 'I saw death in abundance during the war, Inspector. I cannot say that it has inured me to it, but I have a certain stomach for these things. I grieve for James in my own way.'

Her last act of the night was to arrange for the body to be taken to the morgue.

She waited for the ambulance to arrive and looked on as they lifted Herriot's pallid corpse on to a stretcher, threw a white sheet over it, then carried him downstairs and out into the night like pygmies bearing an expired chieftain to the mountain.

As she drove home, just an hour before dawn, a single thought reverberated in her mind. *Why, out of all the police departments in the city, had Lal chosen to call Malabar House?* After all, even if those in power would never openly acknowledge it, *they* knew that they were outsiders, brought together precisely because they had been deemed unfit for any assignment of worth.

The thought followed her into a fitful sleep.

3

1 January 1950

Barely three hours later, Persis awoke to find Akbar in bed beside her, regarding her nonchalantly with the dazzling green eyes that had first won her heart. He leaned his face towards hers, clearly intent on physical intimacy. She grimaced and raised a hand to ward him off. 'I don't think so.'

Offended, he flashed her a cold look, turned his back on her, and snuggled into the soft down of the mattress.

She sat up, stretched, then left the overfed grey tomcat to his sulk as she headed to the bathroom.

The coal heater was out again. The shower, bracingly cold, left her with goose bumps dotting her arms. After dressing quickly in her khaki uniform, she bundled her long black hair into its habitual work-aday bun, tucked her peaked cap under her arm, checked her revolver before slipping it back into its holster, and headed for the living room.

She discovered Aunt Nussie bustling about the kitchen area. 'Sit down, dear,' she sang. 'Almost ready!'

Her father, Sam Wadia, did not bother to look up. He was absorbed in a game of chess with his regular sparring partner, Dr Shaukat Aziz, a kidney specialist of some renown.

'You've got to go easier on the whisky,' Aziz was saying. 'If you're not careful, your liver will blow up like a balloon.'

'Great,' said Sam, plucking up a rook and advancing it belligerently across the board. 'That means there'll be space for more whisky.'

'You're wasting your time, Uncle Aziz,' she said, leaning down and giving her father an affectionate peck on the cheek. 'Happy New Year.'

'How many times have I told you not to call me uncle? I am in the prime of my life. A flâneur, a man about town.'

Aunt Nussie set a pair of steaming plates on the table. Spiced kedgeree. Saliva flooded Persis's mouth. When had she last eaten?

'You didn't have to, Aunt Nussie.'

'What better way to start the new year than a home-cooked breakfast for my only niece?'

'We have a home-cooked breakfast every morning,' muttered Sam. 'Because Krishna cooks it. At home.'

As long as Persis had been aware of it, an unspoken animosity had hovered between her father and her mother's younger sister. It was only after her mother's death that she had discovered the reason why.

Aunt Nussie – and her mother – came from a wealthy Parsee family, the only daughters of Zubin Poonawalla, a shipping magnate who had doted on his girls. Sam Wadia, though also a Parsee, came from earthier stock. His father had run a bookshop, Wadia's Book Emporium, and had made a decent living from it, but had never been a man of any great wealth or influence. Sam himself had studied law before the independence struggle had hijacked his fledgling career. Along with thousands of young men in the country he had thrown himself wholeheartedly into the fight, inspired by the likes of Nehru and Gandhi, but also by his own sense of disillusionment.

Persis had often marvelled at how quickly the British had fallen from their pedestal. For centuries those at the upper levels of Indian society had striven for closeness with their overseers, in the hope that this would allow them to retain some semblance of mastery over their lives. They had shut their eyes to the injustice, the abuse, the cruelties meted out to those at the base of the pyramid. But once the national mood tilted from protest to outright revolution it was only a matter of time. Sam Wadia was just one of millions of educated Indians who had found the scales dashed from their eyes. For Sam Wadia had once admired the British, had held them up as the epitome of all that Indians might aspire to. It had only come to him later in life that this admiration was the result of a sense of self-loathing planted within him by three hundred years of colonial rule.

'Let me look at you,' said Nussie. She reached out and placed her hands either side of the young policewoman's face, a gesture Persis had hated even as a child. 'As lovely as your mother,' she sighed.

This was not so far from the truth.

Persis had seen the photographs; she knew that she closely resembled the tragic beauty who had captured Sam's heart. Jet-black hair, deep brown eyes, full lips and an aquiline nose. There had been times when she had felt the weight of that pulchritude, most notably in the police training college. It seemed that half her time had been spent batting away unwanted advances. It was not that she was immune to romantic longings. It was simply that these were not the desires that commanded her. Sam had not raised her to dream of marrying the first big-chinned wonder who came a-courting. He had encouraged in her a freedom of spirit and thought, of *ambition*, and for this alone she would love him fiercely until the day he died.

Which, if he didn't watch his drinking, would be a day not long in the coming.

She plucked up his glass, walked to the sink and poured it away.

'Are you mad!' howled her father. 'Have you any idea how much that cost?'

'Whisky for breakfast, Papa? Really?' The Bombay Prohibition Act that had come into force the previous year had hardly slowed him down – medical chits granting permission to purchase liquor for health reasons were easy enough to obtain. Even the licensed bars and clubs were forced to use bootleggers to keep the taps flowing.

'The poor girl's only looking out for you,' offered Aziz.

Sam gave his friend a filthy look. 'And what time did *you* get up today?'

'Me? Up at the crack of dawn, as usual.'

'Really? What time did your hangover get up?'

'I'm not the one with a face like a depressed German clown.'

As they glared at one another, Aunt Nussie asked her about the evening before. 'You missed a wonderful party. I mean, really dear, who works on New Year's Eve?'

'Anyone with half a sense of duty,' muttered Sam.

'What use will duty be when she's an old unmarried maid?'

Her mother's younger sister was the other reason Persis had agreed to stand the graveyard shift on New Year's Eve. It was the only way to avoid attending a soirée at Aunt Nussie's home, where, no doubt, she had planned yet another elaborate scheme aimed at thrusting her melon-headed son in Persis's direction. It was not just that Darius Khambatta was her cousin (cousin-marrying within the Parsee community had long been an acceptable practice, responsible, in her private opinion, for their slow waltz to extinction.) It was rather that the sight of a drooling Darius in polished brogues, an ill-fitting three-piece suit, and sporting the expression of a man who looked as if he were about to lay a large egg through a very small hole was enough to put her off marriage for good.

Persis sometimes wondered whether her decision to join the force had been motivated by her desire to prove something to those around her. Following her schooling, it was expected that she would throw herself headlong into the business of marriage and procreation. But in the dead of night her own desires had risen up like smoke to enfold her.

She chose the police force precisely because it seemed a fit for her own sense of morality, a desire to even up the scales in a country where those with wealth and influence could literally get away with murder. In some ways, she was attempting to measure up to the mother she had barely known but whose spectre hovered constantly at her shoulder. By all accounts, Sanaz Wadia had been a woman of great conviction.

As she ate, she found herself sharing the outline of the investigation that lay before her. She reasoned that news of the murder would soon hit the papers; secrecy was pointless. The murder of a million Indians might pass with barely a raised eyebrow in the halls of power, but the death of an Englishman would raise a hue and cry to rouse the gods.

The irony of the situation was not lost on her.

At the beginning of the new decade, the British may have quit India in name, but many remained in the country. More than sixty thousand, at the last estimate. Some had stayed on to live out their remaining days amid the ashes of empire; others had businesses to run or wind down, while others – like Archie Blackfinch – had been tasked to help India find its feet. It was one thing taking the reins of a country as large and unwieldy as the new republic, quite another coming to grips with the monumental task of running her.

Sam's face darkened. He set down his fork and pushed his plate away.

'An Englishman,' he said woodenly. Daylight from the bay window behind him splashed from his bald dome. His greying moustache crinkled as his mouth bent into a grimace. 'You would dishonour your mother by investigating the murder of a Britisher?'

'The British didn't kill my mother,' she countered. 'She should never have been at that rally.'

As soon as the words escaped her mouth she wished she could take them back.

Sam stiffened, a faint tremor of shock passing through him. Without another word, he wheeled his chair around and headed towards his bedroom, the chair's right wheel squeaking in the sudden silence.

As the door closed on him, Aunt Nussie spoke up. 'You shouldn't have said that, Persis.'

Persis refrained from pointing out that her aunt had made the same point on numerous occasions. She wondered what had possessed her to upset her father. Perhaps it was because she had spent part of the night fretting over his reaction to her involvement in the case. Sam might have forgiven the British for many things, but what he could never forgive them for was the death of his wife.

The door to the apartment opened behind them and Krishna, her father's driver and manservant, bundled into the room.

A sixty-year-old south Indian with a potbelly and skin as dark as onyx, Krishna had served the Wadias for the best part of two decades; in some ways, he had been a nanny to Persis. A father of six – all tucked away in a village in the Keralan backwaters, together with his wife, to whom he dutifully posted money orders every month – he was the most inept driver Persis knew. But Sam would never dream of getting rid of him. The two men had shared much, soldier and general.

He turned to her and wheezed, 'There is a man downstairs. He wishes to see you, madam.'

She took the stairs down into the shop, entering it from the rear.

It was the smell that always took her. The unmistakable musk of books, old and new. Arrayed on sagging shelves, piled on trestle tables, built up into drifts eight feet high, to form a haphazard maze that only hardened bibliophiles dared to tread. Over the years, Persis had attempted to impose a semblance of order on the chaos, only to be thwarted by the impracticality of the task. Her father tolerated her efforts with a supercilious expression, knowing full well that no sane person could hope to prevail against the shop's rampant disarray.

'But how can you ever *find* anything?' she would wail.

Sam would grin and tap the side of his forehead. 'It's all in here, daughter of mine.'

The Wadia Book Emporium, tucked away in a corner of Nariman Point at the southern tip of Bombay, flanked on one side by a liquor store and on the other by a cloth merchant, had managed to maintain a loyal clientele throughout the war years. Indeed, though Sam's father, Dastoor Wadia, had openly declared himself for the British at the beginning of the Quit India movement, such was his and the shop's popularity that it had had little effect on the business. It was only later, when the struggle gravitated beyond rhetoric to bloodshed, that father and son were faced with a choice: continue to side with a despotic occupier whose increasingly desperate attempts to maintain the status quo had resulted in shocking acts of cruelty; or join their fellow countrymen.

It had been time to face the truth.

And so the Wadias had thrown in their lot with the revolutionaries. Dastoor became a member of the underground movement, printing and distributing revolutionary propaganda in the shop, holding clandestine meetings with agitators, and, in general, making up for lost time.

Persis retained few memories of her grandfather and none at all of her grandmother – one thing that Sam and his father had shared was the early passing of their wives. Dastoor himself had died one stormy monsoon night, shortly after Persis's eleventh birthday, felled by a heart attack. They found him the next morning, slumped in the battered sofa he kept at the rear of the shop, a copy of Baudelaire's *The Flowers of Evil* still clutched in his grasp. In his latter years, the old *bawa* had taken to wandering down into the shop on restless nights, finding some sense of solace there from the troubles of the time and his own fading health.

It was a habit Persis shared.

As a girl, she had imagined that the books talked to each other in the dark. Papery whispers that gave her comfort through a troubled childhood. The shop became her refuge. Sitting between the shelves, unfashionable reading glasses perched on the end of her nose, she gulped in knowledge. In a very real sense the bookshop had shaped the woman she had become. If she was a police officer today, it was because she had imbibed stories of real-life heroines: aviator Amelia Earhart; Swiss explorer Isabelle Eberhardt, who'd moved to Algeria and dressed as a man to fit in with the locals; British suffragette Emmeline Pankhurst. Indian heroines too: the Rani of Jhansi who'd rebelled against the British; Keladi Chennamma, the 'Pepper Queen' of Karnataka, who'd repelled the Mughal armies of Aurangzeb. These were the women who had inspired her; these were her companions throughout her awkward teenage years.

She had few real friends. Her prickly personality, her refusal to conform, had marked her out as a troublemaker. The other girls at her Anglo school had ostracised her; she had become the focus of their petty cruelties. One day they had rounded on her, teasing her mercilessly until she hurled insults back at them. They held her down and cut off her plaits. The next day, her father's war-cry ringing in her ears, she had returned to the school and ambushed the ringleader, beating the girl black and blue. And so it had continued, until they learned to keep their distance. She had grown to understand loneliness. As with all things, individualism came at a price.

It was a price she was willing to pay.

At the front of the shop she discovered a neatly dressed Indian. She recognised him from Herriot's home: the manservant who had opened the door to her.

'Madam.' He handed her an envelope. 'From Lal Sahib.'

She took the envelope and tore it open.

Lal's handwriting was as immaculate as the man himself; it spiralled over the creamy bond paper in flawless loops.

Inspector Wadia,

Allow me to thank you for your sterling efforts last night. Most impressive. It is my hope that you will continue to head up the investigation into Sir James's death. I have conveyed the same to the commissioner this morning. As per your request please find below a summary of Sir James's recent engagements. I shall be at your disposal. Please do not hesitate to prevail upon me.

Yours faithfully,
Madan Lal

No honorific, she noted. Perhaps the man wasn't quite the stiff she had thought.

Her gaze moved down to the list of Herriot's recent appointments – Lal had been thorough and had covered the past three months – picking out those she thought might be worth following up. There were a number of instances where Herriot had travelled out of the city, but the destinations were not mentioned.

Two recent encounters stood out.

On the morning of his death he had met a Robert Campbell at the Bombay Gymkhana – the only scheduled meeting for that day.

Two days prior to his death, on 29 December, he had met an Adi Shankar. The name stood out because Persis recalled that Herriot had kept a newspaper cutting in his desk of Adi Shankar launching a nightclub in the city. Shankar and Campbell were among those who had left Laburnum House without being interviewed.

A postscript was scrawled at the bottom of the letter.

P.S. I have arranged a meeting for you with K.P. Tilak, the Deputy Home Minister. He is presently in the city celebrating the new year. Tilak will be able to outline for you details of Sir James's work in India. Please report to South Court, Malabar Hill at thirteen hundred hours. A word of warning. Tilak is one of those rare politicos who respects punctuality.

She checked her watch. Almost nine. Plenty of time to get to the office, report in, and then head over to Malabar Hill.

She suspected it was going to be a long day.

4

The station house was a short drive from the bookshop. She took the jeep, navigating the morning traffic – cycle rickshaws weaving in between double-decker buses and rattling trams, hordes of suicidal handcartwallahs vying with the glut of post-Partition automobiles, everywhere the bustle of a city that had rolled up its sleeves, intent on meeting the future head-on.

The war years had made Bombay leaner, she reflected, but now, following independence, migrants were flooding in, forcing the city into a conflict of identity. Always the most cosmopolitan metropolis in the country, it had yet to shed the image of itself that it held most dear. The city of jazz and good times. Of nightclubs and the hedonistic imperialism of the Raj. Thousands of foreigners continued to live the life they had become accustomed to, even as the foundations of that life crumbled around them. Social unrest, protests, a tumultuous push towards Nehru's socialist vision. The ones who thrived now were the ones who had adapted to the new order. For the most part opportunists, though there were genuine sympathisers too. Americans and Europeans, and the occasional Brit willing to stake their claim in the new reality. The Bombay she had known, a city that mixed Portuguese roots with British architecture and native culture, was changing. She wasn't yet sure that the changes were to her liking.

She parked on the main road, before walking along the bustling street towards Malabar House, craning her neck as she approached her home of the past months.

The building was a four-storey Edwardian affair, neoclassical in look and ambition. Built by Scotsman George Wittet – the genius behind the Gateway of India monument – the front façade was a sea of red Malad stone, broken up by a series of horizontal grooves and casement windows. Balustraded balconies fronted some of the windows, and here and there the ugly rear-ends of air conditioners overhung the street. A succession of spouted gargoyles looked down on to passing traffic from the edge of the roof; where water had poured from their mouths, the façade's stonework was discoloured an unsightly yellow. On the ground floor, an arcaded front entrance, emblazoned with the words MALABAR HOUSE, was guarded by a uniformed doorman.

The building housed the only police station in the Malabar Hill area, an affluent enclave overlooking the Back Bay. The region had become home to many Brits when the old Bombay Fort had been demolished a couple of decades earlier. Now it was an acropolis of wealth and power, its inhabitants largely insulated from the whorl of history unfolding around them.

She walked in through the entrance, the doorman salaaming her smartly.

In the lobby – a vision of white marble, terrazzo, lacquered wood and endlessly spinning ceiling fans – a trio of dogs raised their heads, then went back to reclining in the shadows. The dogs were strays who had wandered in one day and made themselves at home. Now, they had become Malabar House's unofficial mascots.

Six months after moving in, it continued to astonish Persis how easily they had fallen into the rhythms of the place. It was as if they were a spoke inserted into a moving wheel or a gasket into a running engine. The building was located on the relatively sedate John Adams Street, owned by, and headquarters to, one of the country's great houses of commerce. Indeed, it was only thanks to the generosity of that particular corporation's patron that they had been given the building's basement as a temporary HQ for their new crime branch unit, set up to handle some of the more sensitive cases overflowing from the state's overworked and under-resourced criminal investigation department, the much maligned CID.

At least that was the story they had been told.

They all knew, of course, that the real reason they had been sent there was because no one knew where else to put them. They were a 'menagerie of misfits', to use the phrase one newspaper had coined. The unwanted and the undesirables. If such a label bothered her, she tried not to show it. She had always known that life as the force's first female police detective would be a trial of prejudice.

She recalled her initial interview at the police recruitment office in Fort. The astonished clerk had at first laughed, and then when he understood that she was serious had led her to a small office. Here she had waited for hours until a senior officer had arrived. As she had explained herself, he had listened intently, then lit a pipe. 'You're not the first woman to have made her way here. Most vanish once they understand what they are up against. What makes you think *you* would be suitable for such a role?'

She had listed for him her capabilities, her sterling education, her physical strengths, her eagerness to pursue justice. He had smiled at her, not unkindly.

'Persis, I don't doubt your enthusiasm. But the fact is that there has never been a female officer in the Indian Police Service. How do you think you will fare in such an environment?'

She had set her jaw defiantly. 'Wouldn't a better question be how will the Indian Police Service fare with *me*?'

He had stared at her then burst into wild laughter.

Three months later she had taken the IPS entrance exams, qualifying in the top one percentile of the country. The physical too she had passed with flying colours – she had spent years in a martial arts class run by a friend of her father's; she was a swimmer, thinking nothing of hurling herself into a hundred laps each morning at the Breach Candy Club pool near her home.

The two years of training had been less of an ordeal than it might have been for another in her shoes. Years of self-reliance and a stubbornness bordering on mania had prepared her well. She had, for the most part, ignored the open hostility.

She made her way down a marbled staircase to the basement, and into the offices of the police unit, where she was pulled up short by the sight of her colleagues already at their desks. She checked her watch.

Impossible.

'What are you all doing here?' It was unusual for her not to be the first in, and even more unusual to find them so alert this early in the day.

'Perhaps *you* can tell *us*, ma'am,' said Sub-Inspector Karim Haq, peering up from his desk. A plate of samosas sat under his nose. Haq's breakfast – a daily affair – went some way to explaining his generous waistline, currently straining the buttons of his khaki shirt. 'The SP called us in. He said for you to go straight in.'

Persis wound her way between the desks and knocked on a door at the very rear of the room.

'Come!'

She entered, closing the door behind her.

Superintendent of Police Roshan Seth looked up from the manila folder open on the desk before him and stared at her, glassy-eyed.

'Good morning, sir,' she said, and then, as an afterthought, 'Happy New Year to you.'

Seth winced. 'Not so loud, for God's sake.' He sat up straight, picked up a glass of water, dropped a tablet into it, then drained the fizzing mixture with an expression of grim distaste.

Persis said nothing. It wasn't the first time she had arrived at Malabar House to find her commanding officer the worse for wear. She stood there, rigid-backed, radiating disapproval.

Roshan Seth was an enigma to her. In the time she had served under him, she had come to appreciate his finer qualities. It wasn't so long ago that Seth's star had shone brightly within the Brihanmumbai Police Service, a man being groomed for the top. And then independence had happened, and Seth – a tear-gas-and-lathi-charge officer, a man who had toed the British line, believing his duty to his uniform to supersede his duty to the cause of his countrymen – had fallen from favour. Not quite labelled a collaborator, he had, nevertheless, been deemed worthy of censure by the mandarins who had taken over from the British. The slide had begun, ending in the transfer to Malabar House. A man who had once commanded the very best was left with those no one else wished to work with. The drinking had soon taken over.

'So,' he began finally, 'you appear to have landed us in the dung-heap.'

She stiffened. 'I'm not certain that I follow.'

'Sir James Herriot. I received a call this morning. At my *home*. ADC Amit Shukla wished to congratulate me on my initiative in taking up the investigation into Sir James's murder. Wanted to know when he might expect me to put the matter to bed. A very sensitive situation, as he was at pains to point out. A political land-mine. I could still hear his laughter when I put down the phone.'

'I don't understand.'

He stared at her. 'No, I don't suppose you do.' The fingers of his right hand drummed the desk. 'Persis, this isn't just another murder. A case like this generates newsprint. Headlines. One wrong move could end our careers, such as they are.'

'I'm confident we can solve this, sir.'

'Are you?' He looked at her sternly. 'Have you any idea *why* they called us? Allow me to explain. Whatever it was that James Herriot was doing for our government, it was a matter of some secrecy. I have made a number of calls this morning – I still have a few friends left – and no one seems to know what he was up to. Do you understand?'

'No.'

'It means that he was involved in something unsavoury, something few people knew about or wish to talk about. Your friend Lal could have called anyone. He could have woken up the commissioner himself and had a crack team sent over from Patnagar's unit.' Ravi Patnagar. Head of the state CID, a former friend of Seth's, now turned bitter enemy. 'But he did not. He called us. Doesn't that strike you as odd?'

'What should I have done, sir? Told him that our dance card was full and directed him elsewhere?'

Seth pursed his lips. 'Do you remember the day Gandhi was shot? I was with a Muslim colleague when we heard the news. He practically swooned into my arms. Because, of course, he, like the rest of us, thought that the assassin had to be a Muslim. Can you imagine the terror *that* would have unleashed? It was a relief to us all when word began to spread that the killer was, in fact, a Hindu. But then, all the Hindus began to panic that it was one of *their* own. Their caste, their tribe, their community. We are a country of a million factions each more than ready to point the finger of blame elsewhere.' He sighed. 'These are turbulent times, Persis. Uncertainty makes people anxious. No one wants to be left holding the baby. And you have just brought the baby home with you.'

Persis stiffened. 'All I ask is that I be allowed to do what I have been trained for.'

'You're an ambitious woman. But ambition has been known to sink whole nations.'

Her eyes flashed. 'Is ambition a virtue in a man and a vice in a woman?'

Seth's eyes softened. 'I did not say that. I have three daughters. India is changing, Persis, but it is not yet ready to be told that it is wrong. At least not by a woman.'

Persis did not trust herself to speak.

The silence stretched and then Seth rose to his feet.

'Call in the rest of them. We may as well let them know what they're in for.'

One by one the team filed in. Persis's fellow inspector, Hemant Oberoi; the trio of sub-inspectors, George Fernandes, Pradeep Birla and Karim Haq; and the two constables, Suresh Subramanium and Rabindranath Ray. They entered in silence, but she could sense their curiosity and trepidation.

She waited for Seth to say something, but he moved to one side. 'You have the floor, Inspector.'

She took a deep breath and quickly summarised the case for them.

When she had finished, they turned as one to look at Seth. A flash of annoyance burned through her.

'This is a political case,' remarked Fernandes, frowning. 'High profile. Why have they given it to *us*?'

'Ours is not to reason why,' replied Seth woodenly.

'Nothing good will come of it,' muttered Birla darkly. 'Mark my words.'

'Why did they take his trousers?' asked Haq, ever to the point.

No further inspiration was forthcoming on the matter of the missing trousers. Oberoi, who had not yet spoken, turned to the SP. 'She shouldn't be heading this investigation.'

Persis narrowed her eyes.

Hemant Oberoi represented everything that was wrong with the force. The very worst aspects of male arrogance, ignorance and privilege distilled into the body of a single man. He hailed from a wealthy Brahmin family, the scion of a former royal, according to one rumour. He certainly acted like it, swanning about the place as if he were some exiled Balkan aristocrat merely passing time on an island prison before being returned to his rightful throne. Tall and blessed with the looks of a matinee idol – complete with a head of lacquered hair and a rakish moustache – he had washed up at Malabar House thanks to an indiscretion, stepping out with the sister of a high-ranking civil servant, a liaison that had ended badly. A career destined for the top – nepotism, after all, favoured the sons of the rich and powerful – had been unceremoniously curtailed, leaving Oberoi in a fury of seething resentment.

'She took the call,' said Seth. 'It's her case.'

'*She* is standing right here,' said Persis coldly. 'Anything you have to say you can say to me.'

Oberoi turned to her. 'You don't deserve this case.'

'And you do?'

'I've been in the service longer than you.'

'Just because a cow stands in a field all day doesn't make it a philosopher.'

Haq sniggered. Oberoi's face bulged with fury; a smile stretched the corners of Seth's mouth.

'What about our other cases?' asked Fernandes, his expression troubled.

'What cases?' said Seth, raising an eyebrow. There was an embarrassed shuffling. The fact was that Malabar House was, quite possibly, the least utilised of the city's police units. And the cases that did come their way were hardly the kind to make headlines.

Persis knew that George Fernandes was a good policeman. He had only ended up at Malabar House because of the sort of tragic error that might have happened to any police officer.

George Fernandes had shot the wrong man.

A raid on a smuggler's den had led to a chase. Fernandes had pursued his quarry down the back alleys of Colaba, eventually cornering and shooting the man. It only later became clear that he had shot dead an innocent bystander who had seen Fernandes hurtling down the road at him waving a revolver and had simply taken off. In the confusion, Fernandes had lost sight of the man he had been chasing and continued to run down the civilian. Smuggler and civilian had both been wearing red shirts that day, one of those fateful cosmic coincidences that no one could legislate for.

'What motive could anyone have had to murder Herriot?' It was Birla who had spoken.

Of all her colleagues, Pradeep Birla was the one Persis found hardest to fathom. A quiet man, Birla was a deeply religious individual who began each morning before the makeshift temple he had set up at the rear of their basement premises. The scent of sandalwood and incense would choke out the office as Birla joined hands respectfully before the various idols crammed into his diorama. The smoke and Birla's voice raised in prayer would inevitably rouse Karim Haq to irritation. In some ways, the two men mirrored the resentments that continued to seethe below the surface of the new republic. Hindu and Muslim were ostensibly equals in India, but the truth was that the bitterness instigated by Partition still echoed in the hearts of millions across the country.

Birla's comment seemed to release the tension, and one by one they began to apply themselves to the task at hand.

'Did he have any enemies?' asked Fernandes.

'None that anyone was willing to tell me about,' replied Persis.

'It's really quite simple,' remarked Oberoi. He gave her a haughty look. Persis dug her nails into her palms. 'Sir James is an Englishman. There are still plenty of agitators who believe that every last Britisher should have been cast out in 1947. Many of them wouldn't think twice about slipping a knife into a man like Herriot. And who's to say they're wrong?'

'Your family did well enough under them,' muttered Haq.

'What's that supposed to mean?' bristled Oberoi.

The two men glared at each other, but Haq said no more. There was little love lost between the pair. Then again, Oberoi had a habit of rubbing most of his colleagues up the wrong way.

Persis wondered if the man had a point. Could someone bearing a lingering grudge against the British have picked Herriot as a target?

Following the briefing, she divided up the task of calling on those who had been in attendance at Sir James's ball but had left before she could interview them. She gave each man a set of names and addresses and a list of questions she wished them to ask. She stressed the importance of persistence. 'These are wealthy and powerful people. Don't let them brush you aside.'

In truth, she hated the idea of handing over this aspect of the investigation. But there were simply too many names and not enough time to chase them all over the city. There was no guarantee they would all remain in Bombay for long. Many of Herriot's friends belonged to that elite social circle with interests and homes around the country. The type who summered in Shimla and shopped in Paris while multitudes starved on their doorsteps.

Oberoi was, as she had expected, less than enthusiastic. 'If you think I'm going to run around the city as your personal errand boy, you are mistaken.'

She stared at him stonily. It was pointless asking Seth to intervene. Oberoi was a law unto himself; it had always been the slimmest of probabilities that he would agree to work under her direction.

She returned to her desk. It was almost ten. Three hours before her appointment with the Deputy Home Minister. She cleared her mind and focused on the day before her.

Her meeting with the minister would hopefully shed light on Herriot's work, which in turn might reveal more about the man himself. Following that she hoped to talk to Robert Campbell, the man whom Herriot had met on the morning of his death. An autopsy was scheduled at the Grant Medical College at twelve the following day. With a buzz of irritation, she realised she would have to inform Lal's friend, Archie Blackfinch. The man had seemed competent enough, but she resented the fact that he had been forced on to her. It was going to be difficult enough juggling her own team without having to worry about a clumsy Englishman with a penchant for stating the obvious.

She took out her notebook, flipped through it, and mentally lined up the information she had so far collected.

James Herriot had been murdered at his home. He seemed a well-liked man, comfortable in wealth and influence. Piecing together his life would not be difficult. But what about the circumstances of his death?

Minor details bothered her. The ticket stub. The piece of paper from his jacket with the meaningless jumble of letters and numbers.

She took out the paper from an evidence bag on her desk. BAKSHI. It was a common enough name. Beneath the name: PLT41/85ACRG11. Who was Bakshi? What did the string of characters mean?

Nothing sprang to mind.

She focused on the stamped writing at the top of the page: *By a pool of nectar, at the shrine of the sixty-eight.*

The sheet had clearly been torn from a notepad. She realised that she could just about make out the bottom of a few printed letters along the jagged tear. Possibly a few 'E's, a 'G', an 'L', and an 'O' towards the end. Four words, by her estimation. This suggested to her that the sheet was stamped stationery. Which meant that the line of text – *By a pool of nectar, at the shrine of the sixty-eight*

– was somehow related to the organisation or establishment that had printed the stationery. A motto or identifier. If she could work out the name of the organisation, she might be able to trace Herriot's movements, and so work out what the characters PLT41/85ACRG11 referred to.

She wrote out the letters she thought she could make out, together with dashes to indicate where she suspected there were letters that had been completely torn away:

_ _ E G_ _ _E_ _E_ _L_ _O_ _ _

She struggled with the problem for a while – it was a good bet that the first word might be 'THE' – but got no further forward. The whole thing might have nothing to do with Herriot's killing at all.

She pondered a moment on the open safe and the missing trousers. She could understand that a killer bent on theft might take whatever was in the safe, but why take the trousers? How did he get them out of Laburnum House? The same applied to the murder weapon. Both knife and trousers seemed to have vanished into thin air.

Her mind looped around itself.

5

By the time she left the office, traffic had built up. The road was clogged with cars, tongas and fume-belching trucks, the roadside with hawkers and pedestrians, bookstalls and handcarts.

A herd of goats blocked the Wellington Fountain roundabout, the chaos exacerbated by a gang of striking mill workers, pumping their fists and shouting anti-Congress slogans. Labour unrest had spread like a disease since independence. Nehru's socialist ideals collided spectacularly with a society that, for millennia, had been marked by deep divisions and the rule of kings and conquerors. Only last week, Persis had read about agitation in Delhi, disillusioned steel workers marching in the capital. Four of the workers had doused themselves in kerosene in front of Parliament House and lit a match. Self-immolation had become a terrifying means of protest around the country.

She made good time along Madam Cama Road, then on to Marine Drive, a three-mile-long esplanade housing a succession of art deco towers – the Oceana, the Shalimar, the Chateau Marine – home to corporate moguls, film stars, and wealthy Hindu families recently arrived from Pakistan, taking the tenancy reins from chain-smoking European émigrés who had returned home at the end of the war.

As a girl, she and her father would join the Sunday throng gathered on the jagged strip of seafront at one end of the promenade to watch movies projected on to a giant screen. She recalled those days with fondness, the face of her mother a ghost in the breeze blowing in off the sea.

She parked on Alexander Graham Bell Road, then walked up to South Court.

The building, informally known as Jinnah House, had been built by Mohammed Ali Jinnah, the 'father' of Pakistan. Jinnah, a trained lawyer, had been a leading light within Gandhi's Indian National Congress until their campaign of civil disobedience. Jinnah disliked the idealistic underpinnings of *satyagraha* – literally: 'insistence upon the truth' – describing it as 'political anarchy'. By the forties, he had come to believe that the Muslims of India must have their own country; in 1940 his All-India Muslim League passed the Lahore Resolution demanding a separate nation. Six years later, in August 1946, he announced a day of 'direct action', urging a general strike in support of his Muslim homeland. Three days of mayhem followed. By the time the killing ended, five thousand lay dead in Calcutta alone. The prospect of continued sectarian violence on such a scale shook even the British out of their torpor. That was the moment Partition became inevitable.

Persis was met at the arched gateway by a dark-suited civil serv-ant introducing himself as Prasad. He greeted her warmly, then led her past petunia beds and mango trees, through the garden where Mountbatten had once strolled planning the dissolution of empire, and into the mansion proper.

In the dining room, she found the Deputy Home Minister at one end of a long, polished table, leafing intently through a set of papers. Mounds of similar papers were piled up around the table like sandbags.

The minister waved her into a seat beside him.

She sat, recalling that K.P. Tilak was another of those to whom the independence movement had been kind. A small, avuncular presence, dressed in a plain white kurta and leggings, he seemed at ease with his place in the new scheme of things.

'Thank you for joining me, Inspector. May I offer you a cup of tea?' He indicated the porcelain tea set at his elbow. 'Please don't refuse. Tea is one of those British refinements that simply cannot be partaken on one's own.'

Not quite sure what to say, Persis did as she had been asked, pouring herself a cup of fragrant Darjeeling.

He smiled at her, his eyes crinkling at the corners as he sipped at his tea. 'I have been wishing to meet you for quite some time,' he began. 'Our nation's first female IPS officer! You know, one day they will read about you in the history books. The likes of myself will fade into the darkness, Persis, but you will live for ever. Such is the fate of all pioneers.'

She did not know how to respond to this. Blushing, she hid behind her tea. Tilak's reputation as a charmer was well deserved.

'But now, you find yourself caught between the crosshairs of fate, an uncomfortable place at the best of times.'

He followed this enigmatic comment with a moment of silence, staring up at the wall where a picture of Gandhi looked down upon them. Beside it was a photograph of Jinnah. She wondered what it was still doing there, and then recalled that the home now belonged to the British. In Indian hands, no doubt, any sign of Jinnah would have been excised from the mansion.

'He knew him, you know. Or rather, they knew each other. Jinnah and Herriot. They'd sparred over the years. Jinnah was always a cold fish; he never really warmed to anyone. But Herriot, there was a man who knew what made people tick. Do *you* know, Persis?'

She set down her tea. 'No, sir.'

'Passion, Inspector. Inflame a man's passion and you can make him do anything. Jinnah liked to appeal to people's intellectualism. The fact is that most cannot see past the ends of their own noses. But tell them they stand to regain their souls, and they'll burn down an empire for you.' He smiled grimly. 'India is a dream, Persis. A dream we all agreed to dream together. But dreams evaporate upon awakening. It might be strange for you to hear the Deputy Home Minister say this, but the truth is that harmony in our new republic is all but impossible. We are too divided, too factionalised, too fractured by our recent experiences. And yet we must make the effort. For we cannot move forward without it.'

'Sir, how is this relevant to the death of Sir James?'

He smiled again. 'I had heard that you were impatient.' He set down his cup, his expression now serious. 'On January 26th, India officially becomes a republic. Twenty-five days, that is how long you have to solve this case, Persis. Let me tell you why. Sir James was working on a matter of great import to our government, to our nation. To move into the future, one must first bury the past. That is what Sir James was doing for us.'

'I don't follow.'

'Four months ago, we asked Sir James to take on a secret commission, a commission to investigate atrocities committed during Partition. It was his task to examine reports of brutalities that occurred during that turbulent time and, where possible, identify individuals guilty of actions that might be tried in a court of law. Rape, murder, incitement to murder. Crimes against humanity. The fact is, Inspector, that there are numerous individuals who have gained power in the new India whose souls are stained with blood, a canker at the heart of the country's economic and political machinery.'

Persis absorbed this silently. Finally, something concrete had emerged from the fog. Sir James Herriot had been given a task that, by its very nature, would have set him on a path of conflict with those who wished their crimes to remain hidden.

'Did you know him well?' she asked.

'Sir James? Yes, I knew him well enough. We'd crossed paths before, during the struggle. He'd always been open about his support for Indian Home Rule.'

'So he was a good man? In your opinion?'

The question seemed to surprise him. 'My opinion, for what it is worth, is that Sir James Herriot was one of those men who endeavoured to do good, and if in the doing of that good he might help himself, so much the better.' He nodded at the picture of Gandhi. 'He was certainly no mahatma.'

Mahatma, thought Persis. *Mahaan aatma.* Meaning 'great soul'.

'What sort of man *was* he?'

'Intelligent. Gregarious. A man who liked the finer things in life. He loved India, not just for what it was, but because of what it made him: a man of consequence. Politically, he was a fierce negotiator. A dog with a bone once something got under his skin. It is one of the reasons we picked him for the Partition Commission.'

'How many people knew of this commission?'

'Only a handful of us within the government. It was believed that if it became common knowledge, it would not only incite a great hue and cry, but might also drive those we sought underground, or to rashness of action. Witnesses to such crimes might have been exposed to danger.'

'And Sir James himself? Was he sworn to secrecy?'

'To a great extent. Of course, any investigation of this magnitude will generate ripples, as I am sure you will soon discover.'

'I would like to see the material he collected during his investigation.'

'I'm afraid that will be difficult.'

Persis frowned. 'Sir, if you wish me to proceed, I must have access to all available information.'

'You don't understand,' said Tilak. 'Sir James had yet to file a report. He kept his documents at his home. And, from what I have been told, those documents may now have been destroyed.'

6

The Bombay Gymkhana. As one of the oldest clubs in the city the Gymkhana enjoyed a certain cachet among Bombay's elite. Initially set up to enable British gentlemen to congregate with the intention of enjoying sporting pursuits – ranging from archery and polo to tennis and shooting – membership had become a must-have symbol of success. Now the wait for an invitation might stretch into years. This alone made the place irresistible to a certain type of Bombayite. It was here that Persis had arranged to see Robert Campbell, the man Herriot had met on the morning of the 31st.

On the drive over from South Court her thoughts had lingered on the meeting with Tilak.

'Sir James had many friends in the British government,' he had said, as he walked her out to the gate. 'They will demand answers. I hope you understand?'

She understood well enough. Tilak was gently warning her that failure would not be looked upon kindly.

She had asked him for a copy of the original dossier handed to Sir James, detailing the alleged incidents of Partition atrocities that he had been tasked to investigate. He informed her that a copy of the documents was held in Delhi. He would arrange for the files to be sent to her.

'I have one last question, sir.' She hesitated. 'Why Malabar House? Why have you not passed the case to one of the bigger units?'

Tilak had replied easily. 'Madan Lal seems to have great faith in you, Inspector. He was Sir James's right-hand man. If he trusts you, who am I to argue?'

She left her jeep in the car park, then made her way to the front entrance where a concierge in a club blazer led her through the lobby, a fetish of panelled oak and marble, through a smoke-filled billiards room, and out to the rear, where they swiftly arrived at the tennis courts.

On the nearest court a robust-looking white gentleman – she guessed him to be in his fifties – was thrashing a ball over the net at a young redhead. The woman, long-limbed and immaculate in tennis whites, bounced up and down on the soles of her feet before returning the ball with pinpoint precision. Her opponent heaved himself across the court like a three-legged wildebeest, fenced at the ball as it whizzed past, then collapsed to the ground in a shower of phlegm and curses.

'Game, set and match,' said the young woman breezily, skipping over to the other side of the net. Persis could not help but note that she was striking, with high, sweat-sheened cheekbones and piercing blue eyes.

The girl stuck out a hand, offering to help up her defeated opponent, but he batted it away with his racquet and struggled to his feet unaided, his face raw and ruddy.

'That ball was out.'

'Afraid not, Pater. You lost fair and square.'

The man – Robert Campbell, Persis presumed – scowled. He was a bear, with thick shoulders, a head of bristly, greying hair, prominent jowls and a sort of menacing pout. His eyes were the same blue as his daughter's.

He was about to retort but Persis stepped forward to interrupt him.

Campbell seemed momentarily puzzled, and then recalled that he had agreed to the appointment.

'Come on,' he said, 'let's do this in the bar. I need a drink.'

Five minutes later, the Scotsman was hunkered into a leather seat, still in his whites, nursing a beer with one hand while holding a cold compress on his right knee with the other. His daughter, Elizabeth, stood behind him, a glass of pomegranate juice in her hand. Neither had offered their visitor a drink.

Around them, a number of gentlemen chatted, smoked and drank in similar chairs scattered around the bar. The majority were elderly and Indian, accompanied by a smattering of English, Americans and Europeans. Curious glances had been directed their way, no doubt attracted by Persis's uniform.

'Desperately bad business,' Campbell muttered. 'A man's no' safe in his own house any more.' His Scottish accent had been leavened by a long stay on the subcontinent, but was still jarring to Persis.

'How well did you know Sir James?'

'Known him the best part of two decades,' replied Campbell. 'We were business partners. Stuck it out when a lot of the old crowd moved back in 1947.'

'What sort of business?'

'Construction,' said Campbell. 'To be precise, *I* own a construction company. James was a consultant to the firm.'

'What does that mean exactly?'

'It means that it was his job to go out and find us contracts. I'm a trained engineer. I build things. I've never been the type to press the flesh, to talk a man into buying what he plainly doesn't need. James said I had all the tact of a bull in a china shop. Where I'm from, we call it plain-speaking.'

'Where *are* you from, if you don't mind me asking?'

He grunted, a humourless smile. 'I dare say the same place you're from, Inspector. I was born right here. Bombay. Breach Candy Hospital. My father was an old India hand. It was him who set up the firm. Came out here with the Royal Fusiliers, helped build the railways. I was born just before the turn of the century. He'd seen enough by then to know he didn't want his only son growing up among the heathen, so he sent me back home while I was still a bairn. To *his* home. Glasgow. I don't suppose you've ever been?'

She shook her head, ignoring Campbell's casual racism.

'I didn't think so. You Indians aren't much for travelling. Well, let me tell you, Scotland is as far a cry from this place as you could wish for. Burns said it best: "The birthplace of valour; the country of worth." I grew up among my own people, Inspector. I learned what it means to be Scottish.'

'And what would that be?'

He leaned forward, his intense blue eyes staring through her. 'It means not to suffer fools.' He sat back, satisfied with his little outburst.

'What about your daughter?'

'What about her?'

'Were you also born in India?' Persis asked, looking directly at Elizabeth.

'Can you no' tell from her voice?' growled Campbell.

'I was born in Glasgow,' replied Elizabeth, 'but moved to an English finishing school at the age of eleven. Elocution was high on the curriculum. I don't think my father approves.'

'Never saw the need for it. If it hadn't been for her mother insisting on it . . .'

An uncomfortable silence passed.

'You were at his home last night. For the party. Both of you.'

'Aye. We were.'

'But you left early. I mean, I didn't get a chance to speak to you.'

'I wasn't about to wait around all night to be interviewed like some common hoodlum.'

'I noticed that Mrs Campbell was not on the list of attendees.'

'What's that got to do with anything?'

Elizabeth squeezed her father's shoulder. Campbell subsided, staring down angrily into his glass.

'My mother has been unwell for rather a long time, Inspector,' explained the girl. 'Consumption. She returned to Scotland almost two years ago, for treatment at a private clinic. And for the air.' This last part was said with a trace of sardonic amusement, and Persis once again found herself wondering at the stiffness between them, a sense of needle that communicated itself via the tone of voice they used with each other, their body language.

'Do you usually accompany your father to parties?'

'Sometimes,' said Elizabeth. 'There's plenty of eligible young bachelors at these things. Father is ever so keen to see me married off. To the right sort, of course.'

'For God's sakes, girl,' muttered Campbell, loud enough to turn heads. The compress balanced on his leg slipped and fell to the floor.

Persis leaned forward, picked it up and held it out to the dour Scot. He snatched it from her and slapped it back on his knee.

'You had a meeting with Sir James that morning. What was it about?'

'Ach. It was just a business meeting. Routine.'

'What did you talk about?'

'We didn't. We were supposed to meet here at ten. James didn't show.'

'Why not?'

Campbell scowled. 'James was his own man. A cancelled meeting was hardly the end of the world. I was due to see him at the ball that evening anyhow.'

Persis paused, then: 'What sort of man was he?'

Campbell twitched in his seat. 'He was smart. Knew how to get what he wanted.'

'Everyone tells me that he was well liked, that he had no enemies.'

Campbell snorted. 'You're no' so naïve as to believe a man as powerful as James hadn't any enemies, Inspector.'

'Is there anyone specific you can think of?'

'I'm no' the man to be asking.'

'Then who should I be asking?'

'That aide of his. Lal. He's the man James trusted with his secrets.'

'I've already spoken to Lal.'

Campbell grimaced. 'What did you make of him?'

'I'm not sure what you mean. He seemed competent.'

'Don't be fooled, Inspector. There's more than meets the eye there. Did he tell you about his war years?'

'He mentioned that he'd fought in Burma.'

Something gleamed in Campbell's eyes. 'Did he by any chance mention that he was court-martialled while he was out there? That if it hadn't been for James, he'd probably still be in a military stockade?'

Persis was silent, unsure of how to reply.

'The trouble with men like Lal, Inspector, is that they bury their true natures deep inside. It wasn't Gandhi who got rid of the British. It was the Lals of this world. The placid ones who, when history came calling, took up the sword and chopped each other to pieces in the streets. That was what the mandarins back home couldn't stomach. Rivers of blood and them being blamed for it.'

The Scot lumbered to his feet. A powerful smell of sweat wafted from him. Standing before her, she was conscious of the raw strength he projected, the muscles cording his forearms, his thick-fingered hands, the girth of his thighs. And the anger. His rage was a palpable thing.

'I have another appointment. I must be away,' he announced.

Persis stood. 'Thank you for your time.'

Campbell began to walk off stiffly, then stopped and turned. 'Whatever happened to James, the one thing I can tell you is this: he deserved better from this country.' He waved at the club. 'India is a sovereign power now, and James helped to make that a reality. But the truth is, we've put this place in the hands of men who haven't a clue what they're doing.'

'And the British did?' The words came out reflexively; she was barely conscious of the annoyance that lay behind them.

'Whatever our faults, Inspector, we transformed this country. We're leaving it for the better.'

'The British *looted* our country for three hundred years. Millions died, millions more have been beggared. The nation has been divided, in more ways than you probably realise. You call that leaving us for the better?'

'What of economic advancement?' growled Campbell, a scarlet blush racing from his cheeks to the tips of his ears. 'We built industries for you; ports, roads, railways. We lifted you from the dirt and gave you a place in the world.'

Her own face grew hot. It wasn't the first time she had heard such sentiments. There were many like Campbell, nursing their resentment openly. She realised that others had paused their conversations to listen. She wondered why none of them rose up to challenge him, why they allowed him to remain a member of the club when he so openly espoused such views.

But then, institutions such as the Bombay Gymkhana had begun as bastions of British insularity. Once upon a time, Indians would not even have been allowed inside the premises. Nor dogs. As for Indians *with* dogs ... The worst of it was that a man like

Campbell did not even understand what it was that was so wrong with his way of looking at the world. He was so steeped in the mythology of colonialism, the belief that the British were not only superior but knew what was best for others, that he could conceive of nothing else.

A stray thought flashed a fin at the back of her mind. Had the Scotsman's views caused friction with James Herriot, an open advocate of Indian independence?

She found words in her mouth. "'You do well, my son, to cry like a woman, for what you could not defend as a man.'"

Campbell's brow corrugated into a frown. 'What? What was that?'

'They were the words that Boabdil's mother said to him as they left Granada, driven out after seven centuries of Muslim rule.'

Understanding came slowly to the Scot. He rolled on the balls of his feet, his face turning the colour of beetroot. Then he turned and stormed from the room.

'Well done,' murmured a voice by her ear.

She turned to find Elizabeth Campbell smiling beside her.

'It takes a lot to rattle my father. I should know.'

With that she followed him out, leaving behind a cloud of gossip and laughter that rose quickly to engulf the young policewoman.

7

It was late in the afternoon by the time she arrived back at the station, her shirt sticking to her back. She discovered Constable Ray half asleep at his desk. 'Sorry, madam.' He grinned queasily. 'I didn't get much rest last night.'

She knew that Ray, the station's *stick havaldar* – a nomenclature from the Raj era, referring to the constable at any of the city's ninety-three police stations who first attended to complainants – had just had a child; his fifth. She wondered what it must be like in their home. Somewhere between a zoo and a lunatic asylum. She had often wondered at the mores of a society that compelled women to act as little more than birthing machines, pumping out one child after another, often into homes that could barely support them. Her father labelled it ignorance, not unkindly. Persis wasn't so sure. It seemed as if something in the very fabric of life on the subcontinent was stoking this blind urge to procreate. Lust couldn't explain it; nor economic necessity. She thought of it as a contagion, a virulent madness that infected so many of her countrymen.

She sat at her desk, set down her cap, sent the office peon, Gopal, scurrying off to fetch a glass of fresh lime, then settled down to write up her notes.

The day had gone as well as she could have hoped. She had learned much, not least of which was that Sir James Herriot had lived a life more complex than apparent at first glance. He had been tasked to investigate a matter of national importance, and in that task lay a possible motive for his killing. Added to this was his relationship with Robert Campbell, ostensibly a friend, but she had sensed something unspoken there worth investigating further.

And last there was Campbell's own insinuation that Madan Lal was not a man to be trusted.

The investigation was barely a day old and already the onion skin was unravelling, revealing layer upon layer.

One by one her fellow officers drifted in and reported back.

Lal had provided her with a list of all those who had attended the ball. She now added to this her own notes from the interviews she had conducted, and the new information supplied by her colleagues. For the most part this information was bland and led her to mentally dismiss the interviewees in question from her thoughts as either credible suspects or sources of relevant information.

In some cases, she made notes for herself to follow up.

There were two testimonies that stood out.

Sub-Inspector Haq, flopping into a seat beside her, had peered down at his notebook, deciphering his own barely legible handwriting with some difficulty. 'An American woman named Jennifer Macey says that she saw Sir James and his aide, Madan Lal, arguing. They'd stepped into an alcove and she could hear raised voices. She couldn't make out what they were saying, but Lal shot past her a minute later like a dog with its tail on fire.'

Persis felt troubled by the revelation.

Lal had neglected to mention any such argument. Perhaps it was a minor matter and he had considered it immaterial to the investigation. Her own perception of Lal had been positive. She had found him helpful and genuine in his desire to find Herriot's killer. Then again, there was Robert Campbell's claim that Lal was a man with a hidden past. And Tilak had indicated that Herriot's Partition documents were missing, possibly destroyed. Her thoughts went to the burned paper she had found in the Englishman's study. Could those ashes be all that remained of the documents? How would Tilak know of this if not from Lal?

She called Lal but was informed by the housekeeper, Mrs Gupta, that he was out. Gupta told her that Lal would be available in his office the following afternoon.

The second point of detail came via Sub-Inspector George Fernandes. Perched on the edge of his own desk, saddlebags of sweat staining his khaki dress shirt, he had relayed his day's efforts. Persis was impressed. Fernandes had been meticulous and detailed. She imagined that being grilled by the man, with his intense expression and bristling moustache, would be an unsettling experience.

'Claude Derrida, a French Jew, architect by profession. Claims that he walked in on Sir James in his study talking to a man named Vishal Mistry. He knows that was his name because he saw it on a card on the desk. Says they were looking at something on the desk that Sir James quickly covered up with a handkerchief. He didn't get a good look, but he thinks it was "shiny".'

'What was Derrida doing there?'

'He'd arrived early for the party. He wanted to ask Sir James's advice on a personal matter. He's travelling to England in the spring and wanted to know the name of Sir James's tailor there.' Fernandes shook his head. 'I told him to save his money. The best tailors are right here in Bombay. Walk in a beggar, walk out a prince. And all at a fraction of the cost.'

She considered the incident. In and of itself, it seemed inconsequential. But Derrida had seen something. What had Herriot been trying to hide from him? If it had been something valuable, then where was it now? Could it have been whatever the murderer had taken from the safe? She added these questions to her growing list.

'Who is Vishal Mistry?' she asked.

'I don't know. He wasn't on the list of names you gave me.'

Persis frowned and went back through her master list. She realised that Mistry wasn't on the official guest list or the list of staff that Lal had given her. Curious. Clearly, Mistry had been at the house the previous evening.

She stopped by the SP's office before heading home.

She waited patiently as Seth finished haranguing someone on the telephone. Having set the receiver down, he sighed wearily, removed a bottle from his desk and poured himself a drink.

'Have you started drinking yet?' he enquired.

'No.'

'Give it a few days.' He knocked back the whisky, grimaced, then said, 'That was Aalam Channa from the *Indian Chronicle*. He wants to interview you. I told him there wasn't a chance in hell. Congratulations, Persis. You wanted fame. Now you have it. Be careful what you wish for.'

It was getting on for dusk when she parked the jeep in the narrow alley behind the bookshop. She got out and walked back around to the front, where she stopped for a moment and looked over the façade.

She knew that it was in urgent need of repair. The succession of ornamental Doric columns that fronted the glass windows were crumbling, the sandstone pitted and worn by decades of monsoon bombardment and midnight drunks urinating on the bases of the pillars. The windows were plastered with posters for books – all but crowded out by propaganda for her father's various political affiliations, including an announcement for an upcoming Congress Party rally. Above the shopfront, an ornamental frieze displayed both the shop's name and aggressive scenes from Zoroastrian mythology: fabled birds, white horses and the prophet Zoroaster perched atop a mountain, bathed in holy fire. At either edge of the frieze, perched on out-jutting plinths, were two stone vultures, peering down at passers-by with seemingly malevolent intent. These overtly Parsee emblems had bothered her increasingly as she moved towards adulthood – religion had never played a significant part in her life, but she understood how it held sway over so many of her countrymen; during the Partition years, she had seen first-hand the havoc misguided faith could cause.

It was strange, she had often thought, how emancipated India in so many ways mirrored the society of its erstwhile rulers.

She remembered, as a naïve twenty-year-old, listening to Gandhi's thrilling 'Quit India' speech, back in 1942. An under-pressure Churchill, seeking India's continued support in the war, had sent Sir Stafford Cripps to discuss a change to India's political status. But Churchill had proved duplicitous and his overtures were rejected by Gandhi and Jinnah. In a meeting of the Congress Party in Bombay, Gandhi's words became a rallying cry for the nation: *Here is a mantra, a short one, that I give to you. You may imprint it on your hearts and let every breath of yours give expression to it. The mantra is 'Do or Die.' We shall either free India or die in the attempt; we shall not live to see the perpetuation of our slavery.*

Persis had thrown herself into the fight. She had attended rallies and spoken out in college debates. When Gandhi had been imprisoned, she had marched with thousands of others demanding his release.

But now, those days seemed a distant memory. The spirit of national unity had fractured and the old divisions had arisen anew.

Caste prejudice, religious strife, economic inequality. The rich fought tooth-and-nail to hold on to what they had; the poor lashed out in mindless fury, victims of their own ignorance.

Gandhi would have wept, she thought.

The front door, as ever, was unlocked. Her father had always reasoned that if anyone was minded enough to steal books, either they were in dire need of them but could not afford them – in which case they were welcome to them – or, if they happened to be confused thieves, then it was better to have well-read thieves roaming the city than illiterate ones.

The lights had been dimmed, pitching the shop into semi-gloom.

There was no one by the counter. Opening and closing times at the Wadia Book Emporium were haphazard, dictated by her father's moods. The shop had the confidence born of a solid reputation. Word of mouth had spread the gospel: Sam Wadia was a man who *knew* books. He read them, he understood them; he pressed them on to his customers, or snatched them out of their startled hands as they browsed the store.

This one is not for you. Try this one.

The funny thing was, he was invariably right.

Such was the shop's fame that celebrities made a point of frequenting the place. Even Prime Minister Jawaharlal Nehru had dropped in during his frequent visits to the city before Delhi tightened its grip on him. Persis remembered his white Ambassador turning up late one night, Nehru's tall, gaunt figure ambling inside as his security guard fretted beside him. Her father had introduced her. Nehru had smiled, shaken her seventeen-year-old hand, asked her what she had been reading. Shyly, she had shown him the battered copy of *Doctor Zhivago* that had been her constant companion for the past week. Her father claimed that the book had been banned in its native Russia.

Nehru had bought a dozen copies on the spot.

She navigated her way to the rear of the shop where she discovered Sam stretched out on the sofa behind *Historical & Archaeology*, his fistulous legs propped on cushions, head lolling back, a line of drool snaking from the corner of his mouth. His chest lifted in an erratic pumping motion as he gently snored. The wheelchair lay temporarily abandoned. She knew that he was adept at manoeuvring himself in and out of the contraption, but was prone to occasionally spilling himself on to the floor in a tangle of limbs and curses.

A pang of guilt twinged at her insides.

Had she really needed to be so harsh with him? The truth was that she knew too little about the facts of her mother's death to condemn anyone, let alone her own father. Sam had kept the truth bottled inside him, her entreaties over the years falling on deaf ears. Her instincts told her that the bare-boned explanation of her mother's demise at an independence rally was not all that had transpired that day. But each time she probed, Sam's eyes would cloud over, his mouth would set itself into a grim line; he would slam the doors of his mind shut and retreat into himself, not emerging for hours, sometimes days.

They had met at a society ball. Sam had sneaked in with a friend, and it was on the dance floor that he had encountered his future wife. To hear him tell the tale, it was love at first sight. Realising that no ordinary approach would work on a woman in such demand, Sam mounted the stage and bribed the band to play his favourite ragtime melody. He had been quite the dancer, by his own account. The stunt had worked and before long Sanaz and Sam were an item, much to the horror of her father, who had forbidden the match. Undeterred, the pair had eloped.

Sanaz had been promptly cut out of her father's will.

When she died, old man Poonawalla had slipped into a precipitous decline and followed her into the fire.

Persis wished she could have known her father then; that, indeed, she might have witnessed the dance that had won her mother's heart. To see him now, trapped in his wheelchair, was almost more than she could bear.

She decided not to disturb him. It would not be the first time he had slept down in the shop. It was a haven for him as much as for her. The one thing he had always been willing to share with her was his love of books, or, rather, her mother's love of them. It was Sanaz who had persuaded Sam to make a go of running the place, *her* passion that had ignited his lukewarm commitment after the passing of his father. Her mother had loved the written word, had fancied herself a writer in the making. She had not lived long enough to see any of her work published, but the fact that this was the star she had chosen to follow somehow added to her enduring mystery.

Persis had asked her father if any of that work still existed. He had been evasive; she suspected that it was something he wished to retain solely for himself. As a girl she had begrudged him this but now she understood. She knew that Sam would willingly have given what remained of his broken body to bring her mother back. Sadness had infected him, like gangrene; yet he could not cut out his heart to save himself, for that was where Sanaz Wadia continued to reside, preserved like a fly in amber.

She leaned forward and gently pressed her lips to his forehead. His eyelids fluttered, a murmur escaped him, but he did not wake. A shaft of moonlight falling in from a porthole window struck the top of his balding head, illuminating the network of small scars that had, over the ticking of the years, been rudely exposed as his hair fell away. Her heart swelled with a curious melancholia. She understood that it was only in dreams that her father truly became himself, that as he sailed on those fantastical oceans of night, he was once again with the only woman he had loved and lost.

8

Her father had been the first to slap a newspaper down in front of her, at the breakfast table, grimacing but not saying a word. By the time Persis arrived at Malabar House the place was alight with the news. Seth had been right. Herriot's murder had commandeered the front pages. She wondered briefly if the senior echelons of the service would continue to leave matters in the hands of the Malabar House team. A fierce determination smouldered inside her. This was *her* case. She would not give it up without a fight.

A photograph of Laburnum House graced the front of the *Times of India*. Inset was a picture of Sir James Herriot speaking at a lectern. The headline:

TOP BRITISH DIPLOMAT
MURDERED AT NEW YEAR'S EVE BALL

She scanned the article. There was little information, merely a sober profile of Herriot and his demise. Thankfully, she could find no mention of the Partition investigation he had been engaged in. The piece ended by stating that the case was now being investigated by a police unit based at Malabar House, led by Inspector Persis Wadia. The *Indian Chronicle* was not as restrained:

BRITISH POLITICO SLAIN AT MARINE DRIVE
RESIDENCE AS BOMBAY ELITE DANCE ON

The journalist, Aalam Channa, painted a grisly picture of Herriot's killing, speculating freely on the motives of the murderer. An unnamed witness confirmed that Sir James had been discovered 'in a pool of his own blood and in a state of undress'. Alongside the obligatory photograph of Herriot was a smaller photograph of 'Inspector Persis Wadia, the female police detective given charge of the case'. Channa mused on the wisdom of handing over such a high-profile investigation to an officer with such little experience. He did not explicitly bring up the matter of her gender, but the implications were unflattering.

She rolled up the paper and threw it into the waste bin.

The remainder of the morning was spent in this way, with interruptions from journalists pursuing the case; a couple even arrived at Malabar House demanding that she meet them. After a while of being ignored, they went away. She did not doubt that they would return. Vultures rarely flew far from the carcass. A Parsee, more than anyone, understood this.

Persis continued to collate her notes, sifting through the new information for further lines of enquiry.

She pulled out the curious note she had found in Herriot's jacket with the name, BAKSHI, and the string of characters. PLT41/85ACRG11. The paper itself, she was certain, was headed stationery.

She focused on the line: *By a pool of nectar, at the shrine of the sixty-eight.*

Something about those words now raised the flag of memory.

She called Pradeep Birla over, handed him the note. His homely features creased in concentration. 'Means nothing to me. Though . . .' She waited. 'Well, the shrine of the sixty-eight. For us

Hindus, devout ones, at any rate, we believe that there are sixty-eight key places of pilgrimage in the country. Going to each one confers different spiritual benefits. For instance, a pilgrimage to Ayodhya absolves your sins. A dip in the Panchganga at Varanasi frees us from the cycle of rebirth. And so on.'

'Are you suggesting Herriot went to these sixty-eight shrines?'

'No. Of course not. Completing such a task is difficult even for Hindus.'

She was pleased, at least, that he seemed genuinely willing to help.

Of all her colleagues at Malabar House, Pradeep Birla was the only one who had made any real attempt at acceptance, the closest to an ally that she had. The others had reacted to her arrival with indignation, antipathy or outright embarrassment, regarding her presence among them as the final proof of their fall from grace. Birla was phlegmatic. 'Madam, you're the only one of us who is here through no fault of her own. That has to count for something.'

At the age of fifty Birla's was a career distinguished by mediocrity. Nevertheless, he had successfully navigated the upheavals of the Partition years – until a single incident had put him in bad odour with a senior officer. 'The man wanted to marry my daughter,' he told Persis. 'She told him she'd rather marry an ass. He took it badly.'

Birla was not unintelligent, she had discovered, far from it. His approach to police work was methodical and, in its own way, effective. Given enough time, he tended to gravitate towards a solution, though she found him wholly lacking in imagination. Perhaps this was due to his religious convictions, which tended to colour his decision-making.

He had grown up in the Maharashtrian hinterlands, moving to Bombay as a child. Brought up in poverty, educated out of necessity, he had never quite lost his rustic way of framing a problem. Nevertheless, Persis was glad of his presence. He, at least, treated her with a semblance of respect, though sometimes she felt this was less because she outranked him and more because she reminded him of his daughter.

She regarded him now, a small man, with dark, pitted cheeks, thick eyebrows, a moustache that looked as if it had been cut from a rug and glued on to his lip, and a head of short peppery hair. Birla had a store of religious sermons at his fingertips and would often illustrate his point by dipping into the Vedic scriptures. It was the one aspect of his personality that never failed to irritate her.

An hour later she left Malabar House to make her way towards Byculla and her lunchtime date with Herriot's corpse.

The Grant Medical College, as one of the oldest medical institutions in the city, exuded a sense of self-importance that Persis had always found mildly patronising. Established in 1845 to teach Indians of the Bombay Presidency the theoretical and practical aspects of western medicine, its very existence promulgated the notion that India's own brand of ancient therapeutic care was both irrelevant and somehow outdated.

She discovered the pathologist, Dr Raj Bhoomi, in the autopsy suite on the first floor, tuning a new Bakelite to All India Radio as he ate noisily from a steel plate.

Bhoomi, a small, round man, with messy whiskers and half-moon spectacles perched on a bulbous nose, stood to greet her, the tray slipping from his lap and scattering rice and lentils on to the white-tiled floor. 'Apologies!' he said brightly and bent down in an ungainly manner to attend to the mess. As she watched the man scooping glutinous handfuls of his lunch back on to his plate, Persis could not help but feel a sense of loss for Bhoomi's predecessor, Dr Galt.

John Galt had been everything a pathologist should be. A cadaverous Englishman, he had approached the business of dealing with death in the manner of an accountant, precisely and with a sense of sobriety that was wholly missing from his successor. She had only met Galt the once, during an investigation into the death of a man cut down in the street by a runaway circus elephant, and had been impressed by him. Following his recent death, the younger man had taken on the role of chief pathologist for the city. She wondered how he had achieved this rank at his age; nepotism, she reasoned, must extend even to such a grim profession as this.

Bhoomi set his tray down next to the radio, which continued to squeal and hiss like an overwrought infant. 'Can't get the damned thing to work,' he said, thumping the instrument. 'I was hoping to catch Bombay playing Baroda in the Ranji Trophy.'

Persis leaned forward and switched the radio off. 'Perhaps we can attend to the matter at hand.'

Bhoomi glanced at her in surprise. Noting her expression, he nervously pushed his spectacles back up his nose. 'Of course, of course.'

He turned and led her deeper into the suite where, on a metal autopsy table, lay Sir James Herriot. His body was covered by a white cloth, but his face, slack in repose, was open to the elements.

She waited as Bhoomi washed his hands.

The acrid stench of formaldehyde expanded to fill the room. Her nose twitched. The sight or smell of death had never bothered her, but there was something inherently mawkish about an autopsy room that set her teeth on edge. If the notion of souls be true, it was here that they must be most at a loss. Tied and yet no longer tied to their erstwhile earthly forms. Like being thrown out of one's home, clattering around the gates, hoping to be let back in, before gradually realising there was nothing for it but to turn and face the darkness.

The door opened behind her.

Turning, she saw the Englishman Archie Blackfinch flapping his way into the room. He wore the same suit as he had worn on the night she had first encountered him, his tie once again inexpertly knotted. His face shone with sweat, his brilliantined dark hair straggling over his forehead, dishevelled by exposure to the blowtorch of the midday sun.

'You're late,' she said.

'Yes, I'm sorry,' he said, pushing a hand through his hair. 'There was a problem with my driver. He, ah, managed to run the car into the back of a bus. I had to catch a rickshaw.'

'Archie!' Dr Bhoomi returned to the fray, clad now in a bottle-green apron and gloves.

'How are you, Raj?' Blackfinch held out a hand which Bhoomi cranked up and down enthusiastically as if he were pumping water from a well.

'Couldn't be busier. The citizens of Bombay appear to be dying with alarming regularity.'

'It's called mortality, old friend. How did the Galt autopsy go?'

'Stupendously,' beamed Bhoomi. 'Mr Galt appears to have died of unaccustomed physical exertion. Hardly surprising. I was called over to Madame Gabor's at two in the morning. Who knew the old goat had it in him? Dropped down dead in the middle of a particularly strenuous demonstration of the lotus—'

Blackfinch coughed, cutting his eyes towards Persis.

Bhoomi stuttered to a halt, realisation flooding his homely features. 'Of course, of course. A lady is present. My apologies. At any rate, there are not many pathologists who can claim to have autopsied their immediate predecessor. I shall dine out on the tale for years.' He turned to the body of Sir James Herriot. 'A powerful man, from what I can gather.'

Bhoomi waited while Blackfinch set up his photographic equipment.

The pathologist moved to the autopsy table, grabbed the white cloth covering Herriot's body, glanced at Persis once, then yanked it away in the manner of a magician's reveal. Blackfinch photographed the body from the front, then waited as Bhoomi – with the help of a mortuary assistant – turned it over, and took further pictures of the rear.

The body was once again turned unceremoniously on to its back, the fleshy arms slapping on to the metal. Persis resisted the urge to wince. She had not known Herriot, but to see his corpse manhandled in this fashion brought home to her, once again, the evanescence of life. Like it or not, she was now the custodian of all that Herriot had once been, his past and her future now inextricably linked.

She hoped she might do justice to them both.

Bhoomi began by noting the basic physical details of the body and then proceeded to take various measurements, before conducting a fingertip search over Herriot's skin, face bent close to the cadaver, searching for anything out of the ordinary. His assistant duly recorded his observations, scratching them into a leather-bound journal. Blackfinch continued to take photographs, the flash popping with eye-watering brightness in the low-ceilinged room. Bhoomi took extra care while examining the wound under Herriot's jaw, the entry point for the knife that had killed him.

When he had completed his inspection, he straightened and provided a summary. 'Other than the principal knife wound, there are no cuts, bruises or abrasions; nothing on the hands that might indicate defensive injuries.'

This tallied with Persis's own observations on the night.

Bhoomi now returned to his bank of instruments, picked up a saw, twanged the blade theatrically, set it down, picked up a knife instead, then bent to the business of opening up the body.

Persis glanced at Blackfinch. The man seemed unperturbed. She recalled her first autopsy, during her training at the academy. A number of her fellow cadets had turned green; one had emptied his stomach on to the pathologist's shoes, another had fallen into a dead faint over the cadaver. For her part, the grisly procedure had raised no real anxiety. Dead flesh was hardly something to be squeamish about. Of far greater interest to her were the rituals men invented to deal with their post-mortal remains. Burying, burning and, in the case of her own community, leaving the dead to be consumed by vultures in Bombay's notorious Towers of Silence. Such mindless adherence to ceremony had always seemed to her the most desperate expression of mankind's ulti-mate ignorance. Her failure to exhibit the appropriate levels of empathy in such matters had only added to her reputation as a cold fish.

She watched now as Bhoomi extracted Herriot's internal organs, set each on a scale, and called out the weight to his assis-tant. He packaged those of the organs to be sent for further analy-sis, then placed a body block under Herriot's head. Making an incision from behind one ear, across the crown, to a point behind the other, he peeled back the scalp. Next, he took a saw and hacked out a cap of bone. Pulling off the cap he exposed the brain, before scooping it out, weighing it, then setting it down on a steel tray. Returning to his tray of instruments, he selected a scalpel, then, carefully, cut into the mass of brain tissue.

Finally, he stepped away, and ran a sleeve over his brow. Turning, he walked to the sink. They waited as the sound of water trickled over his bloodied gloves. 'My understanding is that the case is somewhat political,' he sang over his shoulder.

'That's an understatement,' said Blackfinch, as he packed up his photographic equipment. 'Did you catch the newspapers this morning?'

'Indeed,' said Bhoomi, making his way back towards them. He had divested himself of the gloves and was rolling down the sleeves of his shirt. 'I shall endeavour to get the report to you by tomorrow. Essentially, it will repeat what I have already told you. Death was caused by exsanguination. Both the carotid and jugular arteries were cleanly severed. The wound profile in the neck appears to indicate a long blade of approximately nine inches, and slightly curved.'

'A curved blade?' said Persis, in surprise.

'Yes. It's unusual, but not unduly so. I've seen the like before. Carving knives, Mughal hunting knives, ceremonial *khanjars* from Persia.'

They thanked Bhoomi, then made their way back to the college's forecourt where Persis had parked her jeep.

'I don't suppose you could give me a lift, could you?' said Blackfinch as they walked out into the sun.

Persis hesitated. 'Where do you wish to go?'

'To tell you the truth, I'm rather hungry. I was going to have lunch. In fact, would you care to join me?'

She blinked. 'I – ah – I have work to do.'

'Surely you have to eat? Besides, there are a couple of things about the case I'd like to go over.'

She considered the proposal. She *was* hungry, and he was right in that there were matters that needed to be discussed. 'Very well.'

Half an hour later they were seated inside Britannia & Co, a Parsee restaurant that Persis and her father frequented. The place had been around since the twenties, run by an Iranian Zoroastrian, a smallish affair on Sprott Road, situated beneath drooping willow trees, with an open frontage, red-checked tables and a distinctly heritage atmosphere. On the walls were pictures of King George and Gandhi, side by side; a British flag set above the green, white and saffron pennant of the new republic. The juxtaposition of the two flags was demonstrative, she had often thought, of how some still viewed Britain's time in India.

Blackfinch sent the waiter scurrying off to fetch a cold beer to begin proceedings. Persis settled for lime water. She watched as the Englishman shrugged off his jacket, set it neatly on the back of his chair, then pulled off his spectacles and wiped them with a tablecloth. A fan directly above the table cooled the sweat on his forehead.

She looked on in mild amusement as he picked up and replaced his fork, knife and spoon with exacting precision, then set the condiments in a regimented line that wouldn't have looked out of place on a parade ground. He twisted the salt shaker three times clockwise, then did the same with the pepper shaker.

'What are you doing?'

He seemed to realise that his actions had provoked her curiosity. 'Oh, nothing, nothing,' he muttered.

'I suppose you're one of those people who have to have things just so.'

'Something like that,' he murmured, not meeting her eyes. She realised that he was embarrassed by this revelation. She couldn't imagine why. Most men she knew, including her own father, were far from meticulous. Her own temperament gravitated towards clean lines and orderliness; it was a welcome relief to find herself in the company of a kindred spirit.

The thing with the shakers had been a bit odd, however.

Around them conversations ebbed and flowed, punctuated by the clatter of cutlery and the clink of glasses.

Persis discovered an unexpected awkwardness within herself.

There had been other lunches, of course. Dinners too. With men, some of her own choosing, others foisted upon her by Aunt Nussie and other well-wishers who did not stop long enough to ask if she wanted or needed their help. Some of the men she had stepped out with had shone brightly for a while, and then things had simply fizzled out. Something never quite right. Too vain, too dull, too lacking. In what, she was not always able to define, to the exasperation of her aunt.

There *had* been one, three years earlier, just before she had made the decision to join the police service. A fellow Parsee, son of a grandee, but a man who professed to an independence of spirit. He had been neither tall, nor broad, nor classically handsome. Yet he possessed that indefinable quality that some called charisma. Always impeccably dressed, with a cavalryman's moustache, and a habit of smoking expensive Woodbine cigarillos. He fancied himself a littérateur. They had talked long into the night, debating the works of the greats – Dostoevsky, Joyce, Hemingway, the Brontë sisters, Tagore – aggressively comparing their favourite tomes. A decade older, he had seemed wise beyond her ken.

One night, she had given herself to him.

Three weeks later, he had vanished. A month after that, a wedding card arrived, inviting her to his impending nuptials in Delhi.

'You have an interesting name,' she said, seeking a neutral beginning.

'I could say the same about you.'

'Not really. Persis is common enough in the Parsee community.' She explained that Persis meant *from Persia*, alluding to the fact that the Parsees had fled their ancestral homeland centuries earlier as a nascent Islam's grip closed over Iran and its neighbouring states. That heritage hung lightly upon her shoulders. She was a child of Bombay, twenty-seven years old at century's midpoint, and as fiercely patriotic as any of her fellow citizens, a matter that had been put to the test time and again in recent years.

He smiled, his eyes crinkling at the corners in a way that lit up his handsome features. 'My father was a scientist, a chemist. I think naming me Archimedes was his way of saluting one of the greats. I have a brother named Pythagoras. It was worse for him. I could always get away with being Archie. There's not much room with Pythagoras. Boys can be awfully cruel.'

They chatted for a bit, filling in family details, background. She told him about her father.

'Do you still live with him?'

Persis frowned at the question. Where else would she live? Who would look after him if she moved away? She had often wondered if this thought lurked at the back of her mind each time the idea of marriage reared its head. She couldn't imagine Sam on his own; she couldn't imagine not being there to stand vigil with him through his loneliness. Was it such a sacrifice? She did not think so. She was an independent-minded woman; she did not need to prove it by living on her own.

She discovered that Blackfinch had been in the war. 'I didn't see much of the front, mind you. I spent most of my time behind a desk in Whitehall, in the War Office's science division. My background is chemistry – I'd followed in my father's footsteps – and I was part of a team developing what they euphemistically called "modern" weapons. Classified stuff. When the war ended, I needed a change and so I joined the police, trained as a criminalist, a crime scene specialist. I did that for a while, then, a couple of years ago the War Office – now the Ministry of Defence – found me again. They had a special assignment for me, one that I could not rightly refuse. They sent me out to suspected mass graves across the former battlefields of Europe, to gather evidence of war crimes. I was there with a team: pathologists, ballistics experts, the like.' He stopped a moment, his green eyes focused somewhere in the past. 'It was one of the worst things that I have ever had to do, one of the worst things that anyone can be asked to do. You know, in some of those graves, we found women with babies still in their arms.'

She had no idea how to respond to this.

He asked her about her life, her childhood, growing up in India. The questions made her uncomfortable. Those had been difficult years; it wasn't until her late teens that she had made any real friends, ones that she had carried with her into adulthood. But now Jaya was married with a young child and another on the way; Dinaz had moved to Calcutta to work with the Sunderbans Forest Management Division; and Emily had returned to England with her family in 1946. She had remained in touch with all three – sporadic pen letters, or hurried coffee meetings in Jaya's case. They had stood shoulder to shoulder through the grim years of the Quit India movement – even Emily – but now, she felt their absence keenly.

She remembered something Emily had said to her once, 'You're a hedgehog, Persis. You're built to be alone.' She had felt a sense of sadness at the remark, but Emily had not meant it unkindly.

A waiter clattered over to the table, flapping gigantic menus at them. 'Why don't you choose for me?' Blackfinch suggested from somewhere behind his.

She ordered a mutton dhansak and the house speciality, chicken berry pilaf.

He asked her about the case. Quickly, she filled him in.

'You've made quite a bit of progress,' he said.

'Not as much as I might have hoped. I still have no real motive for the killing.'

She realised that other diners were looking their way, sly glances that slipped away as soon as she turned to them. She wondered, briefly, if the lunch had been ill-judged. The Parsee community was a small one; gossip travelled around it at the speed of light, ricocheting from ear to mouth. God knows what Aunt Nussie would make of it. As cosmopolitan as she favoured herself, her aunt was a traditionalist at heart. It would be unthinkable for Persis to entertain an Englishman in *that* way. Not that that was what she was doing. As for her father . . .

'Let's examine what we know,' the Englishman in question suggested. He began ticking off items on the fingers of his right hand.

He has nice hands, she thought. A pianist's hands. She shook the stray thought out of her head, annoyed with herself.

'One: Herriot was killed between midnight and approximately one. His body was discovered at one-ten. Two: he was killed with a knife, a curved blade, which, as far as we can determine, is no longer on the premises. Three: he was murdered by one of sixty-seven people present that evening. Four: I discovered no finger-prints in his study that did not belong to Herriot or to his regular staff. This tells us that his killer was either incredibly careful or wore gloves. Which would not be surprising given that it was a costumed ball.' He smiled. 'Five: he was involved in a government enquiry into crimes committed during Partition. Six: something may have been taken from his safe. We can only speculate as to what that might have been. Valuables, perhaps, or documentation regarding his investigations – documentation that may have subsequently been destroyed.' He stopped, his eyes trained on a fly that had landed on the lip of his glass.

'Seven,' she continued, 'we know that he met a man named Vishal Mistry that evening, a man whose name was absent from the official guest list.'

'Ah, yes.' He seemed annoyed that he had missed something. 'Who is he exactly?'

'I'm not sure. We're still trying to trace him. Eight: Lal and Herriot were overheard fighting that evening. Nine: we have a set of trivial-seeming items that bother me.'

'Such as?'

She explained about the ticket stub and the sheet torn from a notepad. She took out her own notebook and showed him the name, BAKSHI, and the enigmatic set of characters: PLT41/85ACRG11.

'Means nothing to me, I'm afraid,' he said after studying the page. 'What makes you think these have any relevance to Herriot's death?'

'I just don't like not knowing.'

He smiled. 'That makes two of us.'

'There's something else. Point ten . . .' She paused.

'Yes?'

'On the night of Herriot's death, you took a handkerchief from his study.'

Blackfinch set down his fork. 'Yes. I was getting to that.' He cleared his throat. Colour rose faintly to his cheeks.

She wondered again how old he was. She suspected that his unlined face made him younger than his years.

'I found something on the handkerchief. I took it away for testing.'

'But you already suspected what it was?'

'Yes.' He stopped.

'And?'

His gaze slid away. 'Perhaps this isn't the best place to—'

'For God's sake, just spit it out.'

Her reaction stumbled him across the finishing line. 'Very well. There was a male . . .' – he searched for the word – '*discharge* on the hankie.'

'Do you mean semen?' said Persis. 'If you mean semen, then why don't you just say semen?' Her voice had risen; she realised other diners were staring at her. The waiter, returning with dessert menus, was gawking at them open-mouthed. 'Look,' she said, through gritted teeth, 'I appreciate that you bring certain skills to the investigation, but the next time you take evidence from one of my crime scenes without explaining to me precisely what you are doing, I will not be so understanding.'

He stiffened, then nodded. 'Fair enough.' They resumed their meal.

The waiter set down the menus, took their orders, then retreated with haste.

'This *discharge*,' said Persis, 'I suppose it means that Herriot was with a woman that night.'

'Yes,' he managed weakly. 'My tests – acid phosphate-based – indicate vaginal secretion alongside Herriot's . . . semen.'

She looked down at her plate. In spite of her previous sentiment, colour had risen to her cheeks. It wasn't every day one's lunch partner seasoned the conversation with the word *vaginal*. 'So who was his dance partner that night?' she mumbled.

'More importantly, what does it tell us about him?'

'It tells us that somewhere out there is a person who was with him moments before he was killed.'

She recalled the objects on Herriot's desk, how something about them had bothered her. She realised now what that was. They had all been placed towards the edges of the desk, leaving the centre free. 'They used the desk,' she said.

'What?'

'Herriot and his lover. They used the desk for their . . . liaison.'

There seemed little to add to this. The waiter returned with coffees.

'Is there a Mr Wadia?' Blackfinch asked eventually.

'Yes,' she said automatically. 'My father. Sam Wadia.'

'That's not what I meant.'

'I know what you meant.' She sipped her coffee. 'No. There is no *Mr* Wadia.'

A short silence. 'What about you? Is there a Mrs Blackfinch?'

'Not any more.' He stared at her over the top of his cup, light reflecting from his spectacles.

'I'm so sorry,' she mumbled. 'I did not know.'

'What are you sorry about?'

'Your wife's death,' she burbled.

'My wife's dead?' he said. 'Well, in that case I pity the devil. Hell is going to be an uncomfortable place for the rest of eternity.'

She stared at him. 'I see. You did not mean that your wife had passed.'

'I didn't say that, did I?' He gave a disarming grin. 'My wife and I married young. Turns out we were completely unsuited to each other. We spent six miserable years together and then, one day, I discovered that she had taken up with another man. She left me a note. It simply said: *Let's not waste any more of our lives.*'

'She seems like a wise woman.'

'She was a witch. A basilisk.'

'I have only your side of the story. In my experience men are just as capable of duplicity.'

'Do you have a lot of experience?'

She coloured, but did not reply. 'Do you have children?' she asked.

He shook his head. 'That, at least, was one mistake we did not make. Thank God.' Another silence passed. 'What is it like? Being India's first policewoman?'

'I don't think about it. I just want to be allowed to do my job.'

'Fat chance of that.' He grinned. 'We've had them for a while in England. Policewomen, I mean. I met one once. Very bright woman. Also, great teeth.'

She picked up her coffee again. 'How did you end up in India?'

'I'm not entirely sure. I did seven months with the war crimes team, before returning to London. But I couldn't settle. Something had changed, *I* had changed. I rejoined the Met Police, spent six months teaching at a new forensic science training college they'd just set up. One day, I got a call, out of the blue, from a man I'd worked with on the war crimes team, a pathologist. He said he'd been invited out to India. Said they were looking for trained people. Told me I could write my own ticket. I talked to my bosses at the Met. They agreed that it might not be a bad idea for me to spend some time out here.'

'Do you enjoy it? Being here?'

'I'm not sure if enjoy is the word I'd use.' He caught her expression. 'What I mean is, that it's all very different. The heat, the language, the mosquitoes. The lack of attention to things I've always taken for granted.'

'Such as?'

'Such as . . . well, hygiene, for one.' He moved on hastily, as she bristled. 'I'm not saying I dislike it. It's just . . .'

'Different?'

The meal ended on this discordant note, and she found herself wondering what it was about people that inevitably brought her to this pass. Then again, as Aunt Nussie would sometimes tell her, perhaps it wasn't other people.

Perhaps it was her.

Following the lunch, she drove to Marine Drive and Laburnum House to track down Madan Lal. Blackfinch did not accompany her. He had lab work pending on a number of other cases. The Mumbai Police Service was keeping him busy, supervising a team of eager young technicians, training them in the dark arts of forensic science.

Entering Laburnum House for the second time in as many days, Persis was struck by how different the place seemed. Gone was the gaiety of the New Year's Eve ball. The house was all but deserted, accentuating its size. She wondered what it must be like to live in such a vast space. Perhaps her father was right. A home was only a home if you could reach out and touch another human being.

She was escorted to an office on the ground floor where she found Madan Lal scanning a newspaper at his desk. His jacket was off and he sat in a stiff-backed wooden chair in a pressed white shirt and tie. He waved her into the seat before him, then gestured in disgust at the newspaper. 'I sometimes wonder if journalists take a sacred oath to misrepresent the truth. A great man dies and all they can talk about is the fact that Sir James was found in a state of undress.'

'You have to admit, it is unusual.'

'That's hardly the point,' he countered. 'Should a man's life be reduced to the circumstances of his death? Here lies Sir James Herriot, tireless campaigner for Indian independence, consummate diplomat . . . who died without his trousers.'

Persis forbore from replying. She sensed Lal's exasperation.

'At any rate,' he continued, planting his elbows on the desk and fixing her with an earnest gaze, 'how have your enquiries fared?'

She realised what it was about him that she found so attractive. He reminded her of the man she had surrendered herself to, the con artist who had stolen her heart, then trampled it into the dust. Lal had the same physical presence, small and neat, exuding a sense of self-belief that belied his seemingly placid nature.

She debated with herself just how much to tell him.

Lal had no official standing in her investigation; she was not required to report to him. And yet, he had access to information that would be difficult for her to obtain without his cooperation. She would have to tread a careful path.

She supplied him with a summary of her actions since the night of Herriot's death.

'What did you make of Tilak?' he asked, when she had finished.

'He was very open. He explained the work that Sir James was doing for the government. You knew, didn't you?'

Lal nodded slowly. 'Yes. Sir James confided in me. At least the outlines of the task. He could not go into any detail.'

'Why didn't you tell me?'

'Because it was not my place to do so. You must understand, these are highly sensitive matters. Sir James's investigation was of national importance. It is not something that I, or, for that matter, *you* may discuss openly.'

'Then how am I to investigate?'

He leaned back, pulled a packet of cigarettes from his pocket, and lit one with a match. He offered her the packet, but she declined. He allowed the smoke to flare slowly from his nostrils and billow around his eyes. '*Aut viam inveniam aut faciam.* Either find a way or make one.' He grimaced. 'The motto of my old house at University College London.'

Persis reined in her irritation. 'Did you ever get a look at the documents?'

'No. As I said, he kept them from me. Frankly, I thought he could have used my help, but he was paranoid about anyone discovering too much of what he was doing.'

'The ashes in the grate. Could those have been the documents?'

Lal shrugged. 'Possibly.'

'Did you tell the Deputy Home Minister that the documents had been destroyed?'

He blinked. 'He asked me what was the likelihood. I said that it was possible.'

'In the list of recent appointments you provided me with, Sir James was out of the city on a number of occasions. In most of those instances, you did not mention where he travelled.'

'If I did not it was because such trips were in pursuit of his investigations. Again, he insisted on keeping those details to himself, even to the extent of purchasing his own tickets.'

Her thoughts flashed instantly to the ticket stub she had found in Herriot's jacket. Could that pertain to such a trip?

'On the evening of his death, Sir James was seen in his study with a man named Vishal Mistry. Do you know who he is?'

Lal frowned. 'No.'

'I thought you were his aide?'

'I have no record of a scheduled meeting with a Vishal Mistry.'

Was he telling the truth? What reason had he to lie?

'Very well. That same evening you and Sir James were observed arguing. Can you tell me what the argument was about?'

His brow corrugated. 'Arguing? Who told you this?'

'That doesn't matter, does it?'

He seemed perturbed. 'Sir James and I rarely argued. Yes, we might occasionally harbour differences of opinion, or debate certain matters vigorously, but we did not argue. I always considered my role to be more along the lines of an adviser, a confidant, not just an aide. More importantly, he was my employer. He was in charge. The final decision always rested with him.'

'So you cannot shed any light on this argument?'

His face hardened. He stubbed out the cigarette in an ashtray. 'As I said: there was no argument.'

'Very well. What can you tell me about Robert Campbell?'

'Campbell's a tricky fellow. He likes to come across as a bluff Scotsman, a man who speaks his mind, but the truth is that he is not to be trusted. Sir James knew this.'

'I was under the impression they were friends.'

'They were. But Sir James had no illusions as to the sort of man Campbell is.'

'What sort of man *is* that?'

Lal appeared to engage in a subconscious calculus before answering. 'Ruthless. That's the only word to describe him. He'll have you believe it's the Scot in him, but that's not true. I knew many Scots during my time in the army, fine men, honest and warm. They didn't give their friendship easily, but once they did, they'd stand in front of a tank for you. No, it's something else with Campbell. He's one of those men who simply don't see right or wrong. Wealth is the only philosophy he believes in. Wealth and power.

'A year ago, an ugly rumour about him did the rounds. Campbell had been hired to build a bridge in a township just outside Delhi. Six months into the project, with the bridge half built, he fell out with his chief engineer, a young Indian. Apparently, the man grew a conscience and demanded a fair wage for his workers or they would down tools. Without the raw labour Campbell had little chance of completing the work on time.

'That particular stretch of the Yamuna is notorious for the crocodiles that gather along its banks. One evening, so the rumour goes, Campbell had the engineer taken from his home and strung up by the feet from the half-completed bridge. The next morning, when the villagers came down to the river, they found the lower half of the man's body swinging from the rope. The head, shoulders and arms had been devoured.' He paused, his lips pursing into a grimace. 'Robert Campbell is a man lacking in moral fibre, Inspector.'

'You don't like him.'

'No,' he admitted.

'The feeling is mutual,' she said. 'He made some rather unflattering remarks about you.'

Lal's eyes contracted to pinpricks. He pulled out his cigarette packet again and lit another cigarette. 'And what exactly did he have to say?'

'He implied that your time in the army might not have been as straightforward as you led me to believe. That, in fact, you were court-martiall—'

'Enough!' He slapped the surface of the desk, startling her into silence. An uncomfortable moment passed. 'Forgive me,' he said, 'I did not mean to—' He stopped. 'My time in the army is of no relevance to Sir James's death. I would urge you to concentrate on the facts at hand.'

Persis decided not to pursue the matter; at least, for now. There was nothing to be gained by fuelling Lal's angst.

'I'd like to know more about Sir James's financial situation. Who stands to benefit from his death?'

'That can be easily answered. His will is due to be read tomorrow.'

'Do you know what's in it?'

'No. That was another matter Sir James kept to himself.'

'There's something else,' she began. 'We have evidence that Sir James may have been with a woman on the night of his death.'

Lal's eyes blinked in incomprehension behind his spectacles.

'What I mean is that he was intimate with her.'

'You must be mistaken.'

'There's no mistake. The incident took place just before his murder, in his study. So you can understand why it is important that we identify the other party.'

'I cannot imagine—' Lal began, then stopped.

'Was he having an affair?'

'No.'

'A casual encounter then? Someone he might have flirted with that evening?'

'He was a gregarious man. Women were drawn to him.'

'Any woman in particular?'

Lal's discomfort was obvious. 'I honestly cannot say, Inspector. Sir James was his usual self. He had many dance partners that evening. The man knew how to have a good time.'

'Surely, he must have let something slip. Did you not just tell me that you were his confidant?'

His face hardened. 'Not in such matters,' he said sharply. 'He preferred to keep his private life to himself.'

'This assignation took place in his study with a horde of people in the house. Hardly the act of a man of discretion.'

'Nevertheless, I have no idea who his partner might have been.'

Persis left him, clearly perturbed. Her instincts told her that Lal knew more than he was willing to say. As she moved back towards the front of the house, it occurred to her that if Herriot *had* been engaged in an affair, then Lal was not the only one who might have noticed.

She found the housekeeper, Lalita Gupta, in a small office at the rear of the mansion. The woman, once again dressed in a sari, was seated at a desk, writing in a small notebook. On the desk was a framed photograph of an Indian male. She straightened as Persis entered.

Quickly, Persis explained the situation. 'Was Sir James involved with anyone?'

Panic contorted the woman's fine features. 'Please, madam, such matters are not my concern.'

'I disagree,' said Persis. 'Your employer has been murdered. You were his housekeeper. You saw the comings and goings in his home. Your observations might be critical to helping us solve his murder.'

'But I saw nothing!'

'I don't believe you.'

This seemed to startle her. Her fingers entwined themselves and she looked wretchedly at her feet.

'Whatever you tell me shall remain in confidence,' said Persis, her expression softening. 'But I must have an answer. Rest assured, you will not be betraying Sir James.'

'He had many lady friends.' She stopped.

'Go on,' prompted Persis.

'Female visitors came to the house all the time. Sir James used to say that without a woman a house was just four walls and a roof.' A sad smile played over her lips.

'Were there any women whom he was particularly fond of, regular visitors? I'm especially interested in those who were also here on the night of his death.'

Gupta hesitated, then seemed to resign herself. 'Yes. Eve Gatsby. Sir James became very close with her in recent weeks.'

Persis recalled a tall, young American woman, one of those who had protested loudest at being held for interview at Laburnum House. In the end, she had escaped before Persis could speak with her.

'How did you end up here?'

'My husband passed in the war,' replied Gupta. 'Sir James gave me a roof over my head, a job.'

'Your husband was a soldier?'

'Yes.' She whispered the word.

'What was his name?'

She blinked. 'Duleep.' Sadness trembled beneath the surface of her dusky skin.

'Do you have children?'

'A son.'

'Where is he?'

'He is at a boarding school in Panvel.'

'Boarding school?' It seemed unusual, a widow, a housekeeper with presumably limited means.

Gupta seemed to sense the unasked question. 'Sir James was generous enough to pay for his schooling.'

'What happens to you now?'

'I don't know.'

Persis had nothing further to ask the woman. Yet there was something about her, some sense of evasiveness that made her want to know more about Sir James Herriot's housekeeper.

She took her leave and left the house.

Back at Malabar House she found her stomach rumbling again and sent the peon for a plate of spiced dumplings from the Dancing Stomach, a nearby Chinese eatery. She wolfed the snack and considered her next move.

She pulled out the enigmatic note again and sat it next to her plate. *By a pool of nectar, at the shrine of the sixty-eight.* Birla had said that the sixty-eight might refer to sixty-eight pilgrimage sites important to Hindus. This implied a religious interpretation to the sentence.

Very well.

She focused on the first part of the line. *By a pool of nectar.* In the lexicon of faith, *nectar* might be nectar of the gods. Ambrosia. A spark flamed inside her mind like a lit match.

A pool of ambrosia . . . *Ambrosia* . . . And then she had it.

Amritsar.

The northern city's original name Ambarsar literally meant 'pool of ambrosia'. The city had been founded in 1577 by a Sikh guru who had decreed the building of a temple by a natural pool. That temple was now the holiest site in the Sikh religion.

The Golden Temple.

She looked at the jagged edge of the notepaper, at the few letters she had been able to identify.

_ _ E G _ _ _ E _ _ E _ _ L _ _ O _ _ _

The first three words fitted perfectly: The Golden Temple. And now she could make an informed guess at the final word. Hotel.

The sheet had been taken from a notepad at the Golden Temple Hotel, a hotel that was most likely in Amritsar. And Sir James had been there some time before his death.

She allowed herself a moment of quiet satisfaction before approaching Birla. 'Let's step outside.'

The afternoon street was baking and sweat quickly sheened their faces as they walked along the road to the Marolto Coffee House. A fearsome stench arose from an open sewer by the side of the road; a filth-spattered hog rooted in a mound of rubbish.

Persis shivered. One thing freedom hadn't changed was the city's squalor, squalor that sat side by side with magnificence. Bombay was a study in such contrasts, stratified into distinct layers by caste, wealth and social mores. A Brahmin would no more entertain the idea of sitting down to eat with a Dalit than a Parsee would marry off his daughter to a non-Zoroastrian. The fractious unity engendered by the revolution had evaporated during the communal rioting; the post-independence turmoil had seen the old petty prejudices reassert themselves with a vengeance.

And it wasn't just Bombay, she thought. The city of dreams was a mirror for every corner of the new nation, every village, every town, every city. The struggle for freedom had left in its wake a desire to make something of this ancient-new nation of theirs. But for the three hundred million Indians who dwelt within the newly drawn borders, it was anyone's guess how they would achieve that reality. If Partition had shown them anything, it was that India was a nation as liable to war with itself as with a common enemy.

Once inside the coffee shop, she ordered an iced tea; Birla picked up a jug of water and drained it. He mopped the sweat from his brow and turned his face towards the ceiling fan.

'I have a task for you.' Persis quickly explained her discovery of the Golden Temple Hotel. 'I want you to find the place.'

Birla thought about it. 'There's probably a hotel association in Amritsar. I'll contact them. What should I do once I find it?'

'Nothing. I want to speak to them myself.'

Birla nodded, scratched in his notepad.

'Next,' continued Persis, 'I want to find this Vishal Mistry. Fernandes says a Claude Dérrida walked in on Mistry and Sir James. Derrida described Mistry as well dressed. A suit. Wearing rings and an expensive-looking watch. He came to see Sir James about something, or was invited to do so. Given the circles within which Sir James moved, I would guess that Mistry was not some door-to-door salesman. He was a man of substance. That should make it easier to locate him.'

'Where do we begin?'

'I have an idea.'

The Bombay Registry and Electoral Office was a relatively new title for an old institution. This was the office responsible for the country's census, carried out once every decade. The last census had taken place in 1941; the next was due in a year's time, and was particularly exigent given that the nation's first post-independence general election was due in the summer of 1951.

Persis and Birla made their way into the anteroom where a flunky sat beneath a whirring fan. Such was his state of immobility, Persis wondered if perhaps he had expired in his seat and no one had noticed.

She presented her credentials. 'I wish to locate an individual by means of the electoral roll. Can you help me?'

The man stared at her, his dark face as mournful as a depressed toad's. 'I am afraid that any such request must be presented through official channels and in writing together with a copy of form IU89-b. In triplicate.'

Persis counted to ten. It was a trick Aunt Nussie had taught her, a way of managing her temper before flying off the handle. She reached six before the rage took hold of her. She leaned forward, grabbed the man by the lapels of his shirt and hauled him to his feet.

His lizard eyes goggled at her, but he had lost the power of speech.

'My name is Persis Wadia and I have been tasked by the Deputy Home Minister to investigate the death of Sir James Herriot. If you do not help me you will be impeding me in my duty. I shall have you arrested and thrown in jail. An official complaint will reach your superiors. You will be relieved of your position. You will lose your livelihood, and your home. Your family will be forced into the streets. Your wife will leave you. Your children will take to a life of crime. Do you wish to see all this come to pass?'

His head creaked slowly from side to side.

She let him go and he sagged back into his seat. 'Lead the way.'

Fifteen minutes later they were sitting in the records room, a small, stifling space lit by light bulbs and housing bracketed steel shelves weighed down with red ledgers. A stack of ledgers from the previous census covering surnames beginning with *Mi* were arrayed before them on a steel desk.

'I'll say one thing for the British,' muttered Birla. 'They knew how to keep records.'

'Of course they did,' said Persis. 'They wanted to know exactly how much they could steal and from whom.'

Birla acknowledged the truth of this with a grunt. A fly landed on the page before him and he lashed out automatically, squishing it in a burst of blood. Scowling, he wiped the mess from his hand on to his trousers.

Persis went back to her page, running her finger down the list of entries. Each entry was in the name of the head of the household and contained subsidiary information about the other residents within the home, as well as information about each individual's employment and household assets.

Half an hour later they had a complete list of Vishal Mistrys living within the Bombay Presidency at the time of the last census. Eighty-nine in total.

They began to eliminate those who could not possibly be the man they were looking for. This meant all those under the age of forty and over the age of sixty. Although Derrida had guessed Mistry's age to be around fifty, Persis opted for a margin of latitude in her cull.

They were left with forty-three names. Still too many.

She considered the problem, then stepped outside. She walked back to the reception where the flunky quailed as she bore down on him. 'I need a map of Bombay.'

He blinked at her owlishly.

'Now,' she said.

He leaped to his feet as if electrocuted.

Ten minutes later she was back in the records room with the map spread over the desk, the ledgers having been moved to the floor.

'What are you thinking?' asked Birla.

'The man Derrida described was well off. There are sections of the city where I would not expect him to live.' District by district they marked off the forty-three entries. By the time they had removed those districts that might be considered lower on the social scale, they were left with nine names.

'Now let's see who was closest to Herriot.'

Three of the names lived within a two-mile radius of Laburnum House.

She looked at the names. Three Vishal Mistrys. All of the right age group, all of a background that matched the type of person Sir James might have associated with. She wrote out their details on a sheet of paper. Something occurred to her and she went back and looked at the listed occupation for each of the men. The owner of a cigarette packaging plant. A senior accountant in a shipping container firm. A dealer in antiques and heritage jewellery.

Jewellery. Derrida said that he had seen something shiny on Sir James's desk. Could it have been a piece of jewellery?

She straightened. 'I want you to check out the other two names. In fact, check out the other eight, just to be sure. I'm going to pay this jeweller a visit.'

'It would save time if I asked one of the others to help. Perhaps Oberoi.'

'Do this yourself.' She caught his raised eyebrow. 'I don't trust Oberoi. I can't prove it, but I get the feeling he would rather I failed.'

He gave her a sympathetic look. 'You may not believe me, but there are plenty of us rooting for you. The force needs new faces, new ways of thinking. The common man is fed up of cops like Oberoi. They want police officers they can trust. You have the chance to inspire a generation.'

'I didn't ask for that responsibility.'

'Well, you've got it anyway,' he said cheerfully. 'Because of you my daughter is thinking of putting in her papers as a receptionist at the Taj and joining the force. Heaven help us if they actually let her in.'

*　　*　　*

According to the census Vishal Mistry lived on the fifth floor of an apartment tower just a mile from Laburnum House. Or, at least, he had done a decade earlier. It was entirely possible that he had moved in that time, though the brutal realities of life in Bombay meant that once a resident of the city had climbed the social ladder sufficiently to afford a flat in an area as comfortable as Marine Lines, they tended to inhabit the place with a limpet-like tenacity, leaving it only as a wisp of spectral vapour.

Persis drove there with dusk settling on the city, the call to prayer from a local mosque lilting over the road. At a set of traffic lights, she watched as a child beggar glued himself to the side of a peat-grey Buick. The passenger, a white woman, recoiled in horror. New to the city, Persis thought. An American, perhaps. In time her gaze would become deadened, able to take in everything yet not see anything.

The sentry at Blue Jamaica Tower confirmed that the Mistry family did indeed reside there. He gave her an odd look, one that she took with her as she climbed the stairs to the fifth floor. The reason for his curious gaze became apparent only when she knocked on the door to apartment 501 and the door swung back to reveal a dumpy, middle-aged woman wearing a grey sari and an expression of exhausted belligerence.

'At last,' she grimaced. 'You took long enough.'

In the confusion that followed, a dog yelped over the woman's shoulder, the tinny bark of a small animal.

'You knew I was coming?' asked Persis.

'We were promised an update yesterday,' replied the woman angrily.

'An update?' She felt her feet sinking into quicksand.

The woman folded her arms and stared at her. 'I know you. You're the policewoman from the newspapers.' She sniffed. 'Well, at least they're finally taking us seriously.'

Persis straightened her shoulders. 'Madam, I have no idea what you are talking about.'

'You *are* here about the case, aren't you?'

'I am. But how did you know?'

'How did I know?' echoed the woman in disbelief. 'My brother has been missing for over a day and you ask me *how did I know?*'

It transpired that Vishal Mistry had been missing since the previous morning. The woman who had opened the door was his sister, Minnie Shanbag. Once the initial misunderstanding had been cleared up, she turned back into the apartment, flouncing ahead of Persis in disgust. 'Typical!' she said. 'If the police were any more useless they'd be politicians.'

The flat was modern, rather than lavish. Leather sofas, a dining table to one side, floor bolsters in the corner, a walnut sideboard upon which was perched a gramophone. On one wall were the obligatory pictures of Gandhi and Nehru; on the opposite wall, garlanded photographs of two elders, Mistry's deceased parents. A small dog, a white Pomeranian, ducked in at Persis's heels, yapping itself into a frenzy, as she was led to the sofa where another woman, older than Minnie, sat in a maroon sari. She had a patrician air, and a gaze that seemed to stare a few yards past the policewoman.

'This is Varsha, Vishal's wife,' said Minnie, taking a seat beside the woman and waving Persis into a wing chair.

Quickly, Persis explained the reason for her visit. 'When did you realise that your husband was missing?' she asked Mistry's wife.

Varsha stared at her. Before she could reply, Minnie answered: 'My brother went to his office yesterday morning. He never got there.'

'He went to work on New Year's Day?'

'Vishal never takes a day off, not unless he is severely ill. He's been that way ever since we were children.'

'When was he reported missing?'

'My brother is a man of routine. Every day at lunchtime, Varsha sends the houseboy to the shop with a lunch tiffin. When he returned that day and told her that Vishal wasn't there, that he had never reached the shop, she became concerned. It isn't like him to wander off, not without informing her. She called me and together we went to the Colaba station to file a missing persons report.'

'What did they say?'

'The idiot in charge told us that it was too early for the police to do anything. Vishal had probably just gone off on an unexpected errand. When we went back later, he suggested that perhaps my brother had vanished with the turn of the new year. Gone off to live a gala life somewhere else. I was so angry I could have slapped him.'

Persis stared pointedly at Vishal Mistry's wife. 'Is there a reason Varsha cannot answer for herself?'

'My sister-in-law has taken a vow of silence. She will not speak until her husband is found.'

Persis absorbed this, then: 'Was there anything unusual about that morning? Anything unusual about his behaviour? Did he say or do anything out of the ordinary?'

Minnie was nodding slowly. 'As a matter of fact, yes. As I said my brother is a man of exacting routine. And that morning he broke his routine. He left for the office two hours early, at around 6 a.m.'

'That *is* early,' muttered Persis. 'Did you know that he was at Sir James Herriot's house the evening before he went missing?'

'Herriot? The murdered Englishman?' Minnie exchanged glances with her sister-in-law. 'No. We didn't know that. He told Varsha that he was going out to meet a client.'

'A client? On New Year's Eve?'

'My brother doesn't care about such things. He lived for his work.'

'His work as a jeweller?'

She nodded. 'He has a shop on Walsingham Road.'

'Was he in the habit of paying house calls upon his clients?'

'Sometimes, yes. Vishal is very old-fashioned. He believes in providing a discreet, personal service.'

'Was Sir James a client?'

'You'd have to ask Kedarnath.'

'Kedarnath?'

'My brother's assistant. At the shop.'

She caught Kedarnath just as he was closing up the shop, rolling down the steel shutter with a bang. The description of Vishal Mistry's assistant had been accurate. A short, plump man in his forties, balding, bespectacled and with a prognathous jaw that gave him a permanently disgruntled look. He was dressed in a white *kurta pajama* and leather sandals. Black threads hung around his neck and at his wrists. A frayed moustache reclined limply above his upper lip.

Persis asked him to roll the shutter back up. He did so with ill grace, then led her into the interior of the shop.

It was small, but clean and neatly laid out. Three display counters housed selected pieces of jewellery, coins and heritage artefacts inlaid with precious metals.

She explained the reason for her visit. 'Was Sir James a client of Vishal's?'

Kedarnath scratched his cheek. 'Not as far as I know.'

'Do you know why he was visiting Sir James on the night of his death?'

'No.'

'Did he tell you that he was due to visit Sir James that evening?'

'He did not.'

'Does he usually tell you before visiting clients?'

'We keep a record of every commission that we are working on. It is in the ledger. But there is no entry for Sir James. I would remember.'

'Would you check for me anyway?'

'I would remember,' he persisted.

'Please do as I ask.'

Grumbling, he turned away and shuffled through a door at the rear of the shop, then returned with a ledger. Licking a thumb, he opened the ledger then began to riffle through the pages. 'How far back would you like me to check?'

She hesitated. 'Six months.'

'I shall go back a year.'

Fifteen minutes later, he snapped the book shut. 'Nothing,' he said, with a satisfied grunt. 'Sir James Herriot was not our client.'

'And yet Vishal visited him that evening. What possible reason could he have had for that meeting?'

'I do not know. But Vishal is a man of great knowledge. There is little he does not know about heritage jewellery. His family have been in the business of fashioning jewellery and jewelled artefacts for generations. Sometimes people come to him simply for advice.'

On the journey home these new facts swam around Persis's mind like shoals of distressed fish. Where was Vishal Mistry? Could it be a coincidence that he had vanished shortly after meeting Sir James Herriot, on the night Herriot was killed? What exactly had their meeting been about? And why had he kept that meeting a secret from his family and his employee?

The case was winding itself around her.

She had once chanced upon the skeleton of a monkey in the mangrove swamps that lined the Bandra promenade, its small, soft body strangled by creepers. Upon closer inspection, she saw that it had broken a leg and become trapped in the mesh of vines, inadvertently throttling itself. She had wondered at that moment how the poor dumb beast must have felt, thrashing futilely against its own fate, its struggles simply drawing it closer to its death. A small sense of that black dread had begun to seep into her and she found that, contrary to all expectation, she was afraid.

Not of death or injury, but of failure.

She had two further tasks before she could return home. The first was to meet an old friend of her father's, Augustus Silva, a Goan Catholic and military historian. Augustus had spent his youth in the Indian Army, but taken early retirement following a battle injury that had left him with a pronounced limp. He'd spent the past two decades penning books about Indian military history, from the days of standing armies ruled by despotic kings, maharajas, emperors and nawabs, to the modern military apparatus, such as it had been under the British.

Silva held a tenured position at Bombay University.

She tracked him down to his office where she found him sitting behind a teetering barricade of essay papers. He greeted her enthusiastically, a shaggy bear of a man dressed impeccably in white shirt, dark trousers and a knotted tie, sporting slightly incongruous horn-rimmed glasses. Silva was a familiar sight at the Wadia Book Emporium, seeking out obscure military tomes, many of which had to be ordered in. A friendship had sprung up between Sam and the old Goan, though Persis sometimes wished that Silva would refrain from bringing along a bottle of *feni*, which he ordered by the crate from his native state. The fiercely strong liquor was distilled from the toddy palm and the pair would quickly drink themselves into a stupor.

Persis explained her errand, sketching the broad outlines of the investigation into Herriot's murder and her particular interest in his aide, Madan Lal. 'He apparently served in Burma. I'd like to know more about what led him to leave the army.'

'Can't you approach the army directly?' asked Silva.

'I thought about that. But tell me, how much luck do you think I'll have? A woman, asking for the military record of a man like Lal, a man who served his country and went on to serve a British VIP whose murder is now front-page news?'

'I see your dilemma,' said Silva. 'Well, there's more than one way to skin a camel. Leave it with me. It shouldn't be too difficult to get hold of what you need.'

'Thank you,' said Persis. She had known that Silva, with his network of contacts in the Indian military, would be able to help. 'You must come around for dinner soon.'

'I shall,' he said. 'But first I have a deadline to meet. I am working on a treatise about the Siege of Cawnpore. Indian soldiers of the Bengal Cavalry rebelled against their East India Company officers. Massacres followed on both sides, with hundreds of civilians, British and Indian, caught in the crossfire. In one incident almost two hundred European women and children were murdered by rebel sepoys and stuffed into a well in Bibighar. The British responded with the wholesale burning of villages. A particularly bloody episode.'

The second errand took Persis to the Victoria Terminus railway station in Fort.

She parked the jeep down a side street then walked back towards the station, swimming through the crowds clogging the narrow pavement. The station loomed ahead of her. Built in the Gothic revivalist style, a vision of turrets and pointed arches, the place had always conveyed a sense of Britishness that she found increasingly offensive with the passing years.

She was not alone in her thinking.

A statue of Queen Victoria sat beneath the clock, gazing out over what had once been her dominion. There was already talk of having it removed.

She supposed that this was simply another demonstration of how the relationship with the country's erstwhile rulers had entered a state of flux. Throwing off the yoke of oppression was not the same thing as cutting ties. As the Deputy Home Minister had pointed out, economic necessities bound India to Britain, and would do so for a long time to come. And then there were the memories, *shared* memories, many of them painful, but not all.

She remembered Emily, dear Emily, one of the few to have readily befriended her at school.

Emily had loved the bookshop almost as much as Persis. Her parents, civil servants both, had frequented the place, Persis's father wearing their presence with a grace he refused to accord most Brits who came into the shop. At such times, the ghost of her mother would loom large.

But she had never thought of Emily as one of *those* Brits.

One day the pair of them had been wandering back from school and had come across a white policeman mercilessly beating an elderly Indian in the street. The sight had shocked Persis to a standstill. That a young man might rain blows down upon a frail, grey-haired woman seemed the stuff of nightmares. What sort of moral code could justify such villainy?

Emily had not hesitated.

She'd charged across the road and accosted the man. His face, red with exertion, had seemed shocked at the very notion that his actions might be challenged, let alone conceived of as morally repugnant. They had helped the withered old woman to a nearby hospital, Emily paying from her own purse for her treatment. It had been a defining moment for Persis, one of the reasons she had taken to the movement, and later made the decision to join the police force.

In the years that followed, the four of them – Persis, Dinaz, Jaya and Emily – had attended many rallies together, Emily sometimes forced to go in disguise, dressed in a head-to-toe burka; not every Indian welcomed a white face at such gatherings.

It had been a shock when Emily had announced that her parents had decided to return to London in the summer of 1946. With the end of the war, the situation had become untenable. Protests had become a daily occurrence, the threat of violence against Britishers ever present.

They had parted at the docks, a farewell of restrained emotions. Emily and her family had found passage aboard a troopship bound for Liverpool, one of a thousand families departing the country, a cross-section of those who had made their lives on the subcontinent: missionaries, office workers, tea planters, dressmakers, telephonists, typists, engineers and nurses. Some had been in the country five generations.

They were as Indian as Persis.

She quickly made her way to the station's administrative offices, a journey that took longer than she had imagined. Then again Victoria station served as the headquarters for the Grand Peninsular Railway and was the principal exit point for those travelling from Bombay to virtually every part of the country.

Here she met the man in charge, a Subosh Mazumdar. Mazumdar, an ageing walrus with a moustache that seemed to weigh down his head, absorbed her request. He took the ticket stub that she had found in Herriot's jacket from her, and peered closely at it.

'We will have to dig into the records,' he informed her. 'The serial number and series code should be enough to find the information you are looking for. Give me a day or two.'

'I was hoping you could do this immediately.'

He grimaced as if a fishbone had become stuck in his throat. 'The station is running at peak capacity, madam. Searching for a single ticket log will take time. I cannot spare the manpower.'

She arrived home to discover a small crate waiting for her on the dining table. Her father sat in the corner of the room, by the Steinway, a book in hand, reading glasses balanced on the tip of his nose. The Steinway, a polished black affair, was a relic, gifted to Sam's father by a Yorkshireman who'd left the country in a hurry during the Quit India years. The British had surrendered many pianos to India during their retreat.

Persis had learned to play as a child. Her mother had taught her; she had inherited Sanaz's musical chromosome, but with her passing the music too had died.

'What's this?' she asked, setting down her cap.

'Special Delivery from Delhi. The courier is waiting downstairs for your signature. Apparently, whatever is in there is for your eyes only.'

In the bookshop, she found a youngish man with darting eyes and teeth too big for his mouth, exhibiting all the signs of an unpleasant encounter with her father.

Having signed for the delivery, she returned upstairs, picked up the crate from the dining table, took it to her bedroom, and set it down on the end of her bed.

The courier had handed her a letter, which she now opened.

It was from the Deputy Home Minister, K.P. Tilak. In it he explained that he was sending her copies of the original files that had been provided to Sir James Herriot as part of his Partition crimes investigation. He urged her to secrecy, asking her not to discuss the contents with anyone unless absolutely necessary.

She went back into the living room, found a screwdriver, then returned and opened the crate.

There were sixty-four files in total, thin manila folders wrapped in string, each holding a sheaf of papers. On the front of each folder was written the name of the state from which the complaint had originated. She quickly sorted them in this way, making piles on the bed. There were twenty-eight states – a number ratified by the new constitution – and the bed was soon covered. Some states had a single complaint, others, such as Punjab, Bombay and West Bengal, had multiple.

There was a lot of material to cover, she realised. It would take days for her to go through every document, particularly as she wasn't sure exactly what it was she was searching for. Herriot had looked through these files. It was probable that he had stored his copies in the safe in his study, and that they were now missing. Certainly, they had not been found anywhere else at Laburnum House. She wondered, again, at the ashes she had discovered in the fireplace in Herriot's study. Had Herriot burned the documents? Why?

She considered beginning on the documents right away but a wave of exhaustion dissuaded her. Better to start the following day with a clear head.

She didn't want to risk missing anything.

She showered, changed into a pair of Oriental pyjamas that Dr Aziz had gifted her, then joined her father as Krishna served them dinner, a south Indian chicken curry.

'My bowels have turned to concrete,' remarked Sam, biting down on a roti. 'Aziz recommended papaya. An excellent laxative, by all accounts.'

'Thank you for sharing, Papa,' she said. She could sense a stiffness in him. No doubt he was still upset about the fact that she was investigating the death of an Englishman, and the comment she had made about her mother's passing.

'So, are you going to tell me what was in the crate?' he eventually asked.

'I'm afraid I cannot.'

His moustache twitched, but he said nothing. She thought he might ask something further but he did not.

They ate the rest of their meal in silence.

9

She was delayed the next morning by a visit to the vet – Akbar was in need of his annual check-up and injections.

The tomcat fought her tooth and nail. It was always the same, a spitting, hissing ordeal, bundling him into the jeep, driving the twenty minutes to the clinic in Cuffe Parade, getting him from the vehicle to the surgery. And yet, as soon as he was with the vet, a sandy-haired and ever-smiling Scotswoman by the name of Philippa Macallister, he became as docile as a kitten. It was almost flirtatious, the way he acted around her.

Macallister – who insisted on being called Pippa – gave Akbar the once-over, pronounced a clean bill of health, then advanced upon the tomcat with a syringe. Akbar flattened his ears and backed away.

'Don't be such a baby,' muttered Persis and held him down as the jabs were delivered.

'You look like you could do with one of these,' said Macallister, waving the syringe at Persis. 'Case getting you down?'

They chatted for a while.

Persis had always found Macallister to be a forthright and discreet woman. Her love of Bombay's fauna had prevented her from leaving the country, and she was a popular advocate for the city's animal rights organisations. She was also politically astute.

She listened politely, then said, 'It's a lot of responsibility, isn't it? Being a woman in a man's world?'

Persis said nothing.

'Do you know what the secret is?' She arched an eyebrow. 'Pretend that it *isn't* their world. Pretend that it's yours.'

An hour later, Persis walked into Malabar House to discover a subdued atmosphere.

'What's going on?' she asked George Fernandes, who was typing laboriously with one finger on a battered Remington. She knew that both the 'a' and the 'e' were missing from the ancient machine, a handicap that made Fernandes's reports excruciating to read.

'ADC Shukla is here,' he replied without looking up. 'With Ravi Patnagar. You had better go in.'

She dumped the Partition files she had brought from home into the drawer of her desk, locked it carefully, then headed to Roshan Seth's office where she found Additional Deputy Commissioner of Police Amit Shukla seated before Seth's desk, urbanely drinking tea. Patnagar and Seth were standing, facing each other, hackles raised like alley dogs.

'Ah,' said Shukla, 'Inspector Wadia. Good of you to join us. We were just discussing the case.'

She blinked, momentarily unsure of how to respond. She had never met ADC Shukla before – he was one of a raft of senior officers who acted as assistants to Bombay's commissioner of police, all men, all indistinguishable from one another. Portly and balding, he had the face of a favourite uncle or one of those sleepy-eyed Tibetan mastiffs. Yet there was no doubt as to the power he wielded. The fact that even Ravi Patnagar, head of the state CID, was forced to stand in his presence underlined this point. She resisted the urge to salute. 'Sir, if I had known you were coming, I would have been here earlier.'

'I sense an accusation, Inspector,' said Shukla jovially. 'Rest assured, there is nothing sinister to it. I simply decided to drop by on a whim.'

Persis doubted this. From what little she had heard of him, ADC Shukla was a man of considerable heft within the force, a tactician who had not only survived the post-independence cull within the government services, but positively thrived. Two years earlier the city and state police had merged. The new commissioner, Ranjan 'Tiger' Shroff, Bombay's first non-white commissioner of police, had set the tone by surrounding himself with men possessed of a similar cutthroat dynamism. If Shukla's rise had been meteoric, in its wake lay innumerable bodies.

'Roshan tells me that you have thrown yourself wholeheartedly into the investigation.'

'We are pursuing the matter with alacrity, sir.'

'Excellent!' His lidded eyes rested for a moment on the teacup in his hand. 'Of course, I expect that a woman who sailed through the academy will appreciate the delicate balancing act that such a case imposes upon us.'

'Sir?'

He set down the cup. 'Persis, it has been two years since we achieved independence, yet it is only on January 26th that the constitution of India will finally come into effect, a document prepared by Indians, for Indians. It is only then that we truly become masters of our own destiny.' He paused. 'Three hundred million Indians, Persis. Three hundred million unique identities, all locked into the belief that an age of enlightenment is upon us. Cows will talk, hunger will be banished, evil vanquished. Secularism will become the new religion in a nation plagued by millions of gods.' He grimaced. 'When these miracles do not materialise, anarchy will follow. And we, the Indian Police Service, are tasked with the job of maintaining law and order during this turbulent period in our history. How can we possibly achieve such a thing? Given that there are so few of us?'

She exchanged looks with Seth, who shook his head. 'Let silence be thy watchword': a favourite saying of his in the presence of authority.

'No?' said Shukla. 'The answer, as perverse as it might seem, is that we must look to the British. How did they, with only a handful of individuals, rule over our multitudes?' He slapped the desk with unexpected ferocity. 'The British understood that not everyone is equal. A society is composed of those who lead and those who follow.'

Persis began to see the shape of Shukla's point. He was taking her by the hand and leading her around the perfumed gardens of his argument.

'I have been told that you have been making house calls upon some of the most prominent people in the city.'

She felt a rush of anger. 'We have been making enquiries with those who were present at Sir James's home on the night of his death.'

'I understand that, Inspector,' said Shukla patiently. 'But did you stop to think how it reflects upon the service if you and your men turn up on the doorsteps of such luminaries armed with pitchforks?'

'We must be free to pursue our enquiries as we see fit,' said Persis stiffly.

'Freedom is an illusion, Persis. None of us are truly free.' He relented, offering her a smile. 'Sometimes, we best serve by reverting to first principles. For instance, in my experience, the murder of a wealthy, powerful individual is usually traceable to a disgruntled party of lowly rank.'

She heard herself say, 'I shall take that on board. Sir.'

'Excellent!' He slapped both thighs and bounced to his feet to face her. 'Many in the IPS rolled their eyes when they heard that a female had been accepted into the academy. I was not one of them. You are a credit to the women of this country. The eyes of India are upon you.'

'Sir, if I may—' began Patnagar, only to be halted by an upheld hand from the ADC.

'Ravi, we must allow Persis the opportunity to follow through on what she has begun. A fair crack of the whip, as Sir James himself might say.'

'But—'

'This is the will of the commissioner,' said Shukla, allowing a trace of irritation to enter his tone.

Patnagar subsided, glancing at Seth with undisguised hostility.

The ADC turned to Persis. 'Good luck, Inspector. I am sure that our paths will cross again.'

After they had left, Seth collapsed into his seat, pulled a bottle from his desk and poured himself a Scotch. 'Still certain that you don't want one?'

'Why were they here? I thought you said they wanted nothing to do with this case?'

'No,' said Seth. 'What I said was that they did not want the *risks* associated with this case. What did you expect? You're charging around the city like a bull in a china shop. Someone kicked up a stink.'

'He did not need to come to Malabar House to make his point.'

'Have you ever seen a tiger marking out his territory? Shukla is our tiger. And if we are not careful he will devour us all.'

'I still don't understand. If he's so concerned, why doesn't he just give the case to Patnagar?'

'He doesn't *want* to give it to Patnagar. If he gives it to Patnagar and Patnagar fails then the mess is on Shukla's shoes. But if he leaves it with you and *you* fail, he has just enough distance to wash his hands of us.'

Persis sighed. It was barely ten and she could already feel the exhaustion washing through her. Ever since the academy, she had heard rumours of the internal politics that debilitated the Indian Police Service. Yet it was one thing to know of such a thing in the abstract, quite another to confront the reality.

'Not that Patnagar will let it go,' said Seth gloomily. 'I'm afraid you've made an enemy there.'

'But I never said a word to the man!'

'Patnagar is a traditionalist. His views on women in the service could curdle milk. He considers your very existence a personal affront. How do you think it will look if you actually *succeed*?

'There *is* something I don't understand, however,' he continued, holding his glass under his chin. 'How in the hell did they know about the details of your investigation? Patnagar had a lot to say before you showed up. They had it all, every move you've made, what you plan to do next. I suspect, Inspector, that you have a rat on your team.'

Persis emerged from Seth's office and made a beeline for Oberoi's desk. He was leaning back in his chair with his boots up, grinning smugly at the ceiling as he smoked a cigarette. She felt the fury rising, boiling her brain like a kettle until she felt the top of her skull might blow off. Just as she reached him, Constable Subramanium arrived to intercept her.

'Madam,' he said, 'there is a man here to see you.'

She wrenched her furious gaze from the back of Oberoi's lacquered head. 'Who?'

Subramanium handed her an embossed card.

Aalam Channa
Senior Reporter
The Indian Chronicle

Her eyes unfocused and fell to the framed quote on her desk: 'The commissioner's experiment in catapulting a woman into the service might well mirror our fledgling republic's forward-thinking ideals, but what he has failed to consider is that in temperament, intelligence and moral fibre, the female of the species is, and always will be, inferior to the male.' Channa was the author of that particular gem. 'Tell him I am not here.'

'I am afraid it is too late for that,' said Subramanium apologetically.

'Then tell him I am indisposed,' she snapped.

Subramanium opened his mouth, then thought better of it. He pirouetted smartly on his heels and headed for the door.

The interruption had taken the wind out of her sails.

She fell into her chair and stared at a point between Oberoi's shoulder blades, slowly incinerating him with her gaze. What had possessed the man to go behind her back? He was a prime example of the unthinking misogyny that continued to hold sway over Indian society. It was at times like this that she felt most acutely the loneliness of her pedestal. It was all very well being the nation's first female IPS officer; but the fact was that she was still the country's *only* female IPS officer.

A shadow fell over her. She turned to face a tall, graceful man dressed in a white Nehru suit. A pencil moustache graced his upper lip and his wavy black hair shone lustrously. Subramanium trailed behind him, anxiously waving his hands in the air.

'Inspector Wadia.' Aalam Channa held out a hand. 'Delighted to make your acquaintance.'

Persis sprang to her feet. 'I believe I sent word that I was indisposed.'

'This will only take a minute, Inspector. May I call you Persis?'

'No,' she said. 'You may not.'

Channa smiled, unfazed. 'The *Chronicle* is one of the nation's leading dailies. Our readership stretches from coast to coast, from Kashmir to Kanyakumari. Sir James's murder has captured the public imagination, as, indeed, have you, Inspector. India's first female detective, heading up the decade's first major case. Surely, you can appreciate that such a concatenation of circumstances might be newsworthy?'

Channa spoke with a cultured, pleasant accent. He had something of the nawab about him, a princeling of the hinterlands. 'A short interview, Inspector, that is all I am asking. We do not even have to discuss the material facts of the case, not if you do not wish it. My readers are as interested in *you* as they are in the investigation.'

The man was incorrigible. Persis's mouth flapped open, but Channa quickly moved on before she could respond. 'We have a unique opportunity here. Should you wish it, the *Chronicle* might become an ally. Not only during this investigation, but for your subsequent adventures on the force. Think of it, Inspector. We would make a heroine of you. Imagine all those you might inspire around the country. Young girls seeking a place in the new republic. Is that such a bad thing?'

She blinked, suddenly unsure of herself. Channa had a way of simplifying a complex argument that made it seem beguiling . . .

'An investigation cannot be conducted in the public eye.'

'Then do not give me details. My readers will be happy with broad strokes. The key is for us to convince them that the *Indian Chronicle* has a special insight into the goings-on at Malabar House. With us on your side, everything that you do will be portrayed in the most favourable light possible. Surely that is worth something?'

'I thought the press was meant to be objective.'

For an instant, the smile died from his eyes. She saw in that moment something else, a snake-like blink, a predator thwarted of his prey.

'I'm sorry,' said Persis firmly. 'I have nothing to say at this time. And now I must return to my work. Constable Subramanium will see you out.'

Channa shadowboxed with his own confusion, as if not quite believing that his charm offensive had failed. She supposed that with his good looks and demure manner he did not often find his advances rebuffed. As he walked away, he looked back over his shoulder. 'What is it about the press that so frightens you, Inspector?'

She did not bother to answer.

Resuming her seat, she reached for her notes.

Moments later, Oberoi rushed by her, headed for the door. Prodded by an instinctive churning of suspicion, she rose from her desk and followed him out.

She hung just inside the main doors and observed him as he crossed the road and caught up with Channa as the journalist stepped into a waiting tonga. A conversation ensued and then Channa reached into his jacket and handed Oberoi a card.

A flash of heat pulsed at her temples. It was all she could do to stop herself from charging across the street and putting her hands around his throat. Instead, she calmed herself, turned and headed back downstairs.

The next few hours vanished into nothingness. More interviews with those who had been present at Herriot's party came in. She added the information to her notes.

She compiled a list of tasks for the day.

At 2 p.m. she was scheduled to meet Eve Gatsby, the American whom Herriot's housekeeper had suggested might be a close female acquaintance. Might she be the mysterious woman with whom Herriot had had intercourse in his study just prior to his death?

Following that meeting she was due at the offices of the victim's lawyers, for the reading of his will.

Her final task was to continue to track down Adi Shankar, another of those who had left Herriot's ball prior to being interviewed.

She had called the number Lal had given her half a dozen times, but met with little success. Now she dialled again and was put through to his secretary. The woman, far too sharp-tongued for her own good, duelled with her for a while, before placing her on hold. When she returned, she informed Persis that Shankar continued to be indisposed. If the situation changed she would receive a call.

She resisted the urge to hurl the phone across the room. Instead, she unlocked her drawer, took out the Partition files she had brought from home, went to the small interview room at the rear of the office, locked herself in, and spread them out on the lacquered wooden table.

She began with the files pertaining to Bombay, reasoning that Sir James might have begun his investigations close to home.

In each folder, she first read the statements provided by witnesses, almost all anonymous, sometimes conflicting, always harrowing. That was the trouble. These were eyewitness testimonies, and the one thing she had already learned was how dangerous it was to rely on the word of bystanders. *One part truth to three parts fiction*, was how a senior officer at the academy had put it.

Partition! She remembered how the very spectre of it had set Indians at each other's throats.

Once Jinnah had made his position public, the poison spread quickly, the flames fanned by the British, always quick to exploit divisions among their subject populations. Their attempts at holding on to their 'jewel in the crown' finally collapsed following the war. An exhausted Treasury convinced Attlee's government to end British rule in India and, in early 1947, the British Prime Minister announced a transfer of power by June 1948. However, with the British Army unprepared for the spiralling violence in the country, the new viceroy, Louis Mountbatten, advanced the date for the transfer, allowing less than six months for a mutually agreed plan for independence. In June 1947 India's nationalist leaders, including Jinnah, agreed to a partition of the country along religious lines – the Mountbatten Plan. Gandhi absented himself from the talks; he remained bitterly opposed to the division of India until the day of his death. The predominantly Hindu and Sikh regions were assigned to the new India and predominantly Muslim areas to the new nation of Pakistan; the plan included a partition of the Muslim-majority provinces of Punjab and Bengal.

What should have been predicted, but was wholly unprepared for, was the communal violence that accompanied the announcement of the actual line of partition, the Radcliffe Line, and the subsequent transfer of hostile populations.

By the time the dust settled, more than two million lay dead, and ten million displaced. A litany of horror, acts of such inhuman cruelty that it seemed incomprehensible to Persis. Not just wholesale murder and rape, but the fact that those who had carried out these crimes were, by and large, ordinary people. A postman, a clerk, a farmer. She remembered attending a Rotary Club meeting at her father's lodge on Ravelin Street where they'd played clippings of Movietone News, footage of the Delhi riots. Images of citywide curfews, deserted streets and shuttered shops, set against burning buildings and corpses littering the roads.

Such horror! The disembowelling of pregnant women. The crushing of infants' heads against walls of brick and stone. Blind men doused with gasoline and set alight in the streets. She recalled a statement by Mountbatten, in response to the spectre of Partition violence: *At least on this question I shall give you complete assurance. I shall see to it that there is no bloodshed and riot.*

What stupendous lies had been told during those years!

She remembered too Nehru's momentous speech, at the very instant of India's birth, listening to it on her father's Bakelite, the words speaking to something unknown and possibly unknowable inside the heart and mind of every Indian:

Long years ago we made a tryst with destiny, and now the time comes when we shall redeem our pledge, not wholly or in full measure, but very substantially. At the stroke of the midnight hour, when the world sleeps, India will awake to life and freedom. A moment comes, which comes but rarely in history, when we step out from the old to the new, when an age ends, and when the soul of a nation, long suppressed, finds utterance. It is fitting that at this solemn moment we take the pledge of dedication to the service of India and her people and to the still larger cause of humanity.

How hollow those words now sounded.

In some of the files, there were photographs. One image, in particular, stayed with her. Three headless corpses, clearly young, female, murdered in a field, their bodies propped against a well. Where were their heads? she wondered. Had they been thrown in the well?

She recalled a quote from Cicero. *The life of the dead is placed in the memory of the living.*

Who did these girls have to remember them? She might be the last person on earth to speak their names. She had begun this investigation intoxicated by the belief that it might bring her honour, glory and the respect of her peers. But crimes such as these forced her to adjust her perspective. Evil could only flourish if the world colluded with it. Justice went beyond her own ambitions; it was a matter of balancing the scales.

A knock on the door brought her back. It was Birla. 'There are nine hotels in the city of Amritsar named the Golden Temple. Herriot didn't stay in any of them.'

After Birla had left, she pondered on the detail. The enigmatic code written on the sheet continued to bother her. Who was Bakshi? Why had Herriot written down that name? And what did PLT41/85ACRG11 mean? She had hoped that by discovering the location of the Golden Temple Hotel she might unravel the mystery.

Sighing, she returned to her work.

10

The tomb of Haji Ali had been built in the 1400s, a whitewashed monument perched on a tiny islet in the middle of Haji Ali Bay in mid-town Bombay, linked to the city proper by a narrow causeway that was traversable only during low tide. When the tide was up the causeway vanished, promoting the illusion that the Sufi saint's tomb was floating on water.

Persis parked her jeep on the coast road, then walked along the causeway towards the tomb and its accompanying mosque, shimmering in the midday sun. Pilgrims jostled along on all sides, glancing at her, some with curiosity, others with open hostility. For centuries women had been banned from the tomb; even now they were permitted only into its marbled precincts and not into the sanctum sanctorum that lay at its heart, the central shrine where the saint was interred. Recent petitions to the Bombay High Court had fallen on deaf ears. As far as the law was concerned women were still *persona non grata* here, which made it all the more surprising that Eve Gatsby, a woman *and* a foreigner, had been granted access.

She found the American just outside the tomb, in a blazing white courtyard, examining a succession of pillars embellished with artistic mirror work: blue, green and yellow chips of glass arranged in kaleidoscopic patterns interspersed with Arabic calligraphy spelling out the ninety-nine names of Allah.

In deference to the proscription against revealing clothing, Eve had donned a pair of khaki jodhpurs and long boots, below a white blouson, a headscarf and trendy, bug-eyed sunglasses with yellow frames. She resembled a cross between a fashion model and a jungle explorer.

She was bent behind a tripod and camera set-up.

Persis noted a small, intense-looking Indian standing to one side: Eve's official escort inside the tomb, she presumed. The man, dressed in a white shalwar kameez with a white skullcap, exuded a sense of nervousness, as if, perhaps, he had brought a landmine into the complex and was waiting for it to go off.

'Glad you could make it, Inspector,' said Gatsby in the breezy accent of a native New Yorker. 'To tell the truth I was hoping to meet you while I was out here. India's first female detective. And now a celebrity. In fact, if you don't mind, I'd like to get a few shots of you on camera.'

Persis wasn't sure how to respond. The American oozed self-confidence, as if the very possibility of the world not aligning itself with her wishes was something beyond the bounds of imagination. Gatsby was one of those who hadn't bothered to wait around to be interviewed at Laburnum House.

'I came here to ask you about Sir James Herriot.'

Eve smiled, a dazzling white-toothed affair. She was a beautiful woman, tall and chic, with wisps of dark hair poking out from under her headscarf. Persis could easily imagine her gracing the silver screen; she reminded her of a young Olivia de Havilland – Persis had been a fan of the American actress ever since *They Died with Their Boots On.*

Gatsby pulled out a pack of Capstans from her jodhpurs and lit one. Her minder uncrossed his arms and glanced around like a startled rabbit. Persis noted that the pair of them, the only two women in the courtyard, were attracting considerable attention.

On the far side of the courtyard, a group of Sufi singers launched into a bout of maniacal prayer. Their singsong voices rose above the courtyard, mingling with the cawing of gulls.

'You know,' remarked Eve, 'this place is one of the best examples of Indo-Islamic architecture on the subcontinent. Haji Ali was a wealthy merchant. Gave up all his possessions one day and decided to travel the world seeking goodness in his fellow man.' She flashed another breezy smile. 'It's a shame about Sir James. What would you like to know?'

'How did you know him?' asked Persis.

'Through my father. Sir James was in the States last year, on a diplomatic mission, and my father entertained him at our New York home. They became friends. He invited us out to Bombay. My father couldn't come but I was keen.'

'Are you here for business or pleasure?'

'A bit of both. I'm a photographer. Well, to be truthful I'm the daughter of a very wealthy man, one who pays for me to indulge my hobbies. But I like to think that I take it seriously. The subcontinent has always held a particular allure for the lens, *if* you have the eye for it. You don't know who my father is, do you?'

Persis shook her head.

'Truman Gatsby. Noted industrialist and Republican politician. That's his official entry in the *Marquis Who's Who*. My father made a fortune in New York real estate. And now he wants to run for Congress. We have a saying back home: "When a man is tired of common sense he takes up politics."'

'You sound cynical".'

'Let's just say I've seen a little of the world and not all of it is to my liking.'

'Was Sir James to your liking?'

She froze, then pushed her sunglasses on to her forehead, revealing two dark and pretty eyes. 'If I was a betting woman, Inspector, I'd say *that* had a certain bite to it.'

Persis pressed forward. 'I am told that you and Sir James were . . . involved.'

'Involved?' echoed Eve. 'What a curious word. I take it you mean we were engaged in some sort of tawdry liaison.'

'Were you?'

She gave a short bark of laughter. 'No. The man was old enough to be my father. He had his charms, I suppose, but I'm not in the habit of falling into bed with any old fool.'

'Are you saying he was no more than a friend?'

'An acquaintance.'

'We have evidence that he was ... intimate with a woman just before his death. In his study.'

She grimaced. 'It wasn't me. Not for lack of his trying, I'll grant you.'

'He propositioned you?'

'Of course he did. The man was a predator.' She reached out to flick the ash from her cigarette but was stopped by a strangled cry from her minder. The man leaped forward, took off his skullcap, flipped it upside down. She frowned at him, then obliged by flicking the ash into the cloth bowl.

'Why did you attend his party if you disliked him?'

'I didn't dislike him. I just saw him for what he was. Look, James had his uses. He introduced me to a lot of the city's movers and shakers, people I wanted to photograph. It was his idea of foreplay.'

'You don't seem very distraught by his death.'

'As I said, he was just an acquaintance.'

'Do you know who he might have been with that night? In his study?'

'I'm afraid I haven't a clue, Inspector.'

'Do you know of anyone who might have wished him harm?'

She shrugged. 'He was a political animal. As my father is fond of saying, if you swim with the sharks don't be surprised when one of them takes a bite out your ass.'

Persis waited.

Eve sighed. 'I have no idea. You should ask that aide of his, Lal. I don't think he particularly liked his boss.'

Persis dwelt on these words. It was the second time she had heard of a possible animosity between Lal and his employer.

'Is there nothing at all you can tell me?'

'The only thing I can think of is that he recently fell out with his business partner, the Scot.'

Persis perked up. 'Do you mean Robert Campbell?'

'That's the one. Big brute. Rude.'

'Are you suggesting that Sir James and Campbell had a disagreement? Over what?'

'I don't know. It was just gossip at the party. There seemed to be some tension between the pair of them. At least, James looked like he was avoiding the man.'

'Why would he invite Campbell if they'd fallen out?'

'It certainly wasn't to celebrate anything. I've never seen a man so down in the mouth.'

'Campbell was angry?'

'Not at first. But, something happened late on, after the midnight fireworks. He got into some sort of spat with his daughter. Elizabeth.'

'What about?'

'No idea. Then again, they were always at it. Campbell and his daughter, I mean.'

'Why?'

'There was some talk of a beau that Campbell took exception to a while back. Ended badly, apparently. Or rather he ended it for her.'

'Who was this man?'

'I don't know, but I hear he might have been a native. And I thought *I* was the scandalous one.' She grimaced. 'Rumour has it that Campbell resolved the problem through violence.'

Persis recalled the story Lal had told her about an Indian engineer that Campbell had supposedly had killed. Was there more to it than just rumour?

'Do you remember when this was?'

'About a year ago, I believe. They were up in Faridpur, just outside Delhi.'

II

The offices of Merchant, Palonjee and Pettigrew were located on Manekshaw Lane, wedged in between an army and navy store and the premises of an ambiguous commercial enterprise engaged in 'import and export'. The narrow road was choked with cars, tongas, cycle rickshaws and pedestrians. On the pavement a row of typists sat cross-legged on the baking paving slabs, pounding away on typewriters at ferocious speed. They were a common sight around the city, ranked outside government offices, law firms and the municipality's various courts, catering to those in need of swiftly produced legal documentation.

Persis trudged up a narrow flight of stairs to a first-floor reception where a secretary flapped her towards a leather sofa. On the walls were photographs of the firm's trio of lawyers, rubbing shoulders with a roll-call of clients, mainly white men with tailored suits and white-blocked teeth. She suspected that Merchant, Palonjee and Pettigrew was another of those colonial-era enterprises trying desperately to serve two masters: the past and the future. She also suspected that not so long ago the first name on the firm's letterhead might well have been Pettigrew.

The secretary called inside, then led her through to a boardroom overlooking the main road. A conference table ran the length of the room. At one end a portrait of a severe-looking Britisher in a suit gazed out over the table and the four individuals gathered there. The nearest of these was Madan Lal and he rose now to greet her.

'Thank you for coming, Inspector.' Lal waved at the others. 'May I present Inspector Persis Wadia? She is leading the investigation into Sir James's death.'

The obese man in a light grey suit sitting at the head of the table spoke up. 'Rather unusual to have a police presence at the reading of a will. Are you sure this is necessary?'

'Quite necessary, Mr Merchant,' said Lal before Persis could speak.

'Welcome, Inspector,' said the small man to Merchant's left, dressed in a navy-blue suit, a bow tie and eyeglasses. 'My name is Vivek Palonjee. Please, do have a seat.'

Persis moved around the table and sat directly opposite the white man who had observed her arrival with a steady gaze. He was young, sandy-haired and blue-eyed. He wore an Irish linen jacket over a sodden white shirt, his stomach sagging over his belt. There was something vaguely familiar about him . . .

'May I introduce Edmond de Vries?' said Lal. 'He has flown over from the West Indies. He was Sir James's representative there – managing his Caribbean holdings.'

De Vries nodded solemnly and held out his hand. She took it and was immediately repulsed. She wiped the moistness on to her trousers. He noticed this but said nothing.

An itch at the back of her mind. Where had she seen this man before?

The room was unconscionably warm, the ceiling fan whirring above the table fighting a valiant rearguard action against the rising afternoon heat.

Merchant, ladled into a suit that was too small for him, seemed fit to burst from it like a mango squeezed violently from its skin. 'Now that we are all present, I suggest that we commence with our business.' He had a rough, smoker's voice, impassioned by a strange warble, as if a frog had become trapped in his throat. 'For almost two decades the law firm of Merchant, Palonjee and Pettigrew has served distinguished gentlemen – both British and Indian – with dedication, faith and honesty. Indeed, those very words are the motto of our founder and guiding light, Anthony Pettigrew.'

Persis's eyes shifted to the canvas hanging behind Merchant. 'Where *is* Mr Pettigrew?' she asked.

'Our colleague has temporarily returned to England to attend to certain personal affairs,' supplied Palonjee smoothly. 'We expect his return imminently.'

The lie flapped about the room, then vanished through an open window. Persis wondered if the others had sensed it. If she had to guess, Anthony Pettigrew had discovered that post-independence India was a beast not to his liking. In all probability, he had emulated many of his countrymen and fled the new republic, leaving his partners to continue the fiction of his presence.

'As you are all by now aware,' continued Merchant, scowling at the interruption, 'we were retained by the late Sir James for a variety of legal matters including the administering of his will.' He reached towards the manila folder at his elbow. With great ceremony, he unwrapped the string that encased it, then opened it to reveal a sheaf of stamped papers.

'The will of Sir James was prepared on December 15th, 1948,' he began. 'Its provisions relate to all assets, property and chattel that had accrued to him as on the date of his death. Such assets include the property at No. 38 Palmerston Square in London, England; the cash sums present within three bank accounts held in London; a variety of shareholdings and indentured bonds; a rubber plantation located on the Caribbean island of Trinidad; and its associated commercial enterprise, the West Indian Rubber Corporation, incorporated at Companies House, London.' He paused. 'Allow me to continue in the testator's own words: "I, James Edward Herriot, citizen of the British Empire, being of sound mind and body, declare this to be my last will and testament. I hereby revoke all prior wills and codicils. By this, my will, I bequeath the residue of my estate in its entirety to the Bombay Branch of the Royal Asiatic Society. Such estate shall include my property in London, England, the sum of my cash balances and investments, and the sum of my commercial enterprises in Port of Spain, Trinidad.'"

Merchant paused to pluck a handkerchief from his pocket and wipe the sweat from his jowls.

'The value of the estate has now been ascertained. I am afraid the news is not good.' He glanced at Edmond de Vries. 'The fact is that recent financial difficulties mean that Sir James Herriot's estate has been decimated. To put it bluntly, Sir James was all but bankrupt.'

A stunned silence greeted the lawyer's summation.

Lal was the first to speak. 'There has to be some mistake.'

'I assure you, there is no mistake.' Merchant endeavoured to look apologetic and sanguine at the same time, but failed to do either. He ran a fat finger around his collar.

'How did you determine Sir James's financial situation?' persisted Lal.

Persis couldn't help but note that the revelation of Herriot's penury had stunned the mild-mannered aide. Perhaps he was considering the viability of his own position. If there were no estate left to manage, how long could Lal carry on at Laburnum House?

'We spoke to his bookkeeper and contacted his bankers in London,' Merchant replied. 'And we telegrammed Mr de Vries in Port of Spain. He explained the situation to us.'

'What situation?'

All eyes turned to de Vries. He was sweating profusely; a rash of red crawled up his neck.

'Before I answer that question, I'd like to know: how did he die?' He looked at Persis. 'The gory details. The lawyers were very brief in their telegram and one can only glean so much from the dailies.'

She was taken aback by his tone. 'I am sorry for your loss,' she began, but he halted her in her tracks by bursting into a mirthless laugh.

'Don't be. I'm not.'

'I take it you were not on good terms with—' She stopped. Finally, she had it. It was the eyes. They took her back to the portrait she had seen in the murdered man's office, of a younger Sir James Herriot.

'He was your father, wasn't he?'

His face changed. 'Well done, Inspector. It usually takes a few days for people to make the connection. Though we must be careful of bandying around the word *father*. I was his bastard, you see, and he went to great pains to ensure I was kept hidden away. Wouldn't want to put a dent in the old man's golden aura.'

'You disliked him.'

'I *despised* him,' he said matter-of-factly. 'And he despised me. It's lucky I was on the other side of the world otherwise I might have been your prime suspect.'

'What was the reason for the animosity?'

'I am the living evidence of my father's predatory habits. Only on this occasion my mother refused to go along with his plans for me, namely, a backstreet doctor, followed by a gentle shove into the night, a fistful of cash tucked into her hatband. She died when I was nine. Tuberculosis. When she understood that she hadn't much time left she visited Herriot. Threatened to create a scandal if he didn't take me in. They reached a compromise. Herriot would pay for my education, but I would not take his name, nor reveal to anyone that I was his son. He hated me, of course. The feeling was mutual.' He glared at the wall behind her. 'He was, quite simply, a vile man. Utterly self-centred, focused only on his own advancement, his own gratification. He packed me off to boarding school, then Cambridge. When I came back he banished me to the West Indies to run his holdings there. At least in name. He gelded me first. In actuality, the place is run by his man, a Jew by the name of Abrams; or was until he stuck a revolver in his mouth and blew his brains out.'

His watery eyes held her gaze. Was he attempting to shock her? She had no time for a contest of wills. He had been hurt, she did not doubt that. She could not imagine what it would have been like to grow up with a father who did not care.

'Why did Abrams kill himself?'

His long fingers played with a water glass. 'What does a man have to do to get a proper drink around here?'

She recognised the tracery of crapulence around his eyes, the filigree of broken veins.

'Do you know what really irks me?' he continued. 'How he managed to pull the wool over everyone's eyes. Sir James Herriot. Master statesman. Our man in the Orient.' He leaned closer, his ruddy face twisted in anger. 'He ruined my life and my mother's. He was a monster and I'm glad he's dead.'

'Why did Abrams kill himself?' she repeated.

'Because he couldn't live with it.'

'Live with what?'

'The collapse of the plantation. Insect infestation. There was nothing anyone could do. Or there would have been had Abrams not been asleep at the wheel. By the time he cottoned on to what was happening, it was too late. And so he took the honourable way out.' He mimicked a gun with his fingers, the act of blowing his brains out.

'Your father knew this?'

'Yes. I telegrammed him when it happened. Three months ago.'

'Why didn't you return to India at that time?'

He gave a hollow laugh. '*Return* to India? I was never here in the first place. My father didn't want me anywhere near him. Besides, I had my own commitments.' She continued to stare at him. 'If you must know I have a woman out there. She's just given birth to my child. That's the reason I hung on there. I wanted to come to India with my baby and my black mistress. Introduce my father to his bastard grandchild. Sir James Herriot, peer of the realm, grandfather to a mulatto.' His eyes danced with a maniacal light. And then it all went out of him. 'But he outwitted me again. He went and died on me.'

12

The office was quiet. The only one at his desk was Sub-Inspector Haq, painstakingly writing up a progress report on his investigation into an arson attack that had burned down a local jute warehouse. The warehouse had belonged to a politico, a fiery character. The man had jumped up and down in his jackboots demanding the entire city be turned upside down until the perpetrator was apprehended. The case had gradually worked its way around to Malabar House. Haq, for his sins, had been given the investigation and had made slow but steady progress, weathering the eardrum-bursting fury of the politico and a revolving cast of henchmen whose only function appeared to be to turn up at Malabar House at all hours of the day to berate and threaten him.

She fell into her chair, set down her cap, and closed her eyes. The case was becoming more convoluted by the second.

She sat upright, picked up a pen, and pulled out her notebook.

A killer with a curved blade. A midnight tryst. A falling out with a friend. A mysterious jeweller, now missing. A recent bankruptcy. A government commission to investigate the worst of crimes.

How did these seemingly unconnected blocks fit together?

Inspector Hemant Oberoi walked in, did a double-take as he spotted her.

'So, how goes your investigation?'

'You've made it clear that it's no concern of yours.'

His moustache twitched. 'They put you in charge precisely because they know you will fail. They're laughing at you. You're the only one who doesn't know it.' He turned and strutted away.

The anger stayed with her as she took out the Partition files, moved to the interview room, and resumed looking through them.

Oberoi's words hung in her mind. Could there be an element of truth there?

She drove out the insidious thought and bent to her task.

She had finished looking through the files for Bombay, and now took up the batch of testimonies from Bengal, particularly those centred in and around Calcutta, another epicentre of the bloodshed that had been unleashed during Partition. The division of Bengal into Hindu majority West Bengal and the new Muslim East Pakistan had led to a peak in sectarian violence.

The region had had a particularly hard decade. Famine, and the disease that followed, had killed two million during the war alone.

When the Japanese attacked Burma, half a million Indian refugees poured into neighbouring Bengal. The allied troops, pushed into retreat by the rampant Japanese, soon followed, quickly hoovering up the region's limited resources. Anticipating a Japanese invasion via Bengal's eastern border, the British military launched a pre-emptive, scorched-earth policy designed to deny the invaders access to food supplies. Simultaneously, they confiscated tens of thousands of local fishing boats in order to prevent them being used for transportation by the enemy. Together, these policies decimated food production and distribution in the region. Churchill's army took no steps to relieve the situation. Indeed, the Prime Minister's war cabinet actively denied requests for extra rations to feed the starving, requests made by his own commanders on the ground.

The Bengali peasants suffered horribly. Persis still remembered the pictures of naked infants dead in the streets and fields, their bellies swollen with hunger. While the world praised Churchill, in India many continued to think of him as a mass murderer.

She was looking for anything that might have caught Herriot's eye.

Presumably, he had pored over these same witness statements, had begun investigating some of them. She knew from Lal that Herriot had travelled extensively in the past months – some of that travel must have been to the places mentioned in these files, to speak with those involved, to attempt to unpick the truth from the lies.

Had that effort triggered a sequence of events leading to his death?

Time slipped away from her as she became engrossed in her work.

She stopped for a break. A thought occurred to her.

She found Birla in the main room. 'I want you to track something down for me. Around January last year an Indian engineer working on a bridge project in Faridpur died under odd circumstances. Killed by crocodiles. I want you to find out what you can.'

'Something like that would have made the local papers,' mused Birla. 'What's the connection?'

'He worked for a company Sir James was associated with, run by a Scotsman named Robert Campbell.'

'I'll make some calls.'

She entered the bookshop to find her father scribbling furiously on a writing pad at the counter. A camel stood awkwardly before him, the top of its head brushing the ceiling lamp. A trio of students hovered nearby, pretending to browse the shelves and making a valiant attempt at ignoring the hulking beast behind them.

Persis squashed the impulse to pinch herself. She worked her way around the animal. The clothy smell of its hide entered her nostrils and it was all she could do not to sneeze.

'Father,' she said, 'there's a camel in the shop.'

Her father ignored her, his pen continuing apace over the blue vellum.

The camel snorted breathily over her shoulder. She turned and stared up at it. It had a peculiarly sad expression, as if it too could not fathom the cosmic jest that had transported it to this alien element.

'Father!'

Finally, Sam Wadia looked up. 'It's Screwwallah,' he said emphatically.

Understanding dawned.

For the past decade, her father had maintained a bitter feud with a fellow Parsee by the name of Bastar Screwwallah, who ran a competing bookshop, the Magic Lantern, in the nearby Nepean Sea Road area. The origins of the feud had been lost to the mists of time; all that mattered now was that there *was* a feud. The two men vented their hostility by means of acrimonious letters and by visiting upon each other petty acts of mischief.

A month earlier, Sam had paid a peon to paint over the windows of Screwwallah's shopfront.

'How long has it been here?'

'It was here when I came down this morning,' said Sam crisply.

'Are you telling me this animal has been here the *entire* day?'

'If Screwwallah thinks a camel will knock me off my stride he is sorely mistaken. The beast can stay here for all eternity as far as I care.'

She stared at him. 'You know that you're quite mad, don't you?'

A leathery tongue rasped over her cheek. She stifled the urge to yell. Instead, she marched to the rear of the shop and headed upstairs.

*   *   *

Half an hour later, showered and changed out of her uniform into a pair of slacks and an embroidered kurta, she sat down to supper with her father. Krishna had made lamb cutlets and served them with spiced aubergine.

Her father ate stiffly, pretending to read the evening newspaper.

Persis put down her spoon. 'I apologise,' she said.

'I don't see what you have to apologise for,' said Sam stiffly. 'You're a grown woman. A famous police detective. The toast of the town. You can say and do as you please.'

'Papa, I'm sorry. I should never have said what I did. About Mother.'

His lips compressed themselves into a thin line, but he said nothing.

'I just want to know what happened. Don't I have a right to know?'

He pulled off his spectacles and set them down by his plate. 'Yes, you have a right to know. But you are a child. When the time is right, you shall know.'

'You just said I'm a grown woman!'

'To the world, perhaps. But for me, you will always be my girl.'

She resisted the urge to bang the table in frustration. It always ended this way. Her father's Sphinx-like silence on the matter had infuriated her over the years. But why? What could be so terrible that he felt the need to keep it clutched closely to him like some dead knight with his shield?

'Nussie called,' he said. 'She requested that you come out with her this evening.'

Her antennae sprang to attention. 'Why?'

'Darius has requested the pleasure of your company.'

Persis groaned aloud. 'I hope you told her I was unavailable.'

'I did nothing of the sort. I said that you would be delighted to accompany young Darius.'

'Papa! How could you? I won't go!'

'You'll break Nussie's heart.'

'The man's an imbecile.'

'Really? How well do you actually know him?'

'Weren't you the one who said that he was living proof that even God makes mistakes?'

'Nussie tells me he has matured. Ever since he joined Benson and Pryce as a managing agent he has become quite the catch.'

'I can't believe I'm hearing this. From you!'

He looked at her long and hard and then sighed. 'Persis, Nussie is not your enemy. She wants the best for you, as do I. Look at me, my child. I am an old man, trapped in this chair. There is no telling when the fire will come for me. Don't you think that, like any father, I wish to see you settled? A home of your own. A husband. Children.'

Her eyes flashed. 'You know as well as I do that the Indian Police Service does not allow married women to serve. I would have to resign my post.'

'Would that be so terrible?'

'After everything I've been through? You can sit there and say this to me?'

'You were always a wilful child,' he said. 'You refused to marry young, I agreed. You wanted to become a policewoman, I supported you. But now, now you are no longer just India's first female IPS officer. The nation owns you. And, as many have discovered before you, the nation is fickle. Even if you solve this case, all that will happen is that you will be dragged further into the future, further away from the things that matter. Home, hearth, happiness.'

'What makes you think I'm not happy?'

He gave a tired smile. 'Because you are alone, my child. And who better than I knows the price of loneliness?'

A silence yawned between them. As the clock ticked on the wall behind her, Persis saw just how great a cost her father had borne for the life he had chosen. Was it because of her? Is that why he had never remarried? She felt her heart stretch and bend.

O, how she loved him! How she loved this man who had been her whole world for as long as she could remember. His erudition; his earthiness of spirit; his extravagant moods; his full-throated guffaw. The way he inhabited his wheelchair like a turtle in its shell. Those evenings when he invited children from the nearby slums to the bookshop and read to them, shadows gathering around him as he transported them to faraway lands and mystical adventures. They loved him too; how could they not?

She saw his grief, how it subsisted in the valleys of his soul. He lived with it, but it did not diminish him. In many ways, it was what gave him his extraordinary power.

Her anger dissolved. Was he really asking the impossible?

'Very well,' she said. 'I shall spend the evening with Darius. But that is all.'

His avuncular features broke into a smile. 'You aunt will be over the moon.' He frowned. 'The woman will be insufferable, I suppose.'

A short while later, she stood in front of the mirror in her bedroom staring at her reflection. She had put on a knee-length navy dress with white trim and a plunging surplice neckline. 'A dress to seduce any sailor!' the breathless – and brainless, in Persis's opinion – store-girl had trilled. White patent leather shoes, and a white straw disc hat completed the ensemble.

Doubt assailed her. The prospect of dinner with her cousin was hardly terrifying in itself. Darius was an amiable enough soul, though a trifle full of himself, increasingly so as he found his footing in the world. It was more the fact that she had never considered him in anything but a familial light. She still remembered him as the snotty boy in shorts too small for him, invariably picked on by his older cousins. Once, she had found him hiding in his mother's *almirah*, sucking his thumb, wearing nothing but a small bib. His tormentors had stripped him to his skin, crowning his humiliation by forcing him to don the child's apron.

He had been eighteen at the time.

She heard the phone ringing in the living room.

She walked out, found that her father had vanished, picked up the phone and answered curtly, expecting Aunt Nussie, calling ahead to ensure the sacrificial virgin was staked to her rock.

'Yes?'

It was Adi Shankar's secretary. 'Mr Shankar will meet you tonight at his place of business. At 9 p.m.'

'Nine p.m.?' said Persis. 'What sort of office opens at nine in the evening?'

'The sort of office that employs a jazz band,' came the pert reply. 'Mr Shankar runs the Gulmohar Club. Please be prompt. Oh, and Mr Shankar politely requests that you wear something appropriate for the evening. He would prefer that his clientele do not see him questioned by a uniformed officer. I am sure you understand.'

13

Persis climbed out of the taxi and yanked at her dress. She felt acutely self-conscious, strangely naked without her uniform. Around her, late evening revellers spilled from a cavalcade of tongas and motor cars heading towards the magnificent gulmohar tree that had been planted just outside the front doors of the club. Petals from the tree's red crown smattered the pavement, continually kicked up into the air like little puffs of fire.

'Hello! There you are.'

She turned to see Archie Blackfinch advancing along the pavement. He was dressed in an ill-fitting tux, his hair Brylcreemed back over his head, his spectacles reflecting the lights that festooned the club's rose-coloured façade. 'My goodness,' he said, as he drew alongside, 'you look different.' He blinked owlishly at her. 'What I mean to say is that ah, you look very, um, presentable.'

Presentable? She hadn't expected him to remark on her appearance, but *presentable* seemed an odd sort of compliment, if indeed that is what it had been. Children readying themselves for inspection were 'presentable'. An anxious husband headed for an important meeting was 'presentable'.

She coloured and hoped he couldn't see it.

Perhaps it hadn't been such a good idea to call the Englishman and ask him to accompany her. For some unfathomable reason, she had balked at the idea of entering Shankar's jazz club alone, in her navy swing dress, to question the man. Not because she was afraid or felt the need of an accompanying presence; but simply because in a place like the Gulmohar she was a fish out of water.

'Thank you,' she said stiffly. 'You look very presentable also.' He flashed her a smile, oblivious to her sarcasm. His teeth were small and neatly aligned, she saw.

A bovine smell assaulted her nostrils. She turned to find a cow at her elbow, staring at her sadly as it urinated on to the street, droplets splashing her right shoe. It lowed gently then wandered away. She cursed, shook out the shoe, then headed towards the front doors, Blackfinch following close behind.

At the doors two turbaned doormen wielding ceremonial spears nodded their heads as they passed.

The club opened into a vast space, sprawling over two levels. A dance floor took up the centre of the lower floor, crowded on three sides by round tables. On the upper floor couples leaned over the railing, cigarettes and champagne flutes in hand, tapping their feet to the jazz band playing on the stage below. A series of enormous chandeliers hung above the dance floor where a mix of British, Americans, Europeans and Indians swayed to the music.

Persis had rarely been in nightclubs like the Gulmohar, but she imagined there were places like this all over the country, little strongholds of displaced time, where westerners continued to act out the illusion of empire.

A short maître d' in a smart black Nehru suit approached them, bouncing along on the soles of his feet as if gently electrified by the music.

Persis quickly explained their errand. The man led them to an empty table on the edge of the dance floor. 'I will inform Mr Shankar of your arrival. In the meantime, feel free to order refreshments. Compliments of the house.'

Blackfinch ordered a Black Dog; Persis declined. A strange anxiety oozed around her stomach. She realised now that she had made a mistake. She should have come here as herself, as a police-woman. She had surrendered the most vital part of her identity and in so doing had given up the one advantage that someone like her might have in an environment such as this.

She glanced at Blackfinch who was humming along to the music. What was going through his head? Why had he agreed to come with her?

He caught her look and his mouth bent into an awkward smile.

The waiter arrived with his drink. He thanked the man, lifted the glass to his mouth and took a tentative sip. 'Something the matter?'

Before she could reply, a chattering group descended on them. To her astonishment she saw that Robert Campbell and his daughter, Elizabeth, were among the party. Accompanying them were a trio of Indians: a round, jowly man in a dinner jacket too small for him; a tall, good-looking gentleman in a flashy white tux; and a graceful Indian woman in a gold and black sleeveless sari. The tall man, sporting a head of dark hair and a finely groomed moustache, transferred the elegant white cane he was carrying from his right to left hand, and held out his free hand. 'Inspector Wadia, I presume? I am Aditya Shankar – Adi to my friends. Delighted to make your acquaintance. And may I say that your picture in the papers does you no justice.'

She rose to her feet and stretched out her fingers. With a suddenness that shocked her, he ducked in and planted his lips on the back of her hand. A wave of flame swept across her cheeks and she glanced at Blackfinch, but he seemed not to have noticed.

Shankar straightened. 'This is my fiancée, Meenakshi Rai.' He nodded at the beautiful Indian beside him.

Rai smiled and brought her hands together in *pranaam*. Persis recognised her from the newspaper cutting she had found in Herriot's desk.

'I believe you are already acquainted with Mr Campbell and his daughter.' He indicated the pair with a poke of his cane. Persis noticed that it curved towards a jewel-encrusted handle. Shankar was clearly a man of style and not afraid of displaying his obvious wealth.

Campbell grunted, swilling a whisky glass around in his right paw. 'I trust you've got a wee bit further than when we last met, Inspector.'

'Don't be such a bore, Father,' said Elizabeth, aiming a smile at Persis.

The young woman was dressed in a black gown that accentuated her figure. Her bare shoulders, powdered and buffed to a creamy white, gleamed. Her mass of auburn hair was piled into a mound of curves and creases; her lips were carmine; her eyes delicately blue. Having first encountered her on the tennis court, sweating and heaving in the indelicate exertions of sport, Persis saw now Elizabeth Campbell in her element. Here, in the Gulmohar Club, she was a quite perfect thing of beauty.

'Lovely to see you again, Inspector,' she continued. 'And may I say how wonderful you look. One would hardly recognise you as the same woman.'

'Thank you,' mumbled Persis. 'Ah, you look very beautiful too.'

'And who is this?' asked the Scotswoman, turning her gaze to Blackfinch.

'This is my colleague, Archie Blackfinch,' supplied Persis. 'He is a criminalist.'

'A criminalist?'

'Ah, yes,' stammered Blackfinch. 'I, ah, examine crime scenes.'

'You poke around cadavers and the like?'

'Well, no. That would be a pathologist. But I encounter them routinely. Occupational hazard.'

'How intriguing.'

Blackfinch blushed. 'If you should die in the open the first insect to arrive at your corpse will be a blowfly.'

'Fascinating.'

'They lay eggs, you see,' he burbled. 'Maggots will emerge within two days.' He blinked at her from behind his spectacles.

'May I introduce Ram Acharya?' interrupted Shankar, gesturing at the overweight man beside him. 'He will be fighting for Mumbai North Ward on behalf of Panditji's Congress in next year's elections. A man to watch.'

Acharya gave her a dull look. 'So you are the famous lady police officer?' His tone indicated a distinct lack of enthusiasm. 'Well, at least they picked an attractive one.'

The retort sprang to her lips instinctively. 'Thank you. Unfortunately, I cannot say the same for your seniors in the Congress Party.'

Acharya blinked owlishly, as if he hadn't quite heard. And then his brain caught up with his ears. His thick eyebrows lunged ferociously towards each other; his moustache danced above his lip. Before he could speak, Campbell let out a great bark of laughter, defusing the tension.

Shankar swept them back into their seats. A waiter leaped to attention and drinks were ordered. Once again, Persis declined.

'Surely, you're no longer on duty?' protested Shankar.

'I did not come here for personal reasons,' said Persis stiffly.

'There is no harm in mixing business with pleasure.'

'Hear, hear,' growled Campbell. 'This Indian desire for formality is killing the entrepreneurial spirit. Time was a man could get things done with a handshake and a word in the right ear. Now it's all forms in triplicate and enough red tape to strangle a horse. We're all at the mercy of the bloody *babus*.'

'These *babus* you refer to,' retorted Acharya, 'are simply continuing in the best traditions of the British. You established a monolithic structure of administration – so that every anna you looted from the subcontinent might be accounted for. Well, sir, the boot is now on the other neck.'

'Looted?' bristled Campbell. 'I never took a penny from this country that wasn't earned. I'll no' be slandered by the likes of you, Acharya.'

'Gentlemen, calm yourselves. This is a nightclub, not a debating chamber.' Shankar turned to Persis as the Scot subsided, still glowering.

Acharya, for his part, exhumed a tobacco pouch from his pocket and rolled himself a cheroot, tamping it down into the paper with the thumb of one hand as he held it in the palm of the other. His first puff of acrid smoke collapsed Blackfinch, seated beside him, into a coughing wreck.

'Are you okay, old chap?' asked Shankar.

'I'm afraid the smoke bothers me.'

'What kind of man can't handle a little tobacco?' muttered Campbell suspiciously. His tone indicated that no better might be expected from an Englishman.

'Inspector, perhaps we should get to your questions?' said Shankar.

'I was hoping for somewhere more private.'

'This is a nightclub, Inspector. I'm afraid this is about as private as it gets.'

She frowned, then nodded. 'Of course. But before I do may I ask why Mr Campbell is here?'

'Some law against me being here?' bristled Campbell.

'What I meant was that I am surprised to find you both together.'

'It's no secret,' said Campbell brusquely. 'Adi and I are going into business together.'

'You know each other?'

'We met at James's ball, as a matter of fact. Adi is one of those rare Indians who kens that old saw about the baby and the bathwater.'

'What Robert means,' supplied Shankar, 'is that we live in a time of great opportunity. After centuries India has the chance to redefine itself. Where once the British were our oppressors, we now have the opportunity to make them our partners.'

Acharya snorted loudly. 'So speaks the new face of India!'

'Come now, Acharya. There is no one way to achieve *Indianness*. Your way, Pandit Nehru's way, is to herd the masses towards a future they do not have the capability to understand. But men like me, we are not sheep to be herded. We make our own future. And in so doing, the nation benefits.'

'Quite right,' agreed Campbell. 'If we listened to the likes of you, Acharya, the whole country would be overrun by the Reds. You ask me, there's a bit of the Commie in Nehru. He seems to relish all this land-grabbing. Won't be content until every man of substance in India is beggared in the streets.'

'The Congress is the party of the people,' retorted Acharya. 'We are merely returning to the people what was long ago taken from the people.' He emphasised his point by puffing on his cheroot, and knocking back his gin.

'One might ask what a man of the bloody people is doing juiced to the eyeballs in a nightclub,' growled Campbell. 'Unless I'm much mistaken, you Congresswallahs have done bloody well out of this new utopia of yours.'

Before the pair could launch into a hot dispute, Shankar intervened. 'As Robert says, Inspector, we are venturing into business together. I invited him here tonight. I thought he might help with your enquiries, in case my own memory isn't up to the task.'

She frowned but realised she had no choice but to forge ahead. 'How well did you know Sir James?'

'I have known him for these past couple of months. We met here, shortly after the Gulmohar opened. He introduced himself and we hit it off. I would like to believe that we became friends.'

'He came to see you prior to his death. On December 29th. What was that meeting about?'

His warm brown eyes rested on her. 'It was a private matter.'

'I would still like to know.'

He hesitated, then: 'Very well. Sir James wished to discuss a matter of investment.'

'What sort of investment?'

'He was considering taking a stake in the Gulmohar.'

Her surprise was evident. 'You're looking to sell?'

'Not exactly. But it does no harm to my future interests to have a man like Sir James as a partner. India may be Indian now, Inspector, but a white face still counts for something.'

Elizabeth Campbell gave a gentle laugh that irked Persis. She ran the rim of a long finger around her champagne flute. 'I, for one, believe that greater mixing of whites and natives is all for the best.'

Campbell gave her a look that would have curdled milk. Persis's thoughts flashed again to the story of the Indian engineer the Scotsman was rumoured to have had killed up near Delhi, a man his daughter may have courted.

Her mind churned. Was Shankar telling the truth? Why would Sir James Herriot be flirting with the idea of investing in the club? How could he afford it? Supposedly, he was bankrupt. At least this explained why he had held on to that newspaper article about the Gulmohar's opening.

The thought bothered her. Herriot had been engaged in a serious endeavour, the investigation of historical crimes. Surely, he had had more important matters on his plate than investing in a nightclub?

Perhaps he had been planning ahead, for life after the investigation. He had maintained business interests abroad; perhaps he wished to expand his empire into India, a country he knew well. Everywhere you turned these days people talked of the endless opportunities unleashed by independence. Why shouldn't an Englishman loyal to the subcontinent benefit from those same opportunities?

Persis turned to Campbell. 'Are *you* also investing in the Gulmohar?'

'No,' said Campbell, a little too abruptly. 'I have no interest in running a club. Shankar wants to get in on the construction business. He has contacts in the north that might be of use to me. So here we are.'

'The old pecking order has gone,' elucidated Shankar. 'Take a look at that chap over there.' He waved his glass at a nearby table. She turned and saw a slim, youngish Indian in a dinner jacket laughing with a group of friends. 'He's heading up a new division at Godrej, manufacturing ballot boxes for independent India's first general elections. Two years ago, he was a junior assistant to an Englishman who hadn't the brains he has in his right finger. Independence has thrust us into the spotlight. Some will sink while others swim. But at least it will be on our own merits.'

'Many people died to earn this independence,' she said.

'Doesn't freedom always come at a price?'

'Tell that to those killed by their own countrymen. I doubt that anyone expected the bill for independence to include the dead of Partition.'

Shankar's expression froze. For an instant something else looked out at her from behind his eyes, something dark and haunted. And then he smiled and she wondered if she had seen it at all. 'You're an intelligent woman, Inspector. Partition was the by-product of vested interests.'

'Well, those Muslims are getting it in the neck now,' piped up Acharya. 'I hear conditions are terrible in their Land of the Pure, this Pak-i-stan.'

'Some might say the same for many Muslims in India,' said Persis. Her hackles were up. Perhaps it was the odour of ignorance and unthinking partisanship. 'We've hardly made them welcome.'

'Welcome!' Acharya snorted in disgust. 'Subversives and ingrates. If it had been up to me, I would have rounded up the lot of them and dumped them over the border. Let them live in their stinking new country. Leave India to the real patriots.'

'You mean Hindus?'

'I mean those who did not turn against the motherland.' He punctuated this by thumping his fist against his knee. 'In my opinion, Nehru's first order of business should have been to confiscate every wealthy Muslim's property. Snap off their tails and watch them run to Pakistan.'

'Then it's a good thing Pandit Nehru has more sense than you.'

The band boomed into life behind them.

'The foxtrot!' said Elizabeth, with obvious delight. She rose to her feet, held out a hand towards Blackfinch. 'Perhaps you'd care to take the floor?'

Blackfinch, who had been rubbing at a wine spot on his shirt, coloured. 'Oh, no,' he said. 'I don't dance, I'm afraid.'

'Just follow my lead. There's nothing to it.' She grabbed his hand, hauled him to his feet and led him on to the dance floor, still protesting.

Persis watched them, a splinter of glass working its way under her ribs.

'They make a good-looking couple,' commented Acharya sourly.

'Don't they just?' said Meenakshi, raising a wine glass to her lips.

Persis said nothing. What did she care if he made a fool of himself?

She looked on as Blackfinch blinked in the confusion of lights and music, then slowly began to move, an ungainly, arrhythmic shuffling that reminded her of a man caught in the throes of a fit. Elizabeth yelped as he trod on her foot. He stepped backwards, apologising profusely, and bumped heavily into an Indian couple in full flow. The pair spun out of control, careened into another couple, the four of them sprawling to the floor in an untidy tangle of limbs.

'Christ almighty,' growled Campbell. 'The man's got more left feet than a centipede.'

'Dancing is not everyone's forte.' Meenakshi Rai smiled. 'I'm sure Mr Blackfinch has other talents.'

Persis watched the hapless Englishman as he bent to help the fallen, then turned to Campbell.

'As you are here, perhaps I can ask you a question? I have been told that you and Sir James may have fallen out recently.'

Campbell reddened. 'Where did you hear that?'

'That's not important. Is it true?'

'Absolute rubbish. James and I had our disagreements, but we've never fallen out. We were friends for twenty years.'

'Why did he fail to show up for your meeting that morning?'

'As I've already told you, the man was busy. There's no more to it than that.'

She stared at him, his obvious discomfort. 'I also understand that you fought with your daughter at the party that evening.'

Another scowl. 'You've been listening to too much gossip, Inspector.'

'So you didn't fight with Elizabeth?'

'No. I did not.'

He glared at her until she returned her attention to Shankar. 'Are you from Bombay? Originally?'

He smiled. 'No. I moved to the city a couple of years ago, once the dust of Partition had settled. My ancestral home is in the north. Delhi state.'

'Do you have family there?'

'Not any more. My parents passed when I was younger. I was an only child.' Another smile.

'How did you come to . . . this?' She indicated the club.

'What do you mean?'

'I mean, how could you afford to buy this club?'

He grinned, revealing perfect white teeth. 'Ancestral wealth. My family had large landholdings. I sensed what was on the horizon – Nehru's plans for the zamindars, I mean – and decided to sell up and move to the city of dreams. I invested in various enterprises, including this club. A wise decision, don't you think?'

Blackfinch returned and collapsed into his seat. His cheeks were red and she suspected it was not from the exertion. Elizabeth Campbell was still on the dance floor, hoofing it up with another partner. The dashing young Indian whirled her around in a tango, the band beat pounding around the room to the accompaniment of stomping feet and catcalls. Persis noted that Robert Campbell's mouth had set into a hard line; he stared at the pair with what could only be described as cold fury.

'You're not a fan of the tango?' she asked.

'It's not the dance I'm no' a fan of,' he mumbled. He knocked back his drink, rose to his feet, then waded on to the dance floor, barging other couples out of the way before rudely cutting in on his daughter. A protest ensued. Persis could not make out what the pair were arguing about, but at one point it looked as if Campbell was ready to tear his daughter's dance partner limb from limb.

Finally, Elizabeth Campbell stormed off, vanishing into the crowd, Campbell in hot pursuit.

'What was that about?' asked Persis.

'Oh, I think when it comes to his daughter Mr Campbell is still a little old-fashioned,' said Shankar, amusement playing over his lips.

'What do you mean?'

'Robert Campbell does not appreciate the fact that his daughter has a penchant for stepping out with the natives.'

'She does?' said Blackfinch.

Persis glanced at him. Did he sound crestfallen?

Adi Shankar stood up. 'My apologies, Inspector, but I'm afraid that I must end our discussion. Pressing business matters.'

She rose to her feet. 'Thank you for seeing me. I may have further questions.'

Shankar gave a short bow. 'I am at your service. I wish to see Sir James's murderer caught. Moreover, if we are to set the right tone in this new republic of ours we cannot allow such transgressions to stand. The rule of law must prevail or what are we?'

They watched him walk away with the politician Acharya, heads bent in discussion.

Persis sat down and turned her attention to Meenakshi Rai. 'When did you two meet?'

'A few months before the launch of the Gulmohar,' she replied. 'He was playing polo for the Amateur Riders' Club at the Mahalaxmi Racecourse ground. I thought he was the most dashing man I'd ever laid eyes on.'

'Love at first sight.'

'You don't believe in it?'

Persis forbore from replying. 'Did you know Sir James?'

'Not really. He came to the club. Met us there. He and Adi got on well. They were of a similar temperament. And, frankly, Adi has an affinity for the British. He's a lot like my father in that respect.'

'Your father?'

She smiled wanly. 'My father was a career soldier. He fought for and with the British. He supported Indian independence, but he could never bring himself to hate them. He always said that in every barrel there are bad apples and good ones. He liked to believe that he had spent most of his time in the company of the good ones.'

Persis had heard such sentiments before. It spoke directly to the mixed feelings that some – particularly those who had prospered during the British era – harboured for their former overlords.

She recalled a recent spat between her father and Dr Aziz. 'What's so great about your new republic?' Aziz had said. 'Just today the postal service put up its rates; train schedules have gone to the dogs; the names of roads and cities are being changed wholesale, and now we are told that we must adopt the metric system. Are we Germans, I ask you?'

'Rome has fallen, old friend,' her father had responded. 'It is best to make peace with that fact.'

'Pah! Whatever their evils at least the British inflicted certainty upon us. What has replaced that? The Congress is infected with feeble-minded sycophants; the country is racked by communal disharmony; and our economy is headed into the crapper. And on the subject of crappers, even our European-style toilets are being replaced with the inferior Indian variety where one is forced to squat for the privilege of defecating into one's own pyjama. How's that for a perverted sense of nationalism?'

'My father passed away three years ago,' continued Meenakshi. 'I suppose, when I met Adi, it felt like a connection to him.'

'Is there anything else you can tell me about Sir James?'

Meenakshi shrugged. 'Only that he believed in the vision of a modern, fairer India. I know many who begrudge the poor of this country their due. But men like Sir James and Adi believe they have as much right to the future as the rest of us.'

'Did you notice anything on the night of his death? Anything untoward?'

She shook her head. Her earrings tinkled. 'He seemed fine. A little drunk perhaps. Adi and I were with the jazz band. Adi recently learned to play the saxophone. He charged up on stage and just sat down. The poor bandleader wasn't given any choice.' She smiled. 'He was playing with them right up until you called the party to a halt. We didn't really notice at what point Sir James slipped away but I don't remember seeing him after the midnight fireworks.'

Persis made a mental note to check Meenakshi's story. If Adi Shankar had indeed been playing with the band from midnight until she arrived at Laburnum House he certainly couldn't have been in Herriot's study at the time of the murder.

'When is the wedding?'

'We're planning for the summer. Just before the monsoon hits.' She smiled brightly. 'You must come, Inspector. I'm sure Adi would be delighted.'

Blackfinch offered her a lift home. For a moment, she hesitated. A puff of annoyance blew along the back of her neck. She dismissed the feeling. What right had she to be irritated with him? She had invited him to the Gulmohar, and in so doing had demonstrated weakness. If there was anyone she should be annoyed with it was herself.

'What did you think?' she asked, after a while.

'An interesting man,' replied Blackfinch, his eyes focused on the road ahead. Each time the driver approached the clattering chicken van in front his spare frame tensed. The chickens, stuffed into battery hutches too small for them, looked back at him with expressions of depressed resignation. 'One of the new breed of young Indians. I see them everywhere.'

She glanced suspiciously at his face. 'It's *our* country. Who else will define it except Indians?'

'I only meant that the old guard superintended the independence movement, but it's the likes of Shankar who will determine what you do with it.'

She stared at him. 'Something about him bothered me. I don't think he was entirely honest about his dealings with Sir James.'

'What makes you say that?'

'Instinct.'

'Ah.'

She glanced at him. 'Ah?'

He indulged her with a condescending smile. 'In my world, there is no room for instinct. Science is about facts. Empirical evidence. A good criminalist does not rely on intuition. Nine times out of ten that little feeling in the gut is incipient diarrhoea, not some mythical flash of deductive genius.'

She bristled, then tacked in another direction. 'Don't you find it curious that Campbell is out partying with Shankar just days after his supposed friend and business partner is brutally murdered?'

'What should he do? Sit at home and mourn him for forty days like a Mahomedan?'

She considered telling him of Eve Gatsby's revelation that Herriot and Campbell might have fallen out, then decided against it. She looked out of the window. A warm breeze feathered her cheek. '*She* was in her element, don't you think?'

'Who?'

'Elizabeth Campbell.'

The merest hesitation. 'I suppose so. She's a young woman, after all.'

'Very beautiful too.'

He waited a moment too long to respond. 'In the right light, one might say she was attractive.'

'It's always the right light for women like her.'

They said no more until she was standing outside the bookshop, glancing across the street at the tan Buick parked in front of the doorway.

Aunt Nussie's car.

She cursed, then walked over to poke the dozing driver in the shoulder. He jerked awake, eyes swimming into focus. 'Is Nussie Madam upstairs?'

'Yes,' he said. 'With Mr Darius.'

She cursed again, then turned back to Blackfinch, who was watching her curiously from inside the Ambassador. An idea gleamed at the back of her mind.

She walked back across the road. 'Would you care to join me for a late supper? My father will be awake. He would appreciate a visitor. He's in a wheelchair and doesn't get to meet as many people as he would like.' This was an outright lie. Her father was a committed misanthrope. A plaque on his desk read: *I once considered suicide. But then I thought it would be better to kill the rest of mankind instead.*

He blinked behind his spectacles, surprised by the suggestion. Climbing out of the car, he said, 'Lead on, MacDuff.'

'A misquotation,' she muttered, turning away. 'The line from *Macbeth* is actually "Lay on, MacDuff", which means to attack, vigorously.'

Aunt Nussie was annoyed. Persis could tell this by the way she smoked her cigarette as if she had a personal vendetta against it, the way she tapped her wine glass brightly with a painted fingernail. Aunt Nussie sat at one end of the dining table, her father at the other, Darius and Sam facing each other across the table's width, a no-man's-land populated with the remnants of supper: cold cuts, reheated dhansak, pilau, cheese and pickle.

Darius had surprised her. She hadn't seen him in almost a year, during which time he had undergone a remarkable transformation.

The sprinkle of pimples that had long blighted his forehead had vanished and the heavy moustache under his nose lent a newfound maturity to his features. His cream linen suit was impeccable, his two-tone Oxfords sparkled, and his darkly groomed hair gave him a halo of the debonair. He spoke with a sense of assurance that was at odds with the man she remembered.

Perhaps Nussie had been right, after all. The new republic was remaking her cousin.

Her decision to sit on Blackfinch's side of the table had not gone down well, however, nor indeed the very fact of his presence. Fortunately, Archie Blackfinch seemed oblivious to the situation.

Could the man truly be so blind? she wondered, looking on as he bumbled his way through the stilted dinner conversation, happily describing his work. 'Did you know,' he asked, forking a chicken niblet into his mouth, 'that arterial blood is a brighter red than other blood and that bloodstains tend to fall in certain patterns based on the relative motion of the attacker and victim?'

'Fascinating,' said Darius, eyes lingering on his cousin.

Aunt Nussie poured herself another glass of sherry, gulping it down with a ferocity that even Persis found unnerving. Her aunt had pointedly refrained from mentioning the fact that Persis had effectively run out on Darius. Persis now wished she had called to cancel, but the thought of having that conversation with her aunt had decided her against it. Darius himself had acted the gentleman, going along with the charade that he had simply come along to pay his respects to Sam. He talked about his new role as a managing agent in Calcutta, over on the far side of the country. His prospects were bright, he assured her. The division was still run by an Englishman but that would surely change.

'But enough of me,' he said briskly, dabbing at his moustache with a napkin. 'You have become quite the celebrity, Persis. Imagine my surprise when I picked up the *Gazette* yesterday and saw your face looking back at me from the front page. To think, the girl I used to play hide and seek with is now the belle of our nation's police service.'

'Belle?' echoed Persis, her eyes narrowing.

'An expression,' said Darius. 'I meant no offence. I have to admit, you have surprised us all.'

'In what way?'

'Well, when I first heard that you were determined to become a police officer, I scoffed. I mean, it's hardly a fitting occupation for a woman, is it? But you followed through and now here you are. Naturally, once you have proven your point, I expect you will step down gracefully.'

She set down her fork. 'Proven my point?'

'That our new nation is built on truly democratic principles. And what could be more democratic than allowing a woman to don the khaki?'

'*Allowing?*' The word came out as a strangled squeak.

'There are some who claim that the country has gone to the dogs since the departure of the British,' continued Darius, warming to his theme. 'I disagree. You are a symbol, Persis. Behold, we are no longer a backward nation! We even allow women to police us!'

She stared at him in astonishment. Was this how she was viewed, not just by her cousin but by millions of men around the country? But if that were true then what right did she have to call herself an officer of the law? She was a token, a puppet serving a purpose.

She rose to her feet with ominous deliberation. 'For a moment, I thought you had changed,' she said. 'But it's only in fairy tales that frogs become princes. I am not a symbol. I am a police officer. I trained as hard as any man at the academy. I ranked top of my class. I was given this case because someone considered me competent enough to handle it.'

Darius stood awkwardly. 'I meant no offence,' he repeated.

'And yet offence is taken. I think it is time for you to leave.'

'Persis!' Aunt Nussie's face was scarlet. 'You cannot speak to him like that.'

'Why not?' said Persis. 'As far as I'm concerned, you can put him back in his box and send him back to Calcutta.'

'That's uncalled for—' began Darius, but Persis whirled back on him.

'I'll never marry you. Not if you were the last man on earth.'

They stared at each other, then Darius straightened. 'I think we should leave, Mother. It's getting rather late and I have an early train to catch.'

He turned to Sam Wadia. 'It has been a pleasure, Uncle. I wish you good health.'

He pirouetted on his heels and walked stiffly from the apartment, Nussie trailing in his wake. She spun around at the door. 'Persis, you are incorrigible. When will you learn to behave like a woman? Even in that dress you cannot change. You may as well have worn your khaki trousers beneath it.'

When they had gone, Persis slumped back in her seat.

'I should probably leave too,' said Blackfinch.

Persis ignored him. She was still white-faced with anger. Partly her fury was directed at herself. She had been unforgivably rude, had upset her aunt, and for what? Had Darius's blundering really offended her so? Why was she so quick to take offence? Tact, caution, these were the hallmarks of a good police officer. A thin skin, a fiery temperament: these qualities rarely went well with deductive reasoning.

'Do you feel better now that you've got it out of your system?' asked Sam.

'Is this where you tell me that you're disappointed in me?'

'If I have to tell you, then it's not worth the telling,' he said. 'Goodnight, Mr Blackfinch. It was nice to make your acquaintance.' He wheeled his chair around and left the room.

The cat Akbar slunk in as the door closed behind him, bounded on to the table and began nibbling at a cold cut of chicken.

Blackfinch carefully folded his napkin into a neat square and set it down on the table. 'It's been a very interesting evening.'

She ignored him, her gazed affixed to some distant point in space and time.

'I'll let myself out then, shall I?'

He waited a second longer, then walked to the door and left the apartment.

14

4 January 1950

The morning proved an exercise in frustration. There was still no sign of the missing jeweller Vishal Mistry, no sign of the missing knife or the missing trousers. She had phoned the Victoria station ticket office and been told that the details of the ticket stub she'd discovered in Herriot's jacket were yet to be recovered. Birla had got no further in finding out where the Golden Temple Hotel might be. They still had no idea who Herriot's female companion had been on the night of his death.

With no new leads, she went back over the testimonies of those she had interviewed. She felt instinctively that there was more there than she was being told.

Because there *was* another truth out there. Of that she was certain. Sir James Herriot was not the man the public believed him to be. The Englishman may have been a consummate diplomat, trusted by the Indian government, but he was also a cad, a cad on the verge of bankruptcy.

Seth arrived shortly after eleven, in a vile temper.

She followed him into his office, where he threw himself into his chair and flung a newspaper on to the desk.

'I've just been to see ADC Shukla,' he revealed. 'To say that he was unhappy with Channa's latest article would be an understatement.' He picked up the paper, snapped it angrily, and read from it. '"The investigation into the death of Sir James Herriot has met with little progress. There are no suspects, no clear lines of enquiry, and no real motive established for the murder. The lead detective has chosen to keep the press in the dark. But the *Chronicle* has discovered that her team of officers are busily interviewing some of the most respected residents of the city, in the hope that rattling cages at random will break open the case. One cannot help but feel that this demonstrates a lack of experience and judgement. The investigation is superintended by Roshan Seth, once a name to watch in the service, but no longer."'

Persis said nothing. She had been expecting it. Channa was not the type to take rejection lying down.

She felt another rush of anger towards Oberoi. No doubt he had been feeding Channa scraps, fanning the flames.

Back at her desk, she resumed working through her notes. She could feel the weight of expectation bearing down on her. It was the first time in her fledgling career that she had felt such pressure. Seth had warned her, but she had ignored him.

For an instant, her mind swarmed with panic. What if she failed? She hadn't even admitted the possibility, but now . . .

She closed her eyes and allowed the case to float around her mind. The things that continued to bother her. Vishal Mistry. The knife. The missing trousers—

A thought wormed its way up her spine. Something Aunt Nussie had said the previous evening. *You may as well have worn your khaki trousers beneath it.*

She opened her eyes, sat very still, allowing the thought to complete itself.

Finally, she stood and went to Seth's office.

The SP was clutching an empty whisky tumbler, staring glassy-eyed at a report open before him.

'I have a theory,' she said. 'It's about the trousers.'

He stared at her blankly. 'The trousers?'

'Herriot's trousers were missing. I think I know what happened to them.'

She drove through the gates of Laburnum House at just after twelve.

The sun beat down on the gravel forecourt as she and Sub-Inspector George Fernandes made their way to the front of the mansion.

The door was answered by a surprised Mrs Gupta.

'I'd like to talk to Maan Singh. Is he here?'

'He's working in the garage.'

The housekeeper led them to the side of the house where a low red-brick shed housed a row of motor vehicles. They found Singh bent inside the hood of a red Bentley. He was wearing a white vest beneath his customary turban, revealing the thickly corded muscles of his arms and neck. A smudge of grease on his burnished right bicep only accentuated his powerful physique.

He straightened as they approached, a spanner clutched in his ham-like fist.

Persis stopped, considered what she was about to say.

Back at Malabar House it had seemed to make sense. But here, facing this hulking giant, the words shrivelled inside her. The theory she had run by Roshan Seth now seemed ludicrous.

She licked her lips and glanced at Fernandes. Curiosity etched his features. She hadn't yet told him why they were here. She would have preferred Birla accompanying her, but he had been out on another case. She wondered what Fernandes, as level-headed a man as she knew, would make of her conjecture.

She took a deep breath, and plunged in. 'By your own admission, you stated that you were the one to discover Sir James's body. Lal was the second person to see the body and he confirmed that Sir James's trousers were missing. So, between the murder and Lal showing up, the trousers went missing. We know that the killer did not leave the premises, not unless he climbed a fifteen-foot-high wall topped with barbed wire. If we assume that Sir James's killer took the trousers, what would he have done with them? He could hardly have wandered around with them, not with a houseful of guests and staff. Someone would be bound to notice. Nor could he have hidden them for later removal from Laburnum House. That would run the risk of them being found by us.'

Singh was silent, staring at her with a curiously deadened expression.

Persis took another breath. 'I believe *you* took the trousers. I think you put them on underneath your own trousers and walked out of Laburnum House with them. You are a big man, as was Sir James. You could have slipped them on with ease.'

For an instant, she thought Singh would erupt. She tensed, her right hand closing around the butt of her revolver. If he charged them, she doubted that even a bullet would stop him.

Singh stepped forward. She heard Fernandes reach for his own weapon.

And then the big Sikh held out his hands, fists facing upwards. 'Yes,' he said. 'I killed Sir James.'

Afterwards, it was the sense of relief with which he said those words that would haunt her.

15

Arthur Road Jail, known as Bombay Central Prison, was the city's oldest place of incarceration. Originally built to house eight hundred inmates, its population had swelled in recent years, the result of post-independence judging zealotry. Within its forbidding walls many luminaries from the struggle had whiled away the changeless hours penning revolutionary epistles or singing themselves softly to sleep with thoughts of martyrdom.

Persis logged in at the guardroom. As she signed the day register, the door opened behind her and a familiar figure walked in.

Madan Lal was dressed smartly, as usual, in fawn trousers and a linen jacket. But a darkness encircled his eyes that hadn't been there a few days ago; Sir James's assistant had been having sleepless nights.

'What are you doing here?' she asked.

'I was told you were coming to question him. I'd like to accompany you.' His voice was cold; she sensed an anger behind his words. She suspected that he had not taken kindly to the fact that Singh had been arrested at Laburnum House while he had been elsewhere.

'You're a civilian. You cannot be present during the questioning of a murder suspect.'

'Rules can always be bent, Inspector,' countered Lal. 'Singh won't speak to you.'

She weighed his words. There was something furtive about Lal's manner that made her hesitate. But her previous encounters with

Singh did not inspire confidence that he would open up to her now. The man had not said a single word since his arrest. Not a word on the ride to the Marine Drive station lock-up. And, from what she had been told, not a word while he had been transferred to Arthur Road Jail as she had returned to Malabar House to update Seth and discuss her next course of action.

The SP's initial shock had mirrored her own. But then he had lifted himself from his seat and clapped her on the shoulder. 'You were right!' he said. 'You did it, Persis.'

She could see the machinery whirring behind his eyes. This was the break he had been waiting for. With a confession in the bank, he could finally get the likes of ADC Shukla off his back.

But something about the situation bothered her. The ease with which Singh had capitulated in the face of a frankly outlandish theory. She had not a shred of proof of her conjecture and yet he had instantly confessed to murder.

Why?

She *needed* Singh to talk.

'Very well.'

Singh had been installed in one of the solitary cells, deep within the bowels of the prison. The warden insisted on escorting them personally. They entered the flagstoned cell to find Singh manacled to a steel desk awaiting their arrival.

His eyes flickered momentarily as he saw Lal follow her in.

Persis turned and ushered the warden out, the man's round face collapsing into an 'o' of disappointment.

They took the two seats on the far side of the battered steel table.

'You have confessed to the murder of Sir James,' began Persis. It was a statement, rather than a question.

Singh said nothing. His eyes moved to Lal. Light falling in from the barred window high on the rear wall reflected from the aide's spectacles.

'You should not have come,' rumbled Singh.

She wasn't sure if he meant herself or Sir James's aide.

'Did you do it?' she asked.

'I have confessed,' growled Singh. 'What more do you want?'

'I want to know why.'

Singh opened his mouth, but then confusion clouded his expression. He seemed to Persis like an actor who, finding himself on stage, facing his audience, forgets his lines. 'Every man earns the death he deserves,' he said finally.

'What did Sir James do to deserve *his* death?'

But Singh simply shook the question away with a thrust of his turbaned head.

'Did he do something to anger you?' she persisted.

Silence.

'Why confess now? Why not on the night of his killing?'

Silence.

'Why did you take the trousers? It makes no sense.'

Silence. Her sense of unease grew. There was something illogical about Singh's actions. If he had killed Sir James, and had intended to confess all along, then why the charade with the trousers? Surely, a wild accusation couldn't have crumbled this giant of a man into accepting guilt for such an enormous crime?

'They will hang you. Do you understand?'

'Yes,' said Singh. 'And I will die a proud son of Punjab.'

'Is that what this is about?' said Persis. 'You killed Sir James to prove a point?'

'You wouldn't understand,' said Singh, and his eyes were full of contempt. 'People like you worship the Anglos. You are no Indian.'

Blood darkened her cheeks. In the old days, she thought, a man espousing that sort of rhetoric would have been whisked away to some covert holding cell run by British intelligence. Marked as an anti-imperialist, he would have been tried, judged and summarily executed.

The trial was important. It wasn't enough for the British to hang a man; they had to ensure everyone knew he *deserved* to be hanged. Due process was paramount, even if the outcome was rigged.

'Where is the knife?' she asked.

'I threw it away.'

'Where?'

'It is gone.'

'I don't believe you.'

Instead of reacting with the fury she had expected, a curious uncertainty entered Singh's eyes. 'What do you mean?'

Emboldened, she leaned forward. 'I don't believe that you killed Sir James. You are lying.'

Lal twisted in his seat and looked at her in astonishment.

Singh merely stared at her in sullen silence. 'I can prove that I killed him,' he said finally.

'How?'

'I have the trousers. They are in my home. You will find them hidden in the bottom of my *almirah*.'

Outside the cell, Lal paced the corridor in agitation. 'What will happen to him now?'

'We will search his home. If we find the trousers, he will be tried and, if he continues to insist on his guilt, he will be convicted. And then they will hang him.'

'Why did you say that you did not believe him?'

'I . . .' She hesitated. How to explain to Lal that something about Singh's manner, at once evasive and belligerent, bothered her? Why had he kept the trousers but thrown away the knife? Why take the trousers in the first place? Why wait to be confronted before confessing? Why not march down into the New Year's Eve party at Laburnum House and brazenly announce his deed?

'Tell me about him,' she said. 'How did he end up at Laburnum House?'

'I was forced to dismiss Sir James's driver a month ago for theft. Singh came to the house looking for work. Sir James was impressed with him. I offered him a trial period.' He looked morose. 'It's my fault, isn't it? I should have checked his background more thoroughly.'

'Has he expressed any sort of nationalist sentiment since he joined?'

'No. He has been a perfect employee. Punctual, committed.'

'Was he dissatisfied with his salary? His circumstances?'

'Not that he mentioned. We paid him a good wage.'

'What about his personal life? Was there a reason for discontent there?'

'Frankly, I don't know much about his private affairs. No wife or acquaintances that he maintained – but I would not expect him to discuss such matters with me.'

'What about family?'

'None in Bombay. I never heard him talk about any elsewhere.'

She paused, her mind churning.

'The Sikh character is a strange one,' Lal continued, his voice calmer now. 'Feuds, vendettas, blood vengeance. These are part and parcel of life. Many years ago, while driving in the Punjab, I witnessed an altercation in the street. Two cars had collided. Words were exchanged. In one of the cars was a Sikh, elderly, small; in the other a big, heavy man, dark-skinned: he looked like he was from the south. The Sikh went to the boot of his car, took out a large sword, and cut the man down right where he stood.'

Persis gazed at his troubled features.

'As hard as it is for me to accept,' said Lal, 'I can only conclude that Singh did kill Sir James. Your case is solved, Inspector. Your work is at an end. It will be a relief for all concerned to put the matter to bed. Life, after all, must go on.'

She returned to Malabar House two hours later, having first driven to Singh's home to carry out a search of the premises. She had called the office from the prison and asked Birla to meet her there.

Singh lived in a small two-room dwelling on a patch of waste ground behind the Walter de Souza Park, crowded with makeshift homes, some built by the municipal authorities, others built by free enterprise and a prayer. Singh's was one of the better ones: brick walls and a tin roof. A small padlock rattled on the plywood door – Birla struck it off easily with the butt of his revolver.

The interior of the home was sparse. Whitewashed walls, a single light bulb, a four-legged charpoy, a small kitchen area with an assortment of mismatched steel pans, plates and cups. A wooden table, barely large enough for two, with a single stool. A steel *almirah* housed Singh's collection of clothes, including three work uniforms. At the bottom of the *almirah*, in an old jute bag, were Sir James's trousers.

She held the soft red fabric in her hand. Darker spots indicated the presence of blood.

'Looks like he did it,' said Birla, staring at the garment.

In a small pouch inside the wardrobe she discovered papers. Among them was a ration card. The card noted a permanent residential address, in the northern city of Amritsar.

She wrote the address in her notebook then added the ration card to the evidence.

*   *   *

174

Back at Malabar House she discovered Oberoi holding court, spinning a story for Sub-Inspector Fernandes and the two constables, Subramanium and Ray. Oberoi's grin vanished as she stalked into the room; he watched her sweep by with uneasy eyes.

Seth was eating, picking at a plate of pilaf with a fork, a napkin tucked under his chin. The radio was on. Cricket.

As she entered he let out a sigh, flicked off the radio, and set down his fork.

'I don't think Singh did it.'

Seth's shoulders fell a little. 'What makes you say that?'

Quickly, she outlined the reasons for her doubt. Why would the man wait to be confronted if he was going to confess so readily? Not even a whimper of protest or denial. Why smuggle the trousers out? It was a strange thing to do.

Seth pulled off the napkin and wiped at his mouth. He had just lost his appetite. 'Let me respond: why would an innocent man confess to murder?'

'I don't know.'

'You're familiar with Occam's razor, no doubt?'

'I am.'

'And yet you prefer not to accept what is in front of your eyes.' He sighed irritably. 'The man held a grudge against the British. He found a way into Sir James's employ, waited until he had the lay of the land, then acted. What is so hard to believe about that? As for the trousers – he took them as a souvenir. Killers have been known to do that.'

'It doesn't explain why he didn't confess right away. Or why he offered no resistance when I confronted him.'

'How about this: he wanted an audience. It was a political killing. He waited for the newspapers to work themselves into a frenzy and then, when you confronted him, he stepped forward and said, "Here I am. I did it."'

She hesitated. Seth made it seem so straightforward. Was she being unreasonable?

'I received a call from Tilak,' Seth continued. 'He wished me to pass on his personal congratulations. Do you understand what this means, Persis? It's not every police officer who is commended by the Deputy Home Minister. How do you think he will react if you now insist that Singh is the wrong man?'

'What about the truth?'

'Truth?' Seth let out a loud bray. 'Persis, for those in our position, the truth is merely a fortuitous side effect of what we do. You talk about missing trousers? Frankly, I don't care if those trousers walked out of there on their own.'

She sensed his past looming over them, the cynicism that had infected him since his fall from grace. Could she accept such a vision of the world?

She drilled her eyes forward. 'I request permission to continue with my investigations.'

'And if I do not give it?'

'Then I will continue anyway.'

His eyes rested on her, and then, to her surprise, he chuckled. 'You're quite fearless, aren't you?'

'Fear has nothing to do with it.'

'I cannot give you my blessing, Persis. Not when the commissioner himself will shortly announce that the murder is solved. However, if you should decide to follow up a few loose ends – for the purposes of the official report – I don't think anyone would begrudge you. You're going to be a famous woman, Inspector. They will lionise you. Beware. Such adulation comes at a price.'

Back at her desk she discovered a message written in Birla's scrawling hand, stating that Augustus Silva had telephoned and wished her to pay a visit to his office as soon as she was able. Birla's note went on, reporting on his investigation into the Indian engineer killed by crocodiles up in Faridpur. He had spoken over the phone to the journalist who had written the story. The dead man's name had been Satyajit Sharma. There had indeed been a rumour that he had been involved with a British woman. But there was nothing to suspect her or her father of involvement in his death. The police had attributed the killing to local bandits.

She pocketed the note, snatched up her cap, and headed for the door.

As she hit the lobby, she encountered Birla on his way in.

'Where have you been?' she asked.

'Seth has already reassigned me,' he revealed. 'I'm working on a very important case.'

'What case?'

He sighed. 'Mrs Battachariya is convinced someone is following her around.'

'Mrs Battachariya is senile,' said Persis.

He lifted off his cap and scratched at his head. His hair was matted with sweat and clung to his scalp. 'Mrs Battachariya is also the sister of the Congress MLA for Colaba. She has made his life a misery and so he has generously passed her on to us.'

'I've got something much more useful for you to do. But Seth cannot know about it.'

A gleam of interest entered his eyes.

'Last night I went to meet a man named Adi Shankar. He runs the Gulmohar Club on Churchgate Street. He knew Sir James Herriot; they had recently become acquainted. I want to know more about him. Apparently, he was sitting with the jazz band on the night of Herriot's death from midnight until I got there. Can you check that out with the bandleader?'

Birla nodded, scratching a note in his pad. 'You want me to follow him around?'

'I want you to find out as much as you can. Officially, the case is over. Singh's confession is a godsend for the top brass. They can draw a line under the affair, try Singh in a kangaroo court, and send him to the gallows.'

'You don't think he did it?'

She hesitated. 'I'm not certain,' she said. 'But if a man is to be hanged then I believe the least we can do is to be sure we're hanging him for the right reasons.'

16

The twenty-minute drive from Malabar House to Bombay University gave Persis plenty of time to reflect on the state of the investigation. Her frustration at Seth began to seep away. A man as compromised as Roshan Seth had long ago narrowed his field of view, until all he could see was what others allowed him to see.

She dwelt on her interrogation of Singh.

Something about him, about his confession and the manner in which it had come about – days after the murder – had infected her with doubt.

She wondered how the papers would react.

Seth had informed her that Channa had already been in touch for an interview with the detective who had cracked the case. He had asked for Oberoi. She had found her face turning scarlet, her body rigid with fury. Seth explained that Channa had somehow found out that Oberoi had proposed a nationalist as the killer right from the beginning.

Found out? Persis thought. Or been told?

Seth had reassured her that she would be named as the lead detective on the investigation. ADC Shukla himself had proposed that she be put forward for a commendation. Persis's immediate impulse was to decline. Unearned merit was not worthy of a police officer. She did not deserve credit where credit was not yet due.

The summons from Augustus Silva had directed her to his office at Bombay University. From there they ventured out to the Blue

Danube, a coffee shop just yards from the campus, one of half a dozen in the area. The place was packed with students. Persis spotted a group of boys in cricket whites, hair gleaming with Trugel, patent leather Saxones on their feet, sly smiles and slinky moustaches on their faces. They were making eyes at a coven of young girls, casting saucy remarks their way and receiving calculated indifference in return.

It was a game, one she had refused to play. Flirtatiousness had never been in her nature. The idea of stepping out with wastrels who could barely tie their own laces and whose idea of romance was badly recited couplets from Chaucer was anathema to her.

There were moments, of course, when she would wonder if that had been a mistake, moments when she was taken by an inexpressible hunger, when the shadows of another life swelled around her. She saw the composition of that other life through a glass, darkly. A man, a partner, an eclipse of the heart. A valve would open inside her and those buried feelings would leak out, upsetting her equilibrium. In such moments, she would hold fast to the central dialectic that ruled her life: good versus evil, justice versus injustice.

That was enough, for now.

Silva ordered a brace of coffees, then recounted the results of his investigation into Madan Lal.

'Your man Lal was indeed in Burma, attached to the 50th Parachute Brigade. How much do you know about that battle?'

'Not a great deal.'

'March 1944. It was a major turning point in the South-East Asian theatre of the war. The Japanese attempted to destroy the Allied forces at Imphal. Back then Imphal was the capital of Manipur, a princely state in India's north-east. The troops barracked there were a mixture of British, Gurkha and Indian battalions. Lal's

Parachute Brigade was conducting advanced jungle manoeuvres north of the city.

'When the Japanese attacked, Lal's unit suffered heavy casualties. Lal himself was wounded. What happened next is a little hazy. The Japanese troops were bolstered by troops from the Indian National Army. If you recall, these were Subhas Chandra Bose's men, fighting *with* the Japanese against British rule, as part of the Azad Hind or Free India movement.'

'Weren't a lot of their senior officers court-martialled back in 1946?'

'Correct,' beamed Silva. 'The so-called Red Fort trials. They ended up dividing public opinion to such an extent that the British had to commute most of the sentences from death to imprisonment. As a footnote, one of the lawyers on the defence team was our dear Panditji.'

'Nehru was on the defence counsel?'

'It wasn't so long ago that he was one of our most prominent lawyers. It's what gives his rhetoric such a litigious flavour.' He smiled. 'To return to Lal: it seems that while he was stumbling around in the heat of battle, he somehow managed to capture three of Bose's men. But rather than take them prisoner he ordered them to kneel down, then stood behind them, and put a bullet in the back of each man's head. The act was witnessed by a fellow soldier who sat on it until after the battle, and then his conscience got the better of him.

'Lal's actions clearly put the brass in a quandary. Technically speaking, he had killed a trio of traitors. On the other hand, he had broken the rules of engagement. The British are sticklers for that sort of thing.

'The decision was made to court-martial Lal. Somehow Sir James got wind of it. He intervened on Lal's behalf and managed to get the charges dropped. The witness conveniently recanted his testimony, though a copy of it remains on record.' He handed her a manila folder. 'It wasn't easy getting this.'

She opened the folder and quickly scanned the papers as Silva sipped his coffee.

There was a picture of Lal in military uniform, looking younger, every bit as neat as in his later years. She scanned his military record, a history of incremental progress up the chain of command. He had distinguished himself in a previous conflict resulting in a citation for valour, following which he had been raised to the rank of major. She finally came to the account of the incident at Imphal, including the eyewitness testimony of his killing of the three Indian soldiers.

'What does it mean?' she murmured.

Believing the question to be directed at him, Silva answered. 'What it means is that your man Lal is a killer. He murdered three men in cold blood.'

She understood the implication. If it could happen once it could happen again. Could Lal possibly have had something to do with Sir James's murder? If so, what would have been his motive? Why would he have turned on a man who had saved his life, a man he held up as a friend and mentor? A man with whom he had, according to one witness, fought on the night of his death.

She picked up a list of names. 'What's this?'

'A list of all the men in Lal's unit.'

She scanned the list – and was immediately struck by a trio of names near the top. Madan Lal and two JCOs – Junior Commissioned Officers: Subedar Maan Singh and Subedar Major Duleep Gupta. She recalled that Sir James's housekeeper, Gupta, had told her that her husband had died in the war. His name had been Duleep. Both names were common on the subcontinent, but this had to be more than a coincidence.

She flicked through the folder. Silva had been thorough. The documents included enlistment photos of the men in the unit.

There was no doubt. Maan Singh was one and the same.

There was a note next to Duleep Gupta's entry: K.I.A. *Killed in action.*

In fact, Gupta had been killed on the same day that Lal had gone berserk. Had the death of his comrade sent Lal over the edge?

'I need to know more about these two men,' she said, tapping the pictures of Maan Singh and Duleep Gupta.

Silva smiled. 'I took the liberty of tracking down the unit's commanding officer. He's retired now, lives not too far from here as a matter of fact. He has agreed to speak to you.'

She found the address without difficulty, a tenth-floor flat on Chowringee Lane, just five minutes away. Lieutenant-Colonel Ram Krishnan was white-haired at fifty-eight, walked with a cane, and lived with his son and daughter-in-law. He had retired honourably, at the end of the Second World War, but now had little to do except read the newspapers and complain about the state of the country's politics.

They sat on the balcony, Krishnan basking in the late afternoon sun.

'Yes, I remember them. The three of them were fast friends. Lal, Singh and Gupta. Especially Lal and Gupta. When Gupta was killed that day, it hit Lal hard. They asked me at the court martial whether Lal had ever exhibited behaviour like that before. Conduct unbecoming. I told them no. But the truth was that Lal had a coldness inside him. A killer's heart. Believe it or not most soldiers don't have that.'

'What about Maan Singh? What kind of man was he?'

'A born foot-soldier. Too simple ever to climb the ranks, but there's no one you'd rather have next to you in a scrap.'

'Did he have a killer's heart, like Lal?'

'No. Not in that way. He was an honourable man. Honour meant more to him than anything. That's why he left the army, in the end.'

'How do you mean?'

'The men found out about something from his past. Something about his family. Just rumours. It was enough for Singh. He said he couldn't serve with men who didn't respect him. Quit. He'd completed his terms of engagement, so he was entitled to leave. I could have forced him to stay, but there was no point. I looked into his eyes and saw a broken man. To this day I cannot figure it out. What could break a man like Singh?'

'What were the rumours about?'

'I don't know. When I asked the men, they clammed up. All claimed not to know. After Singh left, I chalked it down to a twist of fate, and forgot about it. Until your friend Silva called me out of the blue.'

She paused, then: 'Is there anything else you can tell me?'

His eyes crinkled. 'Well, there was the fact that Gupta was married to Singh's sister.'

She felt a current run through her. 'Lalita Gupta is Maan Singh's sister?'

'Lalita. Yes, I believe that was her name.'

'Did you ever meet her?'

'No. Though Gupta did show me a picture taken on their wedding day. Pleasant-looking woman.'

Persis described Sir James's housekeeper.

'Yes, that sounds like her,' agreed the former soldier. 'Though without a photograph I couldn't swear to it.'

Questions continued to plague her as, almost an hour later, she found herself navigating the jeep along the congested Sassoon

Dock Road. At this time of day, vehicles – mainly trucks – moved in a noisy throng to and from the docks, ferrying out the last of the day's catch before the final dregs of daylight fell from the sky.

Madan Lal, Maan Singh and Mrs Gupta. The three of them, at the heart of a nexus of lies. If not outright untruths then, at the least, lies of omission.

But why? Why had Lal kept their prior relationships hidden? Why not just be open about the fact that Singh had once served with him, and that Mrs Gupta had been the wife of their fallen comrade as well as Singh's sister?

If anything, this reinforced her belief that there was more to the story of Sir James's death than Singh's confession would have her believe.

She had driven to Laburnum House but had found both Lal and Gupta absent. She had left a message, then turned the jeep around and come . . . here.

She parked not far from the fish market that had been a fixture on the docks for decades; the stench of fish extended for miles around. In her youth, she had accompanied her father on numerous expeditions to the Sassoon Docks, named after David Sassoon, the one-time leader of the Jewish community in Bombay. Whatever romantic notion Persis might have entertained about the place had swiftly vanished. The docks were no place for the weak-stomached. Overrun by cutthroat Koli fisherwomen, the narrow lanes awash with the blood and guts of dismembered sea creatures, she remembered those visits as loud, volatile and, at times, overwhelming.

God knows what had possessed Archie Blackfinch to set up home here.

She had tracked the Englishman down to a fifth-floor apartment further along the Sassoon Dock Road. Not quite far enough to avoid the smell radiating from the docks, but far enough away to escape the mercantile madness.

He opened the door to her wearing a wide-collared sports shirt in windowpane checks, which he had rolled up to the elbows, and a pair of blue plaid trousers that clashed horrendously with the shirt. Such was the garishness of the outfit that it was a moment before she could speak.

'I'm sorry to disturb you,' she said. 'But I wished to speak to you about the case. May I come in?'

'No need to stand on ceremony,' he said breezily. 'Please.' He waved a hand expansively into the space behind him.

She entered and heard the door close behind her. A sudden nervousness fluttered through her chest. It had been a long time since she had last been inside a bachelor's apartment.

It was surprisingly neat. Clean floors, freshly painted walls, the absence of clutter on any of the surfaces. The colours were muted – whites and greys for the most part – but everything was pristine, tidy and in its place. Her limited experience of men, particularly the solitary kind, was that their habits tended to the slovenly. Clearly, Blackfinch was not of that ilk. Her eye was drawn to a bookshelf, the books neatly ordered, alphabetically, she noted, and in strict progression of height within those alphabetic rankings. A maniacal attention to detail. What had he made of the feverish tumult that characterised the Wadia Book Emporium? she wondered.

'Can I get you something to drink?'

She hesitated, formality pressing on her lips, but then something rebelled. It had been a long and trying day. 'Yes. A whisky. Neat.'

Minutes later they were sitting at the kitchen table, Persis's peaked cap on the checked tablecloth, Blackfinch hunched over a gin, staring at her with disarming curiosity from behind his spectacles. A fan whirred softly above them.

'I suppose congratulations are in order,' he began, raising his glass. 'To the woman who solved the "case of the decade".'

She scowled, unable to tell if he was making fun of her. 'I didn't solve anything.'

'That's not what the papers will say tomorrow.'

'You seem like an intelligent man. Then again, my father has always maintained that looks can be deceiving.' She bit her tongue the moment the words were out of her mouth.

Blackfinch stiffened, then gave a soft chuckle.

'I'm sorry,' she mumbled. 'I shouldn't have said that.'

He sipped at his drink. 'I have to confess, I'm not certain what the problem is. I can sense something is bothering you, but . . .'

'Does it not bother *you*?' she said sharply.

'You don't buy it,' he sighed. 'Singh's confession.' It was a statement, not a question.

'No,' she confirmed. 'I do not, as you say, buy it.'

'But why?'

'Something about Singh's story doesn't ring true.'

'A feeling,' he intoned.

Her eyes flashed. 'Are you calling me irrational?'

'I didn't say that,' he replied mildly. 'I'm merely pointing out that if you do not have clear evidence that he is *not* guilty, then any feeling to the contrary must be based on something other than logic.'

A silence followed in which Persis's uncertainty merely grew. She found it difficult to peg the man down. What was he really thinking? What did he really think of *her*? And why had *that* question become so important to her?

'There's a reason I came here,' she said. She told him about Lal's past, his connection to Singh and Gupta. 'Did you know?'

He seemed shocked. 'No. I mean I knew he was in the war, but I had no idea about the court martial or his connection to Singh. Frankly, I'd never met Singh or Gupta until the night of Herriot's death.' He hesitated. 'Look, surely you don't believe Lal had anything to do with Sir James's death?'

She offered no reply to this.

'You've worked with him before?' she asked finally.

'Not exactly. When I arrived in India a year ago, Sir James was an adviser to a committee tasked with improving the policing infrastructure. I met Lal at one of the committee meetings. We got talking. I found him to be well informed, charming. He'd spent time in England and had an astute sense of British as well as Indian politics.'

'Did you see him socially?'

'No. Frankly, I'm not much good at that sort of thing. Besides, I had my hands full setting up the lab.' He shook his head. 'It's strange. The currents that run inside people. I'd never have believed Lal capable of the things you say he did in Burma.' He lapsed into silence, staring at her.

His scrutiny made her uncomfortable and Persis turned away, pretending to look out of the window. The curtains were open and she had an uninterrupted view to the docks and the sea beyond. Dusk was falling and the mast lights of boats twinkled like fireflies out in the bay.

She wondered again why he had chosen to live here, in such close proximity to the docks. There was a certain perversity to it at odds with the picture of him that she had begun to form. Her father had told her on innumerable occasions that she had a habit of leaping to judgement. It was a weakness of character, she knew.

'Why are you here, Persis?' It was as if he had read her thoughts.

'I can no longer rely on assistance from my colleagues at Malabar House. You, however, are independent. I believe that someone from my team is talking to the newspapers. With the case the way it is, I would not want whatever I do next to be broadcast.'

'Is that the only reason you want my help?'

She blinked. The air had changed in texture. 'What do you mean?'

He continued to stare at her, then looked down at his glass. 'Nothing. I meant nothing.'

She noticed again the clean line of his jaw; the pleasing disposition of his nose, the small scar above and to the right of his upper lip. And his eyes, the liquid way they held the light, a gentleness in them that complemented his obvious intelligence.

She found herself on her feet. 'This was a bad idea.'

She whirled about and stepped smartly to the door. As she reached for the handle she heard him scrape back his chair.

'If it helps, I could have a look at the trousers?'

She turned and looked at him, her eyes moving downwards.

'Not *my* trousers,' he said. 'I meant Sir James's trousers. There might be forensic evidence on them.'

She hesitated, then nodded curtly, before turning and vanishing into the stairwell.

17

5 January 1950

The papers were predictably raucous. Maan Singh's photograph – a still from an identity card – looked out fiercely from the front page of every broadsheet, his stern gaze seeming to underline the accompanying headlines.

Murderer.

Killer.

The conclusion: Singh, a crazed fanatic, had ended the life of a blameless Englishman, a long-time ally of the subcontinent.

Malabar House was subdued. Persis's fellow officers wandered by her desk to offer their congratulations, all except Oberoi, who shot her a sour look. A copy of the *Indian Chronicle* was prominent on his desk. She knew that it referred, as Seth had warned her, to an early hypothesis by a 'detective within the investigative team' that the killing was motivated by a misplaced and belated nationalism.

Yet a night spent turning over the problem had convinced Persis that the truth lay elsewhere.

Setting aside Singh's confession, there was Herriot's unsettling behaviour in the weeks before his death. By all accounts he'd fallen out with his supposed friend, Robert Campbell. If so, over what? A business deal gone sour? Did the Indian entrepreneur Adi Shankar have something to do with that? He claimed that Herriot was to have become his new partner; yet he also claimed the same of Campbell. Perhaps Campbell hadn't liked the idea of sharing

Shankar with his former business partner. But enough to kill him? It seemed far-fetched.

What about Madan Lal? Why had he lied about knowing Singh? Or kept hidden the fact that Herriot's housekeeper was Singh's sister and the wife of a fallen comrade from his war years? How was he so readily able to swallow Singh's confession? Surely, the holes in Singh's story merited further investigation.

But Lal had washed his hands of the affair, drawing a terse line under matters.

Her thoughts circled back to a remark Seth had made at the very beginning.

Why *had* Lal called Malabar House instead of a more senior branch of the service? She recalled too that Lal and Sir James had been witnessed in heated discussion on the evening of his death. But Lal denied that such an argument had ever taken place. And now she knew that Lal was a man capable of the very darkest crimes. Had, by all accounts, murdered three men in cold blood out in the jungles of Imphal. Herriot had saved him. Lal was indebted to the Englishman. Is that how he had ended up as his aide?

There was also the matter of Vishal Mistry, the jeweller who had paid Herriot a visit on the night of his murder and who had now vanished. Why had Mistry been visiting Herriot?

And, finally, there was the investigation by Herriot into crimes committed during Partition. Were the ashes found in his fireplace evidence of destroyed documents from that investigation? If so, who had burned them?

Persis could not be certain of anything; a quiver full of doubt did not add up to a single solid lead that might overturn the version of Sir James's death cementing into place around her, namely that the Englishman's manservant, Maan Singh, had murdered his erstwhile employer. He would be condemned, hanged and then consigned to history, a footnote in the great nationalist struggle.

She knew that she had to speak to Lal, but her calls that morning had gone unanswered.

She passed a quiet hour re-examining her notes. Nothing new leaped out at her.

A courier arrived with a letter from the station-master at Victoria Terminus. Inside she found a short note stating that the ticket stub she had found in Sir James Herriot's jacket had been for a rail journey from Bombay to Pandiala, a small town in the state of Punjab. The train had departed from Bombay on 24 December and returned to the city on 28 December. Travelling to Punjab from Bombay took a day. This meant that Herriot had arrived in Punjab on the 25th and stayed till 27 December before taking the train back. Two days. What had he been doing out there?

She unlocked her drawer and hauled out more of the Partition files she had brought over from home. Looking through them, she took out the ones pertaining to Punjab, locked the rest away, then moved to the interview room and locked the door behind her.

It wasn't until the ninth file that she found her pulse quickening.

The account was patchy and missing vital details. The witness, unnamed, had been vague about the location, saying only that it was a village near Pandiala. The witness claimed that a local Muslim zamindar – a feudal landowner – together with his entire household, had been murdered in cold blood during the Partition rioting. The murderers were not named, merely described as locals. The family had consisted of fifteen individuals, including the man's wife, sons, daughters-in-law, grandchildren and two servants. They had died in a fire that had consumed their ancestral home. The authorities had labelled the fire accidental; the witness insisted it was murder. He also insisted that the true motive for the killing had been theft. The landowner had been looted; a fortune in ancestral jewellery had vanished with the murderers. Here the witness became animated, describing a number of the treasures supposedly taken from the victim. Her thoughts snagged on a description of one of the items, a necklace.

The description sounded familiar. But she couldn't place it.

Why had Sir James been so interested in this case? It was likely that his trip out to Pandiala, just days prior to his death, had been to pursue this matter. Was any of this connected to his death? Or was she simply complicating matters?

Sighing, she returned to her desk and locked away the files.

Sub-Inspector Pradeep Birla arrived, chewing on a sandwich. She pulled him to one side.

'I have another task for you.' Quickly, she explained to him her discovery of the connection between Madan Lal, Maan Singh and Mrs Gupta. 'I want you to find out more about Gupta.'

'Why?'

'Because I don't want you going near Lal, and Maan Singh isn't saying anything right now.'

'I meant why are you continuing to pursue this? We have our killer.'

She hesitated, then quickly explained her doubts. Birla was possibly the only one at the station who might listen to her with an open mind.

He put down his sandwich. 'The man confessed.'

'So everyone keeps telling me.'

He examined her for a moment then seemed to resign himself. 'Where do I start? With Gupta, I mean.'

'She told me that she has a son, at a boarding school in Panvel. See if you can track him down.'

'What exactly am I looking for?'

She hesitated. Should she voice the suspicion that had grown ever since meeting Edmond de Vries? 'Herriot was a man with no scruples. He used women. I'm curious as to why a man like him would pay for his housekeeper's son to be educated at an expensive boarding school.'

Birla made the leap right away. 'You think it might be his child?'

'It had crossed my mind.' She paused. 'By the way, did you find out anything about Adi Shankar?'

'There wasn't much to find. I visited the agency that brokered the sale of the Gulmohar Club. Shankar bought the place in good faith. All above board. I also went to his home, cornered his driver, asked him a few questions. Shankar doesn't have any family in Bombay. Enjoys the high life, throws money around, is good to man and beast alike. Well connected, well liked. Frankly speaking, he's just another wealthy Bombay socialite with too much time on his hands.'

'Did you contact the bandleader? From Herriot's party?'

'Yes. He confirmed that Shankar was on stage with the band from midnight until you turned up. If you had any suspicions about him, you'll have to think again. He couldn't have killed Herriot.'

Her phone rang.

'Inspector Wadia?'

The voice was male, gruff.

'Yes.'

'My name is Inspector Biswas, Colaba station. It is my understanding that you have an interest in the whereabouts of one Vishal Mistry? Or so I have been informed by his family.'

'That is correct. Have you found him?'

'In a way. He is currently at the morgue.'

*   *   *

She entered the basement of Grant Medical College to the familiar series of pips that began the All India Radio broadcast. 'This is All India Radio ... The news read by Mohit Bose.' She stopped and listened for a moment, as Bose launched into a summary of the Herriot case, ending with the conclusive assessment that his killer, a Sikh by the name of Maan Singh, had murdered the Englishman out of a latent nationalist hostility.

The broadcast was interrupted as a power cut shuddered through the morgue. Never infrequent, such power cuts continued to inflict upon the city an intermittent inconvenience that some carped was symptomatic of the country's slide into ruin since the departure of the British. Such sentiments could, in part, be put down to the anti-Congress feeling rising from the middle and feudal classes bracing themselves for the centre's planned reforms. Many had grown fat on the British teat and Nehru's lack of empathy had drawn their ire.

She heard the pathologist Raj Bhoomi cursing in the darkness, the tinkle of steel on concrete, further curses, and then the lights flickered back on.

She made her way into the autopsy room where she discovered the young pathologist scraping tools from the floor, a half-carved cadaver on the autopsy table. He reacted with surprise to her presence. 'Inspector Wadia. Did we have an appointment?'

'No,' she said. 'I came here for Vishal Mistry.'

He seemed mystified, then memory caught up. 'Ah, yes. Elderly gentleman. Knife murder.'

She hesitated. That, at least, answered one of her questions. 'Have you autopsied the body?'

Bhoomi stared at her in stupefaction. 'You cannot be serious?'

'I don't understand.'

'Inspector, we have a system here. I cannot just autopsy the first body that arrives through those doors. I will get to Mistry, but it will take a few days. I am backlogged as it is.'

'But you conducted Herriot's autopsy immediately.'

'That was different.'

'Because he was British?'

'Because he was *important*,' said Bhoomi. 'And because orders came down from on high.'

'Every death is important. And *I* am ordering you to carry out Mistry's autopsy.'

He gave a gentle smile, as one might to a mentally deficient elder. 'I'm afraid your authority doesn't quite cut it.'

She glared at him. 'I see. So unless the dog is kicked by its master it will refuse to fetch his slippers.'

He reddened in the washed-out light. 'You cannot speak to me like that.'

'Hello! Perhaps I might interject?'

They both turned to find Archie Blackfinch advancing into the room. 'Persis, a word, if I may?'

Still glaring at Bhoomi, she followed the Englishman out into the corridor. She had called him before leaving for the morgue.

Blackfinch observed her with a look of mild reproof. 'You can't insult a man and expect his cooperation.'

'I'm merely asking him to do the job that he is paid to do.'

'Raj is a fine pathologist. But he's understaffed and overworked.' His eyes lingered on her, the set of her jaw, her flashing gaze, her fine nose flared in anger. 'You'll have to apologise.'

'Apologise?' The notion hovered in the air like a wasp.

Blackfinch nodded. 'Yes. If you want Raj's cooperation.'

When they returned, she stared woodenly into the middle distance. 'If I have caused offence, it was unintentional.'

Bhoomi looked somewhat mollified.

'Look, Raj,' began Blackfinch, 'this really *is* important. Persis thinks there might be a connection between the Mistry killing and Sir James's murder.'

'But Sir James's murder has been solved,' Bhoomi protested. '*She* solved it. You both did.'

'I'm afraid it's not quite as cut and dried as that. I'm speaking off the record, of course.'

Bhoomi's brow became troubled. 'You have no official sanction for continuing your investigation?'

Blackfinch gave a disarming smile. 'None whatsoever.'

Bhoomi broke into a wide grin of his own. 'Well, why didn't you say so? If a rule is worth breaking, then it's worth breaking properly.'

An hour later the autopsy was complete. Running his hands under the tap, Bhoomi gave them his analysis. 'He died of a knife wound to the chest that penetrated the thorax from the seventh left inter-costal space beside the sternum and punctured the right ventricle of the heart. Death would have been swift. I cannot be completely certain but the wound profile appears similar to that sustained by Sir James. It may very well have been the same weapon.'

'Where did they find the body?' asked Persis.

'It's in the police report,' replied Bhoomi. 'I have a copy of it here.'

He removed his gloves, went into a back office and returned with a copy of the report, reading from it as he walked. 'About half a mile from his home. On a walking route running through the wooded section at the southern edge of the Bori Bunder maidan. Apparently, he used to walk through there every morning, from his home on Wallace Road, on his way to the Marine Drive prom-enade. He'd pay his respects to the sea then double back towards his office on Jamshedji Tata Road.'

They parked at the top of the southern edge of the Bori Bunder maidan, got out, then began to walk along the tree-lined path that skirted the field. At this time of day the path was all but deserted; Persis imagined that early in the morning it would have been even quieter, the perfect spot for an ambush. In between the trees, they caught flashes of children playing cricket on the maidan, the odd sleeping drunk. Stray dogs licked at the patchy grass.

'You haven't asked me about Herriot's trousers.'

She inclined her head but did not look at him or slow her pace. Dried leaves crunched beneath their feet. A pig grunted along the lane, trailed by a litter of piglets.

'I took the liberty of examining them this morning. There are some excellent new techniques in the analysis of blood markings that I thought I would use – the Americans, in particular, have made great progress recently, though the science is still not admissible in a court of law.'

She said nothing, her long legs eating up the path. He found himself hurrying to keep pace.

'There's a significant amount of blood on the trousers, of that there's no doubt. The problem is this: the type of staining does not tally with what I'd expected to find.'

'I don't understand.'

'Sir James was knifed in the throat. Blood from that wound would have projected downwards on to his trousers in the form of arterial spray. The shape of such droplets is dictated by physics – large, individual stains. But what I found on the trousers is more akin to what we call transfer stains, when an object comes into contact with existing bloodstains, leaving pattern transfers such as bootprints or, as in this case, smears. They could not have been deposited at the time Sir James was knifed. Ergo, he could not have been wearing the trousers at that time. It looks as if the killer smeared the trousers in Sir James's blood *after* the fact.'

In the branches of the tree behind her a brainfever bird sounded its piercing three-note call, startling them both.

'Why?' Persis asked.

But Blackfinch had no answer to this.

She worked the problem in her mind. If Singh *had* killed Herriot, then it must have been just after Herriot's tryst, before he had had a chance to dress. If they could find the woman he had been with, perhaps she might have seen something as she departed? It still made no sense to her that Singh had taken the trousers.

That question stayed with her as they rounded a curve and encountered a red flag that had been planted at the base of a sprawling banyan tree. This was all that remained to mark the end of Vishal Mistry. According to the report, his body had been discovered hidden within the coiled lower branches of the banyan. It had lain there for four days before a passing pedestrian had been alerted to it by his dog. This section of the path was screened from prying eyes by banyan trees on either side. The perfect spot for a murder.

They scratched around in the dirt for a while, but there was little to see. Whatever evidence had been here had been swept up by the authorities. She hoped they had been thorough.

'Mistry's sister said that he left home earlier than usual. Yet he did not have any planned appointment, certainly none that his assistant at the shop was aware of. So why was he out here so early in the morning?

'The policeman who notified me that Mistry's body had been found told me something else about him,' she added. 'Apparently, he was known to the authorities. He had come to their attention following Partition as a man willing to deal in stolen jewellery. A lot of that sort of thing happened during the troubles, theft and looting, I mean. Mistry was accused of acting as a link between those in possession of such items and those willing to pay for them. None of this was proved, and Mistry was never charged. But the feeling is that there was no smoke without fire.'

She noticed Blackfinch glancing at his watch. 'Is there somewhere else you have to be?'

A flash of guilt swam over his face. 'I have a luncheon appointment. A lady friend. She doesn't like to be kept waiting.'

Unbidden, an image of Elizabeth Campbell leaped into her mind. Persis turned away. 'Do not let me keep you.' Her tone was cold and she felt instantly embarrassed by her reaction.

'Well. Right. If you're sure,' he said. 'I mean, there really isn't much else to see here anyway.'

'Feel free to leave at any time.'

'Yes.' Still, he hesitated.

She deliberately ignored him, dropping to her haunches and pretending to examine minutely some scat on the ground as if perhaps it held a vital clue to the case.

Finally, she heard him walk away. He stopped at the edge of the clearing. 'Persis?'

She looked up, but did not turn her head.

'A little gratitude never hurt anyone.'

He tramped off, leaving her with a buzzing in her ears. Whether it was from anger or humiliation she could not tell.

Back at Malabar House she parked the jeep then stopped off at Afzal's tea stall, a fixture on the corner of the nearby junction for as long as anyone could remember. The stick-thin old man, dressed in Congress white, bowed exaggeratedly. 'The nation's newest heroine. I am honoured.'

She gave him a withering look. As he prepared her a milky tea and a cucumber and chutney sandwich, her thoughts continued to graze over the case. Facts were piling upon facts. New avenues of investigation opening up. And yet clarity was no nearer.

Was Singh the killer? If not, then who?

The connection to Vishal Mistry was significant; only a fool would deny that. It was too much of a coincidence that the jeweller had been murdered the morning after Herriot's own killing. But what had bound the two men? Was it even correct to assume that the same man had killed both Herriot and Mistry? A similar-looking wound was hardly evidence of that fact.

Seated at her desk, Persis dwelt on the things that continued to bother her. She now knew that Herriot had journeyed north, to Punjab, just before his death. The train ticket stub confirmed this. Thinking of the stub reminded her of the note found in the same jacket. The sheet had been taken from the Golden Temple Hotel. It seemed reasonable that he had written that note while he was doing whatever he was doing in the north.

She pulled out her notebook, where she had copied down the name and the strange annotation.

BAKSHI. PLT41/85ACRG11.

She tried to work the letters and numbers around, but only came up with more meaningless jumbles.

What if she broke up the sequence? She picked up her pen again and rewrote the sequence, this time inserting dashes in the most logical places.

PLT-41/85-ACRG-11

Nothing.

She stared at the wall in frustration. On the wall was a map of Bombay. As she gazed at it a tickle feathered the back of her mind.

She continued to look at the map. The city had been dissected into a cartographic grid; along one axis the letters A–K, along the other the numbers 1–14. Malabar House lay squarely in grid G7. A grid.

She looked back down at the enigmatic code, then rewrote it, this time changing one dash.

PLT-41/85-ACR-G11

G11.

What if this were a grid reference? If so, then it hinted at the meaning of ACR. She had seen the annotation before – on rural field maps. ACR was usually an abbreviation for 'acres'.

Could this code refer to eighty-five acres of land in grid square G11? If so, then it was a good bet that PLT-41 meant 'plot 41', another common way of referring to parcels of land in rural areas. But on what map was the grid? And why would all this have mattered to Herriot?

It was likely that he had scribbled these details down while in Punjab. In which case, it made sense that, if the note did indeed refer to a plot of land, then it would be there.

Who did the plot belong to? Bakshi? If so, who was Bakshi? Did this have something to do with Herriot's work for the Partition Commission? She wrestled with the problem for a while, then surrendered.

There was something else she needed to turn her energies to.

18

The sun was beginning to dip behind Laburnum House as Persis pulled the jeep up to the gates. She waited while the guards leaped into action, then navigated her way up the drive to park beside the exterior fountain, a concrete stallion, raised on hind legs, hooves flailing at the air.

She was greeted by the housekeeper, Lalita Gupta. The woman, dressed in a bottle-green sari, looked apprehensive. She led Persis through to a tobacco-panelled drawing room where Madan Lal was drinking tea as he examined a selection of broadsheets.

His eyes widened, but he recovered quickly. 'Apologies for not returning your calls, Inspector,' he said, gesturing at the sofa opposite, as Gupta left the room. 'I have been a little preoccupied.' He bent his slight frame over the teapot. 'May I pour you a cup? It's a Darjeeling blend. Frightfully expensive. I suspect we won't be ordering more for a while.'

He tinkled the spoon around the porcelain teacup, then handed it to Persis.

'Not that imminent bankruptcy curtailed James's extravagance. Appearances were everything to him.'

He pointed the teaspoon over her shoulder at a tiger skin on the wall. 'This was his cardroom. He and his collection of hangers-on would sit here all night carousing and playing poker. He used to tell people that he shot that tiger in Bengal, on a hunt with a local maharaja. It was a lie, of course. That was the first thing I learned about him, Inspector. James was an accomplished liar. It's what made him such a canny politician.'

She sensed a subtle change in the way Lal spoke about his erstwhile employer. The cloying respect had vanished, to be replaced with an edge of cynicism.

She launched right in. 'Why didn't you tell me that you served with Maan Singh during the war? That he is Mrs Gupta's brother.'

Panic flared in his eyes. Recovering quickly, he said, 'It was not relevant.'

'*Everything* is relevant!' She forced herself to calm. 'You deliberately withheld information.'

'As I said, it was not relevant.'

'He was your comrade, your friend. How is it that you are so ready to believe that he is a murderer?'

His expression hardened. 'Yes, Maan and I fought together; but we were never close. After the war, we lost touch. Then, one day, he called me out of the blue and told me that his sister was looking for work in Bombay. We were in need of a housekeeper and so I offered her the job. Later, when we needed a new driver for Sir James she suggested Maan. I called him and he readily agreed. If I had had any idea that he harboured ill intent towards James . . .'

'Why did you lie about how Singh ended up at Laburnum House?'

'I did not wish to complicate matters. Maan is an intensely private individual. He is very guarded about his past.'

She stared at him. Could she trust this man? She was certain he was not telling her everything.

'We found the body of Vishal Mistry.'

'Who?' He seemed genuinely confused.

'The jeweller Sir James met in his study on the evening of his death. He was murdered the following morning.'

'Why are you telling me this?'

'Doesn't it strike you as an extraordinary coincidence?'

He shrugged. 'I didn't know the man or why James was meeting him.'

She changed tack. 'Did you know that Sir James was planning to take a stake in the Gulmohar Club?'

'You must be mistaken.'

'There's no mistake.'

His mouth drew into a grimace. 'How could he afford that?'

'That's just one of the many questions I'm trying to answer. Perhaps he wasn't as bankrupt as we all believe.'

They stared at each other and then retreated into their teacups like soldiers agreeing a momentary truce.

Lal broke the silence. 'Why are you continuing to pursue this? I mean, you've solved the case, you're being fêted by the nation' – he waved at the newspapers sprawled over the coffee table – 'so why do you care?'

The answer to that question was more complex than Persis could easily put into words.

'You're an idealist,' said Lal, supplying his own answer.

'You say that as if it were an insult.'

Another silence.

'What will you do now?' asked Persis. 'I mean, if there really is no money . . .'

'I don't know,' said Lal, but the manner in which he said this was unconvincing.

'You're not being entirely honest with me.'

Lal merely lifted his teacup back to his mouth.

She tilted her chin. 'Sir James was not quite the man you made him out to be.'

'It behoves no one to speak ill of the dead. Like us all James had his faults. But he was a man who achieved great things.'

'Yes. For one, he saved you from spending a very long time in prison.'

He frowned. 'What do you mean?'

'At Imphal. You murdered three men in cold blood. Somehow Sir James kept you out of a military prison. I suppose that sort of thing can buy a man's loyalty.'

He seemed stricken. When he finally spoke, his voice had risen several octaves. 'You have no right to investigate my past.'

'I have every right to investigate this case in any manner I see fit.'

'This case is over!' he exploded. His fists were clenched and he began to rise.

For an instant, fear beat at her like the wings of a giant bird. Her hand strayed to the revolver at her hip. Perhaps Lal saw the movement, or perhaps he realised that he had lost control of himself. He was a man who hated losing control. Because when he did, the results were terrifying, as those men at Imphal had discovered.

'Didn't you tell me that you wanted to know the truth?' continued Persis. '*I* am not yet certain that Maan Singh killed Sir James.'

His dark eyes contracted to pinpoints of shadow. He ground out: 'I will be lodging an official complaint with your senior officer.'

She found the housekeeper in her office at the rear of the house.

Gupta stood as she entered.

'Why didn't you tell me that you knew Lal and Singh before your employment here? That Singh is your brother?'

She blinked rapidly. 'It – it did not seem important.'

'What else haven't you told me? I want the truth.'

'I assure you—'

'I know that Sir James entertained a woman in his office on the night of his death. Was it you?'

She looked aghast. 'No! How could you think that?'

Persis considered asking about Gupta's son, revealing her suspicions on that front, but then decided to wait until Birla returned with something concrete.

'Then who?' Persis pressed in on the woman. Gupta seemed ready to flee. 'I *will* find out.'

Silence.

'Do the newspapers know that Maan Singh is your brother? I can ensure that they do. By tomorrow, there will be a queue a mile long outside your door. They won't stop until they've torn your life apart. Perhaps you'll be willing to talk then?'

Gupta stared in horror at the policewoman, then lowered her eyes. 'If I tell you, you must promise to keep my relationship to Maan a secret.'

'I promise they will not find out from me.'

A shudder passed through the housekeeper. 'I believe Sir James was involved with Elizabeth Campbell.'

Persis was stunned. 'You must be mistaken.'

'I – I saw them together. Here at the house. Some days before his death. I walked in on them . . . embracing. It was obvious.'

'Why didn't you tell me this before?'

'Because it is none of my business,' she said wretchedly. 'None of this is.'

Gravel ground beneath her feet as she marched from the front porch back to her jeep. Gupta's revelation had shaken her. Why would the beautiful young Scotswoman entertain a man like Herriot? The thought of it made her queasy. But it might explain why Herriot had begun to avoid Robert Campbell. And if Campbell had found out . . .

She heard footsteps and turned to find Madan Lal descending on her. 'Inspector,' he said through a primly pursed mouth, 'I have just been told that you questioned Mrs Gupta.'

'I did.' Persis was intrigued by the PA's ire. What was troubling Lal?

'I must insist that you do not bother her any further.'

'Why? What is it that you're not telling me?'

Lal gazed at her in silent fury.

'What did you and Sir James fight about on the evening of his death?'

Silence.

'Why did you call Malabar House? Was it your hope that the case would not be investigated properly? If so, you made a mistake.' She turned and ducked into the jeep, accelerating away in a clatter of gravel, Lal a neat figure dwindling in her rear-view mirror.

The aide was as good as his word.

She stopped off at Malabar House to inform Seth of all that she had discovered – about Lal and Singh, about Elizabeth Campbell – and was instantly made to regret it.

In the time that she had known him, she had rarely seen Roshan Seth worked up in fury.

'Did you have to poke the tiger in the eye?' he seethed. 'Lal called. Have you any idea how much trouble that man can make for us?'

'I'm going where the case takes me.'

'What case? The case is ended. I asked you to be discreet.'

'Lal cannot be trust—'

Seth slapped the desk. She stared at him. 'You don't get it, do you, Persis? They've already taken away my career. Another wrong move and they'll take away my uniform. What will I do then?' He sighed. 'The problem with you, Persis, is that you're so blinded by your own ambition, your own sense of righteousness, that you don't see anything else. It's my own fault. I keep forgetting that you are young and inexperienced. The young are always selfish, even when they don't think they are.'

The words stung. Was Seth right? What if she was truly so blinkered that she did not see the harm that her actions might cause?

'I think you should take a few days off.'

She gaped at him. 'You're suspending me?'

'No,' he said wearily. 'I'm defusing the situation, perhaps even saving your career. You may be stuck at Malabar House with the rest of us for now, Persis, but mark my words: you're destined for better things. If only you can survive long enough. These people will tolerate a little insubordination, but they will never allow you to embarrass them.'

These words continued to ring in her ears as she made her way back to her desk. She collected the Partition files locked in her drawer, then walked up to the lobby. The anger had passed and in its wake came a deep melancholy.

Is this how it would always be? A constant battle to prove her worth in a world dominated by those who thought in a way that was beyond her. Of all the institutions in the new republic, surely it was the police service that must value truth above all things? How was a nation to establish itself if it could not look itself in the mirror?

Her thoughts were interrupted by Pradeep Birla, heading the other way. His shirt was stained with sweat and he looked harried. He pulled her aside as a trio of corporate executives came barrelling into the building.

'I drove out to Panvel,' he said. 'It's about an hour out of the city. There's only one boarding school there, the Heart of Mary Catholic School. It has a stellar reputation, and the fees are stiff. Gupta does have a child there, a boy named Praveen. Nice-looking kid.'

'Let me guess. He's half-Anglo.'

Birla shook his head. 'Afraid not. The kid's as Indian as you or me.'

She was momentarily taken aback. She had all but convinced herself that Herriot was the father of Gupta's child.

'Did you speak to him?'

'Yes. Not that I learned much. He seems a bit dull to me. But here's the good part. I asked to see the kid's files. You said that Sir James was paying for him to be there.'

'Yes. That's what his mother told me.'

'Well, I met the registrar. Guess who signed the cheques for his fees?'

She waited.

'Your friend, Madan Lal.'

The revelation stunned her.

'The registrar told me that Lal was with her when the boy was enrolled and regularly drives her up to visit. He thought the pair were husband and wife till Lal disabused him of the notion.'

Had she misjudged the relationship between Lal and Herriot's housekeeper, a woman who also happened to be the sister of the man who had confessed to Herriot's killing?

'You said the fees at Heart of Mary were stiff. How stiff?'

He told her. The figure was exorbitant. It beggared belief that a man like Sir James would have agreed to such an outlay for his housekeeper. Could Lal have paid the fees himself?

Unlikely. The sum would have taxed an aide's salary, no matter how well paid.

'I want you to do something,' she said. 'Call Herriot's lawyers. Find out from them who Herriot's bookkeeper was. I want to talk to him.'

19

Her father was down in the bookshop with another of their regular clients.

Pran Manikchand was a retired jurist with a penchant for ordering obscure tomes that proved exceedingly difficult to procure. But procure them Sam Wadia did, for Manikchand always paid, in crisp new banknotes, thinking nothing of throwing a small fortune at an early edition of Ghalib or a book about disused railway saloons in the German Rhineland.

After he had left, she sat with her father as he counted the day's takings. Watching him in silence, the books susurrating around her, a sense of desolation settled on her shoulders.

'What's the matter?' said Sam eventually, without looking up.

She considered not telling him, but then, before she knew what was happening, it spilled out of her, a rush of emotion that caught them both unawares. By the time she had finished, she could not stop the tears from flowing. They were not tears of weakness; she was weeping with rage, the whole damned unfairness of it all.

Sam watched her mutely, until finally he wheeled himself around the counter and fixed her with a stern look. 'Are you done feeling sorry for yourself?'

She looked up at him through bleary eyes.

'Seth is right. You *are* selfish.'

This was not what she had expected to hear. She stiffened.

'You don't like that?' said her father. 'Well, tough. What did you think would happen? You've been champing at the bit ever since they gave you your uniform. You want everyone to know that you're the brightest, most capable officer in the whole damned service. But did you ever stop and think that *they don't care?*' He allowed this to sink in. Her tears had vanished. 'They don't care, Persis. It matters not a jot to them that you might be smarter, more dedicated, more righteous. It only matters that you don't disturb the status quo.' He wheeled himself forward, a strange light in his eye. 'So, tell me, daughter of mine, what do you say to that?'

Her mouth hardened into a line. 'I say to hell with them.'

Over dinner she explained to him the impasse she had arrived at.

'Why are you so convinced that Singh didn't do it?'

She shrugged, forking a mouthful of Hyderabadi biryani from her plate. 'Instinct.'

'Rubbish,' he said sternly. 'Instinct is based on experience. You don't have enough of that to develop instincts.'

She coloured.

'You *want* Singh to be innocent,' continued Sam relentlessly. 'Because then it will give you the excuse to continue with your investigations.'

She set down her fork. Her father's words had thrown salt into the wounds opened by Seth. 'You've always told me to rely on myself. Something inside me is telling me Singh didn't do this.'

'People lie to themselves all the time.'

'Is that what you do?' she said softly. The atmosphere shifted uncomfortably. 'Why will you not tell me what really happened that day?'

Sam stiffened. His eyes dimmed and he looked down at his plate.

'Don't I have a right to know? Aren't I old enough?'

'For some things, you will never be old enough.'

'She wasn't just your wife. She was my mother.'

Silence hummed between them.

'It's strange,' he said eventually. 'She's been gone all these years, yet I still see her everywhere. When we first took over the shop from my father, she said something odd to me: "We're going to see a lot of dead people." I had no idea what she meant, but I soon found out.

'Many of the books we bought came from the estates of those who had recently passed. A loved one – a wife, a daughter – would come into the shop and ask us to look at a collection their husband or their father had left behind. Your mother and I would drive out to their home in our Austin. We'd find whole shelves of books about cheeses of the Pyrenees or the rare birds of Guatemala; it never ceases to amaze me the infinite passions that move people. Your mother used to say that a little piece of a person's soul is left behind in their books.' His eyes grew blurry. 'Your mother's death is the greatest regret of my life. She was a flame that burned brightly and still does, if only in my heart.'

Later, after her father had gone to bed, she spread her notes out on the dining table. It was almost two. On the radio: Schubert, of whom she had always been fond. Akbar hopped up on to the corner of the table, and fixed her with a mildly interested gaze. Behind him, Bombay hung in the window. Already it was gaining a reputation as a night-time city. People continued to stream into the metropolis, swelling the city's ranks on a daily basis, drawn here by the dream of a better life.

Bombay: the new utopia.

She wondered if any of them knew that the literal translation of the word *utopia* came from the Greek *ou-topos*: no place on earth.

The wall clock chimed softly. Akbar closed his eyes and drifted to sleep on his paws.

But Persis couldn't sleep. Her thoughts were being pulled in a dozen different directions.

She padded to the fridge and poured herself a glass of orange juice. On a whim, she raided her father's liquor cabinet and added a generous measure of White Horse to it. She looked down at the glass, then poured in a little more.

She took out her notebook, opened a clean page and began to write.

Sir James Herriot
Murdered on New Year's Eve/early New Year's Day
Murder weapon: curved knife. Knife not found on premises.
Trousers missing. Found in Maan Singh's home.
Herriot working on Partition crimes investigation. Highly sensitive.
Empty safe. What was inside? Partition files? Something else?
Ashes found in fireplace – did Herriot burn Partition files? Why?
Visited Pandiala, in Punjab, just before death, possibly pursuing Partition investigation.
Enigmatic code in jacket. Possible plot reference, plot belonging to a 'Bakshi'. Relevant?
Had relations in his office on the night of. Who with?
Housekeeper says Herriot having affair with Elizabeth Campbell.
Herriot bankrupt.
Buying stake in Gulmohar Club. How can he afford if bankrupt?

Maan Singh
Confesses to murder. But what motive? Nationalism?
Sir James's trousers recovered from his home. Why did he take them?
If killer, what did he do with knife?
Why didn't he confess immediately?

Madan Lal
Known Herriot for years.
Murdered three men at Imphal. Rescued by Herriot.
Quarrelled with Herriot on night of. About what? Denies quarrel.
Did not mention serving with Singh and with Duleep Gupta, husband of Herriot's housekeeper, Mrs Gupta. Why?
Has been helping Gupta and her son. Good Samaritan or something else?

Vishal Mistry
Jeweller.
Visited Herriot on night of. Why?
Neither he nor Herriot told anyone of visit. Why?
Murdered on morning after night of.
Known for fencing stolen jewellery.

She paused, collected her thoughts then added two further notes:

Robert Campbell/Elizabeth Campbell
Former business partner. Possible rift?
Campbell fought with daughter at party – did he discover affair with Herriot?
Was Elizabeth Campbell the woman in Herriot's office before his death?

Adi Shankar
Owner of the Gulmohar Club.
Herriot established friendship. Wished to buy stake in club.
Shankar now friends with Campbell, possible business partners.
With jazz band at time of murder.

She stopped again, then wrote another line.

How did the murderer get the knife out of Laburnum House?

The case had spread, like an infection.

Then again, perhaps her father was right. Perhaps sometimes the obvious answer was the right one. Perhaps Maan Singh *had* killed Sir James, and all her speculation was pointless. An attempt to make herself feel important.

She drained the glass and poured herself another.

She began to go over her notes again. The case was like a piece of music; notes of a melody hung in the air, but the overall composition eluded her.

She focused on Herriot, his actions prior to his death. He had gone north to Punjab. She now knew he had ended up in a place called Pandiala, pursuing one of the Partition crimes that he had been tasked to investigate. If so, the jumble of letters and numbers on the note she had found in his jacket, which she believed referred to a plot of land – might that plot not be somewhere in or near Pandiala? If she could find that plot she might understand why Herriot had taken such an interest in it and in the mysterious 'Bakshi'.

She walked down to the bookshop, switched on the light. Silence reigned in the shop. A soft squeak might have been a mouse. She padded around a pyramid of books about the French Revolution, and along several aisles, until she was standing before a section of reference books and atlases.

She reached up and pulled down a copy of *Collier's Giant Atlas of Hindustan and Imperial Gazeteer*. Atlases depicting the new India and Pakistan would be few and far between. Possibly there remained a lingering suspicion at the back of the minds of cartographers that the situation might be reversed, the lines redrawn. There were many in India who felt this, some who actively demanded that the Indian government pursue the matter with military force.

She took the atlas to her father's counter, laid it down, then opened it. Flipping through the pages she located the section depicting the north-west, her eyes tracking upwards from the Bombay Presidency through the Rajputana Agency and up into the Punjab. In the Collier's map the Punjab region still stretched all the way from Delhi and the United Provinces in the east to Peshawar and the North-West Frontier Province in the west. In 1947 the province had been cleaved in two, into East Punjab and West Punjab, respectively administered by the newly created Union of India and the Dominion of Pakistan. The name Punjab meant 'Land of the Five Waters', a corruption of the original Sanskrit name for the region, Panchnanda, 'Land of the Five Rivers', referring to the rivers Jhelum, Chenab, Ravi, Sutlej and Beas, all tributaries of the great Indus. Punjab had been one of the last regions in India to hold out against the East India Company, finally succumbing in 1849 after the Second Anglo-Sikh War. The Punjabis were known for being fierce warriors – half of the six hundred thousand-odd Indian troops who had participated in the First World War had come from the province.

Punjab was also the scene of some of the worst communal rioting during the Partition years.

At the time, Muslims had comprised the majority in the province. With the creation of Pakistan, widespread hostility had seen sectarian killing – largely between Sikh and Muslim – on an unprecedented scale, whole villages massacred, trains travelling between the two countries stopped in their tracks and burned out, thousands perishing in searing agony. The terror had been incited by partisan newspaper reporting and stoked by local rumours of mobs sweeping the countryside. Even now, the state was convulsed by sporadic ethnic violence.

She located the village of Pandiala. Just twenty miles from Amritsar. A red flag waved in her mind. Amritsar.

She flicked through her notebook. The address that she had taken from Maan Singh's ration card was in Amritsar. Was there a connection?

She went back to the shelves and dug out *Werther's Catalogue of Indian Hotels*. Herriot had stayed in Pandiala for a couple of days, presumably in a hotel. It now seemed reasonable that that stay had been in the Golden Temple Hotel.

Quickly, she located the list of hotels in Punjab. There were forty-three named the Golden Temple Hotel, but only one in Pandiala. The entry consisted of just two lines, an address and a photograph. She scribbled down the address and telephone number on her notepad.

A soft chime sounded through the shop. She looked up. The wall clock had struck two in the morning. It was a novelty clock, a gift from Aunt Nussie. Every hour on the hour, it would chime, the front doors would open, and a turbaned soldier would emerge to stumble out an awkward salute. The accompanying chorus of *God Save the King* no longer functioned, only the chime. There was a metaphor in there, somewhere, she felt.

The realisation crept up on her. There was no blinding epiphany, merely a certainty that appeared to have been waiting for her all along.

She would have to go to Punjab. She would have to retrace Sir James's movements. There was no other way. Staying in Bombay under the present circumstances, with nothing to do but wait for Seth's irritation to subside, was pointless. As far as her seniors were concerned the investigation was over. Her only choice was to accept this or not. But if she accepted it, if she meekly returned to work in a few days' time, moved on to the next case, how would it affect the remainder of her career? Could she live with such a decision?

The answer came from the books, whispering to her as they had always done in such moments. They knew her better than she knew herself.

She would pursue the investigation as far as she was able. There was a sense of pre-determinism to the decision – truthfully, it could not have gone any other way. With this thought, the knot in her stomach dissolved.

Yet the prospect of striking out on her own bothered her, more than she cared to admit. If the Herriot case had taught her anything it was that sooner or later one had to acknowledge the necessity of others. But who?

Framing the question gave her the answer. It had been lurking there, waiting. Perhaps, in a way, the question itself had been thrust up by her subconscious mind, slyly designed for the express purpose of presenting just that answer.

Blackfinch.

The Englishman intrigued her. It was pointless pretending otherwise. Yet she was not even sure that she *liked* him. He was clearly intelligent, with a unique set of skills. But he was also odd. As a younger woman, she had dreamed of sophisticated men, mature, competent and assured. She had thought that such men would recognise her inner strength, her intelligence. She had been wrong.

Blackfinch fell far short of that early idealism.

And yet.

She took out her notebook, flipped through until she found his number. Snatching up the receiver of the shop's telephone, she plunged onwards before she could change her mind.

An eternity later, Blackfinch answered. 'Yes,' he said blearily.

She opened her mouth but a sudden panic gripped her tongue.

'Hello?'

Silence.

'Is anyone there?'

Silence.

'I can hear you breathing, you know. This is rather unedifying, whoever you are.'

The clock chimed on the wall, restarting time. She coughed loudly. 'It's me, Persis,' she said gruffly.

Shock poured from the receiver. 'Persis? Do you know what time it is?'

'Yes.'

Another silence.

'It's two in the morning.'

'Yes. I just told you that I already know this.'

'Oh.'

Silence.

'Um. Is there any particular reason that you're calling me at two in the morning?'

She took a deep breath. 'It is for professional reasons.'

'Oh.' Did he sound faintly disappointed? 'And this couldn't have waited until the morning?'

'No.'

'Well, I suppose you had better tell me, then.'

Quickly, she recounted to him her investigation into Herriot's movements and her plan to travel to Punjab.

He did not immediately reply. She heard him clattering around, the clink of a glass. 'Let me get this straight,' he said finally. 'You've been suspended—'

'I have *not* been suspended,' she said hotly.

'My apologies,' he said, not sounding at all apologetic. 'You've been *encouraged*, by your commanding officer, to take a few days off, and instead of taking a well-earned holiday you intend to risk your career by doing the very thing you have been asked not to do?'

Her knuckles tightened on the receiver but she said nothing.

'What exactly do you hope to find?'

'I want to see if Sir James discovered something that might have a bearing on his death. There is also the fact that Maan Singh's permanent residence was in Amritsar. Amritsar is just a short distance from Pandiala. One must pass through it to get to Pandiala.'

'You want to visit Singh's home?'

'Yes.'

He was silent a moment. 'Are you sure this isn't . . .?' He tailed off.

'Isn't what?'

'Well, I was wondering if this isn't a desire on your part to rebel. To show your superiors that you won't be silenced. To prove to them that you know better, in the hope that they'll recognise this as a virtue. Believe me, Persis, *that* sort of thinking has ended many promising careers.'

She swallowed the response that sprang immediately to the tip of her tongue. Namely, that Blackfinch sounded as condescending as her superiors.

'I am aware of the possible consequences of my actions,' she said grimly. 'But that doesn't change anything. I was given this case and I will see it through. I called you because I felt that your investigative skills might be of some use to me on this journey. But if you don't see the point of it, I will bid you goodnight.'

'Is that really why you called me?' he said softly.

'What? What do you mean?' It was the second time in as many days that he had confronted her with a meaning she couldn't quite fathom. Words as slippery as smoke.

The silence stretched, and then he broke the spell. 'When do you plan to leave?'

'Tomorrow. I will take the two-fifteen Frontier Mail from Ballard Pier Mole station to Delhi, then from there to Amritsar and Pandiala.'

'Fine. I'll meet you there.'

She was momentarily taken aback. 'Very well.'

'Good.'

'Good.'

Silence breezed from the receiver.

'Well, I shall put the phone down now.'

'Great.'

'Yes.'

Another waft of silence.

'Goodnight.'

'And a goodnight to you too, Persis.'

As she slipped into bed, Akbar squirming beside her, lost in dreams of mice and men, she couldn't help but linger on the conversation. Blackfinch was an enigma. He had seemed resolutely opposed to her journey, and then, on the turn of a coin, had agreed to accompany her. The man was . . . odd.

She drifted into a sleep with a tiny coal aglow in her stomach.

It was the strangest feeling.

20

6 January 1950

Birla called her at her home as she was packing. 'Why aren't you at the station? I need to speak to you.'

She hesitated, then told him about her plan to follow in Herriot's footsteps. 'I've told Seth that I'm taking a couple of days' leave.'

'That's probably wise,' said Birla. 'Are you going up there alone? A Punjabi village is hardly the sort of place for a young woman to be wandering about on her own.'

His concern was genuine, and she wondered if she should tell him about Blackfinch. In the end, she decided against it. 'I'll be fine.'

Birla seemed set to argue, then gave up. 'You asked me to find an address for Herriot's bookkeeper. Do you still want it?'

She noted the details, then put down the phone. She looked at her watch. There was plenty of time before her afternoon train. She had made plans for the morning but there was time to fit in a visit to Herriot's bookkeeper.

Blackfinch's words regarding her motivations had been sobering. She had been forced to remind herself that a good detective kept an open mind and followed through on every lead.

Herriot's bookkeeper was one such lead.

The other was Elizabeth Campbell.

*　　*　　*

Andrew Morgan worked from glass-fronted offices on the second floor of a ten-storey tower in Cuffe Parade. He was a sallow, silk-shirted man in his mid-forties, prematurely bald with a rash that extended up his throat towards a weak chin.

'What can I do for you, Inspector?' he said, gesturing at a seat before his desk. He blinked at her from behind steel-rimmed spectacles.

The office, like its occupant, was small, every wall lined with client folders, his desk similarly swamped.

'I want to know more about Sir James's finances.'

'I've already told his lawyers everything they needed to know.'

'The man is dead. I'm investigating his murder. I don't think he will mind.'

His brow furrowed. 'I was under the impression that the murderer was behind bars.'

'There are some loose ends.'

He digested this. 'What would you like to know?'

'Were you in charge of Sir James's finances?'

'In charge? No. I merely kept his books.'

'Where did he derive his income from?'

'Well, he was paid a substantial sum by the Indian government for his work on their behalf. Plus there were various investments and consultancies over the years. His holdings in Britain and overseas. It all amounted to a healthy income.'

'My understanding is that he was in financial difficulty.'

Morgan pursed his lips, as if she had personally insulted him. 'Sir James was an extravagant man. He spent money almost as fast as he made it. But, yes, these past few months have been particularly difficult. He had incurred substantial losses.'

This tallied with the testimony of Edmond de Vries, Herriot's son. The collapse of Herriot's holdings in the West Indies had decimated his finances.

'Was he bankrupt?'

'He hadn't officially declared bankruptcy. But, yes, he was headed that way. He'd had to liquidate assets in England. Move large sums around to cover his debts. It wasn't enough to save the sinking ship.'

'Did he approach you just after Christmas to tell you he'd come into money? That he was investing in a club?'

He frowned. 'No. There was nothing like that.'

It was as Persis had expected. Herriot hadn't shared the fact of his newfound source of wealth with his own bookkeeper, the man he trusted with his finances. Why not?

The answer was obvious. It was not the sort of wealth that could be accounted for legitimately.

She shifted in her seat. 'I want to ask you about a particular expenditure. Regular payments made to a boarding school in Panvel.'

He twitched, his demeanour changing. 'I know the payments you mean. It was that aide of his. Lal.'

'I'm sorry?'

'Madan Lal. The man's a crook.'

'Please explain.'

'He was Sir James's go-between. He'd come and throw his weight around. Tell me that Sir James had asked for this expenditure or that. Usually, it would be large sums of cash. At first, I would double-check with Sir James, but he always confirmed that he'd given Lal the instructions; pretty soon, he began to get annoyed. Accused me of "wasting his time". The truth was that he wanted a degree of separation between himself and that money. That's why he gave Lal power of attorney to sign cheques on his behalf – with my counter-signature. I knew what the cash was for, of course. Bribes. Payoffs. Lal was a glorified gopher. A bagman, as they call them in the States.'

'Who was Sir James paying bribes to?'

'Does it matter? This is India, Inspector. Nothing gets done without someone's palm being greased. Sir James was a political agent, a good one. He knew what it took to make things happen out here. When in Rome, yes? And some of those payments, I suspect, were to women, women he'd got into trouble. Like I said, the man led an extravagant life.'

She absorbed this. 'Tell me about the payments to the school.'

'That was an odd one. Lal came to me in mid-1946 to explain that Sir James wanted to pay for some kid's school fees. Eye-watering sum. By then, I wasn't in the habit of querying him, so I approved the payment. I assumed the kid was the result of Sir James's philandering, another of his dirty little secrets. Each term Lal would come along to sign a new cheque. Regular as clockwork.' He stopped. 'But then, a few weeks before his death, Sir James asked me to go over all his expenditure with a fine-tooth comb. I guess he'd found out about the collapse of his holdings and was seeing where he might economise. I did as I was asked.

'I called him back on New Year's Eve. I'd forgotten he was having a party. I hadn't been invited, of course. No one wants their account-ant where their friends can talk to them.' He flashed a mirthless smile. 'At any rate, I went through a list of things where I thought he could tighten his belt, including the vast sum he was spending on this kid at the Heart of Mary School. He hadn't a clue what I was talking about. It took a moment for the penny to drop.

'Lal had pulled the wool over both our eyes. You almost have to admire the man.'

'And you didn't think it was important to come forward with this information?'

He shrugged. 'No one asked me. And then you caught your man, so it seemed irrelevant.'

*   *   *

The home of Elizabeth Campbell turned out to be a breezy bungalow near the Taj Hotel in Apollo Bundar. Persis was let in by a mousy native housemaid and directed into a drawing room featuring heavy Victorian furniture and thick curtains. The gloom bothered her, and she flung the curtains back to reveal a verdant garden in desperate need of the attentions of a *mali*.

A mynah bird flashed on to a branch of a tree abutting the windows and cocked its head at her.

When Elizabeth arrived, she was dressed in a shapeless bathrobe, and seemed somewhat the worse for wear. The woman had been drinking; her blue eyes were bloodshot and an unsavoury odour wafted from her. Unbidden, the word *louche* flapped its way into Persis's thoughts.

Elizabeth looked at her blankly, then flopped on to a sofa and lit a cigarette. Persis took the chair opposite her.

'Don't you just hate mornings?' said the Scotswoman. She stuck out a leg, wiggled her toes into the Shiraz rug at her feet. 'If God had intended us to rise with the larks, he would have made us earthworms.'

Persis refrained from pointing out that it was almost afternoon.

'Tell me about your affair. With Sir James.'

Her eyes widened, but she said nothing.

'Was it to get back at your father? You blamed him for the death of Satyajit Sharma, a man you loved.'

'How – how did you find out? About James?'

'Mrs Gupta. She saw you with him. At Laburnum House.'

She grimaced. 'Yes. I approached James. This was weeks before his death. I made him believe I wanted him. I knew that he had a wandering eye. I couldn't think of anyone I might be with who would annoy my father more.'

'Were you in his study on the night of the ball? Just before his death?'

She shook her head. 'No. I – I told him that I wanted to. I was ready to go through with it. But—' She bit her lip. 'I just couldn't. The idea of him touching me.' She shuddered.

Persis's thoughts ticked over in the silence. Was she telling the truth?

'Did your father know about this?'

'Not until that night.'

'What do you mean?'

She coloured. 'You have to understand. I was furious at my father. I couldn't stop thinking about Satyajit. So I – I did something foolish.' She lifted her chin. 'I told him that I had slept with James.'

'You lied?'

'Yes. I'm not proud of it. I just – I wanted to hurt him the way he had hurt me.'

Persis paused, mind whirling.

'What did he do?'

'He was livid, of course. He'd already suspected that something was wrong. James had begun to avoid him ever since I'd started making overtures. He didn't want to risk giving the game away. But my father had noticed anyway. He wasn't the only one. Tongues were wagging that they'd fallen out. Even at the party James kept his distance.'

'What did he do that night? After you told him?'

The woman steeled herself. 'He went up to confront James. But he came back down within minutes. He was acting strangely. Said he hadn't found him and that he'd speak to him later.'

Persis paused. 'Do you believe that?'

She did not answer.

Persis waited, then: 'Why now? It's been over a year since Satyajit died.'

'Because I thought that time would make the pain go away. I was wrong.'

Persis looked at her squarely. 'Do you think your father killed Sir James?'

Her face crumpled. 'The truth? I don't know.'

There was no direct train to Pandiala. The Frontier Mail ran north for almost twenty hours to Delhi, stopping there for an hour, then turning north-west towards Amritsar for a further six. They would arrive in the Punjabi city some time on the afternoon of the 7th, halt for another hour, then continue to Pandiala, forty minutes further on.

They met on the platform, a swirling mass of passengers, porters, beggars, lepers and snack vendors. Blackfinch stuck out like a flamingo at a convention of crows. She spotted him, a tall island in the midst of the maelstrom, dressed in cream trousers and a sports jacket, his dark hair flopping around his head. He clutched a single battered-looking suitcase. A group of beggars had formed a ring around him, hands outstretched, beseeching animatedly. He seemed oblivious.

He spotted her and waved enthusiastically as if flagging down a taxi. She was glad he was on time. Bombay operated two distinct time regimes: the city's municipal body followed 'Bombay Time', based on the movement of the sun, while the railways, telegraph system and, frankly, most other parts of the country, followed Indian Standard Time, set by the longitude of the Madras observatory. The thirty-minute time difference gave Bombayites the perfect excuse to turn up late for just about everything.

She fought her way to him. 'Here,' she said. 'I bought tickets for two cabins in the first-class compartment.'

'Well done,' he said, beaming at her. He seemed disconcertingly buoyant. She wondered if he'd been at the Black Dog. His eyes ran over her chosen attire – jodhpurs, ankle boots, a white blouson and a wide-brimmed fedora. She had considered wearing her uniform but Punjab was well out of her jurisdiction. Given her current status, it seemed pointless drawing attention to herself.

'You look all set for a safari.'

She frowned. 'These clothes are practical for the journey.'

Blackfinch's smile faltered. 'Well, of course—'

'They allow me freedom of movement while also being comfortable in the hot weather.'

'I didn't mean—'

'I did not feel the need to dress up just because you were accompanying me.'

'That's not what—'

A series of loud, shrill whistles rescued the Englishman. The chaos on the platform ascended to an elemental pitch. A uniformed ticket-master watched them from the nearest bogie with a phlegmatic expression. His jaw moved rhythmically; he leaned over and shot a jet of betel nut on to the baking tarmac.

Persis shuddered. She had always hated the habit.

They plunged through the swarming throng to the front of the train, beggars clinging to Blackfinch's legs, clambered aboard, and made their way up the corridor to their respective cabins.

'Side by side,' said Blackfinch. 'How convenient.'

'What do you mean?'

He beamed at her. 'Oh, you know, if this was a movie . . .'

She continued to look at him.

His smile dipped in wattage. 'Never mind. I was just being humorous.'

They stared at each other, two singular individuals lost in a maze of their own making.

'I have some work to catch up on,' said Blackfinch eventually. 'How about we meet up for dinner? They have a dining compartment, right?'

'Yes,' said Persis. 'For first-class passengers only.'

'Seven?'

'Seven will be fine.'

Her cabin was small, but tidy. The leather of the long seat taking up one side of the berth was vividly maroon and cracked only in the corners. A mural covered the wall above the seat, disguising storage units containing blankets and bolsters. On the opposite side, a pull-down bunk would serve as her bed for the night portion of the journey. She hoisted her suitcase on to the overhead storage rack.

The cabin was pleasantly warm. Kicking off her shoes, she removed a bolster from the cupboards, and stretched out on the seat with a book.

The book was a strange little thing, published the previous summer in Britain, and only recently making it to Indian shores. Her father had purchased a few copies for the shop, and instantly regretted it. 'It will never sell,' he had told her.

It was called *1984*, by an English author she had never read before: George Orwell. She had found the premise intriguing. A future world where perpetual war reigned, and government had become little more than oppression. The concept of the Thought Police, in particular, bothered her, the idea that individualism and independent thinking might actually be considered a crime.

She had only a few pages to go. She didn't mind that the book was heading towards a bleak ending. What concerned her more was the capitulation of the character of Julia, Winston's lover. Winston, the supposed hero, she had pegged as a coward halfway through the novel. Despite his rebellious thoughts, she had been certain that he would ultimately betray the ideals he claimed to harbour. But in Julia she had seen shades of herself. To have her fold to the Thought Police seemed a misstep by the author. She should have emerged as a heroine, or a martyr, at the least. One line, attributed to Julia, stayed with her – in her present situation it had taken on a new significance: 'Sometimes they threaten you with something, something you can't stand up to, can't even think about. And then you say, "Don't do it to me, do it to somebody else."'

Her eyes became heavy in the afternoon heat, the train's gentle rocking adding to the soporific effect. Her head lolled on her chest, and the book slipped to the floor.

She awoke with a start. Rubbing the sleep from her eyes, she checked her watch. It was twenty past seven.

Cursing, she rose from the bunk, excavated her make-up set from her suitcase, then went into the corridor to visit the bathroom.

Fifteen minutes later, she found Blackfinch in the cramped dining compartment.

'Fashionably late,' he said, without rancour, as she slipped into the seat opposite.

'My apologies,' she said. 'I – uh – became engrossed in some work.'

'Well, no harm done. I have a bad habit of always being on time. In India, this has proven to be somewhat of a handicap. May I order you a drop of firewater?'

'A whisky, please.'

They drank in silence for a bit, the hubbub of conversation rising and falling around them.

'It's magnificent, isn't it?' said Blackfinch eventually. He had shed his sports jacket and rolled up the sleeves of his breezy white shirt. His face glowed with heat and good cheer. She wondered how many drinks he had already had.

'What is?'

'These old trains. There's a sense of majesty, history. Decadence, dare I say. Makes one proud to be British.'

'The British built these trains so that they could plunder the subcontinent. Tens of thousands of Indians died to build them. The rails are literally soaked in blood.'

That strangled the conversation for a while.

A waiter arrived and took their order. Outside the window, fields of yellow mustard made a bright splash of colour. They were somewhere between Surat and Indore, she guessed, a swathe of farmland bursting with winter crops.

She noticed Blackfinch fiddling with the salt and pepper shakers, lining them up.

'Why do you do that?'

He hadn't realised that she was watching him. He coloured and for a moment was lost for words. 'I can't help it,' he finally said, as if confessing to a crime. 'Ever since I was young I've had this compulsion for order, neatness. Straight lines. It used to drive my parents to distraction.'

'It doesn't sound like a bad thing.'

'It does when you throw a fit just because your laces aren't tied the right way, or because the number of peas on your plate isn't precisely the same as the day before.' He gave a brittle smile. 'Therapy has helped me control those instincts to a great degree.'

'You see a therapist?' She couldn't hide her astonishment.

'Saw,' he corrected. 'I didn't have much choice. My behaviour was a great source of shame for my father.' He lifted his glass and gulped his whisky. 'On the bright side, it *has* proved to be a useful trait career-wise. I have a rare ability to notice details, to parse facts from a tumult of raw data. I'm still not very good with people.'

'You seem perfectly fine to me,' she said, and then looked away.

'Thank you. I must admit it's unusual for me to be so comfortable around someone. I usually say or do something awkward that puts them off.'

She realised she knew almost nothing about this man. She found herself asking questions, personal questions that, under normal circumstances, would have eluded her.

'Ah. You want to know what makes me tick.' He smiled good-naturedly. 'Let me see . . . My childhood was unremarkable. I never had many friends – my, ah, *manner* put them off, I suppose. My closest friend was my older brother. Pythagoras. Though he insisted on us calling him Thad. Short for Thaddeus – his middle name. When my father passed away, it was Thad who gave the eulogy even though I was the one who'd followed in his footsteps. Into the sciences, I mean.

'Thad is a farmer. A thousand head of cattle, some sheep, a few chickens. His wife is a no-nonsense country woman. They have twin girls, six years old, blue eyes and carrot-red curls, just like their mother. They adore *me*, of course. Uncle Archie, scientist and world-bestriding Colossus. I usually see them at Christmas.

'What else is there to say? I play cricket – though not very well. I read – mainly science and ancient history. I'm a decent hand at poker. And my marriage failed for reasons that I can neither explain nor find myself overly concerned by.' He smiled brightly. 'I'm actually quite dull, when you think about it.'

He asked about her. 'What do you do when you're not working?'

The question caught her off guard. It wasn't that she didn't have other interests, but the fact was that her career had become all-consuming. Was she missing out on the life that Aunt Nussie claimed awaited her, a life of gaiety, romance, social acceptance?

She didn't think so. She was a policewoman because she believed in something greater than herself, greater than the ambitions that any legion of Aunt Nussies might have held for her. Justice. A precious flame – like the holy fire of Zoroastrianism – to be nurtured and shielded against the tyrannies of those who would subvert the fundamental rules of her world: equality, decency and fair play.

As for what she did when she was not working . . . 'I read,' she said. 'I swim. I practise martial arts. I visit museums. I listen to the radio. I sit with my father. I feed my cat.'

Their food arrived. 'So, tell me,' he said, picking at his chicken ballotine, 'how goes it with your beau?'

'My beau?'

'The chap who's wooing you. Mr Benson and Pryce.'

'Darius?' She frowned. 'He's not my beau. He's my cousin.'

'Well, when has a little incest ever stopped anyone? Haven't you ever heard the term "kissing cousins"?'

'We have never kissed,' she said hotly.

He raised his fork in surrender. 'I was just joking. Christ, you're in a bum humour this evening.'

She glared at him. 'What about you?'

'What about me?'

'How was your lunch date?'

He seemed mystified. 'What lunch date?'

'Yesterday. You left for a lunch date.'

His face broadened into a smile. 'Oh, that. Mrs Saunders.'

She stiffened. 'You had a lunch date with a married woman?'

'There's no law against it.'

She set down her fork. 'Is her husband still alive?' She was not going to be caught out a second time.

'I should hope so. I'm due to play bridge with him next week.'

She looked astonished. 'You maintain a friendship with him while – while *going around* with his wife?' Her eyes smouldered. 'Does he know of this?'

'Of what?'

'That you were having lunch with his wife!'

'Well, I'm not sure if he knew of this *specific* instance of lunch. But the general concept of lunches? Yes, I'd say he was aware of them.'

'And you will continue to see this woman?'

'Mrs Saunders? Yes, of course. She's an absolute riot. We have a lot of fun together.'

'But it is immoral!'

He sipped at his whisky, eyes lit with amusement. 'Really? I had no idea. You have some funny old ways over here. In England, lunching with an old friend of the family is hardly considered a violation of the Ten Commandments.'

'A friend of the family?' she echoed.

'Mrs Saunders is seventy-three. She's a friend of my mother's. She and her husband are wintering out here.'

Persis was momentarily speechless. And then she felt a tug at the corners of her mouth. Against her will, she broke into a smile.

'You see,' he beamed at her. 'It's not that difficult.'

'What isn't that difficult?'

'Enjoying yourself.' His eyes twinkled at her above the glass.

They discussed the case over dessert. She laid out everything she had discovered.

The case had solidified around two sets of suspects. First, the Singh-Lal-Gupta nexus. And then there was Robert Campbell and his daughter.

They threw around various theories about how Singh, Lal and Gupta might have conspired to murder Herriot, but nothing made sense. And why had Singh confessed? Without his confession, they would have had little proof that any of them had been directly involved in the murder.

As for Campbell and his daughter . . . 'I find it difficult to believe that Elizabeth had anything to do with Herriot's death,' said Blackfinch.

'That doesn't surprise me,' she said woodenly.

'What's that supposed to mean?'

'Nothing,' she muttered, flushing.

He stared at her, then carried on. 'If Elizabeth isn't the woman Herriot slept with that night then who?'

'I don't know. I suspected Gupta, but she denies it.'

He leaned back. 'With so many suspects, one might ask why we are heading to Punjab. I mean, don't get me wrong. I'm glad to be here, but Herriot's trip to Pandiala may have had nothing to do with his death.'

She hesitated. 'You're right. But as I told you, there's another reason I wanted to go north.'

'Ah. Yes. A visit to Maan Singh's home. What do you hope to find?'

'I really don't know.'

Night fell, and the train rattled onwards. They stopped around midnight at a rural station. Unable to sleep, she went to the nearest doorway, and was astonished to see a silent stream of locals clambering on to the roof of the train, some with bundles of clothing, one or two with battered old cases. They reminded her of langurs swarming over the ramparts of the Castella de Aguada, the old Portuguese fort in Bombay.

A grey-faced man looked out at her sadly from the stationmaster's office. A sign said: INDIAN RAILWAYS: SAFETY AND PUNCTUALITY.

Already a lie, she thought, on two counts.

Back in the corridor, she wondered if Blackfinch was still awake. She vacillated, contemplating the idea of knocking, but then turned and walked the few steps back to her cabin.

A bat had flown in and settled into a comfortable corner above her bunk. She didn't mind. She had no fear of bats.

She read a little more, then turned out the light.

The bat squeaked gently in the darkness.

21

7 January 1950

The train panted on through the morning, stopping for an hour at Delhi before continuing to Amritsar, arriving around 2 p.m. An hour's rest stop was scheduled before the onward journey to Pandiala.

They took a taxi into the city, the cab nosing its way out towards the periphery. 'The home you are looking for is in one of the poorest sections of Amritsar,' explained their driver. 'Near the old Sultanwind Gate.'

The roads gradually became narrower, the houses less well maintained.

By the time he braked to a halt, they had entered a maze of rundown alleyways, whitewashed houses on either side, a thick stench hanging in the air from the open sewers. They stopped at the mouth of an alley. 'It's too narrow for the taxi, madam. I will wait for you here.'

It took them a further five minutes to find Singh's home.

The door was open.

Persis knocked and then ducked inside, Blackfinch close behind, into the sort of home common in the subcontinent: a bedroom, a living room-cum-kitchen, a bathroom. A woman in traditional shalwar kameez sat cross-legged in the corner, grinding wheat using a *chakki* – a flour mill fashioned from coarse stone.

Her eyes widened as they entered and she scrambled to her feet. 'Who are you?' she asked, in Punjabi, placing her hands on her hips. She was a small but strong-looking woman, dusky, with a hard jaw and incongruously full lips.

Persis had a crude grasp of the dialect – it was not so removed from Hindi that she could not follow it. She discovered that the woman was Maan Singh's wife, Rano.

It became immediately clear that Rano knew of her husband's predicament – how could she not? It had been front page news.

Quickly, Persis explained their presence. 'I'm here to understand why Maan Singh did what he did.'

The woman's face slackened in astonishment. She stared at them, then turned away, racked with emotion. 'How – how is he?'

'He has confessed to murder. Unless he changes his story, he will be tried, convicted and hanged.'

'I knew he would do something like this,' whispered the woman.

'What's she saying?' interrupted Blackfinch.

'She's his wife. She doesn't speak English. You'll have to be patient.'

The Englishman subsided, a look of irritation shading his brow.

'How long have you been married?' asked Persis.

'Five years. We were married when he came home from the army. We've known each other since we were young.'

'Do you have children?'

'Yes. Our son is three years old. He is out with his grandmother.'

'Is he the reason you are here and not in Bombay?'

She grimaced. 'I called the prison. They spoke to him for me. His only message was that I forget him.'

Persis considered her next question. 'Why did he leave the army?'

She did not answer; her gaze fell away.

Persis tried another route. 'What did he do when he returned from the war?'

'Nothing.' She hesitated. 'I mean, he gets occasional work, as a labourer, a doorman, but he has no regular occupation. He's too full of anger to last anywhere.'

'That must have been difficult.'

Rano did not reply.

'Did your husband ever talk about his war years? Specifically, about his fellow soldiers in the last unit he served in? A man named Madan Lal and another named Duleep Gupta?'

Recognition flared in her eyes, but she said nothing. There was something there; Persis could feel it. Lal and Singh had known each other from the war, yet neither man had mentioned that fact. Lal had hired Singh shortly before Herriot had been killed. By their own admission, they were the ones who had found the Englishman's body.

The smoke of conspiracy filtered into her nose.

'Why would your husband leave his wife and a young child to go to Bombay?'

Silence.

Persis stepped closer towards her. 'I'm not convinced that your husband murdered Sir James. At least not on his own. Help me to understand why he would confess to such a thing.'

Rano searched the policewoman's face, seeking a lie. Hope flickered in her eyes. 'He received a call. From Madan Lal. Lal asked him to come to Bombay. He said he had a job for him.'

'That couldn't have been the only reason. I mean, he left you behind. Why?'

The woman bit her lip.

'Did it have something to do with his sister? She was married to Duleep Gupta, wasn't she?'

She nodded. 'Her name is Lalita. Unlike Maan, she studied hard in school. She went to Bombay to find work. That's where she met Duleep. Lal used to invite Maan and Duleep back to his Bombay home while they were on leave from the army. Lalita and Duleep got to know one another. They were married shortly afterwards.'

'And then Duleep died in the war.'

She nodded again. 'Lalita had a child by then. Maan told her to come back to Amritsar with him, but she refused. Bombay was her home. Life was difficult, but she was stubborn. Maan later told Lal, after he too had left the army. Lal contacted Lalita, convinced her to work for him.'

'With Sir James Herriot.' Persis pressed closer. 'Why didn't Lal find Maan Singh work with Sir James at the same time? Why, after all these years, did he call and offer Maan work?'

Her fingers worked the edges of her kameez. 'I don't know. Perhaps he didn't think Maan would accept. That's what I couldn't understand – why he agreed to work for an Englishman now. For as long as I have known him he has hated the British.'

'Why?'

She hesitated, then plunged on. 'Before the war he tried to participate in the Quit India movement but they wouldn't let him.'

'What do you mean? Who wouldn't let him?'

'The people here. The ones who ran the local committees, the ones who organised the protests and the anti-British actions.'

'I don't understand. Why wouldn't they want him to be involved?'

'Because they could not forgive him.'

'Forgive him for what?'

'For his father.'

Persis prompted the woman to expand.

'His father was at Jallianwala Bagh,' explained Rano.

A light began to dawn. Jallianwala Bagh. The incident that had lit the touch-paper for Gandhi's non-cooperation initiative and galvanised the independence movement.

On 13 April 1919 close to a thousand locals had gathered at a walled garden in Amritsar known as Jallianwala Bagh. They had come to celebrate the Sikh festival of Baisakhi, and to peacefully protest against the continued presence of the British. Local British commander Acting Brigadier General Reginald Dyer, having got wind of the situation, and with the recently passed Rowlatt Act in mind – the ruling that banned seditious gatherings – assembled a troop of ninety soldiers from the 9th Gurkhas, the 54th Sikhs and the 59th Sind Rifles. Arriving at the Bagh with armoured vehicles, machine guns and a complement of .303 Lee Enfield bolt-action rifles, Dyer blocked the exits to the Bagh. He then ordered his troops to begin shooting – with no warning – at the densest section of the crowd, later explaining to the British House of Commons that his intent had 'not been to disperse the meeting but to punish the Indians for their disobedience'.

A ceasefire was ordered only when the soldiers' ammunition was spent.

Almost a thousand men, women and children lay dead, including a six-week-old infant.

The consequences of the massacre were far-reaching.

Word spread throughout imperial India, inflaming anti-British passions. In Britain, Dyer was at first fêted, but later, as the truth began to filter through, faced political censure.

'I understand,' said Persis. 'Maan Singh grew up to discover that the British had killed his father at Jallianwala Bagh. Sir James became the target for his rage.'

But the woman was shaking her head. 'You *don't* understand,' she said. 'My husband's father was not killed at Jallianwala Bagh. He is the one who did the killing.'

22

The Golden Temple Hotel wasn't shy of displaying its Raj-era sensibilities: a freshly painted maroon façade, shuttered French windows, and a chandelier the size of an inverted pyramid in the lobby. They had arrived at the hotel just over an hour after returning to their train in Amritsar following the visit to Singh's home.

Persis had called ahead to book two rooms.

At the reception counter, the attendant, a thickset man in a dark suit and heavy moustache, eyed them with a look that she couldn't quite fathom until Blackfinch leaned in and whispered, 'He's probably wondering why we're in separate rooms. My guess is that this is one of those places where British sahibs entertained their Indian mistresses.'

She shot him a look. A smile stretched his features. She scowled, and turned back to the attendant. 'Tell me, have you been working here long?'

'Twenty years, madam. My name is Ondha.'

'Mr Ondha, I am a policewoman. My colleague is a detective from London. We are here to investigate the movements of a British gentleman I believe stayed here recently, a man named Sir James Herriot.'

Ondha smiled. 'Madam, Amritsar may be far from the centre now but we are no backwater. I know who you are.' He paused. 'It was my understanding that you had already concluded the investigation into Sir James's death.'

'We have,' said Blackfinch firmly before Persis could reply. 'We are merely tying up loose ends.'

'Anything we can do to help, sir, we shall be most honoured.'

'Do you recall Sir James?' asked Persis.

'Of course. He stayed with us for two nights. December 25th and 26th. He left on the 27th.'

'Did he say why he was here?'

'No, madam. But it was official business, I believe.'

'What makes you say that?'

'The few Britishers who come here now are rarely here for tourism. If they are, it is because they wish to see the Golden Temple in nearby Amritsar or to participate in a hunt. Wild boar, nilgai, panther. Sir James expressed no such interest.'

'What *did* he do?'

'He requested a touring car. He wished to be driven into the surrounding villages.'

'Do you know where he went?'

'I am afraid not, madam.'

She frowned, glanced at Blackfinch.

'However, there is a way to find out,' continued Ondha. He banged the bell atop the counter. Another man, slimmer and younger, with a clipped moustache and pockmarked cheeks, emerged from a door behind him. 'This is our concierge, Prakash.' He turned to the newcomer. 'Do you remember Sir James?'

'Yes, of course.'

'You procured a car for him during his stay here. Do you remember who the driver was?'

'Yes. Kulraj Singh.'

'Can you please locate him and bring him here?'

'What should I tell him?'

'Tell him that we have passengers for him.'

'One more question,' said Persis. 'Did Sir James meet with anyone while he was here?'

'In the hotel?' Ondha considered this. 'Yes. Now that I recall, there was someone. A local, by the looks of him. He came in very late on the evening of the 25th, after Sir James had returned from his day of touring. Refused to give his name. Just said that he had urgent business with Sir James. I called his room. They spoke on the phone, then Sir James told me to send him up. He came down an hour later.'

'Do you know what they spoke about?'

'I'm afraid not, madam.'

The room was opulent, with a large bed, a carpeted floor and hand-carved teak furniture. She wondered how the hotel continued to survive. Partition had decimated commerce in the region; she suspected that tourism had been one of the hardest hit industries. Perhaps the evergreen popularity of the nearby Golden Temple had something to do with it.

Next to the telephone was a notepad. She feathered her fingertips over the topmost sheet. It was headed with the legend: The Golden Temple Hotel. Just below it, the words: *By a pool of nectar, at the shrine of the sixty-eight.*

Sir James had been here. He'd ripped a sheet from a pad like this and scribbled the name Bakshi on it, and a reference to what she believed was a plot of land. Had his mysterious visitor given him that name? Who was Bakshi? What did the enigmatic note mean?

Persis stowed her luggage, then stepped into the shower.

Fifteen minutes later, she stood in front of the room's full-length mirror, wrapped in a towel, brushing her long dark hair. A worm of excitement stirred in her stomach. She hadn't felt this free in a long time. Just being here, following in Herriot's footsteps, felt like a small victory.

She had already made progress. The revelation that Maan Singh's father had been one of the men who had opened fire on civilians during the Amritsar Massacre had stunned her.

Haridas Singh had been only twenty at the time, father to a one-year-old son – Maan Singh – and had no idea of the crushing judgement of history that awaited him. He had been trained to follow orders, unthinkingly, unquestioningly. But the aftermath of that bloody day at Jallianwala Bagh would haunt him for the remainder of his life.

A year after the massacre he quit the Imperial Army, unable to live with the spectres of his fellow Sikhs; they had begun to follow him around, the men, women and children he had murdered at Dyer's behest. In his neighbourhood, once it became known that he was one of the butchers of Jallianwala Bagh, he became a pariah. He was assaulted on numerous occasions. No one would employ him. He became a drunk. His children suffered. For Maan Singh, the humiliation was particularly brutal. Branded the son of a traitor, excluded from his community, something warped inside him as he grew to adulthood.

Later, the army offered an escape. The irony was not lost on him. His father had killed men for the British. And now Singh would too. Yet it was a way out of the daily humiliation of life in Amritsar, and so he took it. He wanted to fight for something noble, to undo his father's legacy.

But he found no nobility in that war, only more confusion. He had thought the war would rid him of his past, but he had been wrong. The past found him, out in the jungle of Burma, and so he quit.

Back home in Amritsar, the rage festered. Independence arrived, but it was bittersweet. He could take no solace from it, not with his father's crime hanging over the future – his own and the future of his child.

And then, one day, his old comrade-in-arms, Madan Lal, called, asking him to come to Bombay. To work for Sir James Herriot. An Englishman.

It dawned on Persis that perhaps she had misjudged the situation, after all. Could it be that Singh *was* guilty of the murder? Certainly, his possible motive for killing Sir James had become clearer.

A knock startled her out of her contemplation. Without thinking she strode to the door and swung it back, then realised too late that she should have put on a dressing gown.

Blackfinch stood framed in the doorway. He too had showered and changed, his hair neatly swept back for once. He peered in at her and a momentary astonishment crossed his features.

'Well,' he said, his eyes passing quickly over her naked shoulders, her glistening hair, lingering on the tightly wrapped towel around her.

'I was just getting ready.'

'Ondha called me. They've located the driver. He's waiting for us in the lobby.'

'I'll be ready shortly.'

'Right.'

They stared at each other.

'Right. I shall make my way downstairs.'

The driver, Kulraj Singh, was a short, barrel-chested man with a white beard like a prophet's, curling whiskers, and a red turban. His lower half was enveloped in a colourful green cotton lungi, his torso in a cream kurta. He smelled strongly of a spicy aftershave as powerful as mustard gas.

'Do you speak English?' asked Persis.

'Most excellently, madam,' replied Kulraj.

'Do you remember Sir James?' she asked.

'Certainly.'

'And do you recall exactly where you drove him to?'

'I do. Sahib visited the local police *thana* here in Pandiala, and then he drove out to the village of Jalanpur.'

She guessed that Herriot had visited the police station to discover the exact location of the Muslim landowner's murder that had brought him out to Pandiala – it was what she would have done. Even if the investigation had not been based here, word would have reached sister stations in the region. Herriot's enquiries must have led him to the village of Jalanpur.

'Please take us there.'

Kulraj gave a sort of half bow, then turned and led them out towards his waiting vehicle. Persis had been expecting a jeep of some description, but the car parked outside was a Buick Roadmaster, maroon with white-rimmed tyres. The spotless bonnet gleamed in the morning sun.

Blackfinch gave a low whistle. 'What a beauty!'

'A gift from my late master,' explained Kulraj. 'When he left for Pakistan he gave me the car. She is the last memory I have of a good man.'

23

The village of Jalanpur lay five miles to the west of Pandiala, practically on the Pakistan border. The road was rutted, marked by
ancient piles of dung. The Buick bounced along in the late afternoon heat.

They were forced to stop while a herd of goats crossed the road.
A tall Sikh with a staff stared at Blackfinch, then spat into the
dust.

'What was that about?' asked the Englishman.

'Punjab has always been a volatile place,' said their driver, accelerating into a bend at breakneck speed. 'During the struggle, there
were many competing interests here. Those who owned the land
were loyal to the British – the Muslim, Hindu and even Sikh
zamindars. They had everything to lose once the British left. But
when they saw that independence was inevitable they began to
fight among each other. The Muslims chose to stand behind the
Muslim League. They were the majority here, so you can imagine
how much trouble that caused.'

They hummed along.

'By rights Amritsar should be the capital of Punjab,' continued
Kulraj. 'But Nehru will never let that happen. We are too close to
the border. They call us Lahore's twin – it's only fifty miles away.
We should never have let them have it. Amritsar is our religious
heart; but Lahore was our cultural capital. One day we will get it
back.' He glanced in the mirror. 'Do you know where our capital
now lies?'

Blackfinch shook his head.

'In Shimla.' This with an exhalation of disgust. 'The British used Shimla as their summer capital and now the Congress administers Punjab from your old offices there.'

'Cyril Radcliffe was given an impossible task,' mused Blackfinch, speaking of the man who had drawn the Partition line. 'He was just a civil servant, not a politician nor a cartographer. He had never even visited India before. They gave him a month to divide the country. I've always wondered what it must have been like, out here with the raging heat, the mosquitoes, the push and pull of a thousand factional voices, knowing that history was looking over his shoulder. It's a wonder it didn't drive him mad.'

Persis glanced at him. The man seemed oblivious. She wondered if fear was something alien to him, another side effect of that strange quirk in his character. It occurred to her that he was probably in some danger. This wasn't Bombay. She shouldn't have brought him here.

The scenery became increasingly agricultural, field after field of winter crops, broken up by earthen dividers. Oxen yoked to ploughs. Bullock carts. They crossed a muddy river, where a glossy water buffalo was submerged to the shoulder. A motorbike roared by, shattering the illusion of rural serenity.

They drove into the heart of the village, a collection of low, white-washed brick buildings bisected by dusty roads. Kulraj brought the Buick sedately to a stop outside a single-storey structure ornamented with a wooden sign that read: LAND REGISTRY OFFICE.

'Sir James visited this place.'

They got out and walked towards the building. The village quadrangle was deserted, but Persis caught eyes peering at them from the surrounding buildings. News would spread soon enough.

The registry office housed three airless rooms. A peon dozed in a chair at the front, snoring loudly. Persis poked him in the shoulder and he awoke with a start. She explained that they wished to meet the man in charge. He stared at her, then ran off to fetch his superior.

Ten minutes later, a slim man in a dhoti and white shirt arrived. He wore no turban, but his moustache was full and encroached over his lips. A sandalwood-paste caste mark was daubed between his eyebrows. He introduced himself as Nayar, the village *patwari*, a government functionary who acted as the record-keeper for rural hamlets such as Jalanpur. It was his duty to ensure that the land records were continually updated, the particulars of ownership and use of each plot within the village's jurisdiction. With the impending land reform initiative under way, the position of *patwari* had become critical across the country. Her father had grimly forecast that the reality of enacting such reform could well cost Nehru his premiership. Untying the millennia-old knots of feudal landholding would take more than an edict from the centre. No doubt many poor tenants would feel the wrath of their landlords before the war was won.

'Do you remember the Englishman, Sir James? He came here recently. He met with you.'

Nayar was impassive. 'He did.'

'What did he want?'

Nayar hesitated. He did not seem particularly impressed with her authority.

Blackfinch stepped forward. 'She asked you a question.'

Nayar visibly shrank. 'He wished to examine our land records, sahib.'

Persis felt the heat of humiliation, the sting of being a woman in a society that was not only male dominated but that lacked even the basic notion of equality between the sexes. In this northern hinterland, her status as a celebrity police officer meant little. She realised, to her chagrin, that, if nothing else, having Blackfinch here would aid her task immeasurably. Without him, she doubted that she would get very far with men like Nayar.

'We'd like to see those records,' continued Blackfinch. '*Now*,' he added sternly.

The *patwari* hesitated, then nodded and vanished into the rear of the building, returning swiftly with a cloth-bound ledger, three field books and two large cloth maps. He unrolled them on to a wooden table. 'These maps cover all the land within the jurisdiction of Jalanpur.'

Persis scanned the maps, the jigsaw profusion of plot markings, annotations and numbers in red ink. 'Who owns these plots?'

'The majority of these landholdings belonged to the family of the Nawab Sikandar Ali Mumtaz. Unfortunately, the nawab died in a fire some years back. His line was ended there. Since then, the land has come under the governance of the village council. The government has yet to decide on its distribution.'

Persis felt the tingle of revelation. This was the Partition crime that had been in the file, the crime that had drawn Herriot northwards. The murder of a Muslim landowner. And now she had a name. The Nawab Sikandar Ali Mumtaz.

Nayar spoke in a mixture of English and Hindi that Blackfinch found difficult to follow. His head swivelled back and forth between them as if he were a spectator at a tennis match.

'Tell me about the fire,' said Persis. 'My understanding is that it was started deliberately.'

Nayar's eyes widened but he said nothing.

She referred to her notebook again to check the name and sequence that Herriot had scribbled on to the sheet of stationery he had taken from the Golden Temple Hotel.

BAKSHI. PLT41/85ACRG11

She now referred back to the maps and realised that in structure this number mirrored the annotations on them. Excitement fluttered inside her.

'Show me the field books.'

Nayar handed her the first of the three field books. She rifled through it, columns of entries in both English and Hindi, lists of names, acreage, plot use and status of the tenancy. The majority, as Nayar had said, were owned by the nawab's family, and sharecropped by others, or rented by tenants. Each plot was given its own landholding number and a name that denoted the tenant or sharecropper.

It took her just ten minutes to find the entry she was looking for. It might have gone swifter with the *patwari*'s help but she did not trust the man.

And there it was. PLT41/85ACRG11. Herriot had been here, had made a note of this entry. Why?

The plot – plot number 41 – was sizeable, one of the largest on the maps, eighty-five acres. The name in the field ledger was Vikas Bakshi.

Bakshi.

'Tell me about Vikas Bakshi,' Persis said, her finger still on the page.

Nayar blinked. 'He was a longstanding tenant in the village. His family had been here for generations.'

'Was?'

'They died in the rioting,' said Nayar. 'Partition wiped them out.'

Persis absorbed this. Two families destroyed by Partition. One Muslim, one Hindu. And Sir James investigating the death of one of them, had made a precise note of the other. Why?

'Who investigated the fire that killed the nawab and his family?'

'The fire was thoroughly investigated,' said the *patwari*.

'That wasn't the question I asked.'

He hesitated. Blackfinch loomed over him. 'The investigating officer was a local. Sub-Inspector Shergill.'

'Where can I find him?'

The police station was located two hundred yards from the land registry. Sub-Inspector Balwant Shergill had been summoned and was waiting for them, as was a crowd. Word had spread. Curiosity appeared to be the dominant emotion, but Persis thought she could detect an undercurrent of hostility.

Shergill was a big man, turbaned and bearded, in a scruffy khaki uniform. He made no secret of his displeasure at being summoned from his home.

'Why are you here?' he asked tersely, after Persis had introduced them.

'I am following up—'

'I know who you are,' interrupted Shergill. 'Lady police.' His contempt was obvious. 'You investigated the murder of the Englishman. If you ask me they should give Maan Singh a medal.' He glared at Blackfinch with loathing. Here was someone uncowed by the sight of a white man. And yet, Persis did not doubt that Shergill had once worked for the imperial police, had taken orders from men such as Blackfinch. Perhaps his loathing was partly for himself, the same self-hatred that had haunted Maan Singh's father.

Persis straightened. 'If you have a problem with me then we can get the Deputy Home Minister on the line. I am here at his personal behest. Do I make myself understood, *Sub*-Inspector?'

Shergill glowered.

'I wish to see the investigative report into the fire at the nawab's home.'

The report was brought out, a slim folder with a handful of papers wedged inside. She took a wooden seat behind the nearest desk and riffled through it.

It began with a preamble detailing the time and location of the incident, and then a short summary of the purported events of that night, 16 July 1947. Just a month before Partition. News of the fire had been relayed to the *thana* at Jalanpur at around eight-thirty that evening. Sub-Inspector Shergill and two constables, together with a band of locals, had rushed to the scene, only to find the nawab's mansion engulfed in flames. A human chain had been formed to ferry water from a local well, but it was useless. The fire raged out of control until the morning.

The next day they counted the charred remains of fifteen members of the nawab's household. The investigation by Shergill indicated the possibility that a faulty gas canister had caused the fire. There was no evidence to back up this assertion.

'What made you think it was a gas canister?'

Shergill scowled. 'It was the most likely explanation.'

'But you were not sure.'

'I was sure.'

'How?'

'I was sure,' he repeated.

'You did not suspect that the fire might have been started deliberately?'

'No.'

She noticed that faces were crowded in at the door and at the barred windows. Every word was being absorbed and passed back. The entire village would soon know of this conversation.

'Was the nawab well liked?' she asked.

Shergill's face darkened. 'The nawab was a hard man. He and his family became wealthy from the land of Punjab. But when the day came to defend their country, they chose to side with Jinnah and the Muslim League. So, yes, there were those who saw him as an enemy of the nation.'

'Were you one of them?' asked Blackfinch.

Something flared in the Sikh's eyes, but he did not respond.

'How was his relationship with Vikas Bakshi?' asked Persis.

This hit Shergill with the force of a blow. He had not been expecting the question and his face slackened with surprise. 'They – they were friends.'

'Even after the nawab turned towards Pakistan?'

'Bakshi was a true patriot.'

'In which case the nawab's actions would have caused resentment. But Bakshi was a mere tenant; there was little he could do. Legally, at any rate.'

The Sikh drilled his eyes forward. 'You are searching for something that isn't there.'

'Or something that has been carefully hidden.'

His lips compressed into a line.

Back out in the quadrangle, the crowd formed a knot around the Buick. As they approached the vehicle, a small, elderly man moved forward and clutched her arm.

'Hey!' said Blackfinch, but she waved him away. Something about the intensity in the old man's eyes held her.

'It was a lie,' he gasped out. 'A lie and a sacrilege.'

'What do you mean?'

But before he could reply, Shergill was there, dragging him away.

'Stop that!' she cried out.

'He's a drunk,' said Shergill. 'He has nothing to say to you.'

'Let him go.'

Shergill looked furious, but did as he had been commanded.

She approached the man. He was short, balding, with grey fuzz around his pate. Hollow, stubbled cheeks and a hooked nose. His clothes were filthy and stank. A note of alcohol wafted from his breath.

'What did you want to tell me?' she asked.

He looked down at his bare feet, refusing to meet her eyes.

'Don't be afraid,' she said. 'What did you mean? *What* was a lie?'

Silence.

She turned to Shergill. 'Who is he?'

'His name is Mangal. As I told you, he's just a drunk.'

But there was more to it than that. She sensed it with a cold certainty. This was a man who lived in the shadow of fear. Her presence had momentarily broken the shackles that bound him, but now he had retreated into the safety of silence.

As Kulraj Singh manoeuvred the Buick out of the village, she turned in her seat and looked back for the man. But he was gone.

'I'd like to see the nawab's home.'

'There is little left to see, madam,' replied Kulraj. 'And it will soon be dark.'

'Perhaps we should be heading back?' mused Blackfinch.

'You can go,' she said. 'I'll continue on foot.'

Blackfinch stared at her but said no more.

They drove a further ten minutes towards the border until they passed through an orchard of sweet-smelling mango trees. On the far side, the charred and blackened remains of the nawab's bungalow hovered on a shallow rise in the land.

They left the car and walked up the short slope. Dusk was falling, the sun flaming the tops of the trees behind them. Crows lined the fallen walls and mounds of charred bricks. They walked around the sprawling complex, but there was nothing to see.

Nevertheless, something about the place, its numen, communicated itself to her. An atrocity had occurred here, of that she was now certain. Memories of violence, bled into the earth. Men, women and children murdered. All in the name of patriotism.

Or might it have been something else? Could simple human avarice have been at work? She recalled the anonymous account that had brought Herriot out here. How it had speculated that the motive for the nawab's murder had been robbery.

From their vantage point, they could see the land sweep away to the Pakistani border, a hurricane fence topped with barbed wire. On the far side, the land was a mirror, highlighting the arbitrary nature of the division.

'Was the nawab really such a hard man?' she asked.

'I'm not from Jalanpur, madam,' said Kulraj. 'But I have friends here. Until the fire, I had heard little said against the nawab. He was no better or worse than generations of landowners. However, it is certainly true that he sided with Pakistan. That turned many against him.' He shook his head. 'The nawab and his family prospered in this region. They accumulated great wealth over many generations. It is said that he had a treasure room in his home, filled with priceless jewels – he was known for his taste in jewellery. He would think nothing of commissioning pieces from artisans in Jaipur.'

She felt as if she had just passed through a vast web, folds of gossamer feathering her cheek. 'Jewellery?'

'Yes. The nawab had a passion for it.'

Her thoughts entwined themselves. She turned to Blackfinch. 'I want to stay in Jalanpur tonight.'

'I'm not sure that's a good idea. They weren't exactly welcoming.'

'I need to speak to that man, Mangal. And I want to see the Bakshi plot. Herriot made a note of it for a reason.'

'Perhaps this Mangal really is just a drunk.'

'Even a drunk has a story to tell. And he may not be the only one. Something happened here, something that has been covered up.'

'You suspect the fire was no accident.'

'I do.'

'And Sir James came here to discover the truth.'

'He did.'

'Do you believe *that* may have led to his death?'

She hesitated. It was a long leap from Jalanpur to Laburnum House. 'I don't know.'

24

Back in the village they discovered an astonished Nayar at his home. Persis explained that they wished to stay the night and that she expected the *patwari* to make suitable arrangements.

'But there is no hotel here,' he protested.

'That is not my concern.'

He eventually led them to a single-storey dwelling at the very edge of the village, abutting a wheat field. 'This home has been abandoned since Partition. The occupants were murdered by Muslims. You may rest here for the night.' He hesitated. 'If you would like food, you may eat with me.'

They ate in the courtyard, under a blanket of stars. Dusk had fallen, and with the darkness came new sights and sounds. Kerosene lamps were lit, spreading a smoky, thick odour to mingle with the smell of food. Soon insects whirred and clicked around them. The food – simple vegetarian dishes and wheat rotis – was prepared by the *patwari*'s wife, a silent woman, clearly nervous to have them in her home. Word had spread and they were interrupted by a stream of visitors casually dropping by.

Good, thought Persis. Soon the entire village would know that they were back, including the man Mangal.

'What do you hope to achieve?' asked Nayar suddenly. The *patwari* had remained sullenly silent throughout the meal. Persis suspected the offer to eat with him had only been made so that he could keep an eye on them.

She considered her reply before speaking. 'History is a harsh judge, Nayar. It's no easy task building a nation on the ashes of the dead. The only way to do it is to sweep aside the lies and admit what happened.'

'What exactly do you think happened?'

'We all know what happened,' she said. 'The trouble is that a new fiction is being written. Day by day we are rewriting the past.'

'And what do you think they are doing in Pakistan?'

'I'm not a police officer in Pakistan,' replied Persis.

'Nehru talks of an India where Hindu, Muslim and Sikh are equals. He tells us to protect the Muslims. But why should we protect those who betrayed us?'

'History betrayed you, Nayar. And to heal the wounds of history, we must rise above hatred. Isn't that what Gandhi taught us?'

'Gandhi was too soft on them,' spat the *putwari*. 'Because of his weakness, this abomination of Pakistan was permitted to be born.'

Persis was surprised. It was rare to find anyone openly criticising the mahatma, though she knew such sentiments existed in the country. It was the reason the great man had been assassinated by one of his co-religionists.

'You are a Brahmin are you not?' she asked.

'I am,' said Nayar proudly.

'Then you believe that the killing of any life tarnishes the soul? From the smallest creature to the most complex? You call it *ahimsa*.'

'A war against those who threaten our way of life is a just war. *Dharma-yuddha*. It is discussed extensively in the *Mahabharata*.'

'How many actual soldiers were murdered in the riots, Nayar? Those who died were civilians, just like you. Men, women and children.'

'We were not the aggressors,' said Nayar, looking away.

*   *   *

It was past ten by the time they made their way back to their lodgings. Nayar had provided them with kerosene lamps.

As they entered, Blackfinch waved his lamp around, then jumped back in fright as a trio of lizards scuttled along the walls.

'Sorry,' he muttered.

There were two bedrooms, furnished with bare charpoys. It would not be the most comfortable of nights, but Persis didn't care.

'Right, well, I'll take one and you take the other,' said Blackfinch.

She went into her room, set the lamp up on a wooden shelf, then opened the window shutters. Moonlight speared in, illuminating a dusty emptiness. Nothing remained of the prior occupants. Who were they? she wondered.

More victims of the war that wasn't a war.

Blackfinch knocked on the door. 'We have a problem,' he said. 'There's no toilet.'

She smiled grimly. 'Yes, there is.' She waved at the fields outside the window.

'You've got to be joking.'

'You wanted to see India. This is India.'

Nayar had left a bucket of water for them, with a brass *lota*. She filled the spouted water vessel and handed it to the Englishman.

'What am I supposed to do with this?'

'Work it out.'

Understanding dawned. 'Christ,' he muttered. 'This is barbaric.' A nervous look came into his eyes. 'I suppose there are snakes out there.'

'Probably.'

'Scorpions?'

'Definitely.'

'Right.' He stared at the *lota*. 'Best get to it then.' He paused at the door. 'Never imagined that a trip to the lavatory could be such an adventure.'

*   *   *

Persis lay down on the charpoy. It wasn't as uncomfortable as she had imagined, though she wished there had been some covering sheets. This far north, at this time of year, the night temperature plummeted.

She heard the slither of geckos. An owl hooted. Her mind swarmed.

She couldn't sleep.

Restlessness lifted her from the charpoy and she found herself moving through the house, back outside, and then towards the fields. Blackfinch had been gone a while. Worry nibbled at her. He was a fish out of water, a particularly clumsy one.

She walked into the field. The wheat, sown in November, was half grown, almost to the level of her waist, the kernels glimmering softly in the moonlight. She waded through the rows, debating whether or not to call out for him. She suspected he was crouched down somewhere, and had no wish to embarrass him.

Her thoughts became ensnared again. What had Sir James found out here? Did it have anything to do with his death or was she chasing her own tail?

The sound of rushing feet.

Persis whirled around to find two men, lathi sticks in hand, gliding through the wheat. The first reached her, raised his stick, swung it hard towards her. She ducked and it caught her a glancing blow on the shoulder that unbalanced her. As she fell, her training kicked into gear. She rolled with the fall, bounced back to her feet, stepped into the man.

His eyes widened in surprise; perhaps he had expected her to flee.

She gave him no time to react. She landed a brutal chop to his throat with the edge of her right hand; as he fell, choking, she swung her knee up and crushed his nose. Blood spurted on to her trousers.

'You there! What the hell are you doing?'

Blackfinch.

The momentary distraction proved critical. The second attacker's lathi struck her on the back of her skull and she fell forward into the wheat, head ringing. For a moment, she lay inert, spots pin-wheeling before her eyes. A field mouse scampered past her nose. Sounds came from a distance, as if through layers of damp cloth. She waited for more blows, but none came.

Eventually, the ringing subsided. She hauled a deep breath, then rose to her feet, swaying unsteadily.

Blackfinch was down, her assailant looming over him, striking him repeatedly with his lathi. The Englishman took the blows on his arms and legs, crying out in pain.

She looked around, grabbed the staff of the fallen man, then flung herself forward.

The man turned just as she whirled the stick around in a sweeping arc, catching him squarely on the jaw. From the way he went down, she knew he wouldn't be getting back up.

She helped Blackfinch to his feet. He had taken a blow to the face, she saw. His right cheek was swelling, and blood trailed from his mouth.

'Come on.'

'My glasses,' he mumbled groggily.

She looked around, saw moonlight glint off something at her feet. She reached down, scooped the spectacles into her pocket.

Draping his arm around her shoulder, she limped him back to the house, stretched him out on his charpoy, then fetched the water bucket and watched him wash the blood out of his mouth.

'Christ,' he muttered. 'Some knight in shining armour I turned out to be.'

'You were very brave.'

'Yes. I had him right where I wanted.'

'I'm sure you would have turned the tables soon.'

He refused to meet her eyes, humiliation rising from him like smoke.

Persis had long ago discovered that a man's ego was as fragile as the skull of a newly hatched bird. The slightest pressure and it buckled. She placed a hand on his arm. He winced. 'You need medical attention.'

'No.'

'There's no shame in admitting that you need help.'

'I'm fine,' he repeated firmly.

'Very well.' She stood up. 'I'm going to speak to Nayar.'

'Don't bother.'

'What if they come for us again?'

'They won't. This was meant as a warning. If they'd really wanted to harm us they would have come with real weapons.'

She realised that he was right. 'Someone doesn't want us to ask questions.'

He said nothing.

She sat back down. 'I'm sorry for involving you in this.'

He finally looked at her. 'No, you're not. You don't give a damn about anything except getting to your precious truth.'

She began a protest, but he waved it away. 'Where did you learn to fight like that?'

'The academy. I was the only woman there. Every grinning idiot made a joke of how easy it would be to take me on. And so I went as hard as I could at them.'

'I'll bet you did,' he muttered.

A cough sounded from the door and their heads shot around. Persis tensed. But it was an old man, quavering in the smoky light.

Mangal. The man who had tried to talk to her earlier in the day.

'Come in,' she said.

He shuffled into the room, eyes widening as he took in Blackfinch's bruised and battered face.

'I must speak with you,' he began, in English.

'Are you a drunk?' she asked.

Confusion entered his gaze, and then he nodded. 'Yes.'

'Why should I believe you?'

'Because someone has to.'

She stared at him, then nodded.

'I worked for the nawab for years,' he began. 'I was a driver. I have always had a problem with drink, but the nawab never held that against me. He treated me well. He loved the British. He was one of those who truly regretted their departure. But Partition was a different matter. When the nawab began to openly advocate for Pakistan, people began to talk. And then the rioting began.' He stopped. 'On the night he died, I had returned from a visit to my sister's home in a neighbouring village. I saw a trio of men outside the nawab's home. They were armed and I knew there was going to be trouble. I hid in the mango orchard and watched from a distance. I saw the nawab come out with his sons; he had two. He seemed confused. The man who was heading the group was known to him. His name was Surat Bakshi – the elder son of Vikas Bakshi. Surat had been schooled in Amritsar. He was an educated man. I knew why he was there.

'Just days earlier I had driven the nawab to visit his tenants, Bakshi among them. He had told them that they must either purchase their plots from him or vacate his land. He intended to sell up and move to Pakistan. Of course, for many this was impossible. They did not have the funds to buy the land. But the nawab was adamant. He employed ruffians to enforce his decree.

'Vikas Bakshi was his largest tenant. But in the past three years, drought had decimated much of his crops. He had fallen behind in his dues. His arrears were such that the nawab did not believe he would be able to recover. They had fallen out over the matter. And then Partition came along and the issue became muddied with religious rhetoric. It stopped being about landowner and tenant and became Muslim versus Hindu. And when news of killings began to reach us, of Muslim mobs roaming the countryside murdering Sikhs and Hindus, raping their women, the touch-paper was lit.

'I watched Surat argue with the nawab and his sons. He demanded that the nawab sign over his father's land and leave for Pakistan immediately. He called him a traitor and told him that traitors had no right to Indian soil.

'The nawab was furious. He ordered his sons to fetch his hunting rifle. But before they could move Surat fell upon the nawab, running him through with a sword. The others killed the nawab's sons.

'I saw them enter the home. When they returned, their kurtas were slick with blood. They were carrying wooden crates with them. One of them stumbled, and the case broke open. Jewellery fell from it; necklaces, rings, silver goblets, plates. They had stolen the nawab's ancestral treasure. I believe that had been their intent all along.

'I looked on as they set fire to the bungalow. They watched it burn for a while, and then ran into the night.

'Two days later Muslim rioters caught Vikas Bakshi out in the fields and murdered him. Cut him down in cold blood. They killed Surat's brother too. And his mother, who had been delivering food to them. A whole family wiped out. Muslim mobs were out in force after the nawab's death. They suspected the truth, even if the police chose to report a lie.

'Surat vanished that same night. The two men who had accompanied him in the killing of the nawab and his family later turned up dead. I believe Surat murdered them to protect his secret.'

'Why didn't you say all this to the police?'

'I did,' he said. 'I told Shergill. He strung me up for three days in a cell, beat me until I thought I would die.'

'You could have gone to Amritsar, told the authorities there.'

'Who would have protected me? The Muslims of Jalanpur were gone. The village closed ranks. I was just a drunk, the nawab's former driver. They called me traitor. Each night I expected a traitor's death. In the end, I wrote an account of what I had witnessed and sent it to Delhi.'

'Your account lacked many details.'

'I was afraid,' he said. 'If I had been precise, they might have traced it back to me.'

She examined his face, the haunted flicker in his eyes. Mangal had the look of a man confessing a great sin. The sin was not his; nonetheless, his soul demanded absolution. And now he had it.

'Did you tell all this to Sir James when he came here?'

'Yes. He came to Jalanpur, asked questions, but got no answers. That night I went to his hotel in Pandiala.'

'The Golden Temple Hotel?'

He nodded. 'I told him my story.'

Persis imagined Herriot listening to the man, writing down the name Bakshi on a hotel notepad.

'Where did you learn to speak English?'

'The nawab liked to speak it when I drove him around. Whenever a British officer came here he would ask me to drive them around. He paid a tutor to teach me their language.'

'What did Sir James say when you told him about what had happened?'

'He wanted to know more about Surat Bakshi. I told him to ask the *patwari* in Jalanpur.'

That tallied with Herriot's movements, and explained why he had taken such an interest in Bakshi's affairs.

'What did he do after he visited the land registry?'

'He went to see Bakshi's home. They told him it had been abandoned since the Bakshis were killed, but he insisted on going
anyway. He went alone. I followed him.'

'What did he do there?'

'He walked around. Searched the place.'

'Did he find anything?'

'Just some old photographs. Of the family. He took those with
him.'

'Why?'

'I don't know. He asked me which one was Surat. I told him.'

Her heart lurched. Why had Herriot taken those photographs?
Why had he cared what Surat Bakshi looked like?

'Did he say anything else?'

Mangal hesitated. 'He asked me about the things Bakshi had
stolen from the nawab's home. He was particularly interested in a
necklace. I had mentioned it in my account. I wanted to make sure
that when they caught Surat they would know what to look for.
Evidence of his crime.'

'Describe it to me.'

'It was a choker, made of gold, and set with emeralds. In the
centre were two peacocks facing one another.'

She absorbed this silently, clutching at the clue as it wavered in
her mind like a kite in a high wind. Something about the necklace's description . . . but she couldn't quite reel it in.

'Do you know where Bakshi went?'

'No, madam. All I know is that he never came back.'

25

8 January 1950

Kulraj Singh arrived to pick them up early in the morning. He raised an eyebrow at the sight of Blackfinch's swollen face but otherwise made no comment. They returned to the Golden Temple Hotel, checked out, then headed to the station for the train back to Bombay.

On the way to Amritsar, Persis had time to consider all that she had discovered.

Herriot, in the process of investigating the Partition crimes, had come north to Pandiala and then from there to the village of Jalanpur. This was just days prior to his death, at a time when he was battling bankruptcy. Why take such a keen interest in *this* case?

There was only one reason she could think of. The nawab's jewellery. The possibility of being able to track down the nawab's stolen treasure might have been just enough of an incentive for a man facing financial ruin.

But what had convinced him that there was something out here for him to find in the first place?

The answer was obvious. He had seen something in Bombay that connected with Mangal's account of the nawab's death, the account sent to him as part of the Partition Commission documents. The peacock necklace. He had seen the necklace in Bombay. It seemed a big leap, but it fitted the facts at hand, at least as well as any other theory.

If Herriot had indeed seen that necklace in Bombay, his suspicions would have brought him north, seeking confirmation. That was why he had taken Surat Bakshi's photograph. Armed with that picture he had returned to Bombay to track down his quarry. And then what?

Had he found his man? Had he confronted him? But why would Herriot think Bakshi was in Bombay?

Again, the answer was obvious. Because he had seen him there. She felt a surge of excitement. Sir James Herriot had identified Surat Bakshi in Bombay. That *had* to be it.

What then? Had he threatened him? And had *that* led to his death? She couldn't be sure, but the evidence was compelling.

The image of Vishal Mistry rose before her. Mistry had been a jeweller, an expert in heritage jewellery. Jewellery such as the peacock necklace. She understood now why Herriot had met him on the night of his death and why both he and Mistry had told no one of that meeting.

Secrets and lies. Murder and corruption.

She took a deep breath. To continue in Herriot's footsteps, she too needed to know what Surat Bakshi looked like. But how? There had been no photographs of him in Jalanpur.

An idea occurred to her. She discussed it with Blackfinch and they agreed to use the hour-long stop in Amritsar to test out her theory.

Ten minutes after disembarking they reached the offices of the *Amritsar Journal*.

The newspaper's editor-in-chief was only too glad to help. The paper had carried the story of Persis's investigation into Sir James's death and he was intrigued by her ongoing efforts.

'I am looking specifically for reports of the death of Nawab Sikandar Ali Mumtaz and his family.'

'Simple enough,' said the editor. 'I remember the incident. A terrible affair.' He led them to a room in the basement. 'We keep five years' worth of back issues here. Prior to that, we have another three decades' worth in our central storage depot.'

Together, she and Blackfinch went through the stack of newspapers.

They had been filed in a rather haphazard manner and so it took longer to find the dates they were seeking. The front pages around then carried similar headlines.

COMMUNAL RIOTS AT AMRITSAR:
40 DEAD, SHOPS LOOTED

WIDESPREAD DISTURBANCES IN
FIVE VILLAGES NEAR AMRITSAR:
130 MUSLIMS DEAD, 2 SIKHS

476 HINDUS AND SIKHS KILLED IN TRAIN
BURNING ATROCITY NEAR NEW BORDER

Dust swirled up from the pages sending Blackfinch into a fit of violent sneezing.

'Go outside,' said Persis irritably.

The Englishman stumbled out into the corridor, eyes streaming.

Five minutes later, she found what she had been searching for.

JALANPUR NAWAB DIES IN FIRE
TOGETHER WITH FAMILY

The front page carried a picture of the nawab, a round-faced man with a walrus moustache, sporting a grey fur cap of the type favoured by Jinnah.

She turned to the inner pages for the full story. The journalist had quoted verbatim the investigating officer, one Sub-Inspector Shergill, who had labelled the fire an accident, with no further investigation deemed necessary.

Her eyes lingered on the photographs of the nawab's family, a medley of pictures, many taken from society functions. His daughters-in-law were particularly gaudy, decked out in silk shalwar kameezes and finely worked jewellery. The youngest, a woman named Sakina Baig, was particularly striking. Something about her photograph held Persis, that same tickle at the back of her mind that she had experienced when listening to Mangal's account.

And then she had it.

It was the woman's necklace, a bejewelled affair, inset with two golden peacocks, facing each other. It was the necklace Mangal had described in his original account of the nawab's murder, the account that had been sent to the authorities and then to Sir James Herriot. This was the necklace she had conjectured that Herriot had seen in Bombay, and that had then taken him to Jalanpur.

But where could he possibly have seen the piece?

Revelation hovered in the air. She almost had it . . . But it was gone.

She nearly shouted in annoyance, then calmed her thoughts. It would come to her; she was certain of it. She cleared her mind and continued through the article.

Her eye was caught by a picture of a dagger, a slim curved blade with a beautifully wrought ivory handle, encrusted with precious stones. The article referred to it as the 'khanjar of aman' – the dagger of peace. She recalled now that this was another of the pieces that Mangal had mentioned in his account. Stolen by Surat Bakshi.

Her eyes lingered on the picture. Again, there was something familiar about the knife. She felt certain she had seen it before. But, again, she couldn't place it. Her frustration grew.

She returned her attention to the pile of newspapers. Now that she had a firm date to use as a starting point she began to examine the editions from the days following the fire.

She found what she was looking for tucked in the inner pages of the issue dated 18 July 1947. Two days after the incident.

LONGSTANDING JALANPUR TENANT
FAMILY MURDERED BY MUSLIMS

The article detailed the killing of Vikas Bakshi, his son and his wife. The piece was accompanied by a photograph of each of the victims. And another photograph of the son who had gone missing, presumed dead. Surat Bakshi.

As soon as she saw the photograph the world dissolved; she knew instantly that she had made a great discovery.

She understood that Herriot had also made this same discovery. The Englishman too had gazed at the face of Surat Bakshi with recognition dawning. What had happened next? What thread connected this finding to his subsequent death? Or were the two unrelated?

There was only one way to find out.

The answers lay back in Bombay.

26

At Malabar House, she discovered that Seth had taken the day off. This information was relayed to her by the only other officer present, Oberoi.

She sat down at her desk, closed her eyes.

It felt good to be back. There was something about the basement office that instantly filled her with a sense of belonging, of mission. In the short time that she had worked there, Malabar House had become a fixed point in her life, a locus of her ambition, her hopes, her fears. It was more than her place of work. It was as much a part of her existence as the bookshop.

They had arrived back in the metropolis late in the afternoon, parting company at the station. Blackfinch's body had begun to stiffen, the bruises from his beating now in full voice, stiffening his gait, and eliciting a wince with every step. He put on a brave face, but Persis could sense the exhaustion behind his eyes. The man needed medical attention. And rest.

She watched him hail a cab, and then turned and set off for Malabar House.

Now, she sat and thought through her next course of action.

She could strike out alone, follow her suspicions to ground and attempt to apprehend the person she believed might be behind Sir James Herriot's murder. But without official sanction her efforts might prove futile.

The alternative was to share with Seth all that she had learned and hope that he would stand behind her. She doubted it. Seth would be furious that she was still pursuing the investigation. He might well believe her, but his hands were bound by his unwilling-ness to risk what remained of his career.

She scraped back her chair and got to her feet, placed her cap back on her head. She supposed she had known that, in the end, it would come to this. She had always been alone.

'It won't last, you know,' said Oberoi behind her, as she turned to leave.

She turned back, waited for him to complete his thought, knowing that he had to get it out.

'Today, they're fêting you, because it suits a certain political agenda. But the first time you slip up, they'll throw you to the wolves, and they'll do it gladly. You're an aberration. Women have no place in the service.'

She stepped forward until she stood directly before him. His nostrils flared but he said nothing.

'This country is going to change. Whether it wants to or not. And it won't be because of one woman. It will be because of us all. For millennia, we have been told what our role must be: wife, mother, daughter. We are all those things, but we are so much more. Men like you think you can stop us. Go ahead and try. Have you ever tried to stop the monsoon?'

She spun on her feet, and walked away.

As she passed George Fernandes's desk, her eye fell on a note tucked under a manila folder. She had become used to his dense scribble and so instantly recognised the scrawl of numbers. Her brow furrowed, and then she continued towards the exit.

Her next errand took her back to the jewellery shop belonging to the deceased Vishal Mistry. His assistant, Kedarnath, did not seem pleased to see her again. She waited for him to finish tend-ing to a customer, then pulled him to one side and showed him the newspaper cutting she had obtained from the *Amritsar Journal* containing an image of Surat Bakshi. 'Have you seen this man before?'

Kedarnath squinted at the picture. At first, he seemed intent on denial, then his eyes widened. He nodded. 'Yes. This was one of Vishal's private clients. Though he looked somewhat different when I saw him last.'

'What business did he have with Vishal?'

'That I don't know. Vishal dealt with him personally. He said it was just advice. He asked me not to enter it in the ledger.'

Another piece of the puzzle fell into place. She thanked the man, then left.

Superintendent Roshan Seth lived in a whitewashed bungalow just a mile from Colaba Point, at the southernmost tip of Bombay. On one side loomed the lighthouse, on the other lay the old luna-tic asylum and the abandoned British infantry barracks.

She was led through the deserted home by an elderly maid, into a small garden where she discovered her commanding officer on his knees in the dirt, planting a sapling. He was dressed in shorts and a wide-brimmed sunhat. At her approach, he glanced around. His eyes widened, and then he returned to his work.

She watched him for a while. The maid had vanished and it was just the two of them now.

The garden was well tended, with a profusion of flowering plants, bushes and trees. Bougainvillea made vivid splashes of colour. It astonished her that Seth might have been responsible for this. The loucheness with which he approached his work at the station seemed curiously at odds with the regimented dedication she saw around her.

A bead of sweat trickled down her back. She should probably have gone home, showered and changed. After more than a day on a rattling train, she must smell ripe.

Seth finished with the tree and struggled to his feet. He took off his hat and passed a forearm over his sweating brow. 'You have to get the depth just right,' he said. 'Too shallow and it won't hold. Too deep and you'll smother it.'

She wondered briefly if he was being allegorical.

'Let's get into the shade.'

They sat on a swing seat out on the veranda.

Persis explained all that she had discovered, the various criss-crossing theories that now plagued her thoughts.

Seth's expression suggested that he had been stricken with a bout of stomach cramps. 'So you disobeyed a direct order?' he eventually said.

'I took leave as you suggested—' she began, but he waved her into silence.

'Semantics don't suit you, Persis. You've always been a straight talker, too much so for your own good.' He sighed. 'What's done is done. I hope you realise that others will discover what you've been up to. It will not go down well.'

She adopted a look of contriteness.

Seth stared at her, then burst into a bray of laughter. 'If you're going to pretend to look sorry, at least make a half-decent stab at it.'

Her cheeks burned, but she said nothing.

'You could have got hurt,' he said, a little more gently. 'How would that have looked? India's first female detective cut down at the very flowering of her career.'

'You're being melodramatic.'

'Am I? Evil is real, Persis. It lives inside men's hearts, waiting to be unleashed. How else do you explain it? The killings, the rapes, the savage lusts that overtake us? Has history taught you nothing?'

'What if I'm right? What if Maan Singh isn't guilty?'

'What if he is?' Seth shot back.

'If he is, then what will we lose?'

He shook his head. 'You want to fling mud in all directions, hoping that it sticks to – to *someone*, and you sit there and tell me *what will we lose?*'

'I have evidence.'

'You have *supposition*,' snapped Seth. 'It isn't the same thing. Tell me, can you categorically state who *actually* killed Sir James?'

She hesitated. 'No. But—'

'Then how can you expect me to allow you to continue?' His eyes softened. 'Persis, I would support you in a great many things, but don't ask me to light the funeral pyre for both our careers.'

She arrived home seething with rage. Her anger was directed not so much at Seth as it was at the institution that had corralled his thinking, stifling the courage that a truly good investigator needed.

She threw her luggage on to the bed, narrowly missing Akbar, who hissed at her, flung off her sweaty clothes, and walked into the bathroom.

Thirty minutes later, showered, dressed in a short white kimono imprinted with cherry blossom trees, she sat down heavily at the dining room table. Her father looked up from his newspaper.

'Good trip?'

She stared at him, and then sat her chin on her forearms. 'Yes. And no.'

'Do you want to talk about it?'

Akbar had followed her out and jumped on to the table. He took a strategic position at the very corner, in case she flung anything else his way.

She went over her trip north, her thoughts about the case, and her meeting with Seth.

Her father spooned pancakes smothered in Lyle's Golden Syrup into his mouth as he listened, then burped loudly. He pushed his plate away, then looked at her with a mixture of affection and sympathy.

'Your mother was a crusader. I know that you've always thought of me as the one who somehow infected her with my anarchy, but you couldn't be further from the truth. It was she who decided that she wanted to participate in the struggle. And once she made up her mind, even Zoroaster himself couldn't change it.' His eyes softened in memory. 'The day she died I begged her not to go. She was pregnant, you see. Six weeks along. We'd had word of a rally planned at Azad Maidan. The British were panicked, by then. They could sense that the horse had bolted; they were losing control.

'There were thousands there that day. Chanting, shouting, making speeches. It was a blisteringly hot day; I saw people fainting in the press of bodies. I could sense your mother weakening. I tried to make her leave, but she wouldn't go until she'd heard Sardar Patel speak – he was a favourite of hers.

'By the time Patel finished, an electric rage was passing through the crowd. We were in danger of becoming a mob. The British sensed it too, and ordered us to disperse. That didn't go down too well. Everyone was high on Gandhi's spirit of non-cooperation, your mother too. That was when it all went wrong.

'I heard a gunshot. I looked back and saw a British soldier at the very edge of the gathering go down. Everything became a blur after that. I hauled your mother to our car, threw her in and tried to drive out of there. But the roads were congested, people fleeing in panic. I saw British troops firing wildly in all directions.' He stopped, his wheelchair seeming to grow around him until it filled the room. 'I panicked. I went too fast; I didn't pay attention to the road. The car spun out of control. I ran into an oncoming British Army truck. My legs were crushed, but I was conscious long enough to see her die beside me. She murmured your name as she passed.'

Persis sat still in her seat, a fist clenched around her heart.

All these years she had waited for her father to speak, to explain why she had grown up without a mother. And now that he had, she felt as if something had been stolen from her. Whatever else she might hold the British accountable for, she could not blame them for the death of Sanaz Wadia. Her mother was simply another victim of circumstance.

She reached across the table and enclosed his fist with her hands. His skin was warm and seemed to throb. They sat there like this, until finally she arose, kissed him on the forehead, and went back to her room.

She lay in bed, staring at the ceiling fan as it rotated above her.

In the corner of the room Akbar prowled the side of the wardrobe. A mouse had recently begun to torment him.

The case swirled around her. She now had all the pieces. It simply remained to fit them together.

Sir James might have been murdered by any of a number of people. And yet only one was actually responsible. As she lined up the suspects in her mind, she became convinced that it was the Englishman's journey to Jalanpur that lay at the heart of his death. And at the centre of that was ...

She sat upright. The necklace.

Memory arced into her mind with the force of lightning; she realised that she too had encountered the peacock necklace, back at the very beginning of the case. She had seen it precisely where Sir James had also first seen it, *after* he had read the account by Mangal describing it. As she clung to the image, she felt doubt dropping away, answers unfolding before her.

She was now certain that she knew who had murdered Sir James Herriot. *But could she prove it?*

She did not think so. The evidence was there, but, following her meeting with Seth, she did not believe her seniors would entertain anything less than a confession.

So the question was: *how could she force Herriot's killer to admit the crime?*

27

10 January 1950

The Cathedral of St Thomas the Apostle dominated the Fort area. Built in 1718, as the first Anglican church in the city, its original purpose had been to aid in the improvement of the moral fibre of the growing British community in Bombay. They had come to India seeking fame and fortune. Instead they had found malaria, dysentery, heat and monsoon. It was inevitable that some would turn from the righteous path, seeking solace in gin, gambling and infidelity. Many of those early luminaries lay interred within the church's precincts, under marble headstones engraved with moving elegies. Soldiers, clerks, lawyers and company men. Few had anticipated the subcontinent as their final resting place. Yet here they were, banded together for all eternity.

The funeral of Sir James Herriot took place in the afternoon, with the midday heat at its zenith, a dry wind rustling the palms lining the cathedral's courtyard.

Persis arrived in her jeep to discover a line of cars already pulled up along Churchgate Street. She parked, then walked briskly towards the cathedral, glancing up at the white Neo-Gothic façade. Her father had once told her that the roof had been designed to be cannon-proof. She wondered just who it was that the British had expected to fire cannons at their place of worship.

At the entrance to the church she encountered a press of people, Europeans dressed universally in black, Indians in white. This contrast, the plumage each community adopted in the shadow of death, had always struck her as strangely perverse.

She had chosen to attend in uniform.

She wasn't the only one. Police officers of various ranks were among the mourners. She spotted Ravi Patnagar bent towards the ear of the Additional Deputy Commissioner, Amit Shukla. She ducked away as she saw Roshan Seth approaching them. Seth would soon discover that she was here, but she did not want him to order her home before she had had a chance to put into action the plan she had come up with the night before.

The mourners were being greeted by the Bishop of Bombay, William Quinn, a weathered Englishman who had spent three decades broiling in the Indian sun. He met each arrival with a red face and an expression of incipient martyrdom. The bishop was famed for his bombastic sermons, and his fondness of fine wine.

'Wasn't sure if you'd be attending.'

She turned to find Blackfinch at her elbow. The Englishman too was dressed in black, a tight-fitting suit that appeared to elicit a wince each time he moved. The right side of his face had puffed up, giving him a beery look behind his spectacles. He was paler than usual. She guessed he had had a difficult couple of nights.

'Why wouldn't I?' They stared at each other, and then, lowering her voice, she said, 'I need your help.'

'Really? I'm not sure my body can take the prospect of offering you any more help.' He gave a wan smile, but she was in no mood for humour.

Quickly, she outlined her plan.

He sighed. 'Persis, you realise that half the city's brass is here?'

'Yes.'

'You're risking your career.'

'Yes.'

'I mean, you could lose your uniform.'

286

Persis hesitated. It was not that the thought hadn't occurred to her, or that she had blindly committed herself to a suicidal course of action. The fear was real. She simply chose to blank it from her mind, and to follow the instincts that had brought her this far.

'I can't let it go.'

He stared at her with a curious mixture of sympathy and admiration. 'No. I suppose not. How can I help?'

She reached into her pocket and took out the slips of paper she had carefully written out the night before. 'Once the service is over, I need you to hand these to the following individuals. You must be quick, before they leave.' She named each of the recipients.

'Wouldn't it be better to do this at the wake? At Laburnum House.'

She shook her head. 'I can't be sure they will all attend the wake.'

He took the chits from her and stuffed them into his pocket. 'Shall we?'

They walked towards the front door. Persis attempted to brush past the bishop, but he latched on to her, grabbing her by the shoulders and gazing down beatifically into her eyes as if the mother of Christ had risen before him. 'Ah, the lady of the hour.' He flashed her a ruddy beam. 'It is never pleasant to preside over the obsequies of a murdered man, but at least Sir James can go to his rest knowing that his killer will receive earthly justice.'

'Is there another kind?' said Persis tersely.

Quinn's smile dimmed. He looked at Blackfinch as if for support, but the Englishman merely offered him a nod of greeting, then followed the policewoman into the enfolding darkness of the church.

To Persis, the close confines of the nave, packed with bodies, poorly ventilated and badly lit, had the feel of a malarial hospice.

Around her, the city's nobility tugged at their collars, fanned themselves with copies of sermon books, and sweated in sombre solidarity. One of their own had fallen, cut down from his pedestal by the forces that lurked forever at the edge of the forest. If Partition had taught them anything, it was that no man of wealth or power – Indian or British – was ever safe, not out here.

She moved towards the edge of the cathedral, drifting behind a statue of St John the Baptist. From here she could observe proceedings in relative anonymity. Blackfinch made to follow her, but was hailed by an elderly white woman who appeared to know him. Grasping him by the elbow, she wheeled him around to introduce him to an equally ancient male; between the pair of them they propelled him towards a pew, as Quinn ascended the pulpit and called the congregation to order.

Persis looked over the sea of heads, searching for the faces of those she had come for. One by one she picked them out, sitting, like the others, awaiting Quinn's peroration.

Some of the certainty leaked from her. There was no telling how things would go. The only thing she could say with any assurance was that it would soon be over, one way or the other.

A silence descended on the congregation, punctuated by the odd cough.

'Sir James Herriot was a man admired for many qualities,' began Quinn. 'A man of empathy and integrity, an inspiration to those who knew him. Taken from us too soon, he nevertheless leaves behind the richest of legacies. As Isaiah tells us: "The righteous perisheth, and no man layeth it to heart; and merciful men are taken away, none considering that the righteous is taken away from the evil to come."'

Persis resisted the urge to interject. The one thing she now knew about James Herriot was that his integrity, such as it was, had evaporated in the face of circumstance.

She reflected on how swiftly time had passed. It seemed only moments before that the phone had rung summoning her to Laburnum House. She marshalled her initial impressions once again, set them beside all that she had discovered, the pieces of the puzzle that she had assembled.

A shiver ran through her. *What if she was wrong?* What if all her conjecture amounted to no more than a ladder of false assumptions?

Her throat felt dry. She worked some moisture into her mouth.

Quinn had become animated, face red, arms flailing, in serious risk of ventricular strain. She tuned him out. Focus. Everything she had learned pointed her in the direction of the guilty party, but there was no way to be sure. Maan Singh's confession made her task doubly difficult.

Her plan was simple. Bring together all those who might have murdered Herriot, then throw the cat among the pigeons. In the ensuing chaos, she hoped that she could force a confession from the true killer. It wasn't a great plan. She could admit that to herself. But it was all she had.

Quinn had wound down. He muttered words to the effect that the family would not be delivering any eulogies, and then asked for the pallbearers to step forward.

She saw Herriot's son stand up and move reluctantly towards the coffin. Robert Campbell followed him, together with Madan Lal, Adi Shankar and two others whom Persis did not recognise. Brass poles were inserted into the casket, before it was heaved up from its dais by the pallbearers.

They made for the rear exit, out towards the cemetery, a hymn swelling behind them. As soon as they passed through the door, the mourners lifted from their pews and herded out behind them, Persis following in their wake.

Herriot's plot lay next to the grave of a former East India Company director. The hole had already been dug. Two gravediggers awaited, leaning on their shovels. She noticed that ravens lined the branches of the surrounding trees. A langur looked on from a crow's nest at the top of a nearby palm, letting out occasional shrieks.

The casket was swiftly lowered into the earth. Quinn said a few final words, uttered a prayer, then gestured at the diggers.

Earth rained down on the casket and in short order James Herriot – what remained of him – vanished from the world.

The crowd instantly dispersed, racing for the exit without a backward glance, as if pursued by death or the tax man. Persis searched for Blackfinch, saw that he had sprung into action, moving among the mourners, pulling them aside, a terse conversation, then handing over the note, before wheeling away to the next on the list, leaving behind frowns of consternation and anger.

She turned away and hurried back inside the church.

28

They arrived one by one. The church had an annexe attached to its western flank, a small room designed for non-devotional meetings. The room, a functional space bathed in ribbons of light falling from a succession of ogival windows, contained a table and chairs. A filing cabinet lurked in one corner; above it a noticeboard plastered with pamphlets and papers.

Robert Campbell was the first to arrive, with his daughter. He charged into the room, spotted Persis, and took five quick strides towards her, visibly shaking with anger. He flapped the note under her nose. 'What the hell do you mean by this?'

She was given no chance to reply. The door opened again and in came Madan Lal, Lalita Gupta, Adi Shankar and Meenakshi Rai, closely followed by Edmond de Vries. They stood there, looking from Persis to the Campbells and back again. Lal made as if to speak, but this time it was his turn to be interrupted, by the arrival of Archie Blackfinch and Roshan Seth.

Seth wasted no time. He stalked over to Persis and pulled her to one side, lowering his voice and hissing, 'You've gone too far.'

'Sir, I asked Blackfinch to bring you here. If you give me just a little while, I will reveal to you Sir James's true killer.'

He looked at her as if stunned. 'Do you understand what you are doing, Persis? The ADC is out there. Don't you think he will hear of this? You're throwing away your career.'

'I don't believe so,' she said firmly. 'The truth—'

'The truth!' he yelped. 'Why does the damned truth matter so much to you?'

She stared at him. 'The question, sir, is when did it stop mattering to you?'

It was as if she had slapped him. His mouth flapped open, but no words would come. He lowered his eyes. For a moment, she felt her future spin on its axis. And then Seth seemed to gather himself. 'I have tried my best to protect you, Persis. But if this is truly the course of action you feel is right, then I will not stand in your way.' As good as his word, he stepped aside and gave her the floor.

Madan Lal took this as a signal. He brandished the chit Blackfinch had handed him. 'I presume this came from you?' he said. 'It is simply outrageous. Your career is over, Inspector.'

The others immediately launched into similar protests.

Persis waited calmly for the baying to stop, then said, 'Mr Lal, please read out what it says on your chit.'

'I shall do no such thing.'

She turned towards Elizabeth Campbell. 'May I?'

The young woman examined her face, then shrugged and handed over her slip of paper.

Persis held it up. On it, in bold letters, it said:

I KNOW YOU KILLED SIR JAMES.
COME IMMEDIATELY TO THE
CATHEDRAL'S WESTERN ANNEXE.

'I apologise for bringing you here with this simple ruse,' she said. 'But I needed you all present. You see, it is my intention to reveal to you Sir James's true killer.'

'This is ludicrous,' bellowed Robert Campbell. 'James's killer has confessed. Singh will be convicted and hanged, and it will be no more than he deserves.'

'Maan Singh did not kill Sir James.'

'Then why the hell did he confess?' Campbell's face was blotchy, his brows beetled in anger and confusion.

'I will explain,' said Persis. 'But first, allow me to set the stage. We have just heard a great deal about Sir James Herriot. A consummate politician, a man of integrity and so forth. This is not quite the truth. Sir James had his faults and those faults led him ultimately to his death.'

Lal stepped forward, something wild in his eyes. 'I won't stand here and listen to this.'

Persis ignored him. 'Sir James was living a lie on many fronts. His business ventures had bankrupted him. He was estranged from his son.' She glanced at Edmond de Vries, who looked away quickly to his shoes. 'He was a man faced with stark choices. And he made the wrong ones.

'When I first arrived at the scene of his death there were a number of anomalies that bothered me. Aside from the fact that we couldn't find the murder weapon, there was also the strangeness of his missing trousers. We now know that Sir James had an intimate encounter just prior to his death. In his study. That was why he'd taken off his trousers.' She allowed that uncomfortable image to hang in the air. She turned towards Elizabeth Campbell. 'Shall I tell them or would you like to?'

The young woman flushed, but said nothing.

'Elizabeth sought an affair with Sir James not because she loved or admired him, but because she wished to get back at her father. About a year ago Robert Campbell refused to allow her to marry the man she had fallen in love with, an Indian named Satyajit Sharma. Sharma was subsequently murdered. She suspected her father's hand in his death.'

Elizabeth spoke up, unable to hold herself in. 'Satya was a gentle soul. Intelligent and kind. He was educated in England but he'd returned to India to help his country find its feet. We fell in love. He insisted on approaching my father to ask for my hand. I tried to talk him out of it but he wouldn't listen.' Her eyes smarted. 'My father threatened him. When I found out I told him that I didn't care what he thought. I'd run away with Satya.' She stopped. 'A week later he was dead. My father killed him. I know it. I don't care how many times he denies it.'

'For God's sake!' spluttered Robert Campbell.

Persis took up the story. 'On the night of his death, Elizabeth planned to seduce Sir James at the party and tell her father about it. In the end, she couldn't go through with it. Nevertheless, she told her father that she *had* done so. They argued, before he charged off looking for Herriot, intent, I am certain, on murder.'

All eyes turned to the Scotsman.

Robert Campbell cleared his throat. 'I didn't kill James. I wanted to. Believe me, nothing would have given me greater pleasure.' He glanced at his daughter. 'After what had happened with her engineer, Elizabeth couldn't forgive me. It's true I warned him away from her, but I never laid a hand on that boy.' He took a deep breath. 'I think it was James who arranged for his murder. He was the one who'd got me the contract. He had a large commission due on the completion of that bridge. He was livid when I told him it was being delayed by a native. He told me he'd take care of it. I assumed he'd talk to some of his friends in the area, apply some pressure. But the next thing I knew the boy turned up dead.'

Elizabeth stared at him in shock and loathing. 'You knew?' she whispered.

'I wasn't sure,' said Campbell. 'James never admitted any involvement. I'm sorry, I truly am.' He returned his gaze to Persis. 'Yes, Elizabeth lied to me that night. She told me that she and James ... The red mist fell over my eyes. I went upstairs to his office and, heaven help me, I might have killed him. But I didn't. I couldn't have.'

'Why not?' asked Persis.

'Because he was already dead.'

Another round of murmurs sprang up from the group like a flock of startled birds.

'You found him dead and said nothing?' Lal's astonishment was mirrored around the room.

Campbell sank into himself. 'What should I have said? That I went up to throttle the man who I thought had seduced my daughter and found his corpse? That, for an instant, I thought – I thought that perhaps *she* had done it?'

Persis turned to Elizabeth. 'Did you kill Sir James?'

'No! Of course not!'

'No,' echoed Persis. 'I don't believe you had anything to do with his death.'

'Inspector, surely you have your murderer?' said Adi Shankar, speaking for the first time. 'Arrest him and let us be done with this.'

'Not yet, Mr Shankar,' said Persis calmly. 'Robert Campbell isn't the only one here with reason to have wished Sir James ill.' She paused, waiting for them to settle down once more. 'Maan Singh confessed to the killing. From the beginning, I wasn't certain of his guilt. Why hadn't he confessed straight away? Why did he confess without protest when I confronted him about the missing trousers? Why did he keep the trousers at his home but not the knife? Why take the trousers at all? It made no sense. To find answers to these questions I travelled to his real home, in Amritsar, where I spoke to his wife. She told me some interesting facts about her husband.

'Maan Singh was the son of a soldier, one of the men who fired upon his fellow Indians at the behest of Brigadier Dyer at

Jallianwala Bagh on April 13th, 1919. As a consequence Maan Singh grew up an outcast. His whole life he has wished for nothing more than to regain the honour that his father had squandered. Maan Singh has a sister. That sister moved to Bombay, married a soldier named Duleep, had a child. But then her husband died, killed in action at Imphal. He had served with Maan Singh and another man – Madan Lal.' She turned to lock eyes with the aide. 'During the action at Imphal, Lal killed three enemy soldiers *after* they had surrendered. He was due to be court-martialled, but was rescued by Sir James, an old acquaintance. After the war, Lal took up employment with Sir James, though I suspect he had little choice. He became Sir James's aide, but, in truth, he was employed to carry out a host of unsavoury duties. He became a fixer, running errands for Sir James. I have no doubt that he disliked his new situation, but he was bound to the Englishman. The man had saved his life, after all.

'At some point during his time at Laburnum House, Lal discovered – through Maan Singh – that their fallen comrade's widow, Duleep's wife – Maan Singh's sister – was destitute and living in Bombay. And so he convinced Sir James to offer her employment.' A pause. 'Have I got this right so far, Mrs Gupta?'

All eyes turned to the housekeeper. A woman used to blending into the background now found herself thrust into the limelight; she shrank visibly, unable to speak.

'She has nothing to do with this,' said Lal, stepping forward.

Persis ignored him, continuing to look at Gupta. 'When I spoke to you, you told me that you had a son. You said that Sir James had agreed to pay for his education. I found that unusual. After all, why would an Englishman agree to undertake such an expense for the child of a housekeeper? As we have discovered, Sir James's greatness has been greatly exaggerated.' She gave a mirthless smile. 'We traced your son to the Heart of Mary School in Panvel. We discovered that it was Madan Lal who had enrolled him there, that he had lied to Sir James's bookkeeper to organise the payment of your son's fees. That, in fact, he stole the money from his employer.' She switched her attention to Lal. 'Sir James was informed of this fact on the evening he died. By Andrew Morgan, his bookkeeper. This led to an argument between you. My guess is that he was furious. Perhaps he threatened to sack Gupta. This you could not contemplate. Because, of course, you were in love with her.'

It was Lal's turn to become the object of scrutiny. He blinked behind his spectacles, then flashed a look of defiance. His hands clenched by his side.

'Am I wrong?' pushed Persis.

'No,' he said hoarsely. 'You are not wrong.' He stepped to Gupta's side, a protective gesture. 'Duleep was my friend. He saved my life that day, at Imphal. In saving me he lost his own life. I temporarily lost control of my senses. If I could take back what I did that day, in the jungle, I would.

'James rescued me from spending the rest of my life in a military prison. I was indebted to him and so I agreed to work for him. I was glad to. He was a man I had always admired. But there is nothing so ruinous as discovering that your idols have feet of clay. James turned out to be an unscrupulous man. And in return for saving me, he took his pound of flesh.

'A year after I joined Laburnum House, I found out from Maan Singh that Duleep's wife had fallen on hard times in Bombay. I owed it to his memory to help. A debt of honour. I did the best I could for her and her child. I do not regret it. What later happened between Lalita and I was unexpected, unplanned.'

'You were angry with Sir James. By now you were thoroughly disillusioned with him. And now he was threatening the woman you adored.'

'I didn't kill him.'

'Yet killing is second nature to you, isn't it?' continued Persis. 'You owed Sir James. But you were sick of it, sick of the things he was making you do. Yet you couldn't very well do anything to the man. Not with your record. Suspicion would instantly fall on you. Isn't that why you invited Maan Singh to Bombay?'

'What are you talking about?'

'Maan Singh's wife told me that he received a call from you. That you invited him to work in Bombay. Why now? After years of nothing? You knew of his hatred of the English. You knew about his father. It had come out during your time together as soldiers. It was the reason Singh eventually quit the army. Word had got back of his father's part in the Jallianwala Bagh massacre, of what Dyer had made him do. Singh couldn't stand the idea of his comrades questioning his honour. And so he left.

'You twisted that rage to your own purpose. You sacked Sir James's driver, making up an excuse about theft. And you hired Singh in his place. You told him to gain Sir James's trust. My guess is that at some point you planned to light the touch-paper and stand back to watch Singh explode. Finally, you would be free.'

'No!' protested Gupta. 'He wouldn't have done that. He – he called Maan to Bombay because of me.'

'Don't say another word,' interrupted Lal.

Gupta gave him a sad look. 'It's time to tell the truth, Madan.' She took a deep breath. 'Sir James assaulted me. A month ago. He was drunk and I managed to fight him off. Afterwards, he pretended nothing had happened. But I could sense him watching me. I knew it was only a matter of time before he tried again. I'd observed him at close quarters for years. The way he was with women. He'd left me alone until then, but . . . I was afraid. And so I told Madan; I shouldn't have. He became wild with anger, ready to confront Sir James, but I calmed him down. I knew that if Sir James wished it he could have thrown us both into the street, made life impossible for us. I have been destitute before, after my husband died. It is not something I wish ever to experience again. But more importantly, it would have meant my son suffering with me. Expelled from his school, doomed through no fault of his own. This I could not permit.'

'For a while I thought you were the mystery woman in his study on the night of his death. I thought that perhaps, after discovering Lal's duplicity, Sir James had blackmailed you into giving in to his demands. That, perhaps, you had complied to protect your son,' said Persis.

'No! Never.'

'Did you kill him?'

'No.'

Persis looked back at Lal. '*Did* you plan for Maan Singh to murder Sir James that night?'

'I tell you harming Sir James was never my intention.' Lal looked desperately around him. 'You have to believe me.'

'Then what was?'

'I – I just wanted Maan here to protect Lalita. I couldn't be by her side all the time. But by placing Maan next to Sir James I could ensure that *he* was constantly watched. I had to do something, don't you see? The man was a jackal. I'd seen him destroy the lives of a dozen women. Because of his wealth, his reputation, he was untouchable. Any woman who raised a fuss, it was *my* job to make the problem go away.' He shuddered, reliving the life of petty thuggery that Sir James had imposed upon him.

Persis supposed this was not what Lal had expected when he had agreed to work for the Englishman; but once he was ensnared, once Gupta and her son became part of the equation, he could not leave. She had no doubt that Sir James had gone out of his way to rescue Lal at Imphal, precisely so that he might bind him to himself.

'After you argued that evening, you believed that Sir James intended to dismiss Gupta, perhaps dismiss you both. He would have ruined you. He had said as much to his bookkeeper. He demanded you return the money you had stolen. You became desperate. I ask again: did you send Maan Singh up to Sir James's study with the intention of killing him?'

'No.'

'Why did Maan Singh confess to the murder?'

'I – I don't know.'

'Do you believe that he killed Sir James?'

He blinked. 'It's possible.'

Beside him, Gupta began to weep.

Persis continued to hold him with her gaze, but he did not flinch. 'There is more to this story. I have come to believe that the last few months of Sir James's life have a direct bearing on his death. Sir James had been engaged by the Indian government to investigate crimes committed during Partition. Our government is determined to show that history cannot shield those who took advantage of the chaos. They provided Sir James with a list of reported atrocities to investigate. One of these alleged crimes took him to Punjab, to a village called Jalanpur, where the local land-owner, a Nawab Sikandar Ali Mumtaz, and his entire family – men, women, children – died in a fire that burned their ancestral home to the ground. The local police reported it as an accident, but an eyewitness account reached New Delhi claiming that there might have been more to it.

'I followed Sir James's trail to Jalanpur. I spoke with the man who had witnessed the incident. He confirmed that the nawab and his family had been murdered, and he told me why.

'The nawab had been attempting to sell his land and move to Pakistan. In doing so he was making many of his oldest tenants destitute. He was a Muslim; his tenants were largely Sikh and

Hindu. With Partition as the backdrop, it was inevitable that conflict would ensue.

'The eyewitness identified a man named Surat Bakshi, the son of a local tenant, as the ringleader behind the murders. He believed that Bakshi had an ulterior motive – he witnessed him loot the nawab's residence of its ancestral treasure, treasure that included many priceless items of jewellery.

'Bakshi vanished days later when his own family was murdered by a Muslim mob.' She paused. 'The jewellery that he stole lies at the heart of Sir James's murder. Not nationalism, not infidelity, but simple human greed.

'Sir James was bankrupt. His business in the West Indies had collapsed, all but ruining him. He was in debt. And then, one day, he saw a newspaper article in Bombay accompanied by a photo of a woman wearing a dazzling necklace. A necklace of beaten gold, embedded with emeralds, and adorned by two peacocks. The sight electrified Sir James. Because he had encountered that necklace before, or at least a description of it, in the eyewitness account sent to him by Delhi of the murder of the Nawab Sikandar Ali Mumtaz. *What was that necklace doing in Bombay?*

'He proceeded with caution. He approached the woman from the article, and discovered that the necklace had been gifted to her by her fiancé. He befriended this man. And then, when he felt he was on the right track, he travelled to Punjab to search for evidence. Here he confirmed what he had already begun to suspect: that the man he had befriended in Bombay, the owner of the peacock necklace, was none other than Surat Bakshi. Murderer and thief.

'Did Sir James report his findings to the authorities?' She grimaced. 'No. Because for him the critical aspect of Bakshi's crime was not that he had murdered an entire family, but that he had stolen the nawab's ancestral treasure. He returned to Bombay, approached this man, and told him what he knew. Then he made him an offer.

'He asked for the jewellery. In return for his silence.'

'He blackmailed him?' said Campbell, in astonishment.

'Yes. I can only conjecture at this point, but what I believe happened is this: Sir James returned from Punjab on December 28th. A day later he made an appointment to meet the man he believed to be Surat Bakshi. Bakshi became convinced that Sir James knew enough.

'Two days later he attended Sir James's New Year's Eve ball. He brought along a specimen of the stolen jewellery – perhaps even the same peacock necklace. He also invited another man to the ball, a local jeweller named Vishal Mistry, to confirm its value for Sir James. Mistry had a reputation for dealing in stolen jewellery. I confirmed that Bakshi had visited Mistry's jewellery shop on a number of prior occasions; I believe he used Mistry himself as he gradually disposed of the pieces he had stolen from the nawab.

'Mistry was spotted meeting with Sir James in his office early that evening. The next day he was murdered. My guess is that Bakshi did not wish to leave a trail that might lead back to him.' She paused. 'Somewhere along the line Sir James made a miscalculation. The price of his silence became too high. And so Bakshi decided to kill him.'

'Who in the hell is this man?' exclaimed Campbell.

'Before I answer that question, let me describe another of the items stolen from the nawab's treasury. A dagger, an ancestral blade that had been in the nawab's family for generations. A *curved* blade, its ivory hilt encrusted with precious stones. Why is this significant? For two reasons. One, because Sir James was murdered with a curved blade. And two . . . It always bothered me that we couldn't find the murder weapon when we searched his home on the night of his murder. How did the killer get the knife out of

Laburnum House?' She stopped again. 'It wasn't until I saw a photograph of Surat Bakshi that I understood how it had been done. You see, it was at that moment that I realised that I too had already met Bakshi. In Bombay.

'The dagger was fitted into a specially designed cane, serving as its handle. Having committed the murder, Sir James's killer simply slipped the dagger back into place and walked out of Laburnum House with it.

'That was the key,' she continued. 'Many of you in this room had the motive and the opportunity to kill Sir James. But only one of you had the means. Isn't that right, Surat?' She turned to face Adi Shankar.

The room turned with her.

To his credit, Shankar maintained his composure; the only sign that he had heard was the twitching of his shoulders. His right hand tightened around the curved handle of his cane.

'Conjecture, Inspector,' he said eventually. 'That's all you have. Are you forgetting that I couldn't possibly have killed Sir James? I was with the jazz band at the time of his death. There are literally dozens of witnesses.'

'I'll come to the matter of your alibi in a moment. But my theory is more than conjecture.' She reached into her pocket and held up the newspaper cutting she had taken from the *Amritsar Journal*.

'This is a photograph of Surat Bakshi. A good enough likeness, don't you think?'

'That proves nothing,' countered Shankar, but he was visibly shaken. 'Many people come to Bombay and adopt a new identity. It is no crime.'

Persis reached into her pocket again and took out two more cuttings. One showed the peacock necklace around the throat of the nawab's sister, Sakina Baig. 'This is the nawab's murdered sister, wearing the peacock necklace some time before her death in 1947.' She held up another cutting – the cutting she had found in Sir James's desk at the beginning of the investigation. 'This was taken from an article in the *Times of India* dated two months ago, at the opening of the Gulmohar Club. It shows Meenakshi Rai, Adi Shankar's fiancée, wearing the same necklace.' She locked eyes with Shankar. 'How did a dead woman's necklace, a necklace stolen by her murderer, end up around your fiancée's throat?'

'No court would convict me on the basis of some old newspaper cuttings.'

'It isn't these that will convict you. It's the cane.'

'You'd be amazed at the sort of things modern forensic science can detect,' said Archie Blackfinch. 'Microscopic traces of blood are particularly difficult to get rid of. I have no doubt that once I examine your cane we'll be able to tie you to the murder.'

There was a stunned silence. Shankar's face was set in stone and then he seemed to arrive at a decision.

'It never ceases to amaze me,' he spat. 'We will happily slaughter thousands to defend our gods, but murder a man for profit and it becomes a national crisis of conscience. Yes, I killed the nawab and his family. He deserved such a death. He and his ilk made a fortune from the suffering of men like my father. He was a traitor. I took his treasure – why not? I had a right to it.' He grimaced. 'None of this would have happened if I hadn't given Meenakshi the necklace to wear on the night of the Gulmohar's opening. It was a moment of weakness.

'That was what started it all. You were right, Inspector. He saw the necklace in that article. And once he began to suspect that it was the same piece he had read about in his files, he decided to investigate. He *befriended* me. And then he went to Jalanpur and found his answers. He found Surat Bakshi. He found me.'

'What really happened?'

'He came to my home on the 29th. He showed me the picture he had of me as Surat Bakshi. He told me about his files, his investigation. And then he told me the price for his silence. Half of the stolen jewellery, and a 50 per cent stake in the club. You see, that part was true. I knew then that I would have to kill him. He thought that he was being reasonable, asking for only half, but a man like that would never stop, not until he had taken everything I had.'

'He told me to come to his ball and to bring the peacock necklace with me. I was to give him my answer that very evening. Of course, there was only one answer he expected to hear. I agreed, if only to give myself time to think.

'On the evening of the ball, I handed him the necklace. I had arranged for Vishal Mistry to visit at the same time, to confirm its value for him. And yes, afterwards, I couldn't leave Mistry alive. He was a loose end.'

'So *you* killed Sir James?' she said.

'Yes. He insisted that I stay for the party. That I pretend to be his friend so that afterwards when he announced that he had taken a stake in my club it would seem a natural progression of our friendship.'

'There's just one problem with your scenario,' said Persis. 'Your alibi. As you rightly pointed out, you *couldn't* have killed Sir James.'

'I tell you it was me. I killed him with the dagger in my cane. I confess.'

'No. You couldn't have done it. But there was another at the ball who could have. Someone you had confided in. Someone whose life stood to be destroyed by Sir James's blackmail.' She turned to Meenakshi Rai. '*You* killed Sir James,' she said softly. 'To protect the man you loved.'

They all turned to stare at her, standing frozen in her black sari. Her cheeks trembled.

'Meenakshi, don't say a word.' Shankar looked at her desperately.

'It was lies,' she whispered. 'All lies.'

'Meenakshi!'

She ignored him. 'He told me that he had killed a man in self-defence during the Partition riots. That no one would believe him, and so he had run to Bombay and changed his name. He told me that Sir James had found out and was trying to blackmail him; that he had found an old photograph of him, that he had compiled a file of evidence, and that he wanted Adi's ancestral treasure, including the necklace that he had given me for our engagement. He told me that this man would not stop until he had ruined our lives.

'When Adi went up on stage with the band he handed me his cane. He told me again what I needed to do. We'd talked about it beforehand. *He'd* talked about it. I had balked, at first, but in the end Adi convinced me this was the only way.

'I found Sir James and whispered in his ear. I told him that I wanted him. I told him that I would meet him alone in his study. I had seen the way he looked at me. I knew he would not resist.

'He was waiting for me. Before I knew it, he was all over me. I pushed him back. I told him that I wanted to wear my necklace one last time. Adi had told me that he had given it to him that evening. Sir James was amused, but did as I asked. He took down a painting behind his desk and opened a safe. As he did so I saw a stack of files inside. He took out the necklace and placed it around my throat. It sickened me to feel his touch but I couldn't back out. I had to see it through.

'When we had finished he barely gave me a second glance. Just sat there, smoking, eyes closed. His trousers were on the floor. He was naked, vulnerable.

'I picked up the cane, unscrewed the dagger.

'He opened his eyes, saw me, and smiled. That terrible grin of his. He believed that he was in control, that he held the power.

'I stabbed him in the throat. He died quickly.

'I searched the safe. Inside, I found the photograph of Surat Bakshi, and the files of Sir James's investigations. I had no time to check which file was the one he had compiled on Adi and I couldn't take them all with me without being noticed. So I burned them and the photograph in the fireplace. It only took a few minutes but I was beginning to panic. I shut the safe, not bothering to lock it. I hung the painting in front of it, then fled the room and rejoined the party.'

Persis ran through the sequence of events in her mind.

Four months ago, Sir James Herriot had been tasked to investigate crimes committed during Partition and given files pertaining to these crimes. While reading these documents he had come across the account of the murder of the Nawab Sikandar Ali Mumtaz. In that account, he had read of the nawab's priceless treasure being looted, including the peacock necklace.

Soon afterwards, he had discovered that his holdings in the West Indies had collapsed, pushing him into crippling debt. He was on the verge of bankruptcy.

And then, a lifeline. He saw an article in a Bombay newspaper, a picture of a woman wearing a necklace – the peacock necklace. That was the real reason he had kept the article. He traced the necklace back to Adi Shankar, owner of the Gulmohar Club. He visited the club, befriended Shankar. His suspicions were aroused – his next act had been to travel north, to Punjab, where the witness account had originated, to confirm those suspicions.

Here, he followed the trail to the village of Jalanpur. He visited Jalanpur on December 25th. Word spread throughout the village that an Englishman was asking questions about the death of the nawab.

Later that night, he was visited at the Golden Temple Hotel by Mangal, the author of the eyewitness account. Mangal told him everything, all the details that he had left out of the report, including the name of the nawab's killer.

Surat Bakshi.

Herriot had scribbled Bakshi's name on a notepad from the hotel.

The next day he tore off the chit, and took it with him back to Jalanpur, intent on finding out more about Bakshi. He went through the land record books and wrote down details of the Bakshi family plot. He then visited the plot and searched the abandoned Bakshi home. She suspected that he had been searching for the treasure that Bakshi had looted; perhaps he thought the man hadn't had time to take it all with him when he fled the village after the death of his own family.

He found no treasure, but instead discovered something just as valuable.

A picture of Surat Bakshi.

Herriot returned to Bombay and used that picture to blackmail Adi Shankar, the man Bakshi had become. He invited Shankar/Bakshi to his ball to seal the deal, believing that he had the man at his mercy.

But what he hadn't counted on was Adi Shankar using Meenakshi Rai, his fiancée, a woman from a military family. Persis did not doubt that her father had taught her to handle weapons such as the dagger with which she had killed Sir James in his study.

Shortly afterwards, Robert Campbell had come charging into the office, to find his business partner dead. Believing that he or his daughter might be incriminated – because of the affair with Herriot that she had claimed – he had simply backed out and not said a word.

And moments after *that*, Maan Singh had shown up.

The big Sikh's reaction to Sir James's death had been equally curious. She couldn't be sure that he had ever intended to harm Sir

James, but, faced with the dead Englishman that night, he had seen an unexpected opportunity of regaining his family honour. Acting on instinct, he had stolen Sir James's trousers, wiping them in the man's blood first – so that they might serve as incriminating evidence – and reported the death to Lal, who had been left to consider the best way to ensure the investigation did not turn towards himself, given his fractured relations with Herriot. Perhaps he suspected Singh of the killing. Perhaps Singh told him he intended to confess. Either way Lal would have told him not to say a word. Not with Gupta's future at stake – Singh's sister and Lal's lover.

That was why Singh had not confessed right away. That and because he couldn't be certain that the true murderer might not be apprehended in the days to come.

It was also why Lal had called Malabar House. Lal had hoped that the most inexperienced and maligned unit in the service would make little headway and the whole thing might die a quiet death, Sir James's murder blamed on a non-existent intruder.

And then, days later, she had confronted Singh about the trousers. He had realised at that moment that she was desperate, that she had no other leads. He had confessed instantly, knowing that the full weight of the law would fall upon him, shutting down further investigation. He *wanted* to be known as the man who killed Sir James Herriot and she had given that to him.

His confession had thrown Lal into a panic. That was why he had insisted on being present when she had questioned Singh. But, to Lal's relief, Singh had remained tight-lipped, incriminating none but himself. In effect, he had solved all of Lal's problems – as long as the investigation went no further. That was why Lal had been so adamant in shutting her down and letting Singh accept the burden of guilt.

But why *had* Singh confessed to a crime he did not commit? She supposed that in his own mind, the Sikh had become a martyr.

The logic was twisted, but in an oblique way she could understand what had moved him to act as he had. By killing a Britisher he had avenged the dead of Jallianwala Bagh; he had regained his family's honour.

She realised she still had unanswered questions. She turned back to Meenakshi. 'What did you do with the necklace?'

'I walked out of Laburnum House wearing it.'

'We found no fingerprints in Sir James's study that didn't belong there.'

'Gloves,' she said simply. 'They were part of my costume.'

'Meenakshi—' began Shankar.

She whirled on him, her face wet. 'You lied to me! You murdered an entire family. You murdered . . . children.' Her voice hitched. 'And you made a murderer of me. You – you're a monster.'

'Don't say that!'

But she turned away, and said no more.

Shankar gave a howl of anguish.

Blackfinch moved towards him and held out his hand. 'Give me the cane.'

Shankar's eyes narrowed. And then his face transformed into a snarl. His hands moved quickly, working the top of the cane. Before anyone could react, he had grabbed Blackfinch by the wrist, whirled him around, whipped an arm around his throat, and set the dagger against it with his other hand. The Englishman cried out in alarm, flapping at Shankar's grip, but he was held fast.

Shankar began to back away to the door. 'Don't follow me. One dead Englishman is enough, don't you think?'

Persis did not waste her breath by telling him to stop. Her mind whirled, mapping out Shankar's exit route. He would have to drag Blackfinch along a narrow path that looped back out to the front where, presumably, his car was parked. At that point, he would either kill him or let him go. She couldn't see a good reason for

Shankar *not* to let Blackfinch go. But the man was desperate and desperate men made bad decisions.

Shankar halted at the door. 'Meenakshi. Wait for me. I'll find you. We *will* be together.'

She stared at him with hollow eyes.

He vanished through the door with his hostage, leaving the gathering gaping after him.

Persis moved into gear. 'Hold her here!' she yelled, pointing at Meenakshi Rai, then sprinted towards the door, grabbing her revolver from its holster. She barrelled out into blinding sunlight. A second's pause to get her bearings, and then she set off around the other side of the building, so that she could cut Shankar off before he reached his car.

Moments later, she found herself standing beside a granite statue of Mary, eyes focused on the path that wound around the cathedral's eastern flank. She settled into a shooting stance, bracing herself against the statue. Warmth from the stone radiated into her shoulder. She breathed in, attempted to restore a centre of calm.

Shankar appeared around the edge of the cathedral, still dragging Blackfinch. She realised that she could shoot him in the back now and end this. But what if the bullet travelled through him and into his hostage?

She sighted down the barrel. A twig cracked under her foot, the sound like a rifle shot in the silence.

Shankar whipped around, pulling Blackfinch with him, a curse escaping the Englishman.

Shankar's eyes widened. He pressed the tip of the knife against Blackfinch's throat. A bead of blood slid down the blade. There was something wild in the man's eyes. Persis recognised the blood-lust that had led Shankar to murder an entire family. This was not a man to be reasoned with. Surat Bakshi may have transformed himself into the urbane Adi Shankar, but at his core he would remain a deeply fearful man, ruled by a savagery of nature that was part and parcel of his character.

And a man's character was his fate.

Persis sighted down the barrel of her revolver and squeezed the trigger.

29

25 January 1950

Malabar House was unnaturally quiet. She had expected no less. It was the day before Republic Day. Most of the team had begged time off to spend with their families preparing for the celebrations. She had considered staying away, but somehow it had not worked out like that. Her suspension had ended the night before and she had found herself overtaken by an irrational desire to be at her desk, if only for a few short hours.

Suspension. The sting of it still lingered. On an intellectual level, she understood the inevitability of it. The events at St Thomas Cathedral had left her superiors with little choice.

Two days after she had confronted Shankar, she had been hauled before a panel of senior officers. The panel had been chaired by Additional Deputy Commissioner of Police Amit Shukla. Ravi Patnagar, head of the state CID, had also been present.

To her surprise the atmosphere had been subdued. She had expected the worst; the night before, terror had paralysed her, the fear that she would be stripped of her uniform.

It quickly dawned on her that a different dynamic was at work. They were not there to condemn her; they were gathered to find a way to save themselves.

Seth had been right. The fact that she had become a national celebrity during the Herriot investigation, the fact that they had lauded her, now made it all but impossible for them to condemn her without condemning themselves. They couldn't release Maan Singh and declare his innocence without a significant loss of face. Nor could they ignore the evidence that her renegade investigation had uncovered.

They had spent hours poring over that investigation. To her surprise ADC Shukla had displayed a policeman's curiosity; his manner grew animated as she detailed how she had pieced together the events that had led to Sir James's death. Patnagar seemed less impressed.

When they were done, they asked her to step outside.

An hour later, she had been invited to return. That hour had been the loneliest of her life. She could only imagine the debate that had raged behind those doors. Her heart leaped into her mouth as she entered the room; she stared at their faces, attempting to read the verdict from their expressions.

'You have left us with quite a dilemma, Inspector,' said Shukla. 'You have disobeyed direct orders, pursued an enquiry you were explicitly told not to pursue. Can you imagine the chaos if every officer acted as you have?' He paused and she had to restrain herself from yelling into the silence. How could they be so – so *blind*?

Shukla appeared to read her mind. 'You are young. I don't mean that as a criticism. Your ideals are the ideals that underpin this service. Do you remember Bhagat Singh? The martyr? He once wrote: "The sanctity of the law can be maintained only so long as it is the will of the people." But the people are fickle, Inspector. They believe in myths and legends, heroes and villains. We don't share the Greek love of tragedy; we prefer our heroes to be infallible.' He sighed. 'It is the decision of this panel that you will be suspended from duty for a short period but will face no further censure. Upon your return, you will remain at Malabar House in your present capacity until we can decide what to do with you. Personally, I think you are too good an officer to waste your time there. But it is too early to judge whether that promise will be fulfilled. You are headstrong, Persis, and while I may privately applaud you for it, the fact remains that you cannot be trusted.'

She straightened her shoulders. 'What of Maan Singh? What of the investigation?'

It was Patnagar who spoke. 'The investigation is closed. It will not be re-opened.'

She stared at him in confusion. 'I don't understand.'

'You don't have to underst—' began Patnagar angrily, but Shukla waved him into silence.

'Did I not just tell you that the public are unwilling to accept weakness in their heroes? How can they trust us to maintain law and order if we admit that we are wrong?'

'But—' she began, only to be cut off by Shukla's raised hand.

'Be content that you have solved the case. The guilty party is no more.'

'But what of Maan Singh?' she repeated. 'He must be set free, exonerated.'

'I have spoken with Singh, explained the facts of the matter. He does not wish to be released.'

The words were deafening in her ears. 'Impossible!'

Shukla raised an eyebrow. 'I assure you, the man wishes only to be remembered as the killer of Sir James. By his own twisted logic, his acceptance of guilt shall release his family from the disgrace brought upon them by his father.'

'But he will hang for a crime he did not commit! How is this justice?'

Shukla gave a sad smile. 'Justice can take many forms, Persis.'

She gaped at the man. 'What of Meenakshi Rai? Her confession?'

Shukla exchanged glances with Patnagar. 'I take it you haven't heard?' He shifted in his seat. 'Meenakshi Rai committed suicide in her cell yesterday. She strangled herself with the *dupatta* of her sari.'

Shock rooted her to the spot.

'We managed to keep her arrest out of the newspapers. As far as the press are concerned, Adi Shankar shot himself because of financial problems at his club. His heartbroken fiancée, Meenakshi Rai, then committed suicide.'

'You can't do this,' she whispered.

'It is already done.'

'What about Lal, Campbell, all the others who heard their confession?'

'All have been spoken to. They have seen the wisdom in our chosen course of action.'

She wrestled with her desire to scream. To shout. To give vent to the anger and frustration that threatened to burst out of her and burn down the room.

Instead, she took a deep breath. Her father had warned her that there would come a moment during the hearing upon which would pivot her whole future. What she said and did then would determine her fate. Along one path would be rage and perhaps a moment's satisfaction; along the other: suppression of her will, but the chance to continue to do good in the world.

She stared straight ahead, into the future.

'Yes, sir,' she said.

She stirred from her thoughts as Pradeep Birla entered the office. A smile cracked his dark features as he spotted her.

'So, how does it feel? You solved the case.'

She realised that no one else had asked her this question, not even her father. She had focused so intently on the hearing and subsequent suspension that she had not had the opportunity to reflect on the fact that, ultimately, she had achieved the task that she had set herself – to unmask Sir James Herriot's killer.

She blinked. 'I feel – I feel . . .' She tailed off, seized by a sudden melancholy. They had given her the case believing that she would fail. They had obstructed her at every turn. And still she had prevailed.

And yet ... the death of Meenakshi Rai, killer though she be, churned uneasily inside her. The beautiful socialite had been lied to, manipulated, and had ultimately committed the worst of crimes, believing that she was protecting the man she loved.

Meanwhile, Singh would hang for a crime he did not commit.

The truth had been subverted; it left a bitter taste in her mouth.

Perhaps this, more than anything, affirmed for her that she had chosen wisely. She was more than just India's first female IPS officer. She was an instrument of the law.

'My wife would like to invite you to dinner,' said Birla. 'She is quite taken by the fact that you outrank me. She is a very progressive woman.' He seemed pained by this revelation.

The invitation surprised her, and she found herself staring at him. But he seemed sincere.

'Thank you. I accept.'

After Birla had left, Persis lingered for a moment, enjoying the moment of unusual quiet.

George Fernandes entered the office. He froze as he spotted her, then nodded, took off his cap and sat down heavily at his desk.

'I hadn't expected you back until after Republic Day,' he said.

'I hadn't expected you back at all,' she replied.

He stared at her in confusion.

'I saw the number on your notepad. Aalam Channa's number.'

His eyes widened, but he said nothing. His hand fidgeted on his knee.

'It wasn't Oberoi feeding him information. It was you.'

He couldn't meet her eyes.

'Why did you do it?'

'You wouldn't understand.'

'Try me.'

He raised his chin, something defiant in his eyes now. 'I've given my life to the force. I did everything they asked of me. And then, one mistake, and I am condemned. Cast aside, to live out the remainder of my career . . . here. Channa promised me a way back. He has contacts at state CID – Ravi Patnagar. I was told that if I could provide information about what you were doing, that if ultimately it might lead to you – to you being removed from the force, I would be transferred back to a central unit.'

'You tried to sabotage my career,' she said flatly.

'You have no right to be here!' he exploded. 'You are a publicity stunt. Policing is not for women. What future do you think you have? Do you really believe that men will ever follow your orders?'

She was taken aback. She had never guessed that such currents of prejudice ran through the seemingly mild-mannered Fernandes. It was another valuable lesson.

Her face hardened, then she stood, placed her cap upon her head. 'I conveyed my suspicions to ADC Shukla. You will be investigated. If I were you I would begin praying that you don't lose your liberty as well as your career.'

She considered saying more, but then realised that she had said enough.

Exactly enough.

30

26 January 1950 – Republic Day

The langur sat above the hoarding – a technicolour poster for the latest Bollywood blockbuster, somewhat defaced by trails of pigeon excrement – watching her closely as she parked the jeep and stepped outside into the afternoon sun. The grey-brick building before her reminded her of a Gothic mausoleum, looming darkly over the city.

She walked briskly into the entrance, spoke briefly to the security guard, then made her way down into the bowels of the building.

Pausing momentarily outside a door marked FORENSIC SCIENCE LABORATORY, she gathered her thoughts. She smoothed down the front of her blouse, pushed a frond of hair behind her ear, then stepped inside.

Blackfinch was bent over a workstation, in flannel trousers and a white shirt rolled to the elbows, peering into a microscope, his spectacles pushed back into his hair. He appeared not to have heard her enter. She waited, debating with herself how best to interrupt him.

The decision was made for her by a loud clacking at the window. She turned to see a crow land on the windowsill, pecking at the pane.

Blackfinch looked around, saw her, and stiffened. She noticed that a bandage still obscured his right ear. He stared at her, then turned back to his microscope.

She moved forward into the room, feeling acutely conscious of her appearance. Perhaps it had been a bad idea to put on a dress, and these uncomfortable – yet undeniably stylish – shoes that Aunt Nussie had gifted her a year ago.

'I'm surprised to see you here,' she said. 'I'd have thought you'd be out celebrating the birth of a nation with your old friend from England.'

'It's not my nation,' he said stiffly, without turning around.

'I disagree. Locard's principle, right? No contact fails to leave a trace. The British were here three hundred years. That's a lot of contact.'

He grunted. She attempted to move around into his line of sight, but he shifted himself so that he maintained his back to her, lighthouse fashion.

She sighed. 'I take it you're still upset with me?'

'Why would I be upset with you? I mean, it's not as if you shot me. Oh wait. That's precisely what you did.'

'What do you want me to say? I apologise. I didn't mean to shoot part of your ear off.'

'You could have killed me!'

'I took a calculated risk. If Shankar had got you to his car who knows what he might have done. You were never in any danger from me. I scored 96 per cent in my pistol proficiency test at the academy.'

'That's heartening to know,' he muttered.

'I'm sorry,' she repeated. 'You twitched at the last second, otherwise I wouldn't have hit your ear.'

'So it's *my* fault?' He turned to face her, his cheeks red.

She thought it might be amusing to tell him that he looked attractive when he was angry, but restrained herself. She suspected he wouldn't appreciate the sentiment.

'You're reckless, Persis,' he fumed. 'And one day it's going to get someone killed. Someone you actually care about.'

Something rose unbidden to her lips. She bit down on her tongue. The confusion of feelings that had brought her here seemed suddenly daunting, a complexity beyond her ability to unravel. Perhaps it would have been better to have stayed away.

'I wish you a speedy recovery,' she said stiffly. 'Thank you for your assistance with the investigation.' She turned and walked out of the lab, her heels clacking on the tiles.

Outside, the langur eyed her stonily from his perch as she stalked back to the jeep, swore, then got inside, and swore again. She closed her eyes, leaned back momentarily.

A thumping on the window. Blackfinch's face peered in at her. She rolled down the window, waited for him to speak.

'I've been invited to attend fireworks and whatnot. Six p.m. at the 360 Club. I don't suppose you'd care to attend? There'll be supper and speeches. Possibly dancing.'

She looked away, her gaze alighting on a woman by the side of the road feeding her child from her breast, her eyes the milky white so common to poverty in the new republic.

'Let me think about it,' she said.

Author's Note:
The Ghosts of Partition

We often think of Partition as a matter of historical importance involving nation states, macro-level politics, and major world figures. But the truth is that Partition had – and continues to have – an enduring effect on individual lives. Millions died, millions more lost their homes, their businesses, the lives that they had known. Studies have estimated that between two to three million people went missing in the state of Punjab during the movement of populations and have never been accounted for.

The chaos of Partition cannot be blamed solely on Mountbatten and British policy. Subcontinental politicians must shoulder their share of the blame. And individuals too. Those ordinary citizens who allowed themselves to be incited into hatred and religious xenophobia, who set aside decades, sometimes centuries of friendship, who took up sword and flame to terrorise their neighbours and compatriots, to murder men, women, and children in a frenzy of bloodlust that even now is difficult to comprehend.

My own father retained hazy memories of being forced from his village in Punjab as a boy. He was one of the fortunate ones. The violence passed him by and he settled in a village in Pakistan, a mirror image of the one that he had left behind. In his twenties, fortune brought him to the UK where he settled in London, where I was born.

My father passed away last year at the age of 82, having spent many more years in Britain than on the subcontinent. He identified as a Brit and a Pakistani but he never forgot the India that he claimed was his birthplace. When I, at the age of 23, found myself travelling to live and work in that country (I stayed for a decade), he was overjoyed. My mother was somewhat less enthused. She had been born in Pakistan and had grown up with the hateful rhetoric that even now pits the two neighbours against one another at regular intervals.

That is the true legacy of Partition. The way it has coloured the perceptions of two peoples who were essentially one, the way it continues to serve as a means by which political interests on both sides of the border can employ hatred and prejudice as a means of deflecting criticism of their regimes.

One can only hope that the wounds of history are healed in the fullness of time. Only then might the ghosts of Partition, the millions of dead and missing, find peace.

Vaseem Khan
London, March 2020

Acknowledgements

Beginning a new series is always daunting. To breathe life into new characters, invent new plots, and then hope that others will fall in love with your creations all over again. I am grateful to all those who have helped evolve Persis Wadia from an idea glimmering at the back of my mind to a living breathing reality.

So thank you to my agent Euan Thorneycroft at A.M. Heath, my editor Jo Dickinson and my publicity team of Steven Cooper and Maddy Marshall. A thank you too to Ruth Tross and Kerry Hood who were there at the beginning.

I would also like to thank the rest of the team at Hodder, Rachel Southey in production and Dom Gribben in audiobooks. Similar thanks go to Euan's assistant Jessica Sinyor. And thank you too to Jack Smyth for a terrific cover.

Finally, a heartfelt thank you to the Red Hot Chilli Writers, Abir Mukherjee, Ayisha Malik, Amit Dhand, Imran Mahmood and Alex Caan, not just for your sterling work on the Red Hot Chilli Writers podcast (tune in if you haven't yet heard us!) but for being the therapy group that every writer needs.

This book marks the start of what I hope will be an exhilarating new journey.

I'm ready. Are you?

Order the next book in Vaseem Khan's
exciting historical crime series . . .

The Dying Days

Bombay, 1950

India's first female police detective, Persis Wadia, is
summoned to the 150-year-old Bombay Royal Asiatic
Society at Horniman Circle. The society's preeminent
treasure, a priceless manuscript of Dante's *Divine Comedy*,
has vanished, as has the society's head curator, William
Huxley, an Englishman with a passion for Indian history.

Tasked to recover an item for which Benito Mussolini
once offered one million pounds, Persis soon uncovers a
series of murders, and a trail of tantalising coded clues
that lead her into the dark heart of conspiracy . . .

**Gripping, immersive, and full of Vaseem Khan's
trademark wit, this is historical fiction at its finest.**

HODDER

And the fun never stops . . . Listen to bestselling crime authors Vaseem Khan and Abir Mukherjee on the Red Hot Chilli Writers podcast

A podcast that discusses books and writing, as well as the creative arts, pop culture, risqué humour and Big Fat Asian weddings. The podcast features big name interviews, alongside offering advice, on-air therapy and lashings of cultural anarchy. Listen in on iTunes, Spotify, Spreaker or visit WWW.REDHOTCHILLIWRITERS.COM

You can also keep up to date with Vaseem's work by joining his newsletter. It goes out quarterly and includes:

*Extracts from Vaseem's next book *Exclusive short stories and articles *News of forthcoming events and signings *Competitions – win signed copies of books *Writing advice *Latest forensic and crime science articles *Vaseem's reading recommendations

You can join the newsletter in just a few seconds at Vaseem's website:

WWW. VASEEMKHAN.COM